Atelier Marie and Elie
Zarlburg Alchemist

VOLUME 3

Created By
Yoshihiko Ochi

HAMBURG // LONDON // LOS ANGELES // TOKYO

Atelier Marie and Elie -Zarlburg Alchemist- Volume 3
Story and Art by Yoshihiko Ochi

Translation - Alethea & Athena Nibley
English Adaption - Barb Lien-Cooper
Retouch and Lettering - Star Print Brokers
Production Artist - Katherine Schilling
Graphic Design - Jennifer Carbajal

Editor - Katherine Schilling
Digital Imaging Manager - Chris Buford
Pre-Production Supervisor - Erika Terriquez
Production Manager - Elisabeth Brizzi
Managing Editor - Vy Nguyen
Creative Director - Anne Marie Horne
Editor-in-Chief - Rob Tokar
Publisher - Mike Kiley
President and C.O.O. - John Parker
C.E.O. and Chief Creative Officer - Stuart Levy

A  Manga

TOKYOPOP and are trademarks or registered trademarks of TOKYOPOP Inc.

TOKYOPOP Inc.
5900 Wilshire Blvd. Suite 2000
Los Angeles, CA 90036

E-mail: info@TOKYOPOP.com
Come visit us online at www.TOKYOPOP.com

©1997/2001 GUST Co., LTD./Imagineer Co., Ltd
illustration: Kohime Ose
©1998/2001 GUST Co., LTD./Imagineer Co., Ltd
illustration: Isaemon Yamagata
All rights reserved.
First published in Japan in 2001 by ENTERBRAIN, INC., Tokyo. English translation rights arranged with ENTERBRAIN, INC. through Tuttle-Mori Agency, Inc., Tokyo.
English text copyright © 2008 TOKYOPOP Inc.

All rights reserved. No portion of this book may be reproduced or transmitted in any form or by any means without written permission from the copyright holders. This manga is a work of fiction. Any resemblance to actual events or locales or persons, living or dead, is entirely coincidental.

ISBN: 978-1-59816-527-2

First TOKYOPOP printing: April 2008
10 9 8 7 6 5 4 3 2 1
Printed in the USA

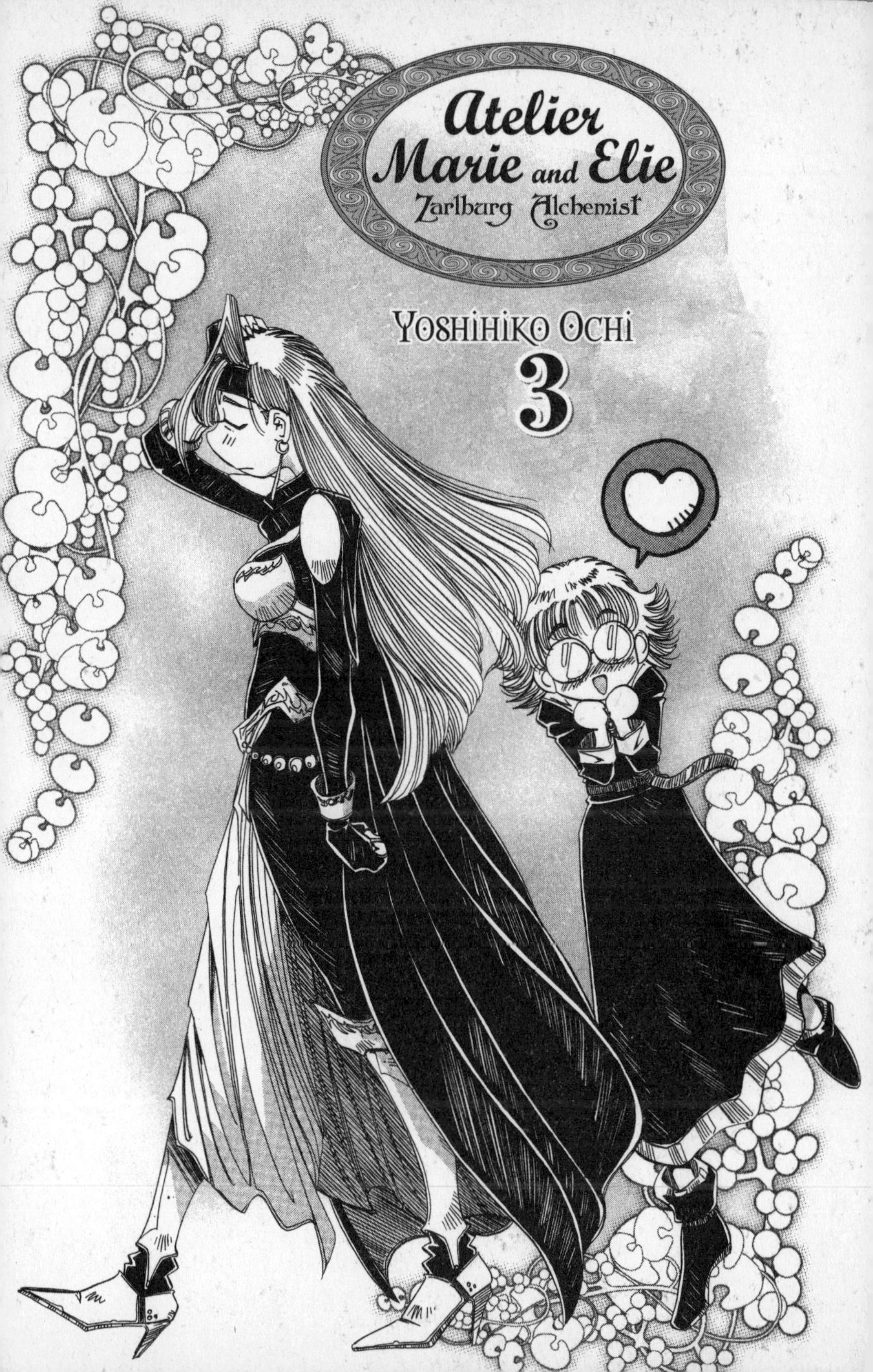
Atelier
Marie and Elie
Zarlburg Alchemist
YOSHIHIKO OCHI
3

A Good Cast is Worth Repeating

Character & Stories

Elfir [Elie]

Marie's protégé. After Marie saved her life using alchemy, young Elfir just knew she'd follow in our goofy alchemist's offbeat footsteps. Elfir may be young and naive, but rumor has it that she might be more capable in some matters than her eccentric mentor.

Marlone [Marie]

A downright goofy alchemist who returned to the magical Academy in Zarlburg after a long journey to perfect her magical skills. Can she put her reputation as a failed student behind her at last?

Passek and Prusha

These two shrimps came to Zarlburg from the Forest of Elves in order to study alchemy with Marie. The one with short hair is Passek, while the one with long hair is Prusha.

Our Story So Far

In the peaceful town of Zarlburg, two eager alchemists named Marie and Elie have opened their own alchemy workshop. Throw in a couple of elves who, by strange coincidence, are their only students, and the entire town is up to its proverbial navel in magical adventures. One day, while out gathering alchemy ingredients in the forest, Elie helps an injured woman she finds collapsed on the ground. Interestingly enough, that same woman is Marie's former adventuring companion, Kyrielich (nickname: Kyrie).

To make a long story short, with the addition of Kyrie, it looks like the workshop has gained another resident. But will Lady Kyrie's demons come back to haunt her...?!

Professor Helmina

A teacher at the Academy. She's a bit of an odd duck, specializing as she does in somewhat dubious alchemy. Is Professor Helmina Professor Ingrid's rival?

Millcassee

A cleric at the temple of the goddess Althena, Millcassee is a person of great charity and faith. The demon hound Strafe has taken an interest in her, though. Watch out, Millcassee!

Professor Ingrid

Marie and Elie's most honorable teacher. She's somewhat intimidating at first glance, but the truth is she is actually very kind and helpful. But will this teacher end up an old maid?

Demon Hound Strafe

A demon hound who came from the demon world chasing after Lady Kyrie after she'd escaped to the human world. Are the vertical stripes tattooed on his forehead his trademark, or is this dog just a fashion victim?

Black Knight

An unbelievably strong demon, the Black Knight has come to the human world. Is the dark one here to chase Lady Kyrie, or are ulterior motives in play?

Kyrielich (Kyrie)

A half-human, half-demonic adventurer. Chased out of the demon world by those plotting to revive the demon king, she is currently staying at Marie and Elie's house.

Contents

- Chapter 13: "Shinachiku fencing sticks"? 7
- Chapter 14: "...Oops... I did it again!" 23
- Chapter 15: "That's why Zarlburg is my kind of town." 55
- Chapter 16: "I can't teach you in words." 87
- Chapter 17: "When you cut me down, it hurt." 111
- Chapter 18: "Ack, how embarrassing!" 143

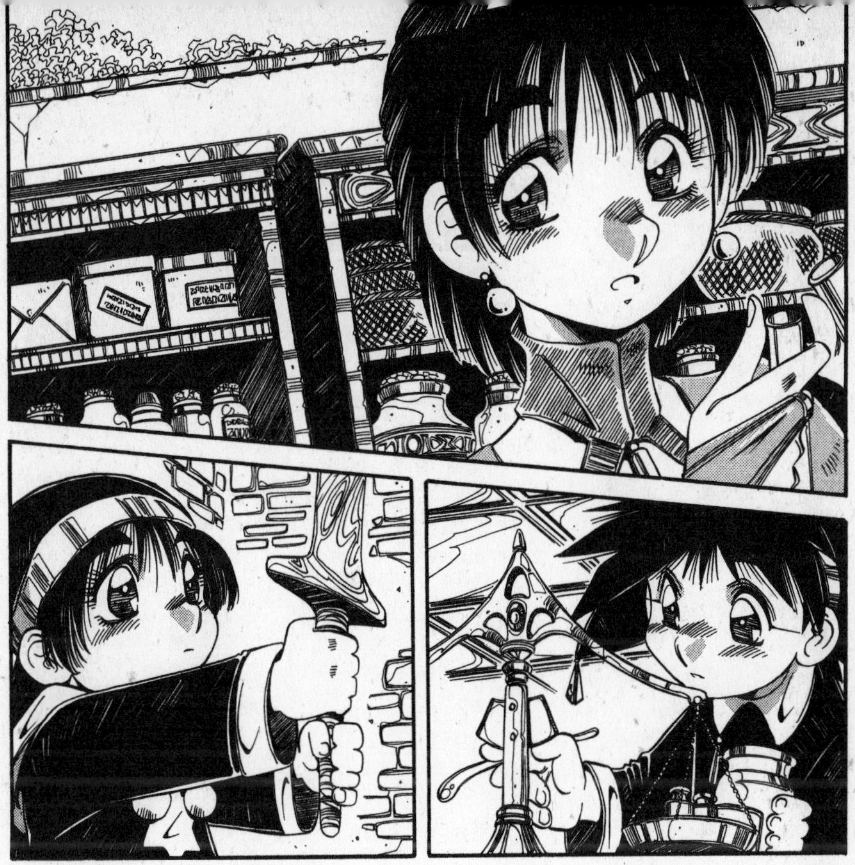

Chapter 13
"Shinachiku fencing sticks"?

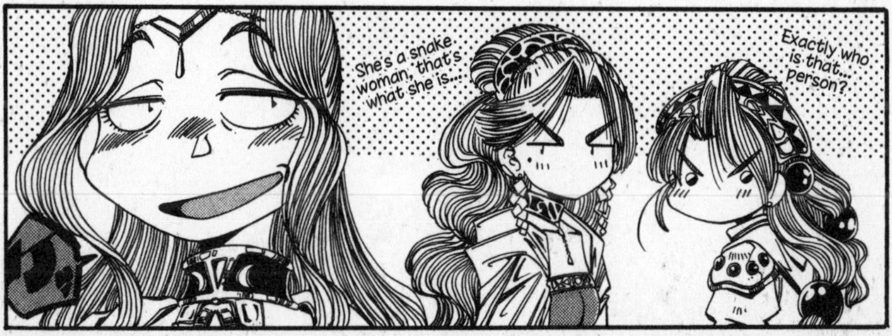
Exactly who is that... person?
She's a snake woman, that's what she is...

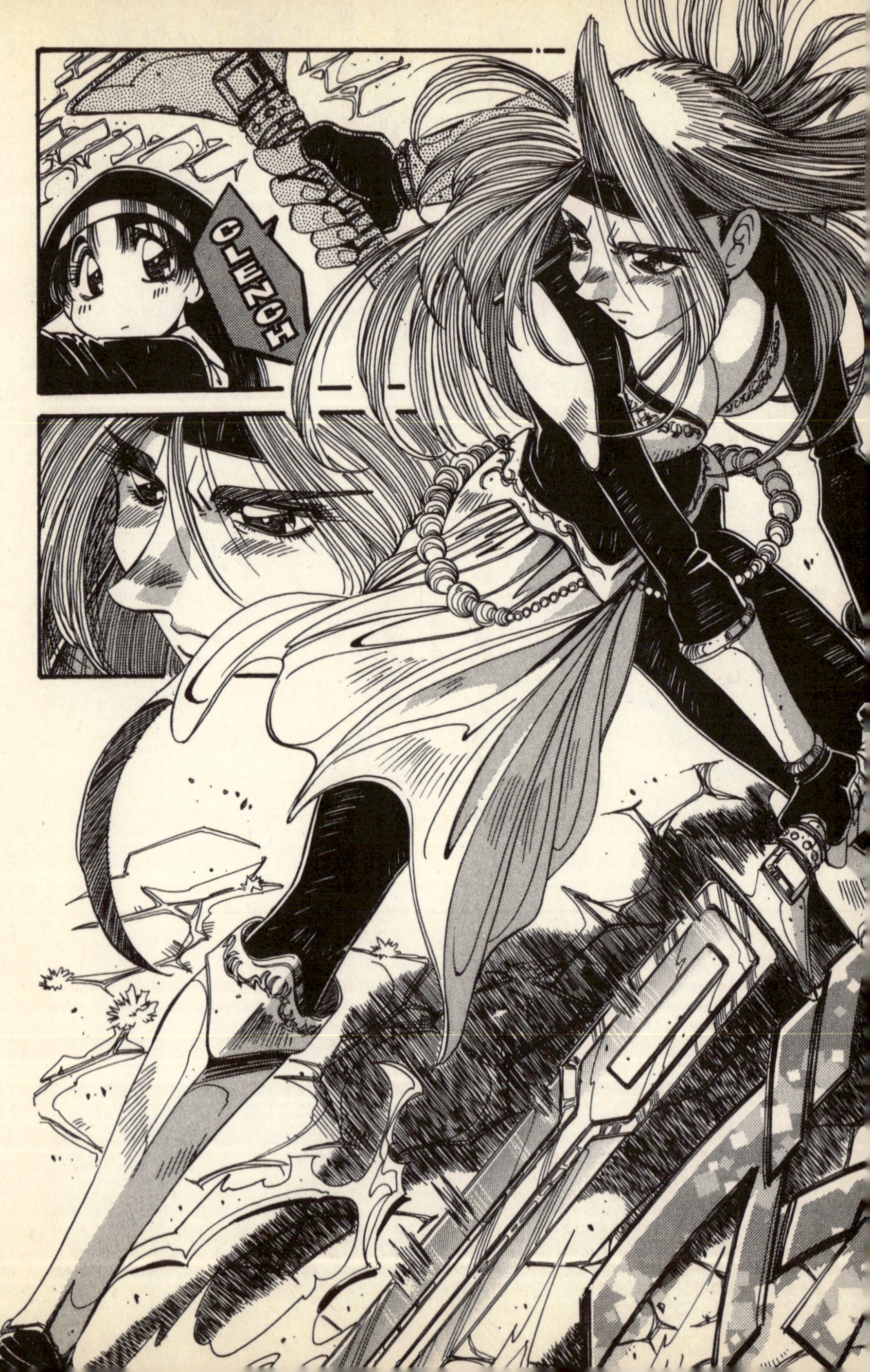
CLENCH

OOH...
SIGH...
COME ON! DON'T JUST STAND THERE STARING-- KEEP SWINGING!
Y-YES, MA'AM!
EXACTLY WHAT ARE YOU HERE FOR?
UM, UM, THAT IS, YOU KNOW HOW IT IS...
I WANT TO BE A STRONG FEMALE ROLE MODEL, JUST LIKE YOU, LADY KYRIE!
SO I'D LIKE TO LEARN HOW TO USE A SWORD...

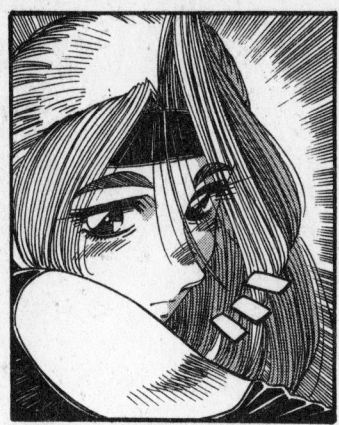

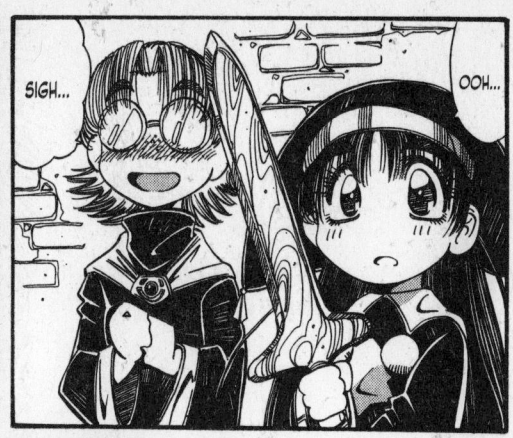

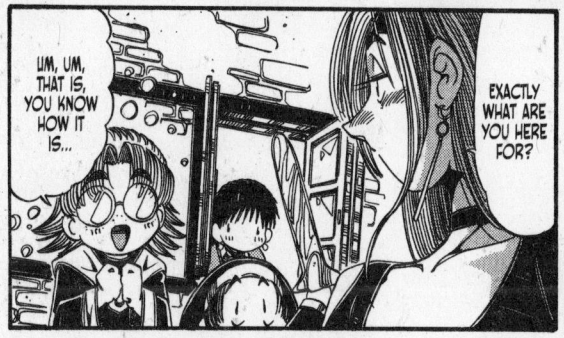

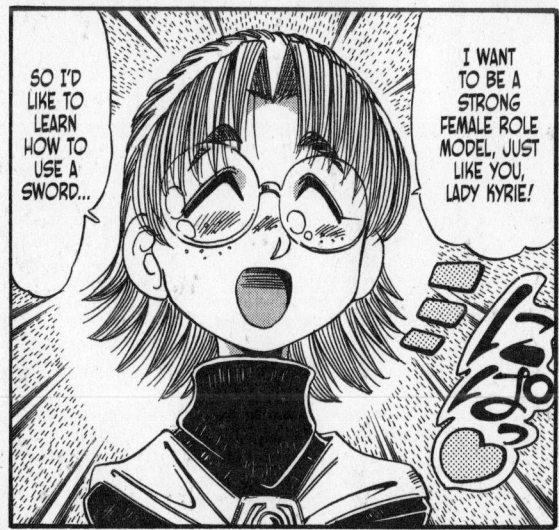

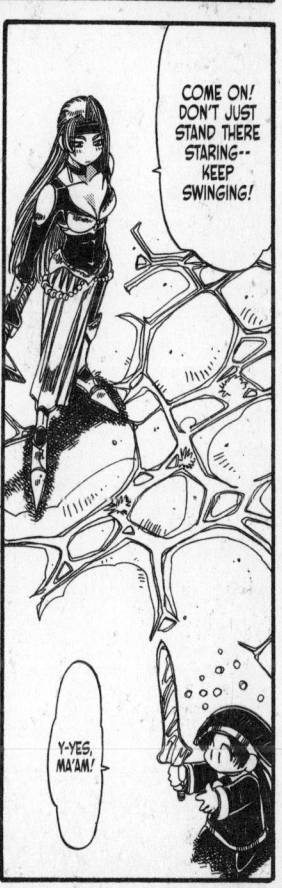

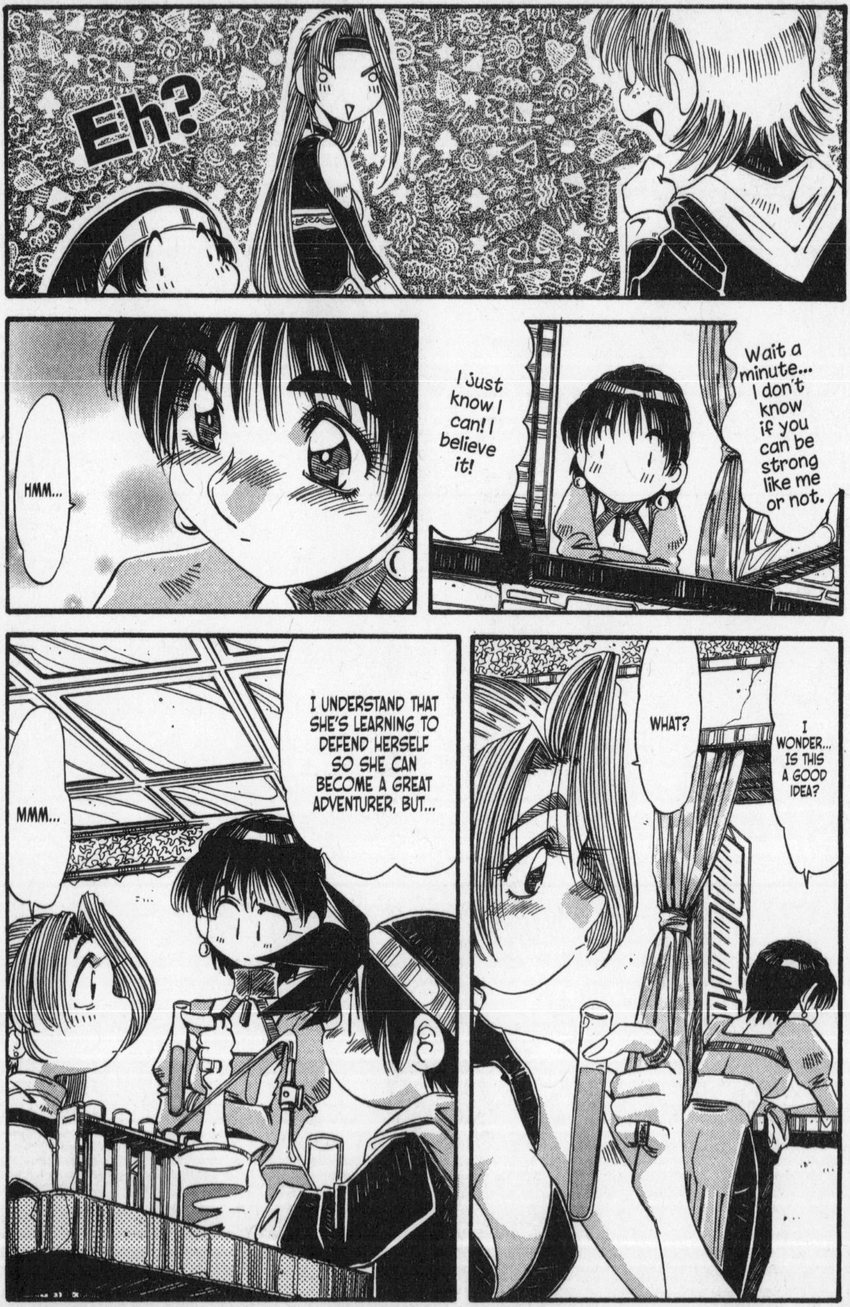
Eh?
Wait a minute... I don't know if you can be strong like me or not.
I just know I can! I believe it!
HMM...
I WONDER... IS THIS A GOOD IDEA?
WHAT?
I UNDERSTAND THAT SHE'S LEARNING TO DEFEND HERSELF SO SHE CAN BECOME A GREAT ADVENTURER, BUT...
MMM...

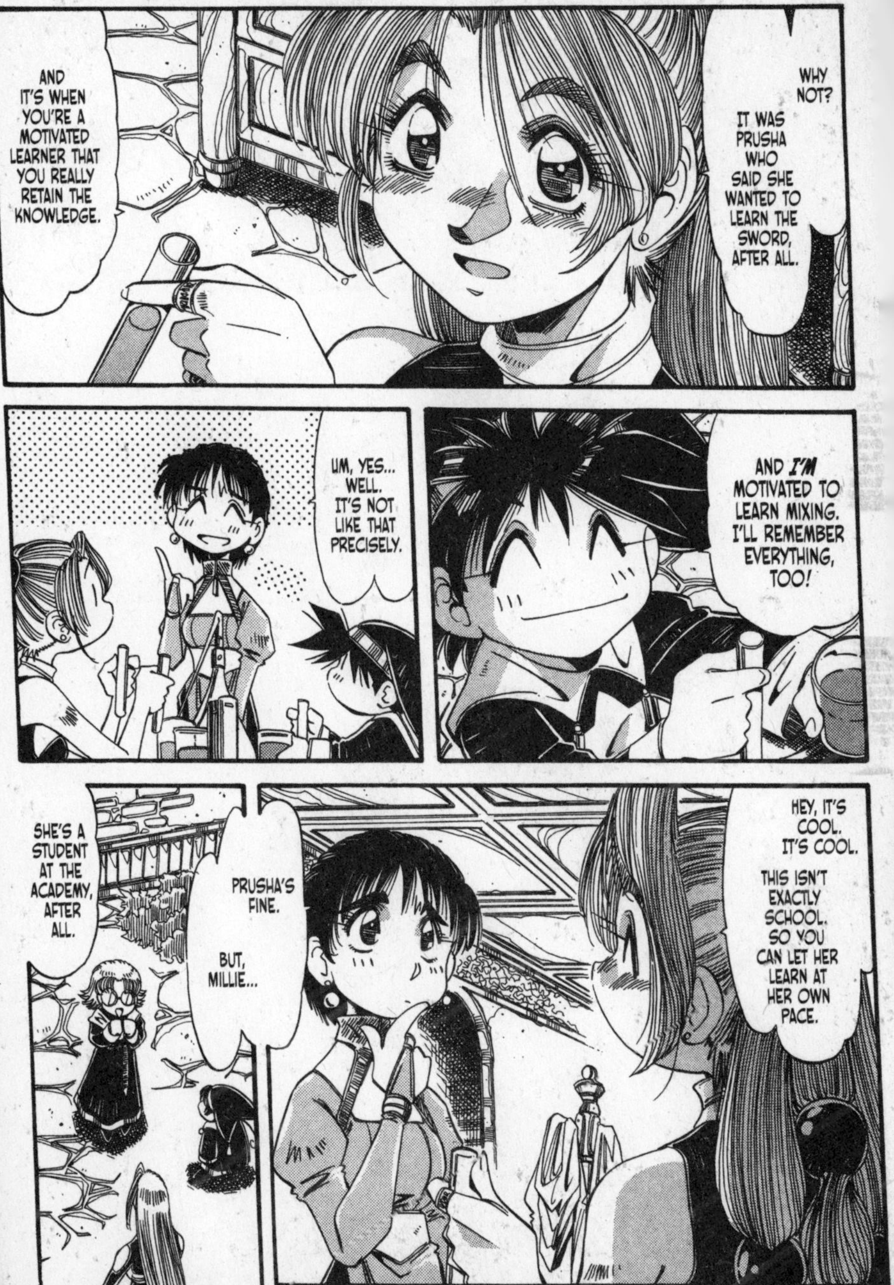
WHY NOT? IT WAS PRUSHA WHO SAID SHE WANTED TO LEARN THE SWORD, AFTER ALL.
AND IT'S WHEN YOU'RE A MOTIVATED LEARNER THAT YOU REALLY RETAIN THE KNOWLEDGE.
AND *I'M* MOTIVATED TO LEARN MIXING. I'LL REMEMBER EVERYTHING, TOO!
UM, YES... WELL. IT'S NOT LIKE THAT PRECISELY.
HEY, IT'S COOL. IT'S COOL.
THIS ISN'T EXACTLY SCHOOL. SO YOU CAN LET HER LEARN AT HER OWN PACE.
PRUSHA'S FINE.
BUT, MILLIE...
SHE'S A STUDENT AT THE ACADEMY, AFTER ALL.

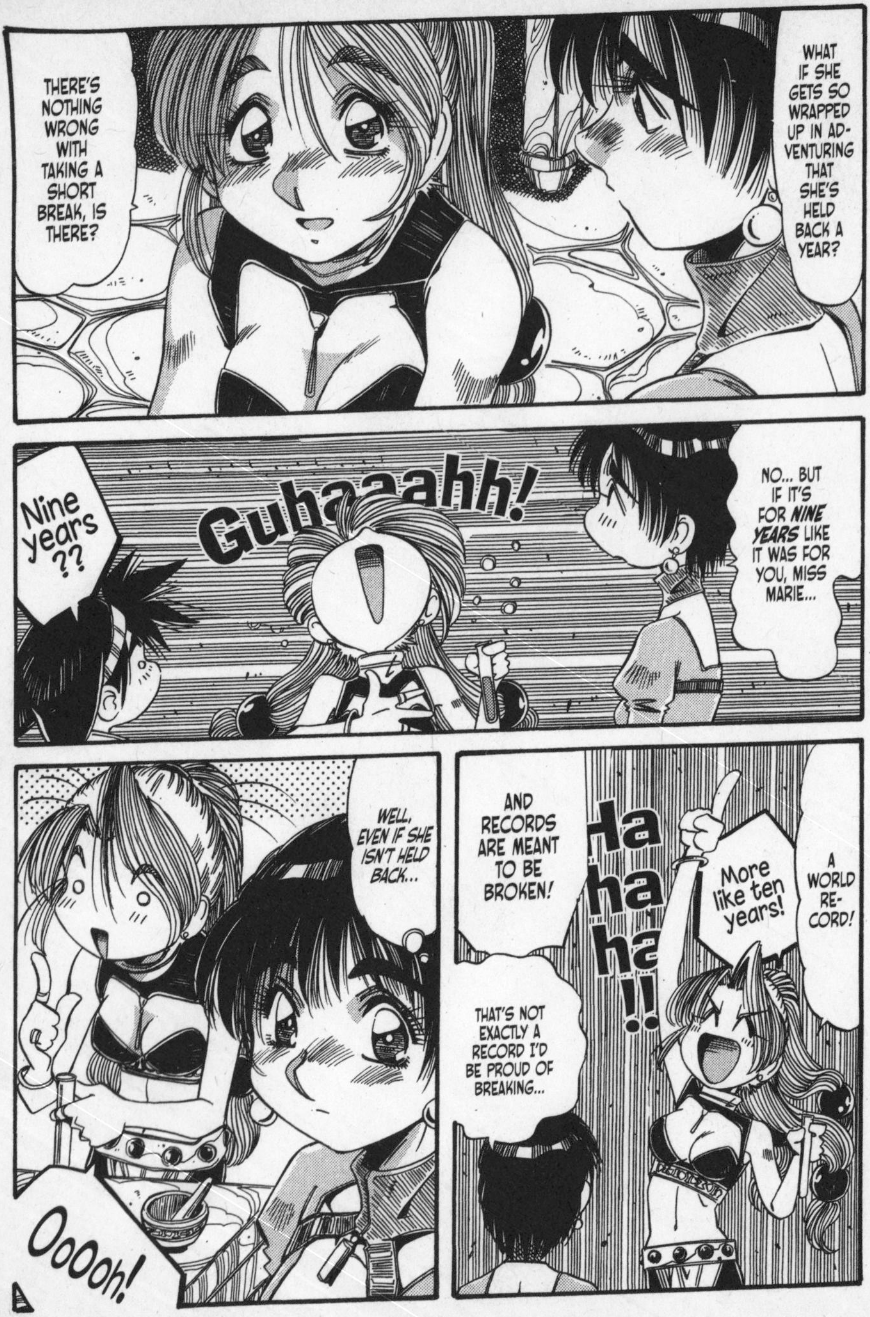
WHAT IF SHE GETS SO WRAPPED UP IN AD-VENTURING THAT SHE'S HELD BACK A YEAR?
THERE'S NOTHING WRONG WITH TAKING A SHORT BREAK, IS THERE?
NO... BUT IF IT'S FOR *NINE YEARS* LIKE IT WAS FOR YOU, MISS MARIE...
Guhaaaahh!
Nine years??
A WORLD RE-CORD!
More like ten years!
Ha ha ha!!
AND RECORDS ARE MEANT TO BE BROKEN!
THAT'S NOT EXACTLY A RECORD I'D BE PROUD OF BREAKING...
WELL, EVEN IF SHE ISN'T HELD BACK...
Ooooh!

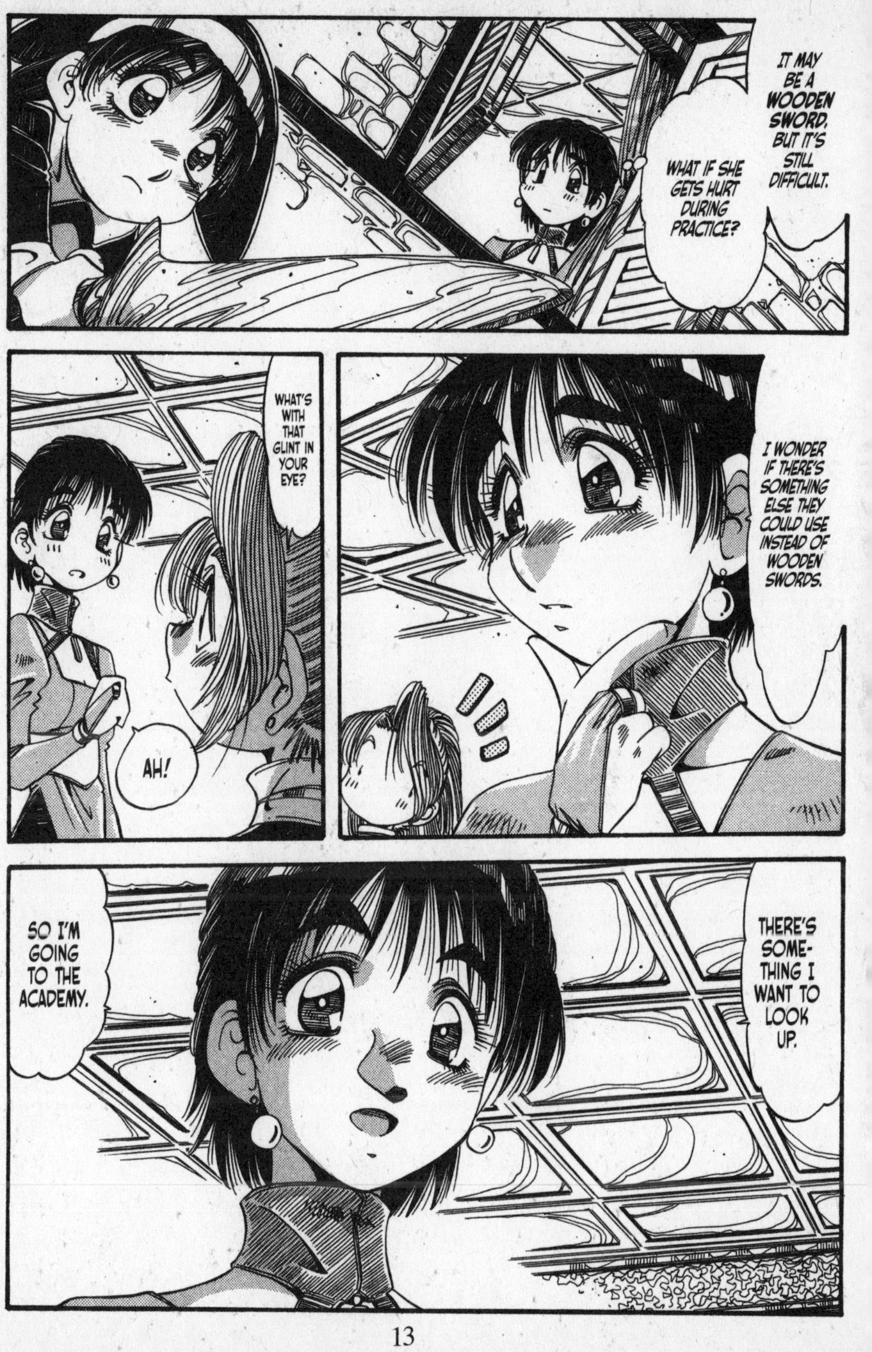
IT MAY BE A WOODEN SWORD, BUT IT'S STILL DIFFICULT.
WHAT IF SHE GETS HURT DURING PRACTICE?
I WONDER IF THERE'S SOMETHING ELSE THEY COULD USE INSTEAD OF WOODEN SWORDS.
WHAT'S WITH THAT GLINT IN YOUR EYE?
AH!
THERE'S SOME-THING I WANT TO LOOK UP.
SO I'M GOING TO THE ACADEMY.

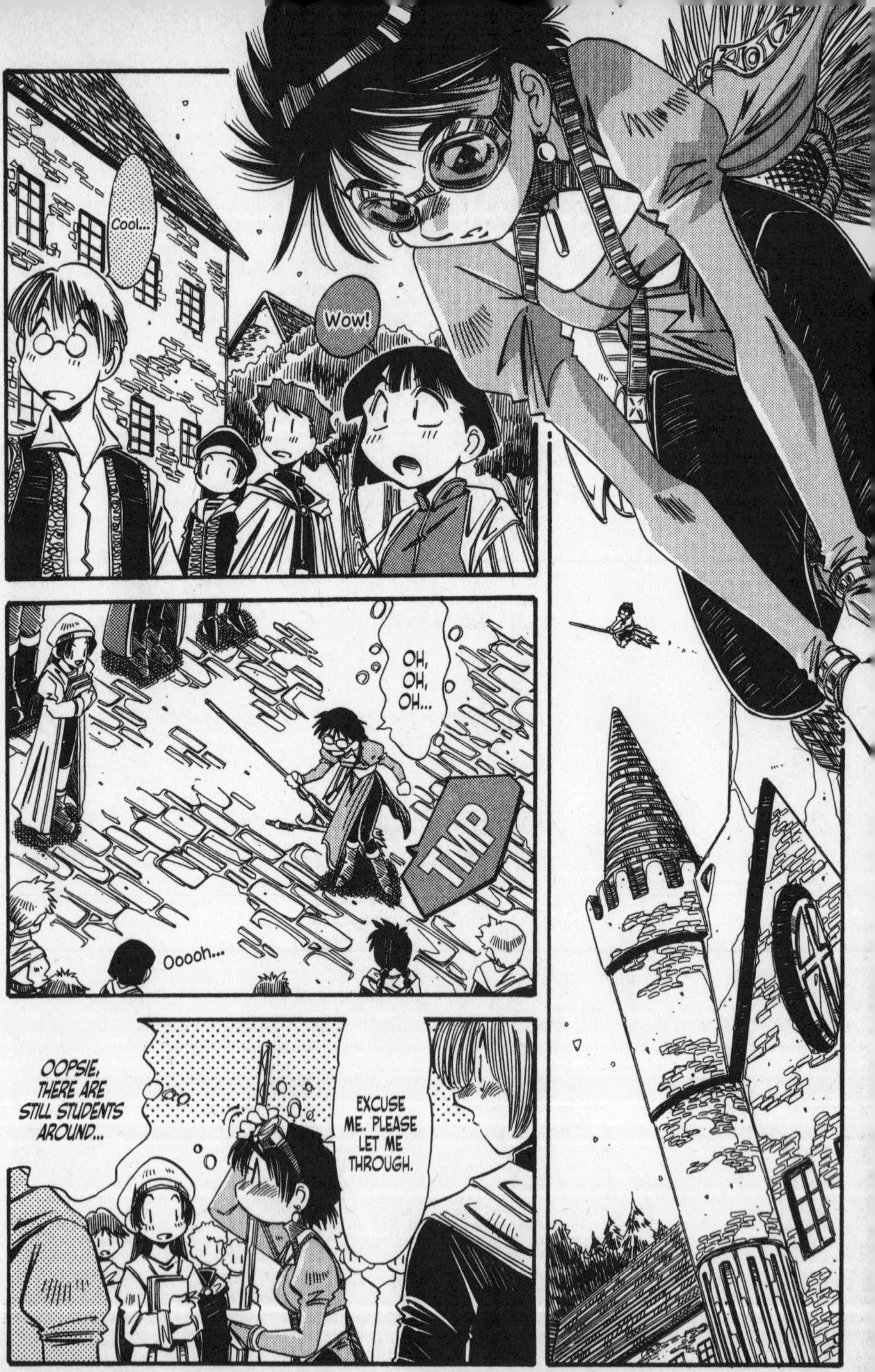
Cool...
Wow!
OH, OH, OH...
TMP
Ooooh...
EXCUSE ME. PLEASE LET ME THROUGH.
OOPSIE, THERE ARE STILL STUDENTS AROUND...

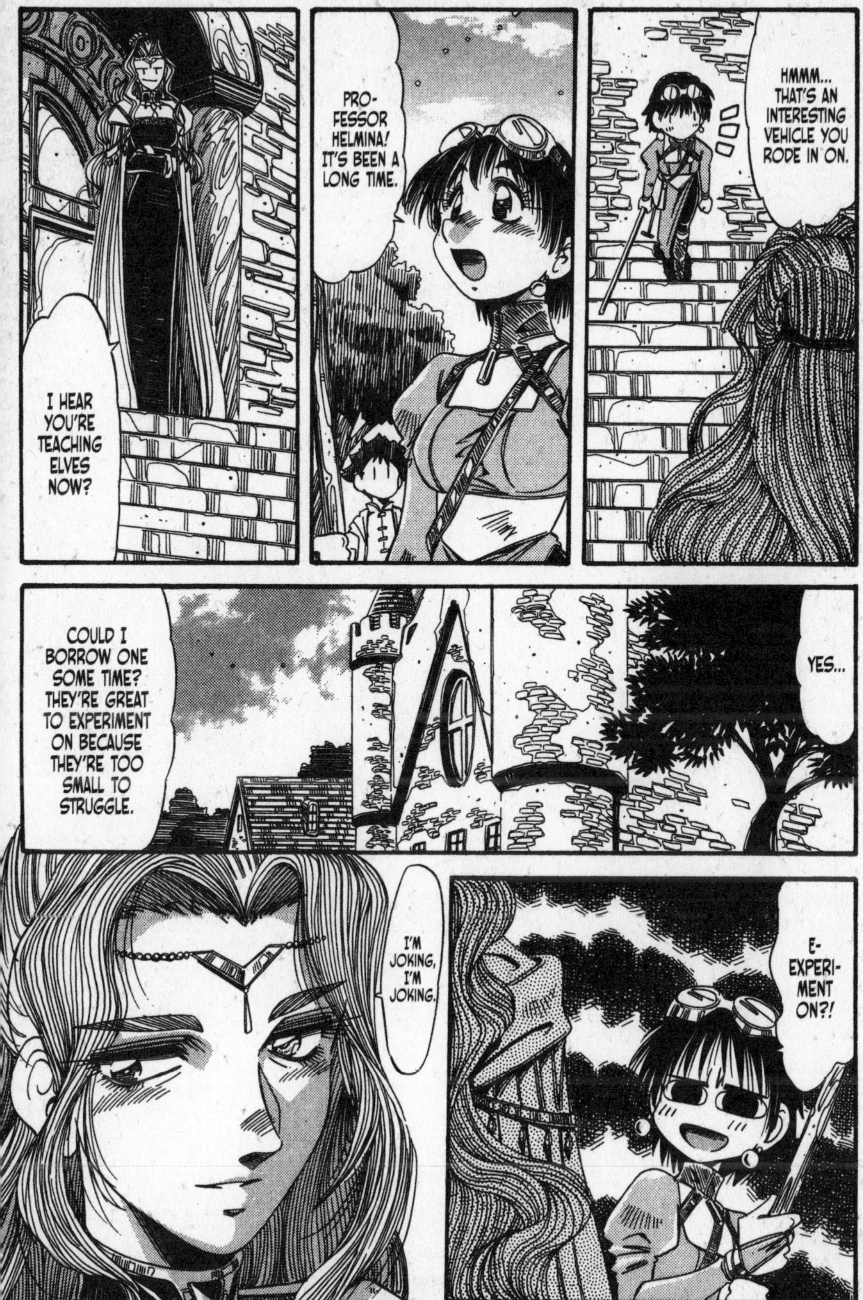
HMMM... THAT'S AN INTERESTING VEHICLE YOU RODE IN ON.
PRO-FESSOR HELMINA! IT'S BEEN A LONG TIME.
I HEAR YOU'RE TEACHING ELVES NOW?
YES...
COULD I BORROW ONE SOME TIME? THEY'RE GREAT TO EXPERIMENT ON BECAUSE THEY'RE TOO SMALL TO STRUGGLE.
E-EXPERI-MENT ON?!
I'M JOKING, I'M JOKING.

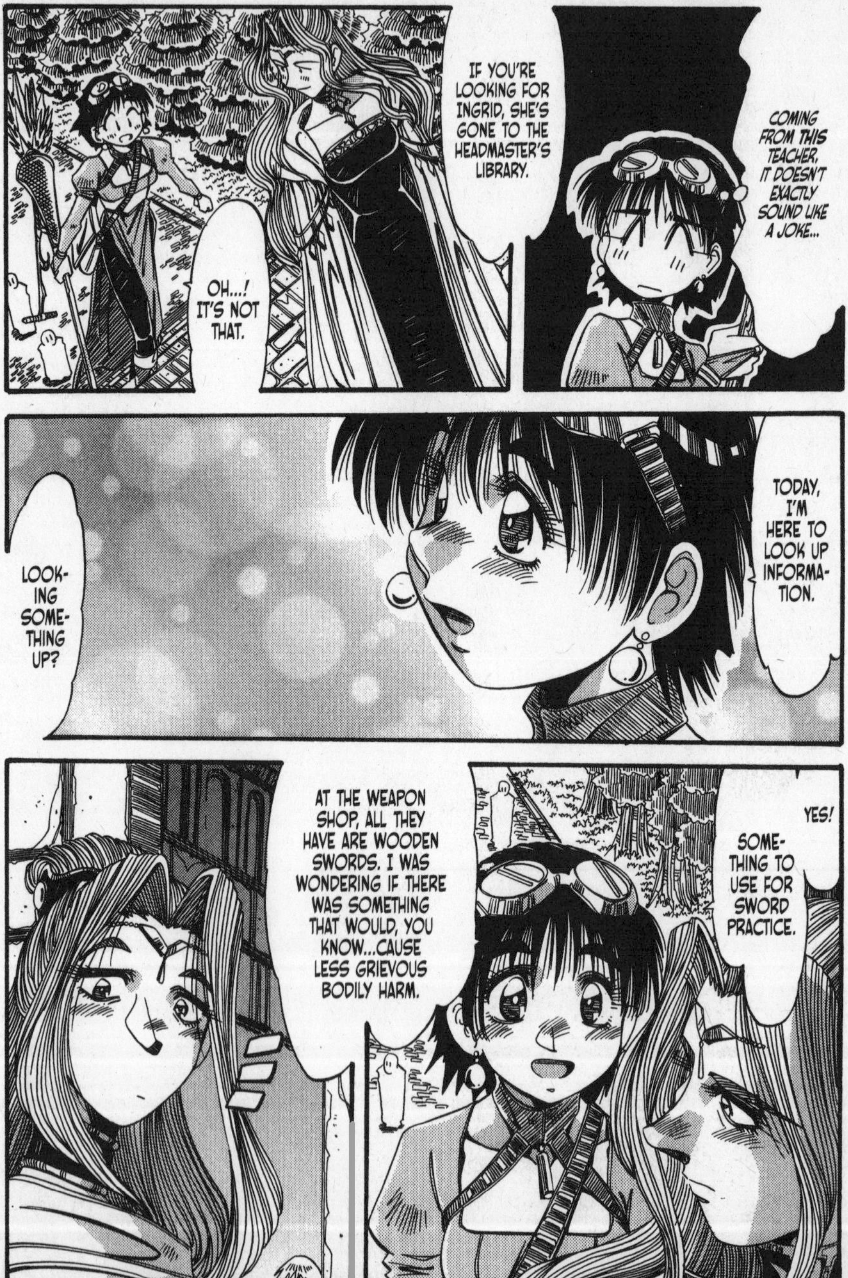
COMING FROM THIS TEACHER, IT DOESN'T EXACTLY SOUND LIKE A JOKE...
IF YOU'RE LOOKING FOR INGRID, SHE'S GONE TO THE HEADMASTER'S LIBRARY.
OH...! IT'S NOT THAT.
TODAY, I'M HERE TO LOOK UP INFORMA-TION.
LOOK-ING SOME-THING UP?
YES!
SOME-THING TO USE FOR SWORD PRACTICE.
AT THE WEAPON SHOP, ALL THEY HAVE ARE WOODEN SWORDS. I WAS WONDERING IF THERE WAS SOMETHING THAT WOULD, YOU KNOW...CAUSE LESS GRIEVOUS BODILY HARM.

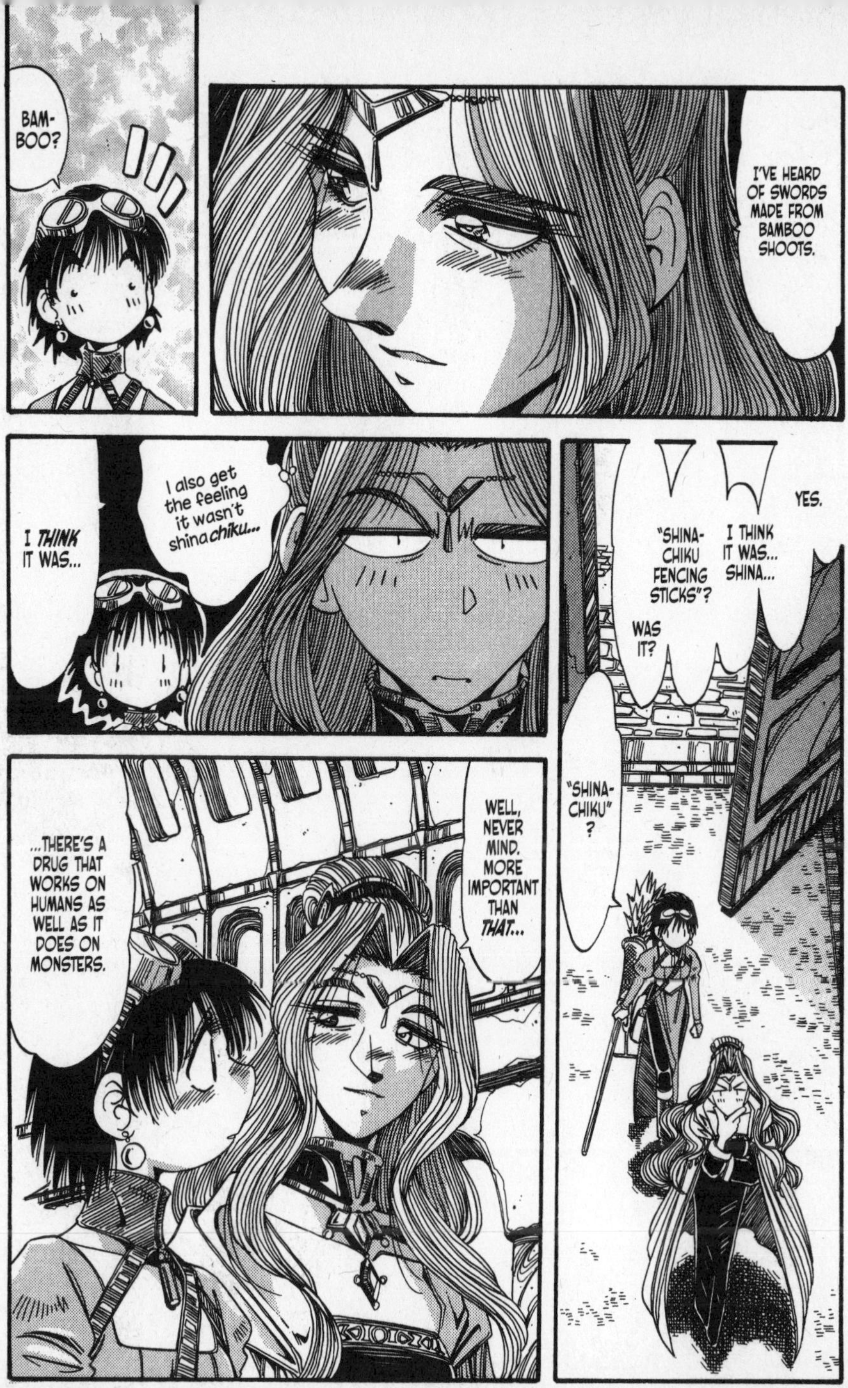
I'VE HEARD OF SWORDS MADE FROM BAMBOO SHOOTS.
BAM-BOO?
YES.
I THINK IT WAS... SHINA...
"SHINA-CHIKU FENCING STICKS"?
WAS IT?
"SHINA-CHIKU" ?
I also get the feeling it wasn't shina*chiku*...
I *THINK* IT WAS...
WELL, NEVER MIND. MORE IMPORTANT THAN *THAT*...
...THERE'S A DRUG THAT WORKS ON HUMANS AS WELL AS IT DOES ON MONSTERS.

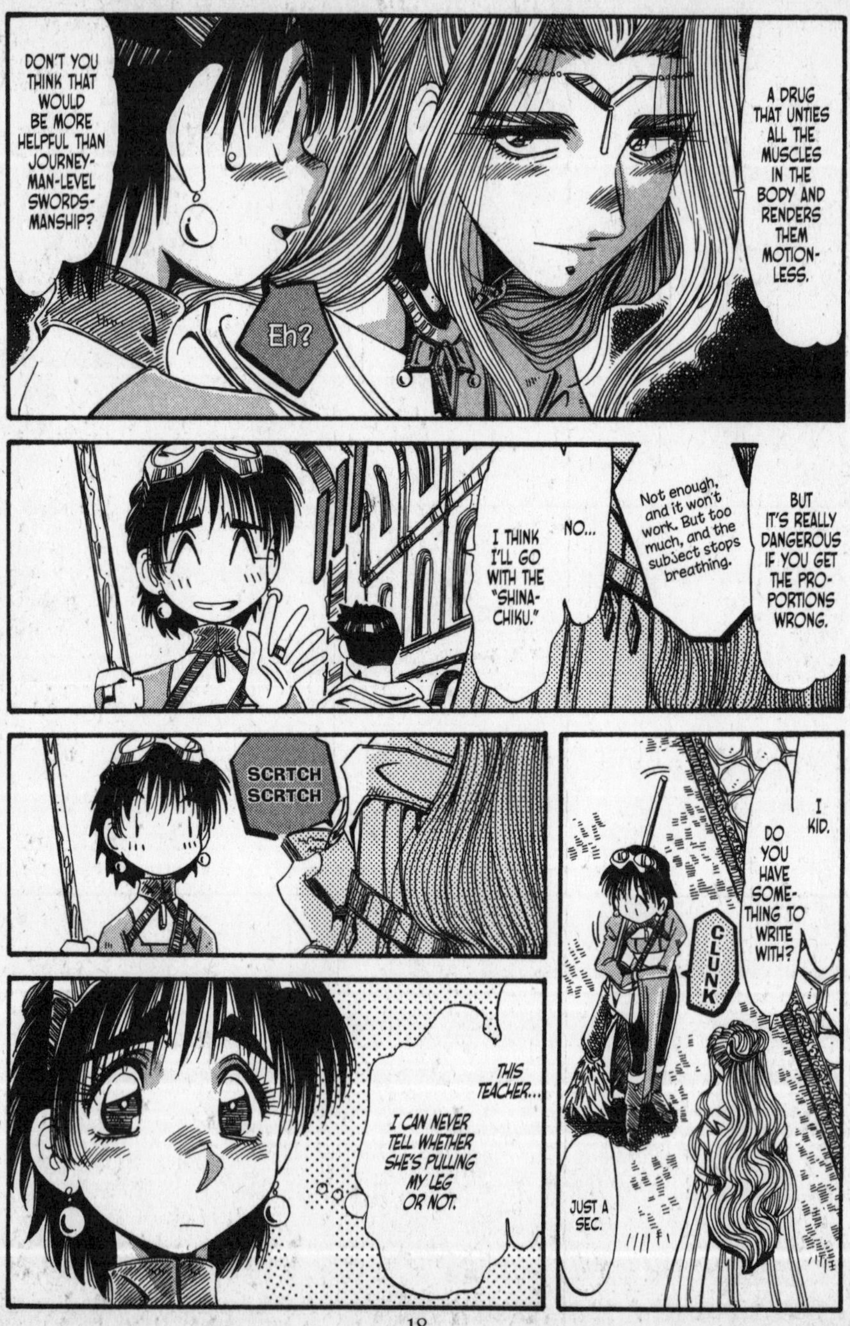
A DRUG THAT UNTIES ALL THE MUSCLES IN THE BODY AND RENDERS THEM MOTIONLESS.
DON'T YOU THINK THAT WOULD BE MORE HELPFUL THAN JOURNEYMAN-LEVEL SWORDSMANSHIP?
Eh?
BUT IT'S REALLY DANGEROUS IF YOU GET THE PROPORTIONS WRONG.
Not enough, and it won't work. But too much, and the subject stops breathing.
NO...
I THINK I'LL GO WITH THE "SHINA-CHIKU."
I KID.
DO YOU HAVE SOMETHING TO WRITE WITH?
CLUNK
JUST A SEC.
SCRTCH SCRTCH
THIS TEACHER...
I CAN NEVER TELL WHETHER SHE'S PULLING MY LEG OR NOT.

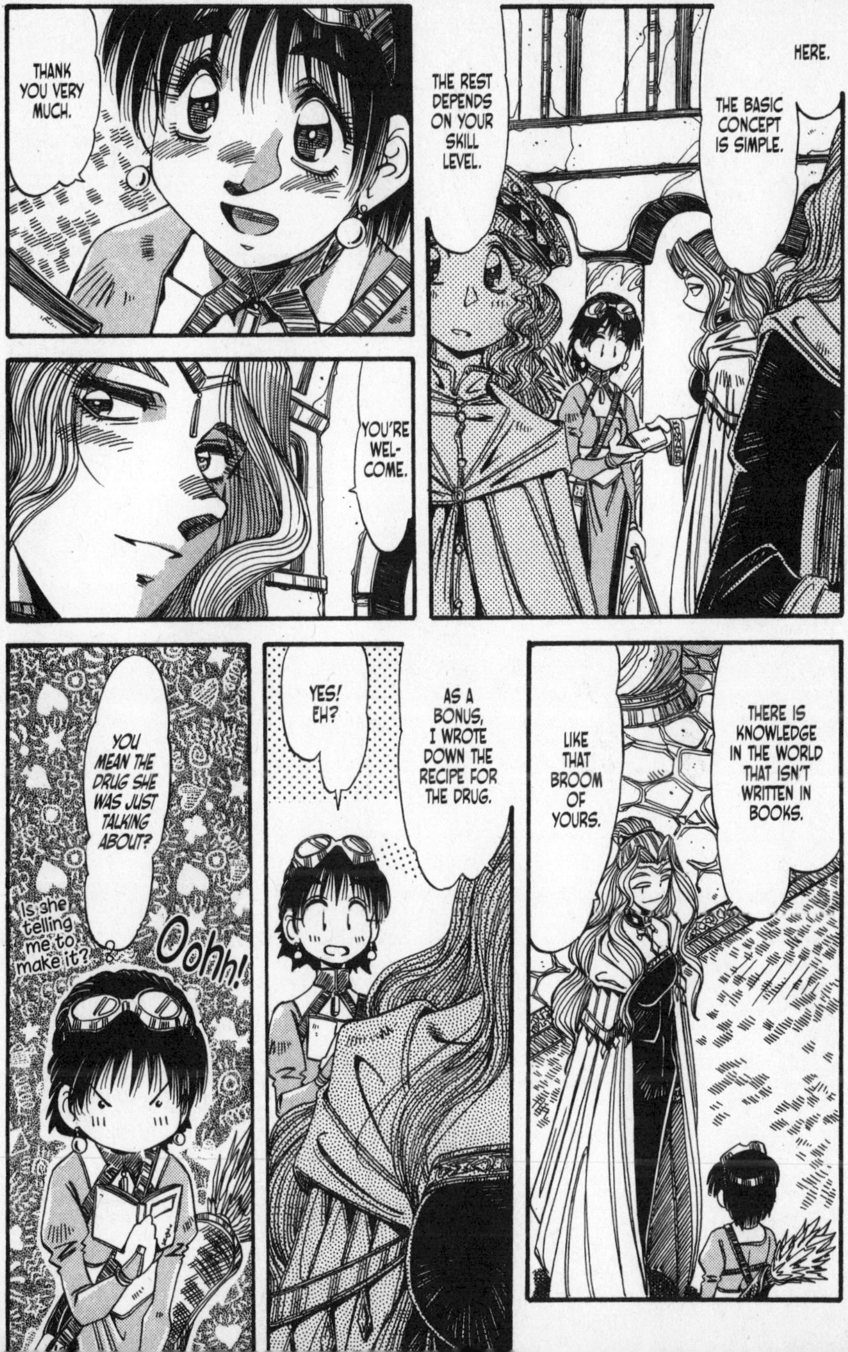
HERE.
THE BASIC CONCEPT IS SIMPLE.
THE REST DEPENDS ON YOUR SKILL LEVEL.
THANK YOU VERY MUCH.
YOU'RE WEL-COME.
THERE IS KNOWLEDGE IN THE WORLD THAT ISN'T WRITTEN IN BOOKS.
LIKE THAT BROOM OF YOURS.
AS A BONUS, I WROTE DOWN THE RECIPE FOR THE DRUG.
YES! EH?
YOU MEAN THE DRUG SHE WAS JUST TALKING ABOUT?
Oohh!
Is she telling me to make it?

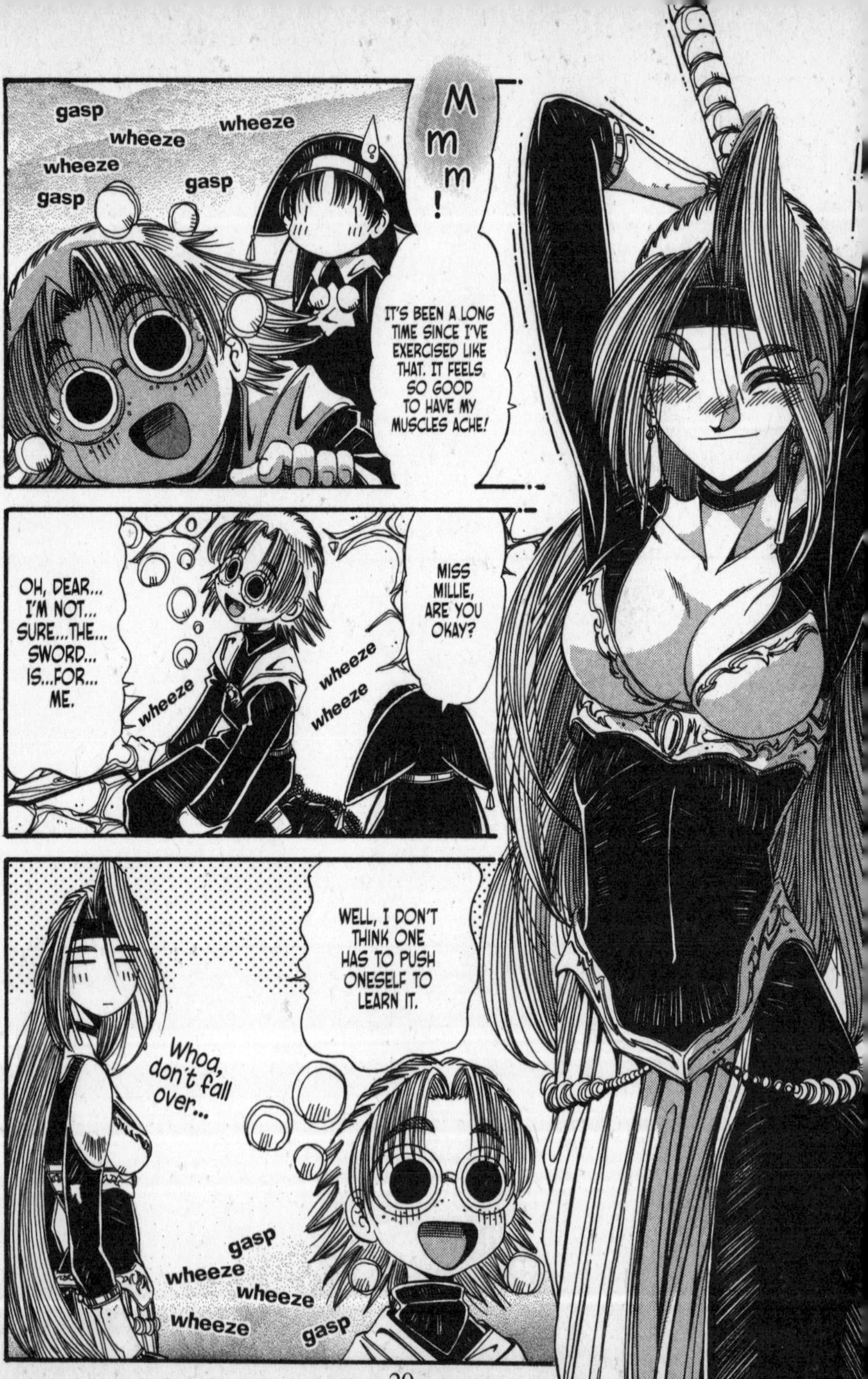
Mmm!
IT'S BEEN A LONG TIME SINCE I'VE EXERCISED LIKE THAT. IT FEELS SO GOOD TO HAVE MY MUSCLES ACHE!
wheeze
gasp
wheeze
gasp
wheeze
gasp
MISS MILLIE, ARE YOU OKAY?
wheeze
wheeze
OH, DEAR... I'M NOT... SURE...THE... SWORD... IS...FOR... ME.
wheeze
WELL, I DON'T THINK ONE HAS TO PUSH ONESELF TO LEARN IT.
Whoa, don't fall over...
gasp
wheeze
wheeze
wheeze
gasp

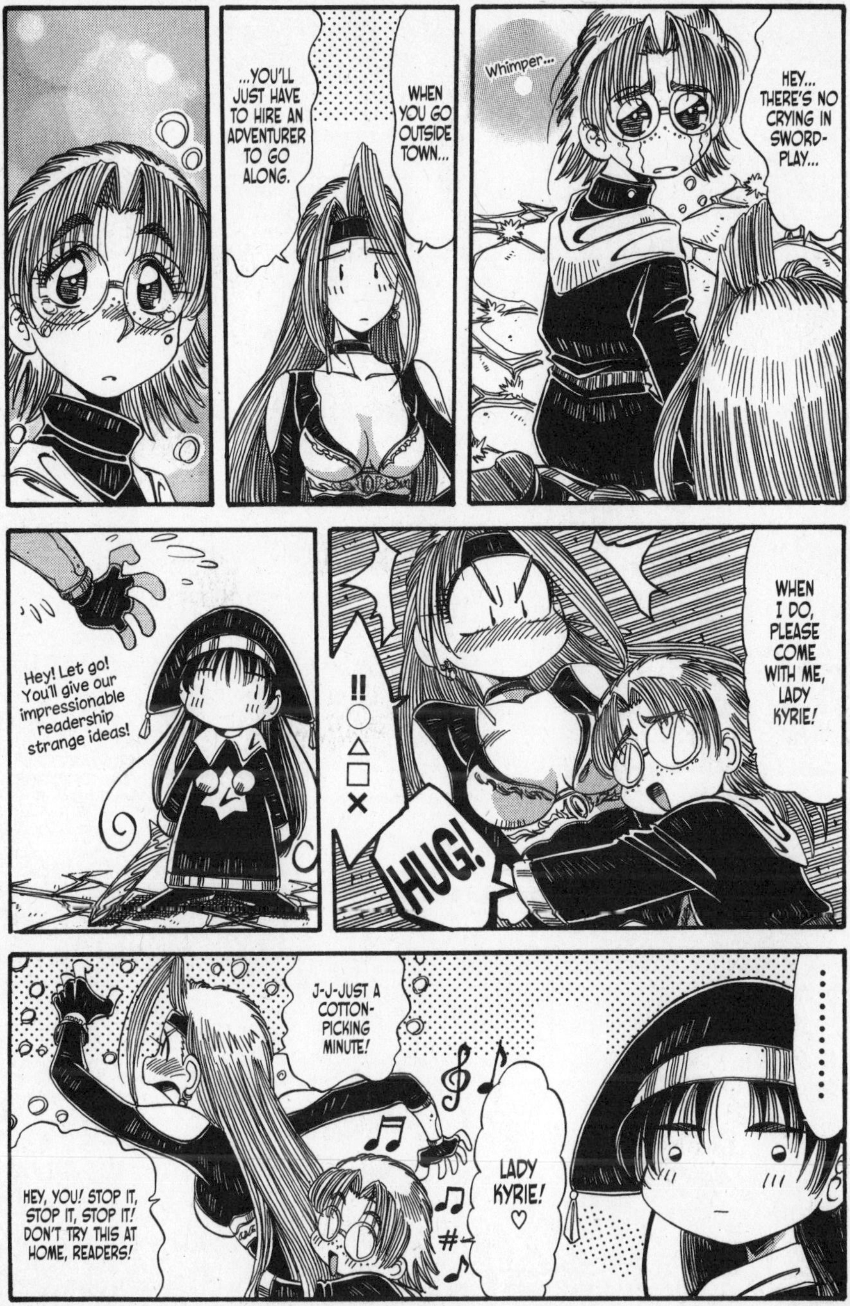
HEY... THERE'S NO CRYING IN SWORD-PLAY...
Whimper...
WHEN YOU GO OUTSIDE TOWN...
...YOU'LL JUST HAVE TO HIRE AN ADVENTURER TO GO ALONG.
WHEN I DO, PLEASE COME WITH ME, LADY KYRIE!
!! ○ △ □ ×
HUG!
Hey! Let go! You'll give our impressionable readership strange ideas!
......
LADY KYRIE! ♡
J-J-JUST A COTTON-PICKING MINUTE!
HEY, YOU! STOP IT, STOP IT, STOP IT! DON'T TRY THIS AT HOME, READERS!

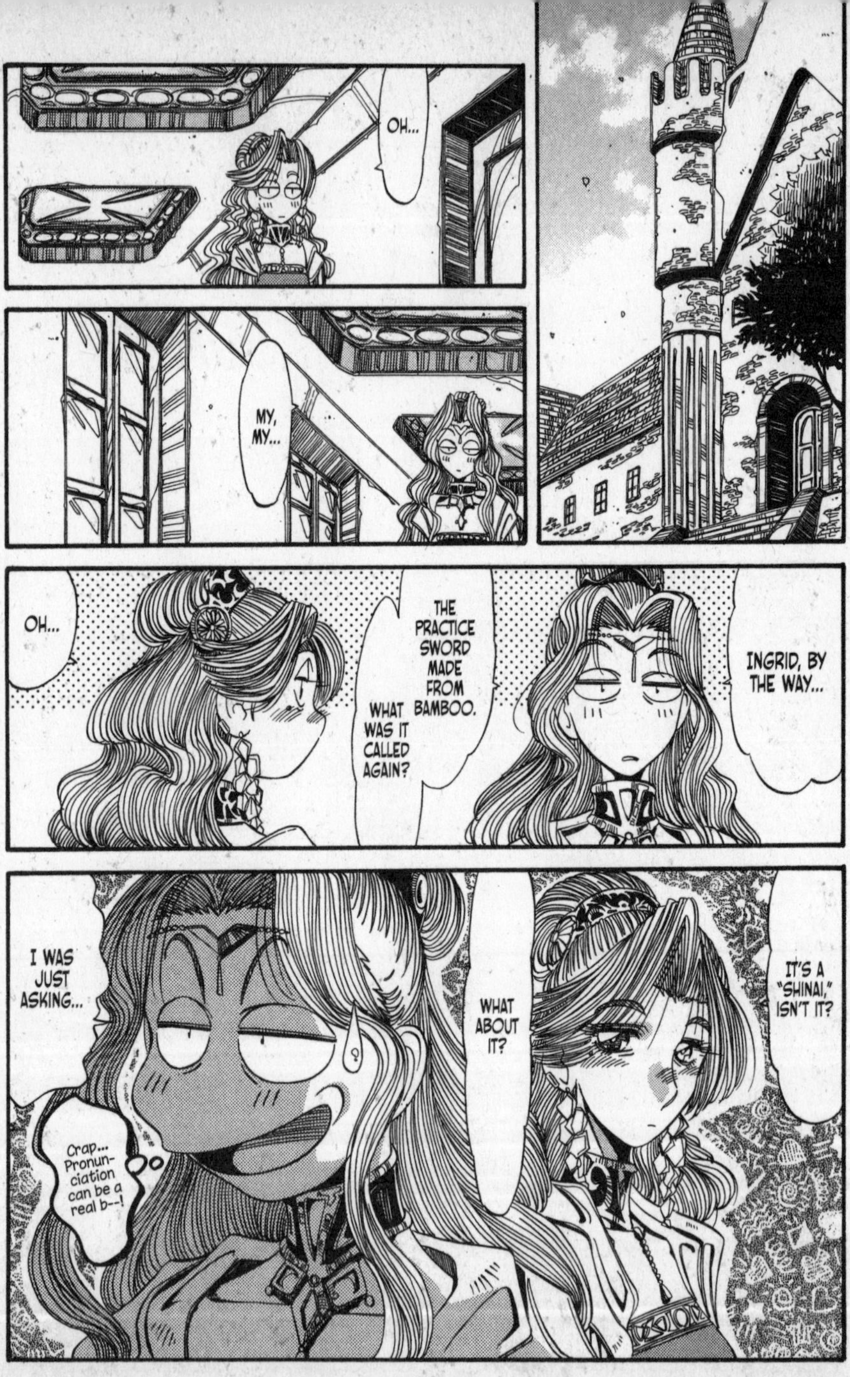
OH...
MY, MY...
INGRID, BY THE WAY...
THE PRACTICE SWORD MADE FROM BAMBOO.
WHAT WAS IT CALLED AGAIN?
OH...
IT'S A "SHINAI," ISN'T IT?
WHAT ABOUT IT?
I WAS JUST ASKING...
Crap... Pronunciation can be a real b--!

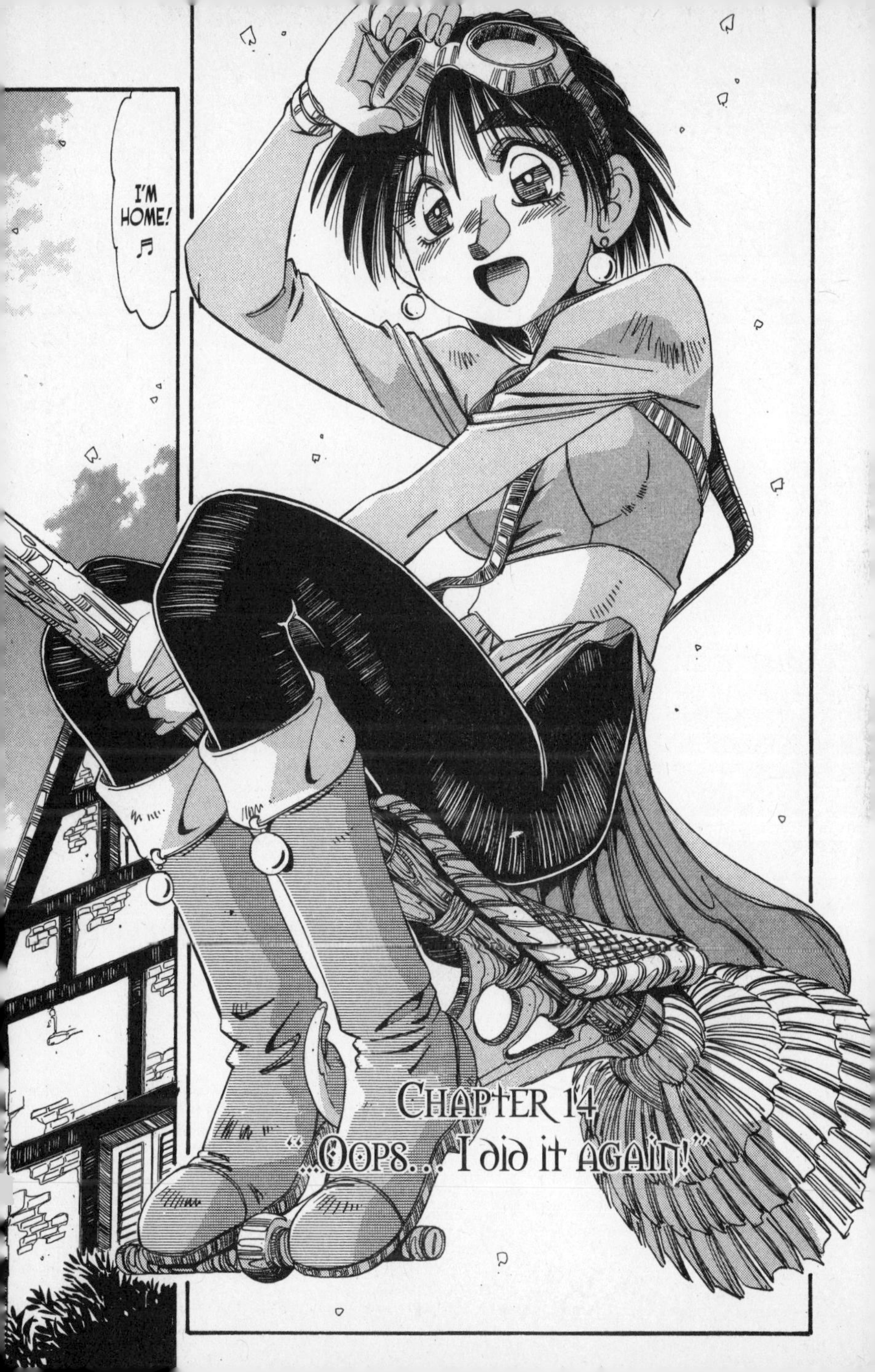
I'M HOME! ♫
CHAPTER 14
"...OOPS... I DID IT AGAIN!"

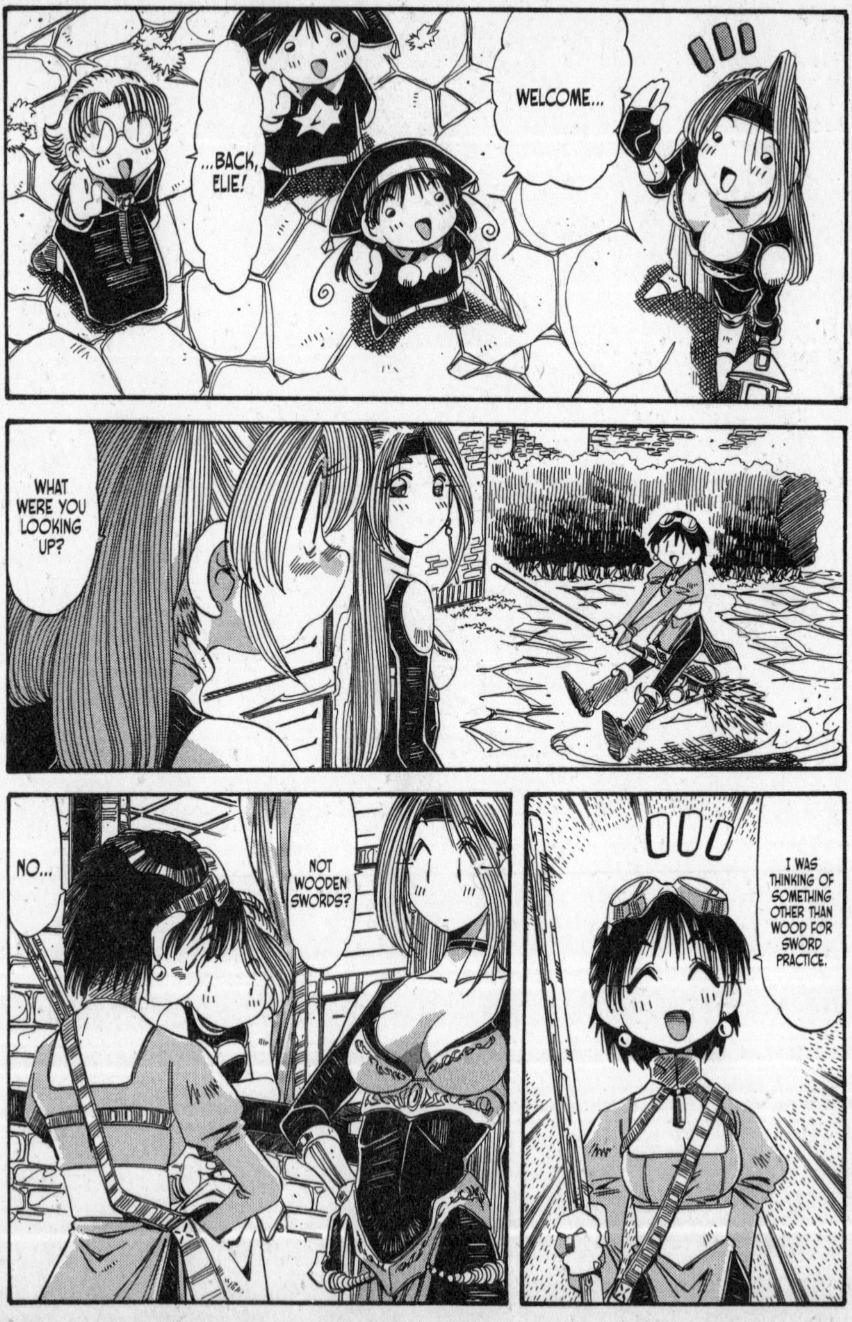
WELCOME...
...BACK, ELIE!
WHAT WERE YOU LOOKING UP?
I WAS THINKING OF SOMETHING OTHER THAN WOOD FOR SWORD PRACTICE.
NOT WOODEN SWORDS?
NO...

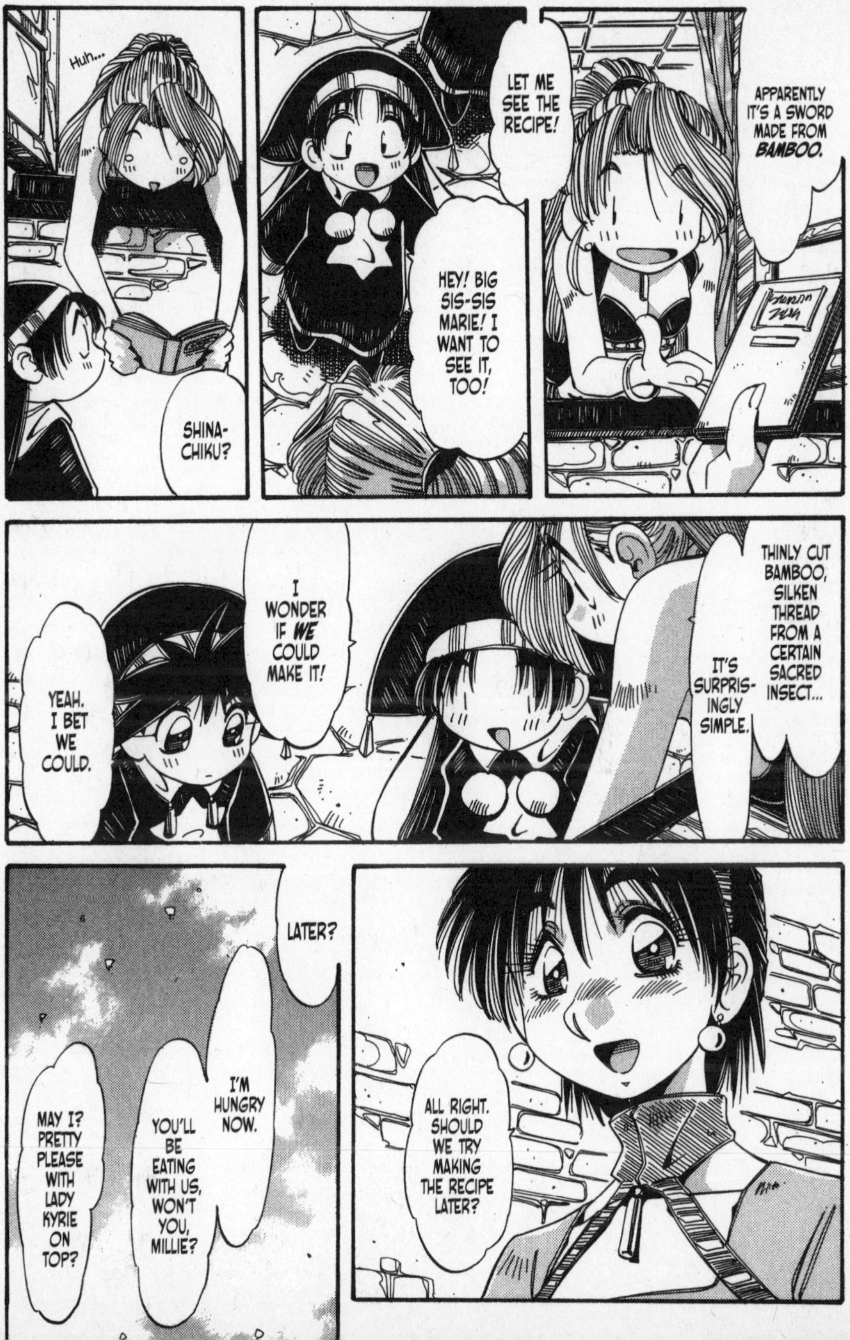
APPARENTLY IT'S A SWORD MADE FROM BAMBOO.
LET ME SEE THE RECIPE!
HEY! BIG SIS-SIS MARIE! I WANT TO SEE IT, TOO!
Huh...
SHINA-CHIKU?
THINLY CUT BAMBOO, SILKEN THREAD FROM A CERTAIN SACRED INSECT...
IT'S SURPRIS-INGLY SIMPLE.
I WONDER IF WE COULD MAKE IT!
YEAH. I BET WE COULD.
ALL RIGHT. SHOULD WE TRY MAKING THE RECIPE LATER?
LATER?
I'M HUNGRY NOW.
YOU'LL BE EATING WITH US, WON'T YOU, MILLIE?
MAY I? PRETTY PLEASE WITH LADY KYRIE ON TOP?

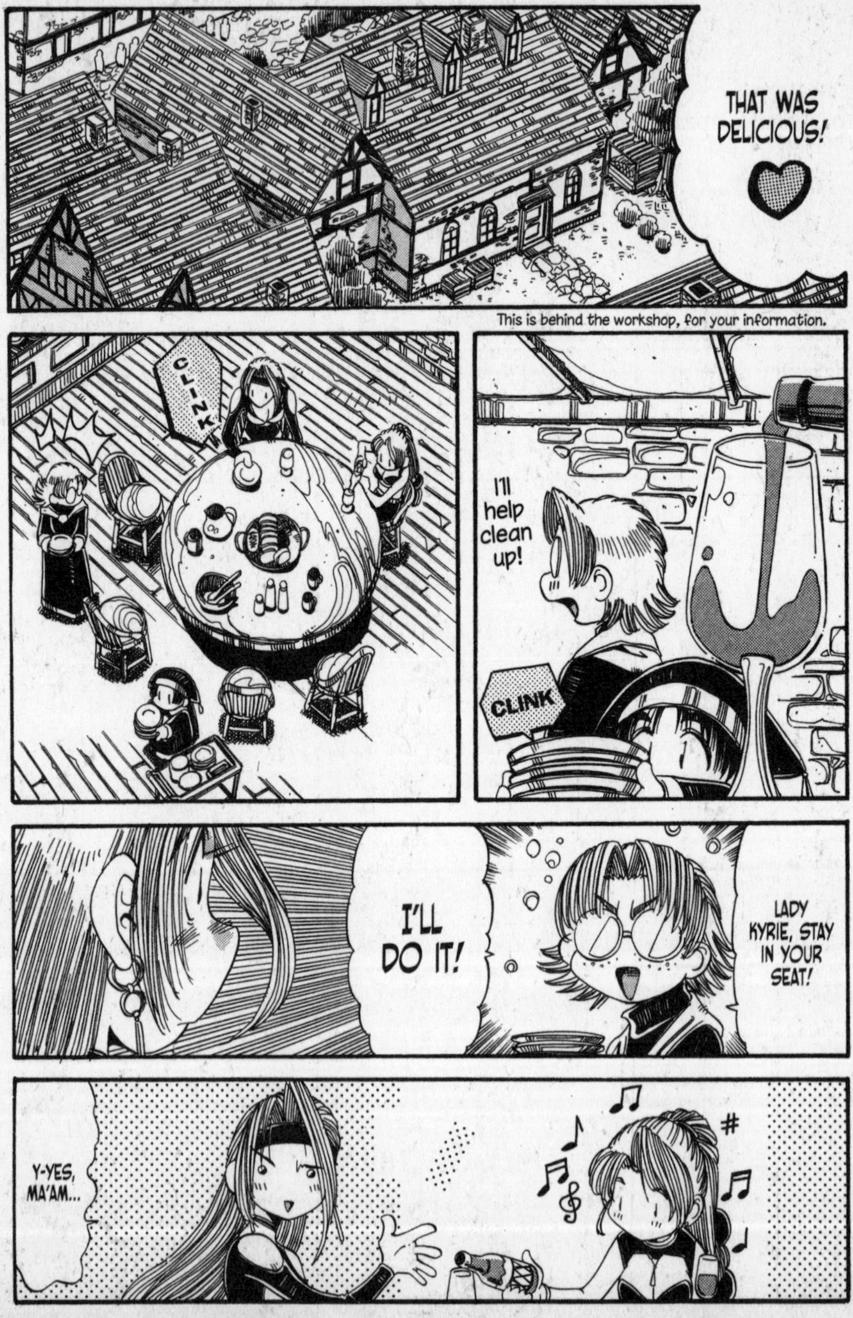
THAT WAS DELICIOUS!
This is behind the workshop, for your information.
I'll help clean up!
CLINK
CLINK
LADY KYRIE, STAY IN YOUR SEAT!
I'LL DO IT!
Y-YES, MA'AM...

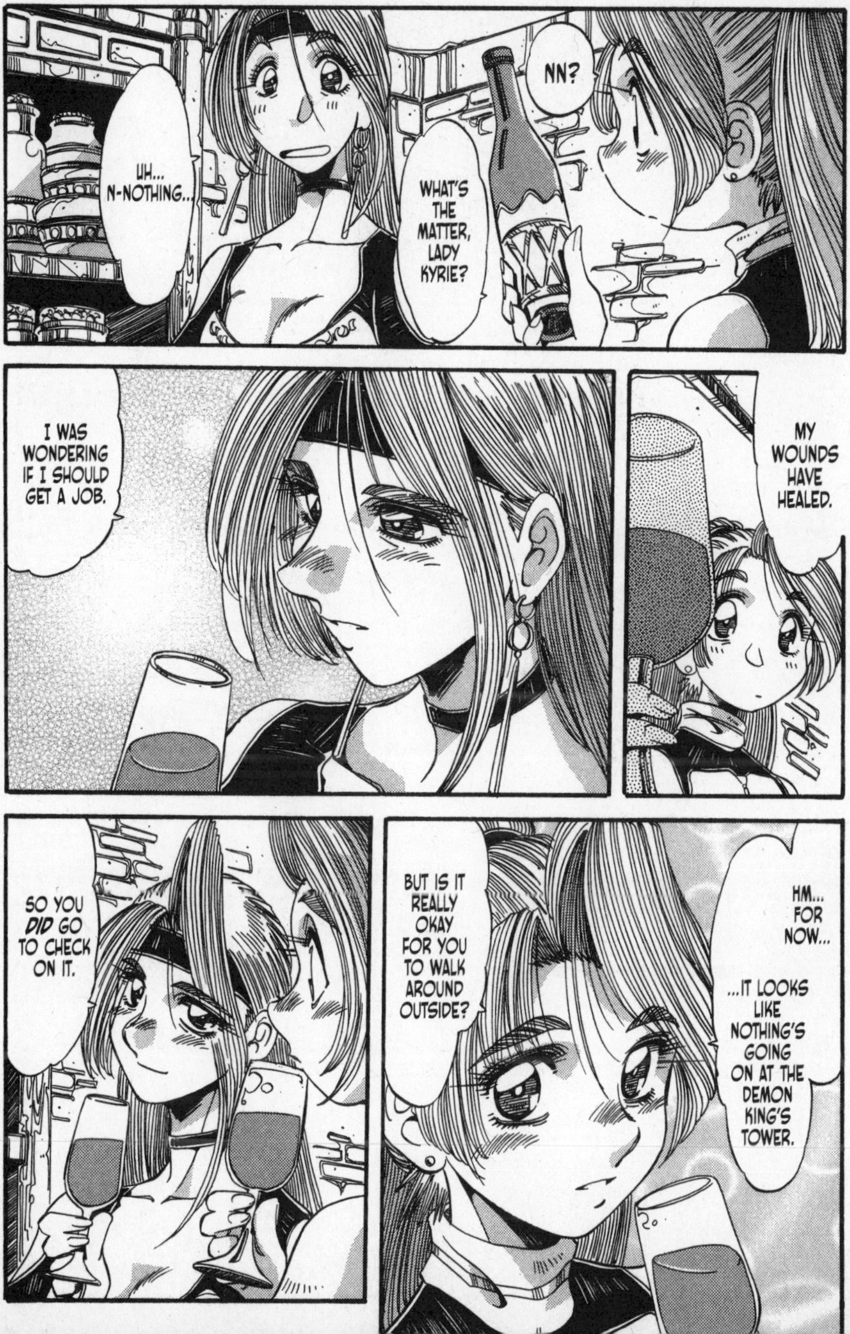
NN?
WHAT'S THE MATTER, LADY KYRIE?
UH... N-NOTHING...
MY WOUNDS HAVE HEALED.
I WAS WONDERING IF I SHOULD GET A JOB.
HM... FOR NOW...
...IT LOOKS LIKE NOTHING'S GOING ON AT THE DEMON KING'S TOWER.
BUT IS IT REALLY OKAY FOR YOU TO WALK AROUND OUTSIDE?
SO YOU *DID* GO TO CHECK ON IT.

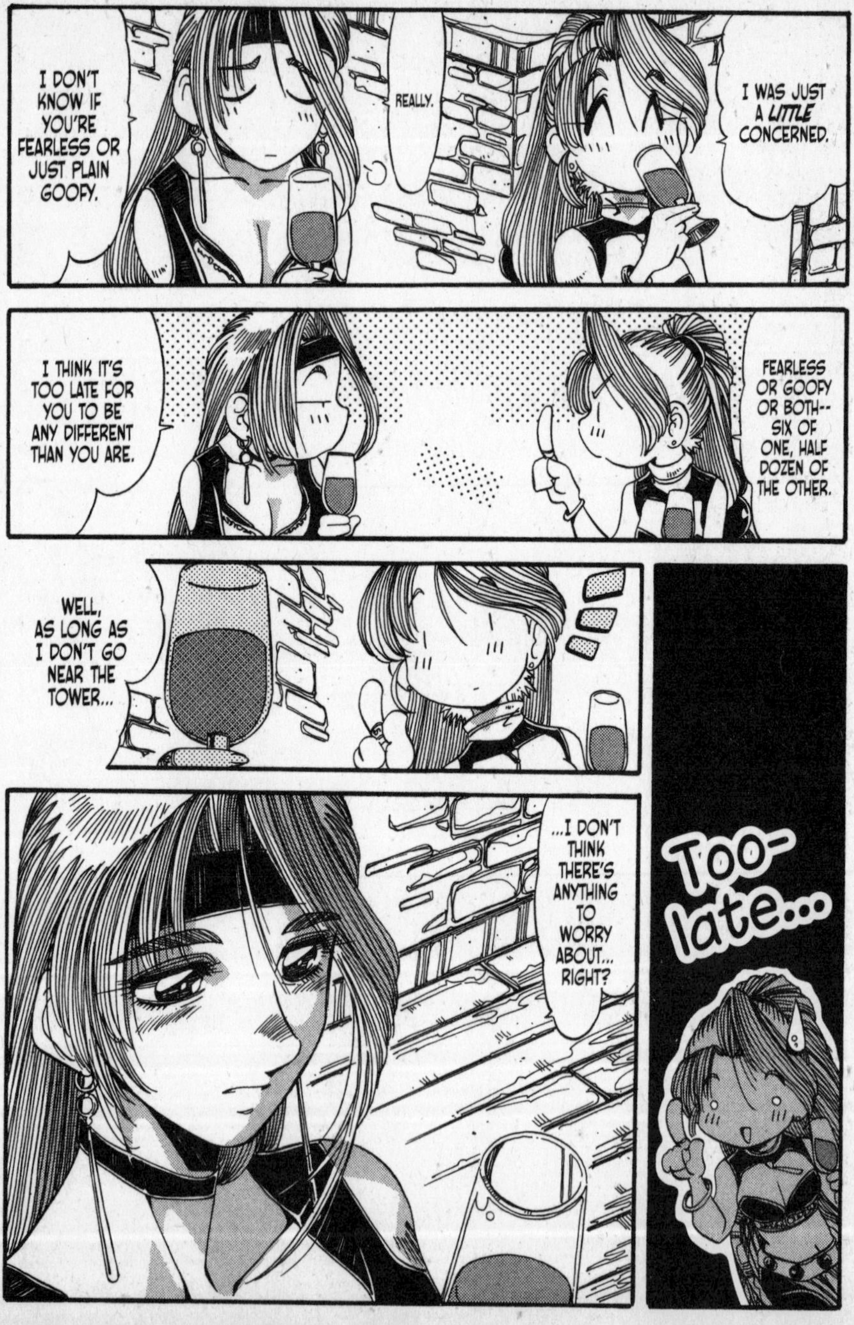
I WAS JUST A LITTLE CONCERNED.
REALLY.
I DON'T KNOW IF YOU'RE FEARLESS OR JUST PLAIN GOOFY.
FEARLESS OR GOOFY OR BOTH--SIX OF ONE, HALF DOZEN OF THE OTHER.
I THINK IT'S TOO LATE FOR YOU TO BE ANY DIFFERENT THAN YOU ARE.
Too-late...
WELL, AS LONG AS I DON'T GO NEAR THE TOWER...
...I DON'T THINK THERE'S ANYTHING TO WORRY ABOUT... RIGHT?

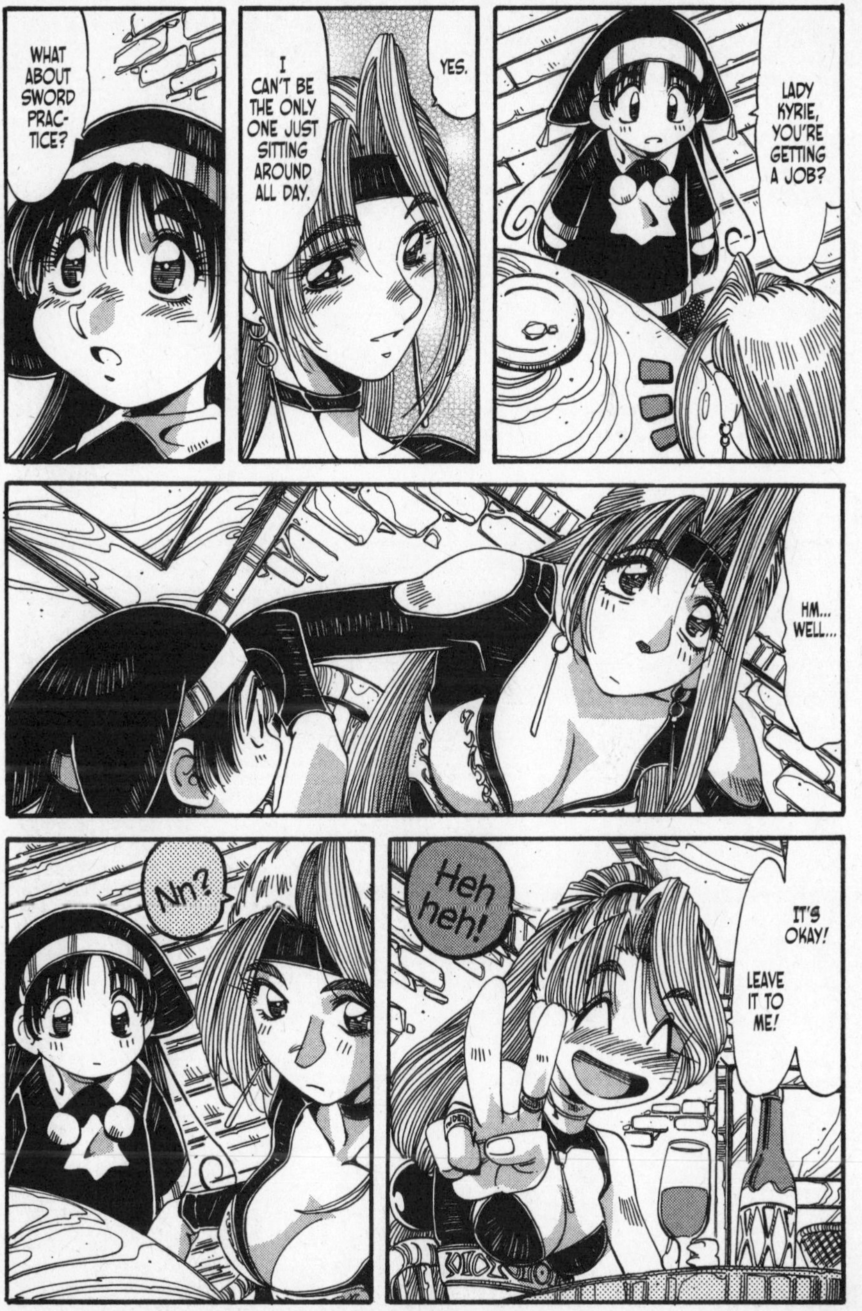
LADY KYRIE, YOU'RE GETTING A JOB?
YES.
I CAN'T BE THE ONLY ONE JUST SITTING AROUND ALL DAY.
WHAT ABOUT SWORD PRAC-TICE?
HM... WELL...
IT'S OKAY!
LEAVE IT TO ME!
Heh heh!
Nn?

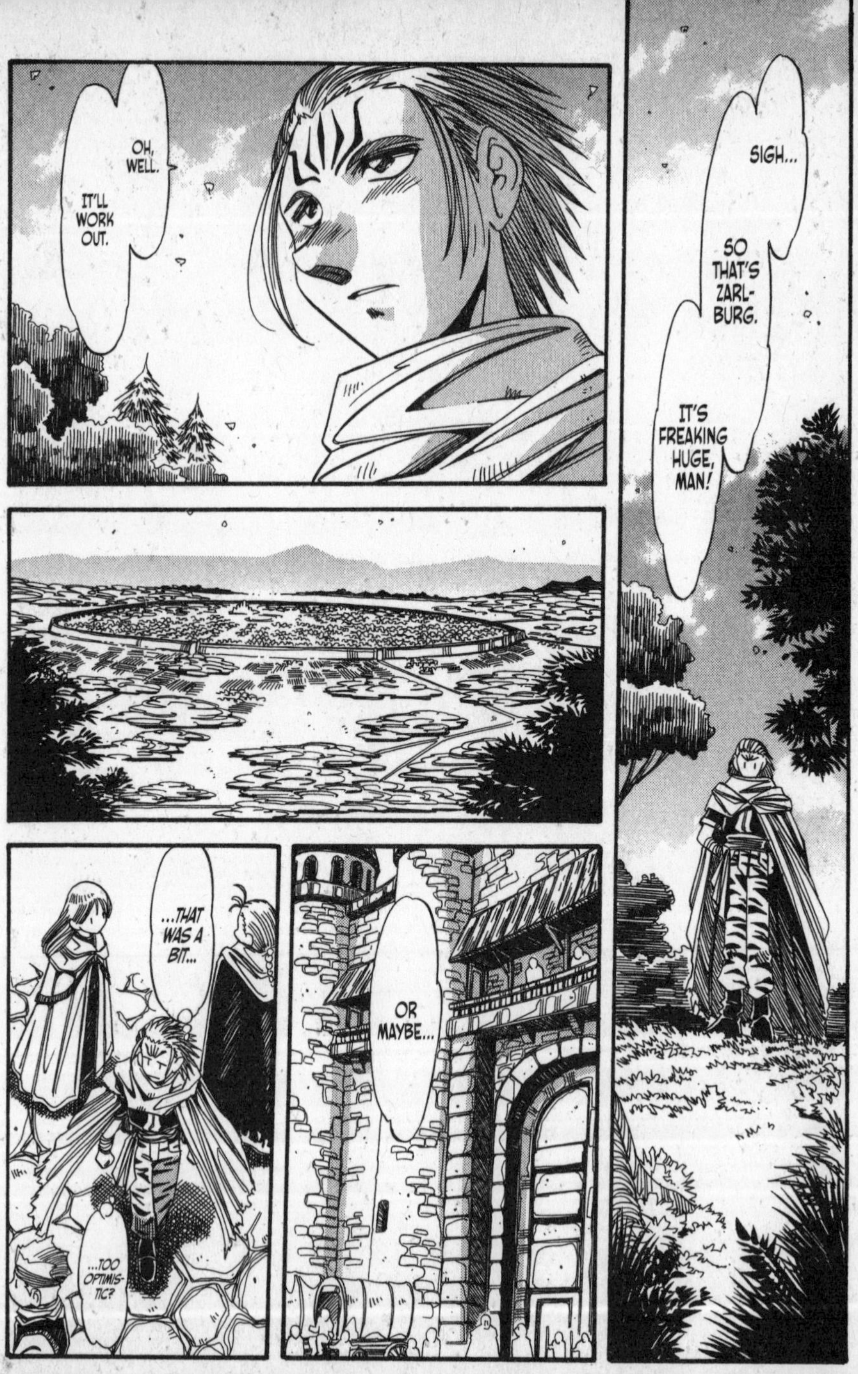
SIGH...
SO THAT'S ZARL-BURG.
IT'S FREAKING HUGE, MAN!
OH, WELL.
IT'LL WORK OUT.
OR MAYBE...
...THAT WAS A BIT...
...TOO OPTIMIS-TIC?

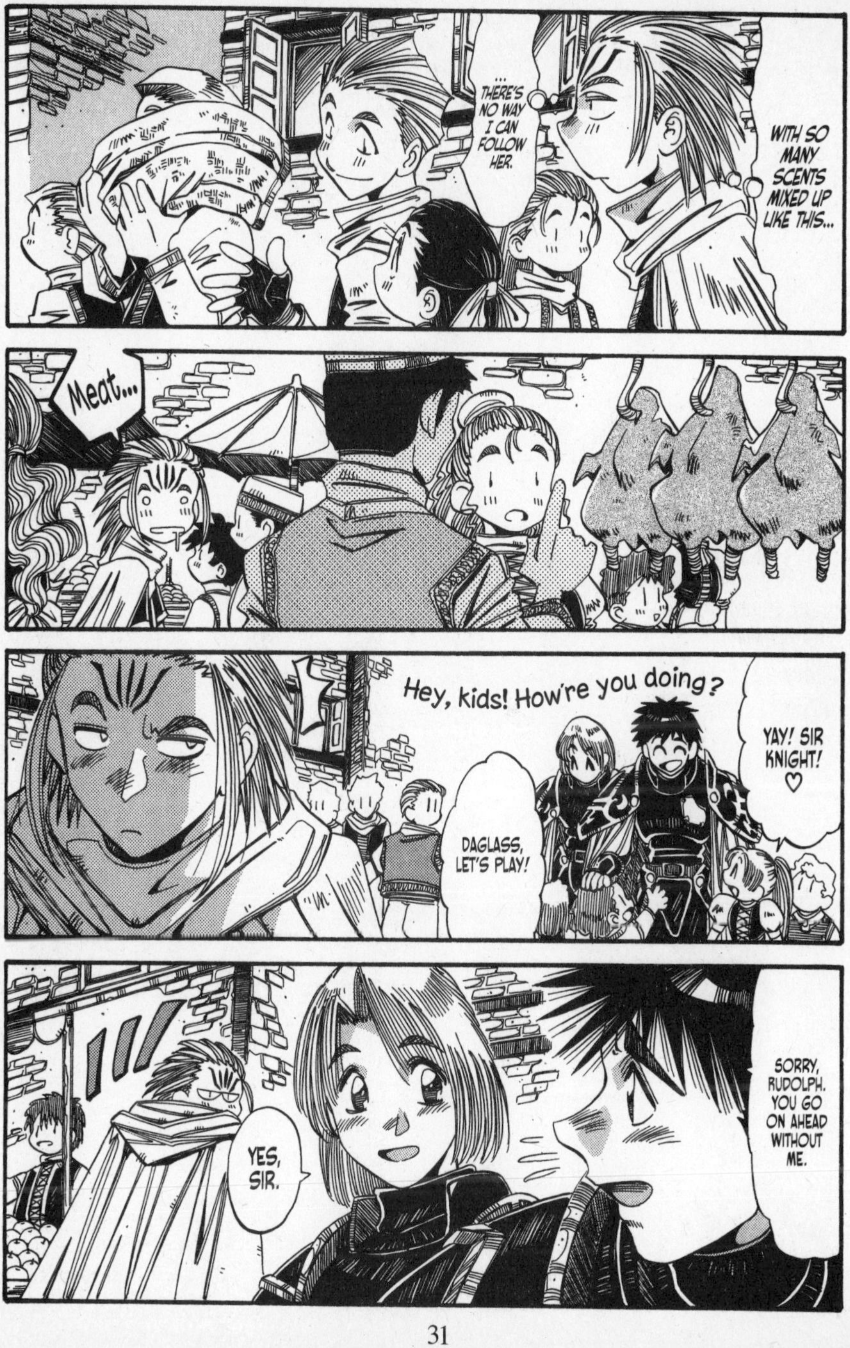
WITH SO MANY SCENTS MIXED UP LIKE THIS...
... THERE'S NO WAY I CAN FOLLOW HER.
Meat...
YAY! SIR KNIGHT! ♡
Hey, kids! How're you doing?
DAGLASS, LET'S PLAY!
SORRY, RUDOLPH. YOU GO ON AHEAD WITHOUT ME.
YES, SIR.

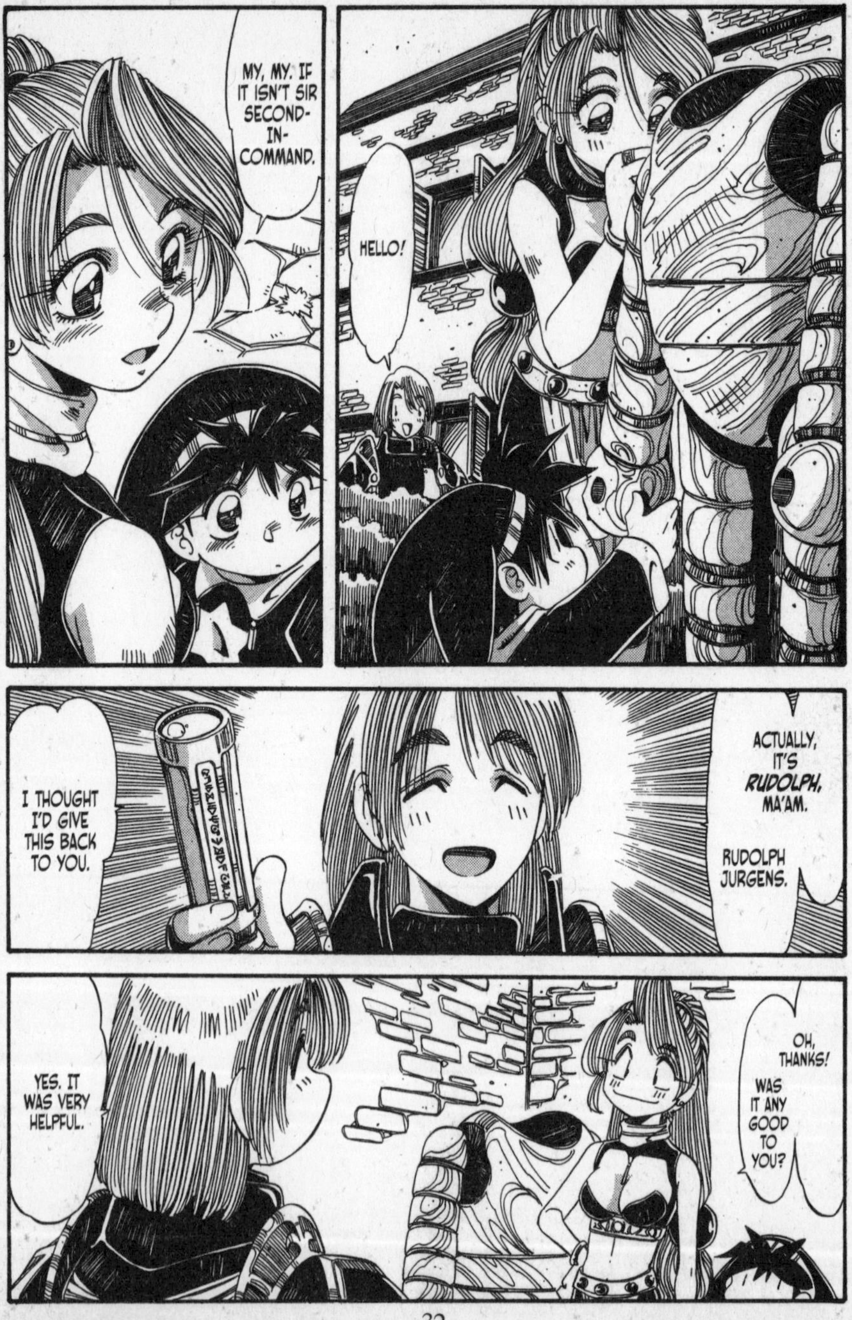
HELLO!
MY, MY. IF IT ISN'T SIR SECOND-IN-COMMAND.
ACTUALLY, IT'S RUDOLPH, MA'AM.
RUDOLPH JURGENS.
I THOUGHT I'D GIVE THIS BACK TO YOU.
OH, THANKS!
WAS IT ANY GOOD TO YOU?
YES. IT WAS VERY HELPFUL.

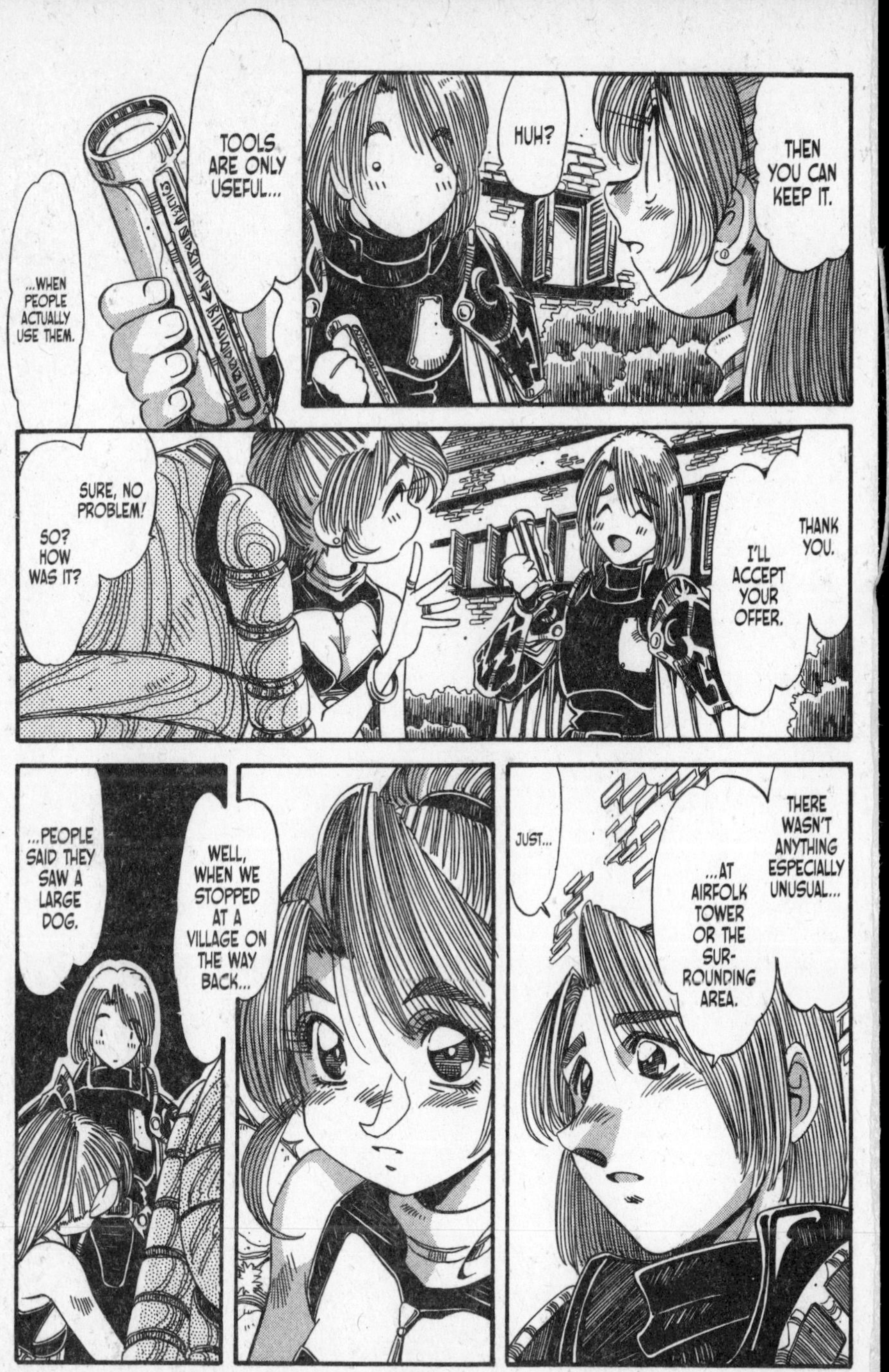
THEN YOU CAN KEEP IT.
HUH?
TOOLS ARE ONLY USEFUL...
...WHEN PEOPLE ACTUALLY USE THEM.
THANK YOU.
I'LL ACCEPT YOUR OFFER.
SURE, NO PROBLEM!
SO? HOW WAS IT?
THERE WASN'T ANYTHING ESPECIALLY UNUSUAL...
...AT AIRFOLK TOWER OR THE SUR-ROUNDING AREA.
JUST...
WELL, WHEN WE STOPPED AT A VILLAGE ON THE WAY BACK...
...PEOPLE SAID THEY SAW A LARGE DOG.

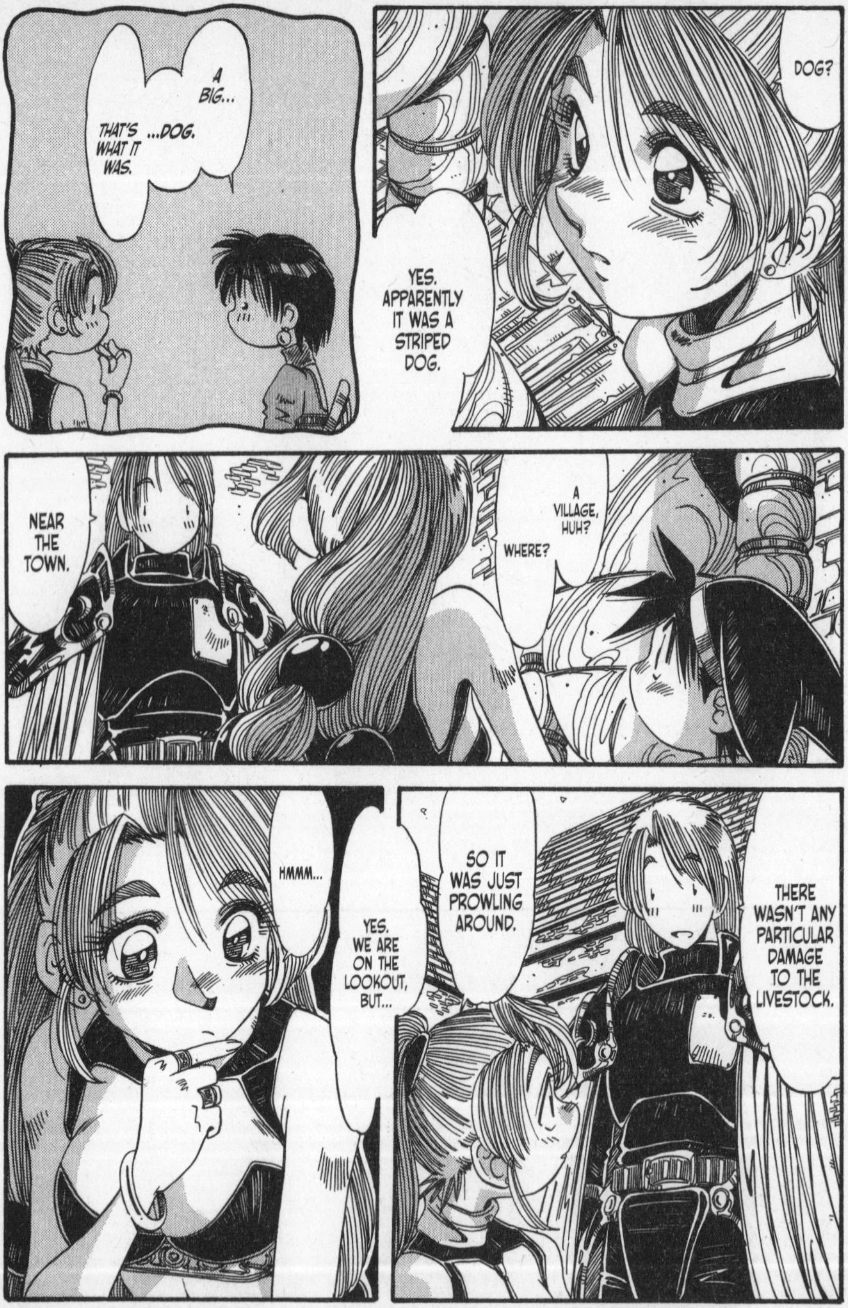
DOG?
YES. APPARENTLY IT WAS A STRIPED DOG.
A BIG...
...DOG.
THAT'S WHAT IT WAS.
A VILLAGE, HUH?
WHERE?
NEAR THE TOWN.
THERE WASN'T ANY PARTICULAR DAMAGE TO THE LIVESTOCK.
SO IT WAS JUST PROWLING AROUND.
YES. WE ARE ON THE LOOKOUT, BUT...
HMMM...

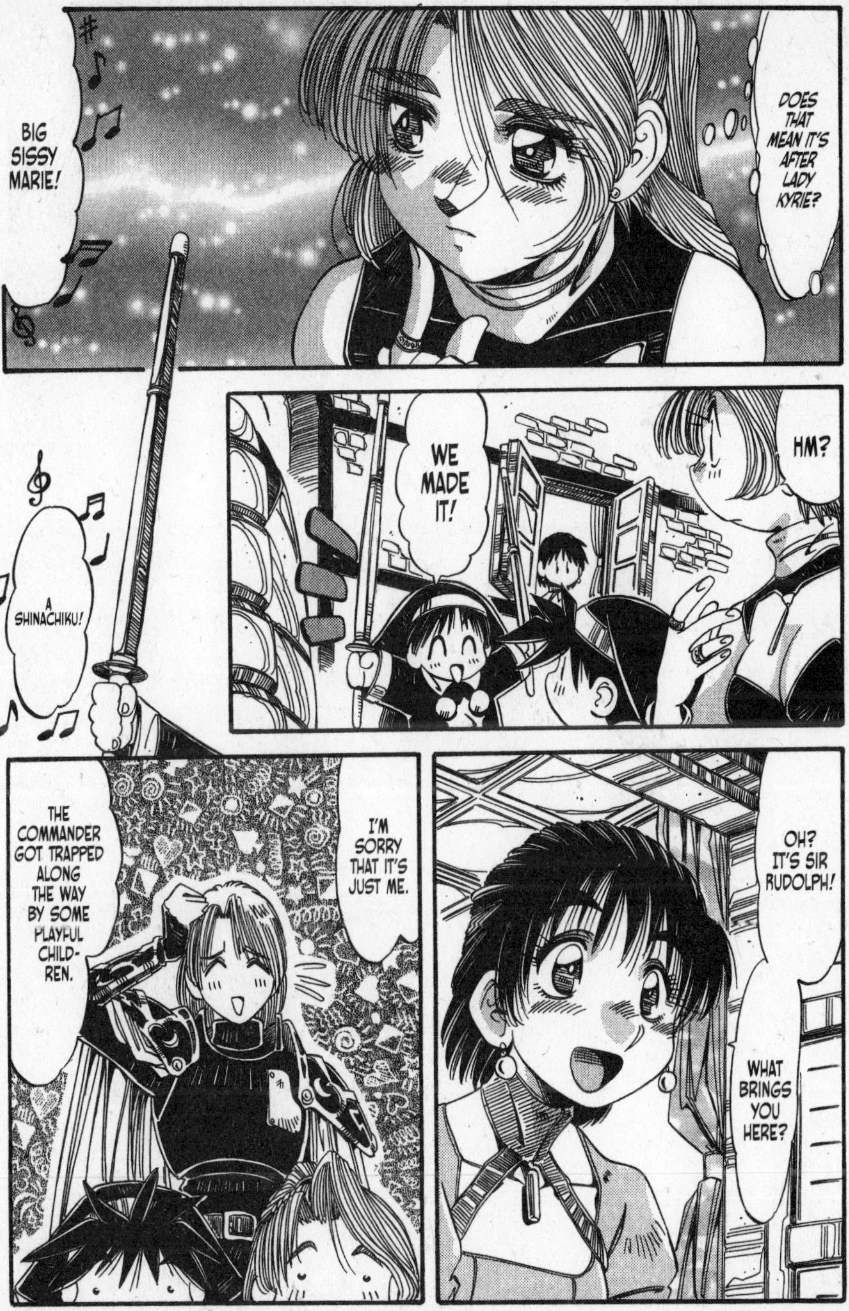
DOES THAT MEAN IT'S AFTER LADY KYRIE?
BIG SISSY MARIE!
HM?
WE MADE IT!
A SHINACHIKU!
OH? IT'S SIR RUDOLPH!
WHAT BRINGS YOU HERE?
I'M SORRY THAT IT'S JUST ME.
THE COMMANDER GOT TRAPPED ALONG THE WAY BY SOME PLAYFUL CHILD-REN.

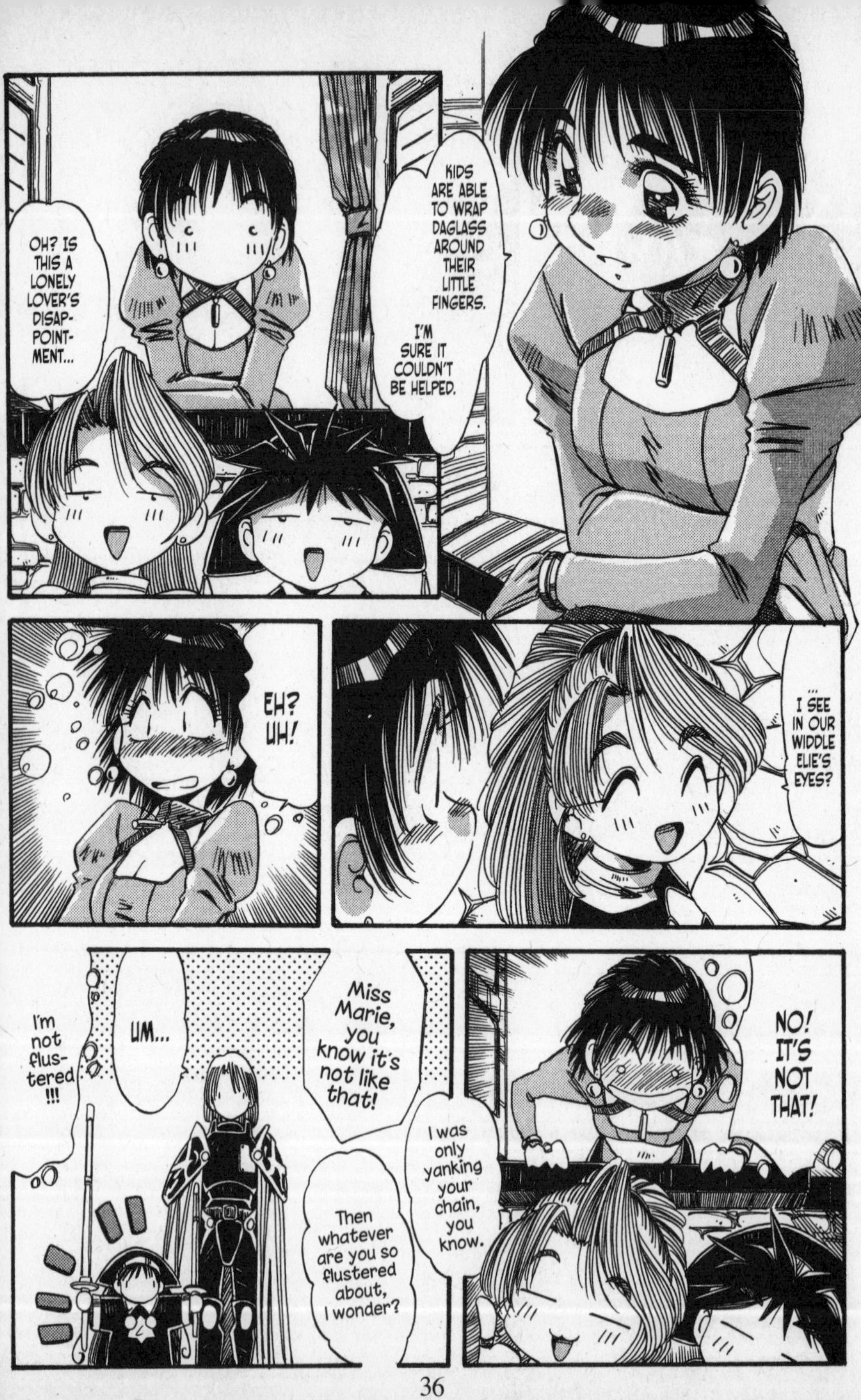
KIDS ARE ABLE TO WRAP DAGLASS AROUND THEIR LITTLE FINGERS.
I'M SURE IT COULDN'T BE HELPED.
OH? IS THIS A LONELY LOVER'S DISAPP-POINT-MENT...
... I SEE IN OUR WIDDLE ELIE'S EYES?
EH? UH!
NO! IT'S NOT THAT!
Miss Marie, you know it's not like that!
I was only yanking your chain, you know.
Then whatever are you so flustered about, I wonder?
UM...
I'm not flus-tered!!!

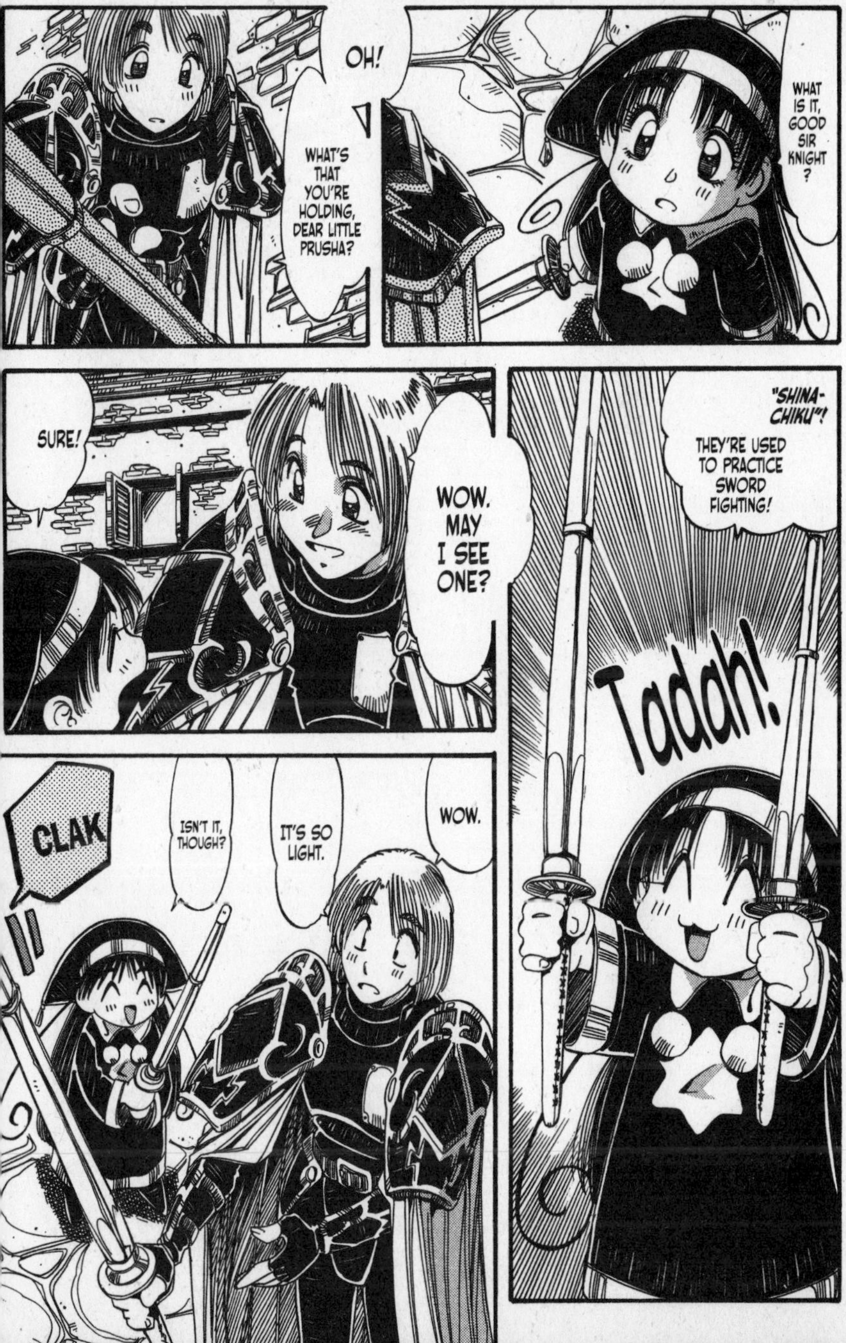
WHAT IS IT, GOOD SIR KNIGHT?
OH!
WHAT'S THAT YOU'RE HOLDING, DEAR LITTLE PRUSHA?
"SHINA-CHIKU"! THEY'RE USED TO PRACTICE SWORD FIGHTING!
Tadah!
WOW. MAY I SEE ONE?
SURE!
WOW.
IT'S SO LIGHT.
ISN'T IT, THOUGH?
CLAK

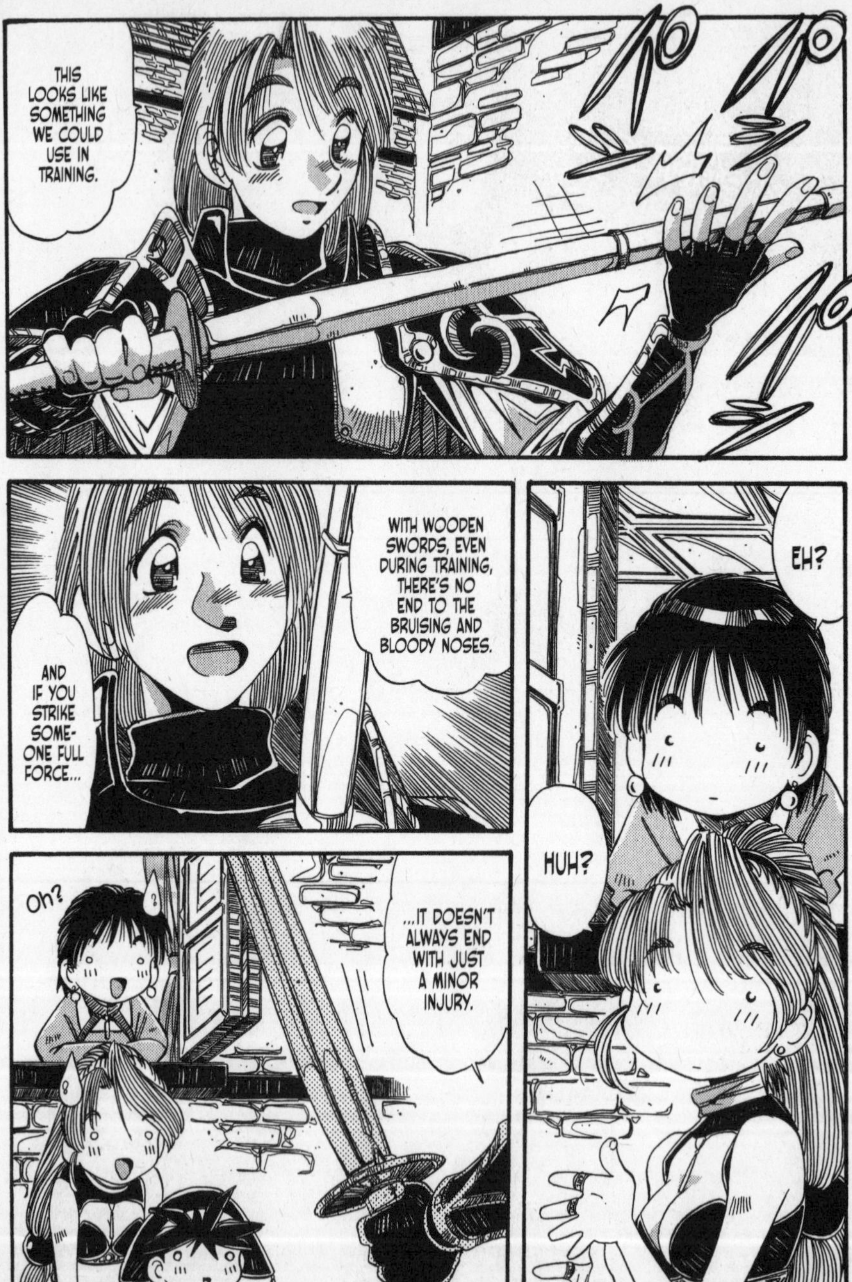
THIS LOOKS LIKE SOMETHING WE COULD USE IN TRAINING.
EH?
HUH?
WITH WOODEN SWORDS, EVEN DURING TRAINING, THERE'S NO END TO THE BRUISING AND BLOODY NOSES.
AND IF YOU STRIKE SOME-ONE FULL FORCE...
...IT DOESN'T ALWAYS END WITH JUST A MINOR INJURY.
Oh?

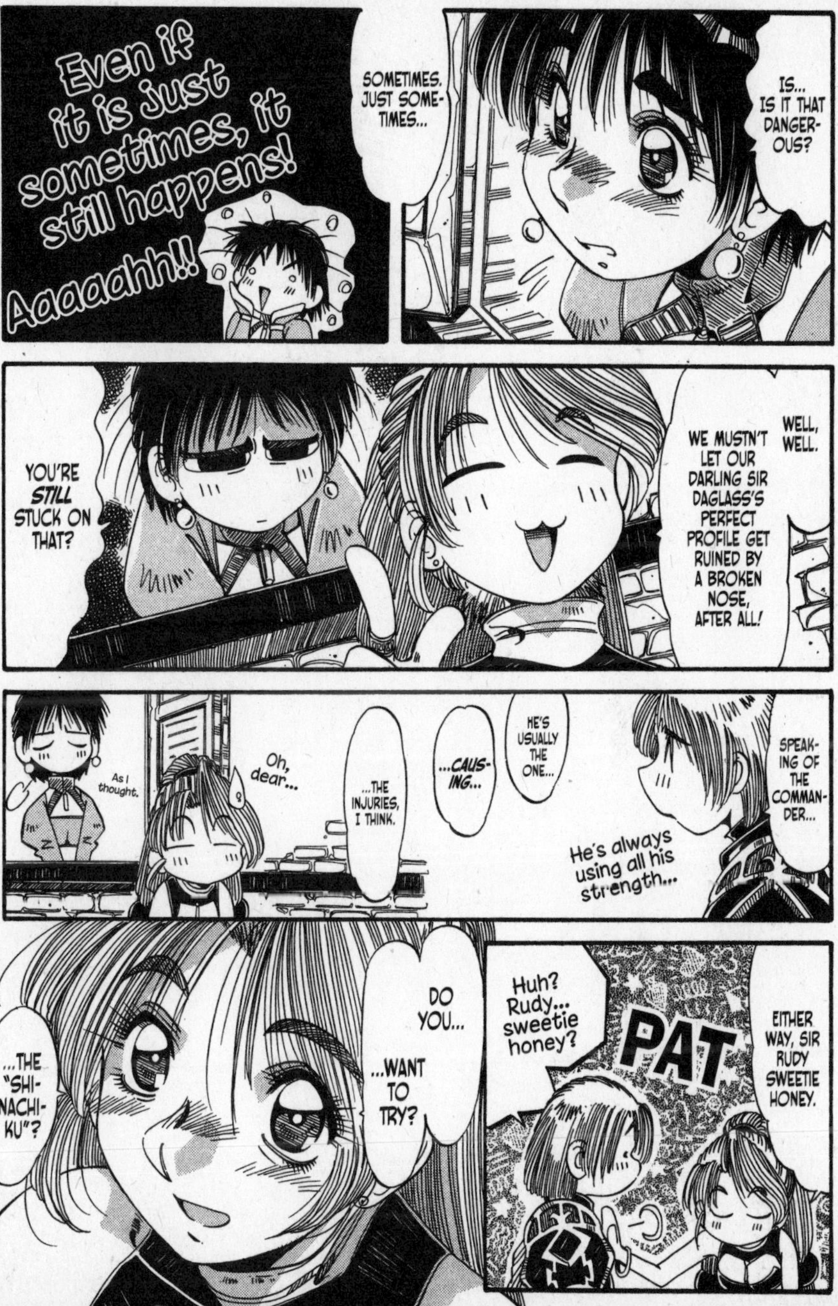
IS... IS IT THAT DANGEROUS?
SOMETIMES. JUST SOMETIMES...
Even if it is just sometimes, it still happens!
Aaaaahh!!
WELL, WELL.
WE MUSTN'T LET OUR DARLING SIR DAGLASS'S PERFECT PROFILE GET RUINED BY A BROKEN NOSE, AFTER ALL!
YOU'RE *STILL* STUCK ON THAT?
SPEAKING OF THE COMMANDER...
He's always using all his strength...
HE'S USUALLY THE ONE...
...CAUSING...
...THE INJURIES, I THINK.
Oh, dear...
As I thought.
EITHER WAY, SIR RUDY SWEETIE HONEY.
PAT
Huh? Rudy... sweetie honey?
DO YOU...
...WANT TO TRY?
...THE "SHINACHIKU"?

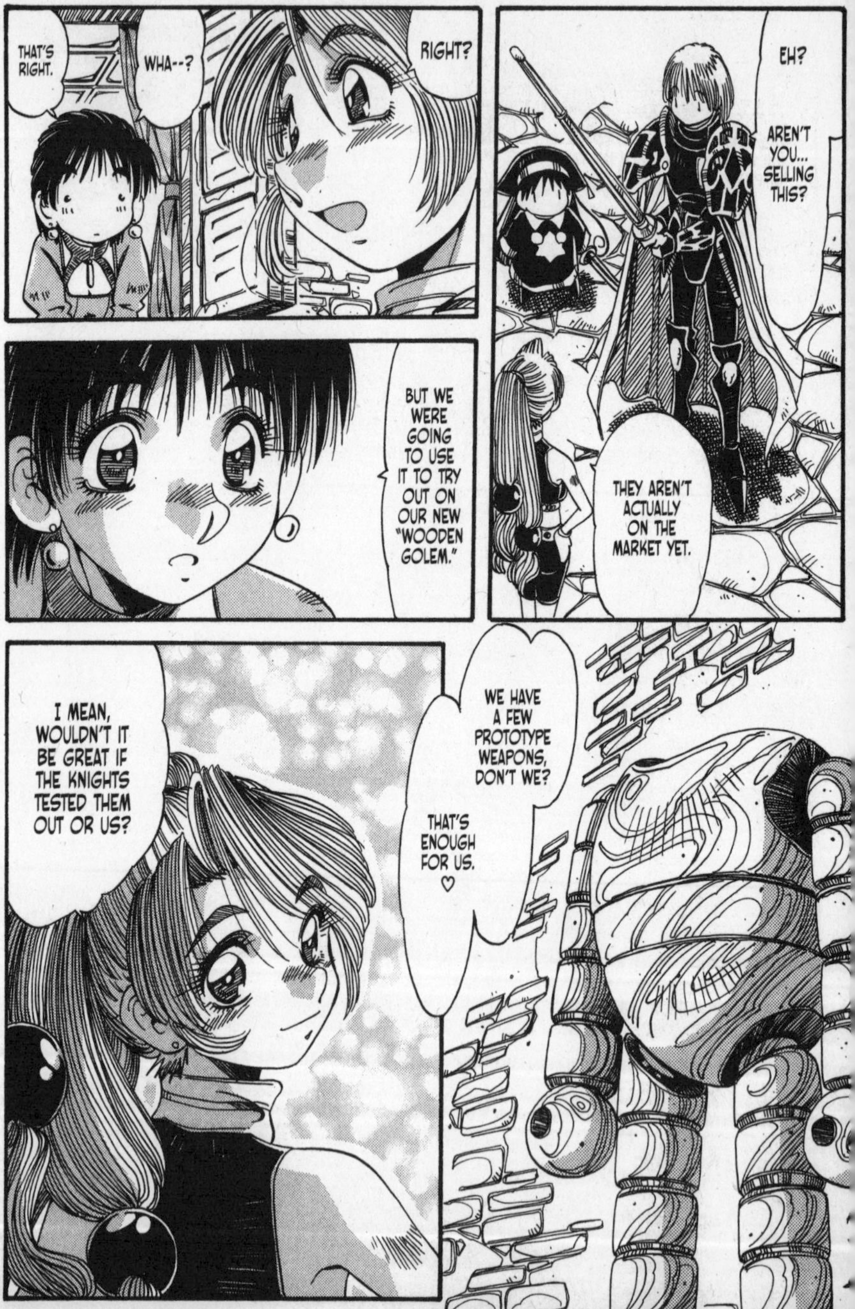
EH?
AREN'T YOU... SELLING THIS?
THEY AREN'T ACTUALLY ON THE MARKET YET.
RIGHT?
WHA--?
THAT'S RIGHT.
BUT WE WERE GOING TO USE IT TO TRY OUT ON OUR NEW "WOODEN GOLEM."
WE HAVE A FEW PROTOTYPE WEAPONS, DON'T WE?
THAT'S ENOUGH FOR US. ♡
I MEAN, WOULDN'T IT BE GREAT IF THE KNIGHTS TESTED THEM OUT OR US?

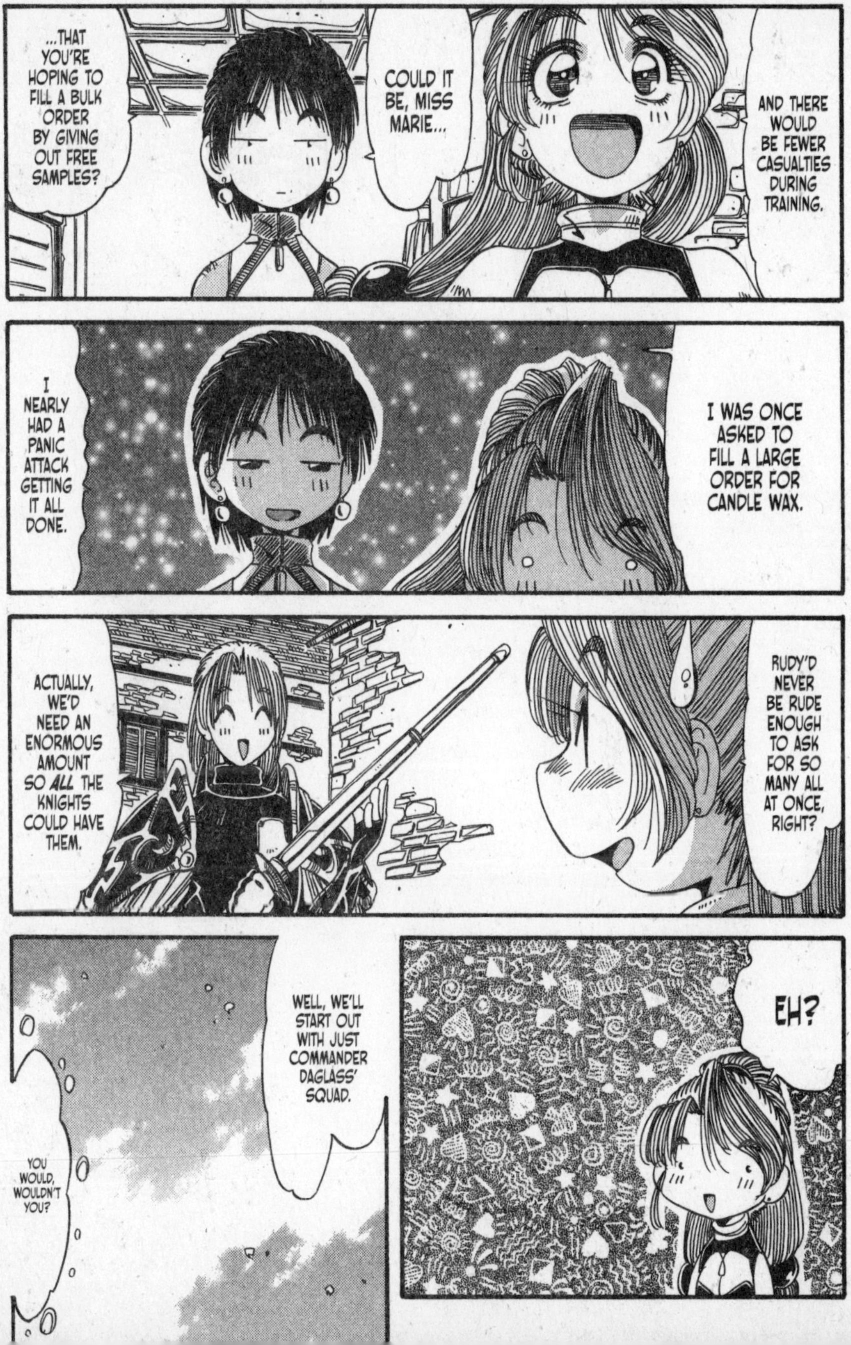
AND THERE WOULD BE FEWER CASUALTIES DURING TRAINING.
COULD IT BE, MISS MARIE...
...THAT YOU'RE HOPING TO FILL A BULK ORDER BY GIVING OUT FREE SAMPLES?
I WAS ONCE ASKED TO FILL A LARGE ORDER FOR CANDLE WAX.
I NEARLY HAD A PANIC ATTACK GETTING IT ALL DONE.
RUDY'D NEVER BE RUDE ENOUGH TO ASK FOR SO MANY ALL AT ONCE, RIGHT?
ACTUALLY, WE'D NEED AN ENORMOUS AMOUNT SO *ALL* THE KNIGHTS COULD HAVE THEM.
EH?
WELL, WE'LL START OUT WITH JUST COMMANDER DAGLASS' SQUAD.
YOU WOULD, WOULDN'T YOU?

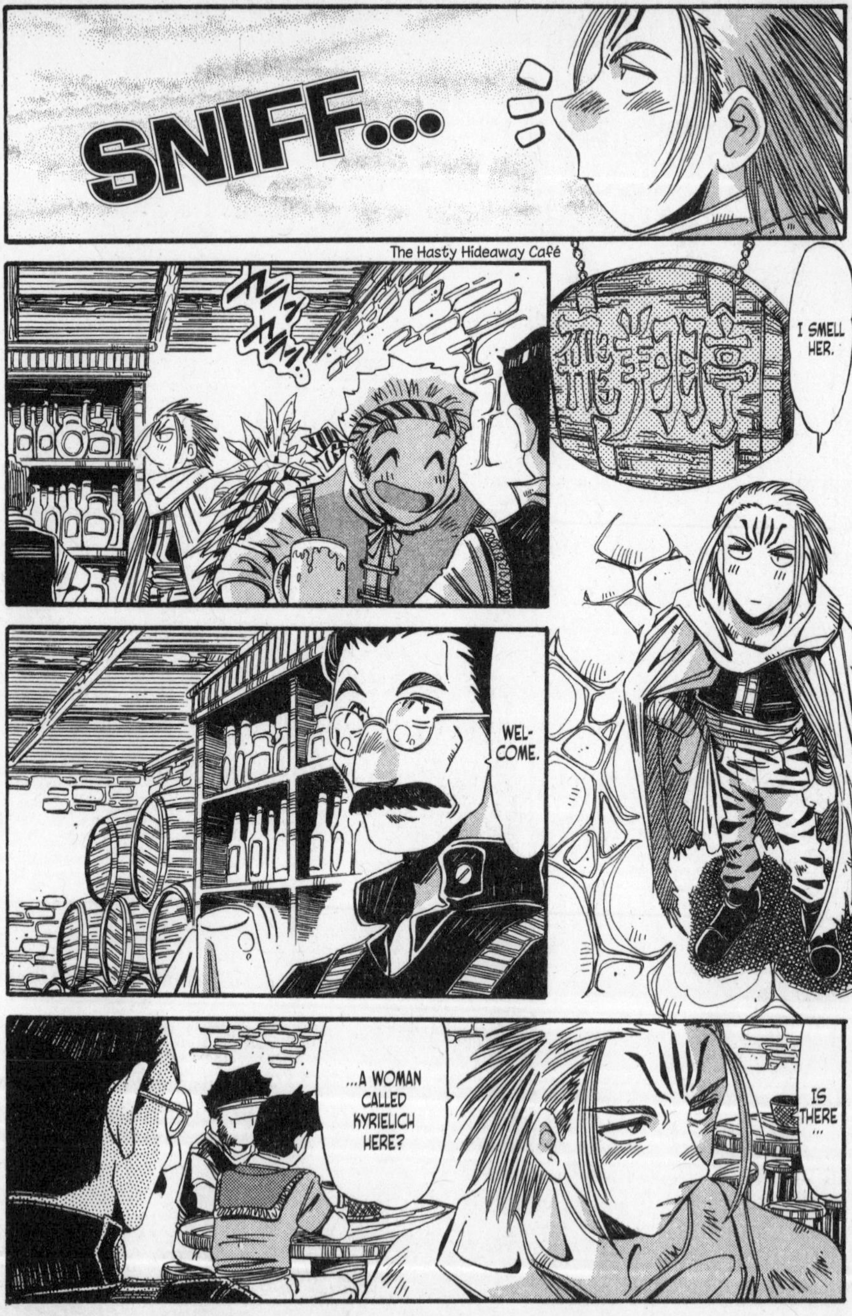
SNIFF...
The Hasty Hideaway Café
I SMELL HER.
WEL-COME.
IS THERE ...
...A WOMAN CALLED KYRIELICH HERE?

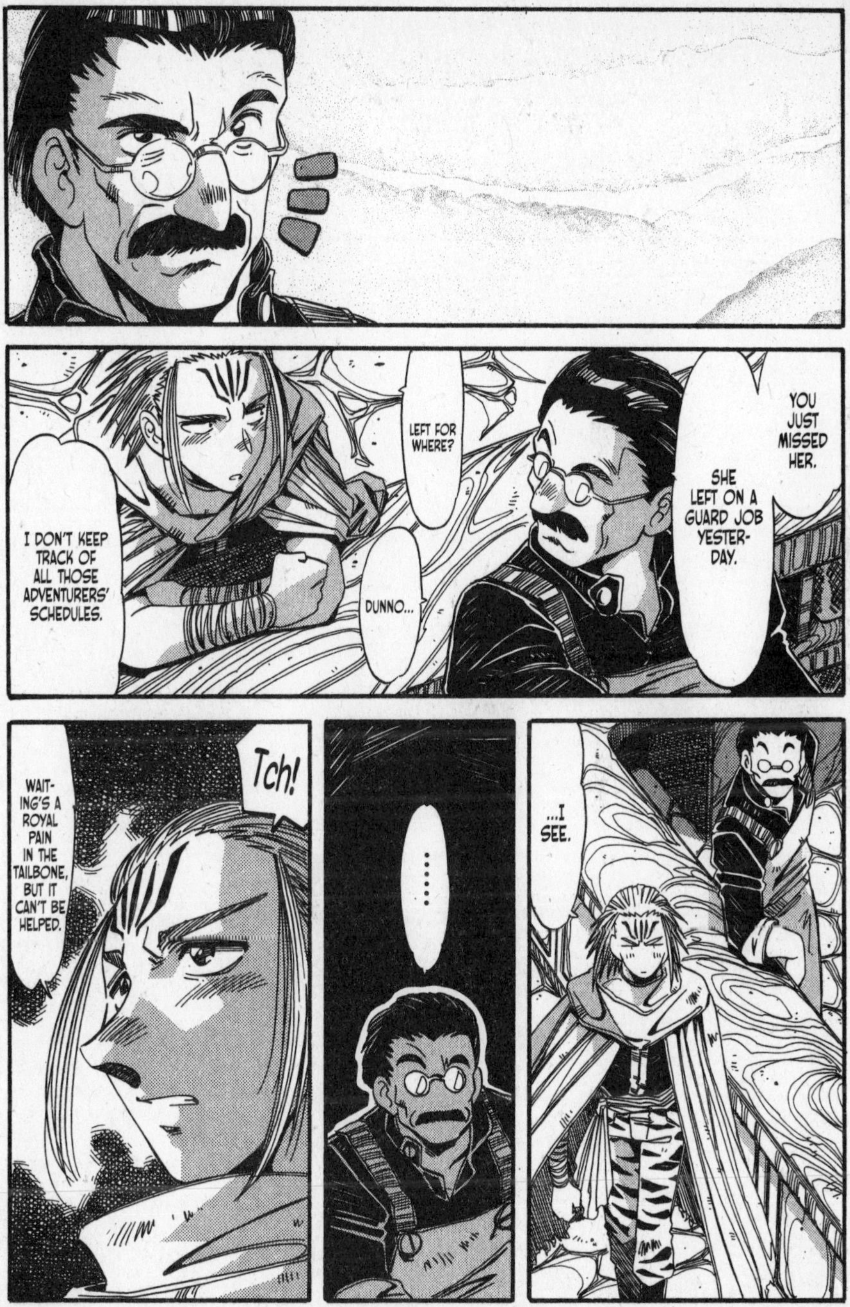
YOU JUST MISSED HER.
SHE LEFT ON A GUARD JOB YESTERDAY.
LEFT FOR WHERE?
DUNNO...
I DON'T KEEP TRACK OF ALL THOSE ADVENTURERS' SCHEDULES.
...I SEE.
......
Tch!
WAITING'S A ROYAL PAIN IN THE TAILBONE, BUT IT CAN'T BE HELPED.

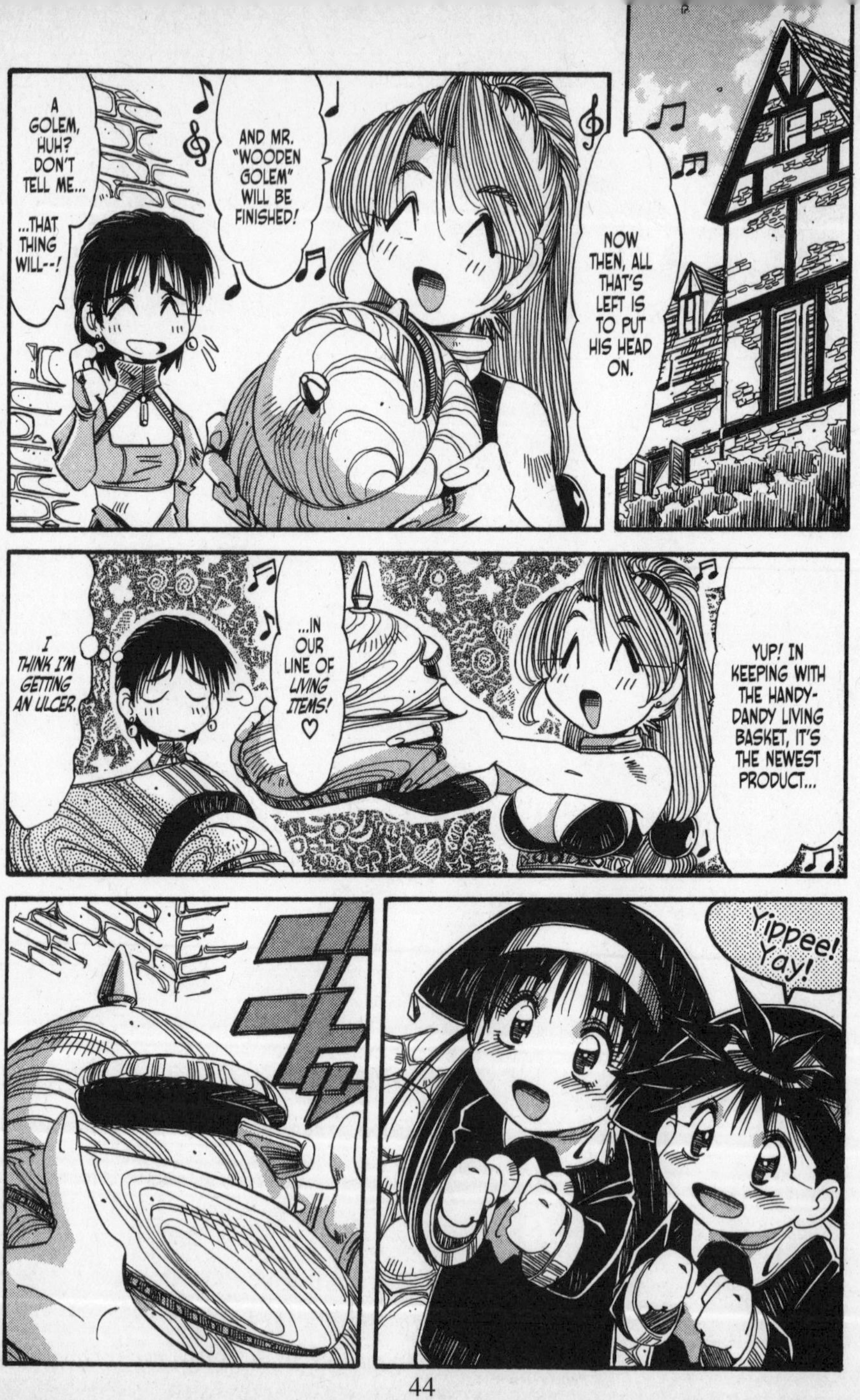
NOW THEN, ALL THAT'S LEFT IS TO PUT HIS HEAD ON.
AND MR. "WOODEN GOLEM" WILL BE FINISHED!
A GOLEM, HUH? DON'T TELL ME...
...THAT THING WILL--!
YUP! IN KEEPING WITH THE HANDY-DANDY LIVING BASKET, IT'S THE NEWEST PRODUCT...
...IN OUR LINE OF LIVING ITEMS! ♡
I THINK I'M GETTING AN ULCER.
Yippee! Yay!

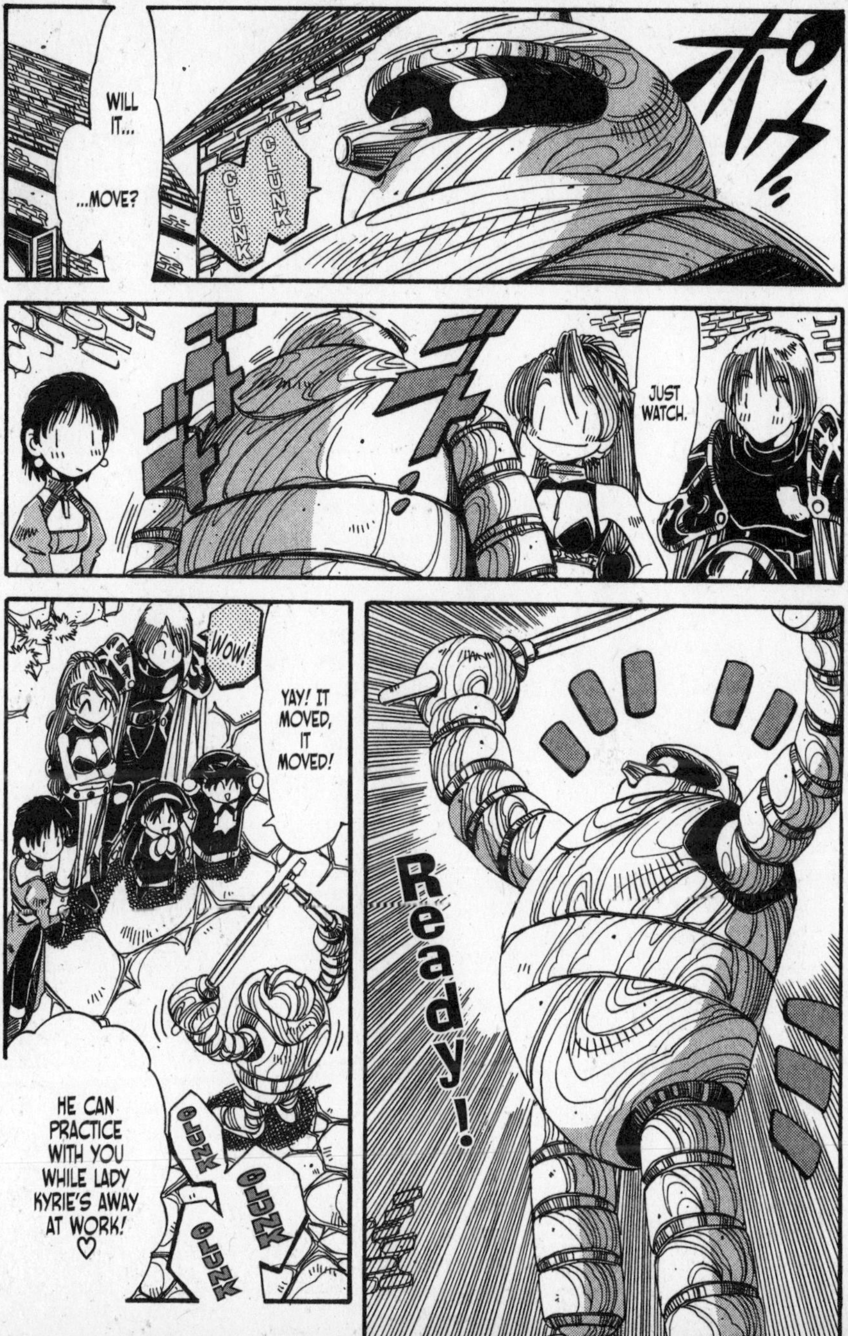

CLUNK
CLUNK
WILL IT...
...MOVE?
JUST WATCH.
Ready!
WOW!
YAY! IT MOVED, IT MOVED!
HE CAN PRACTICE WITH YOU WHILE LADY KYRIE'S AWAY AT WORK! ♡
CLUNK
CLUNK
CLUNK

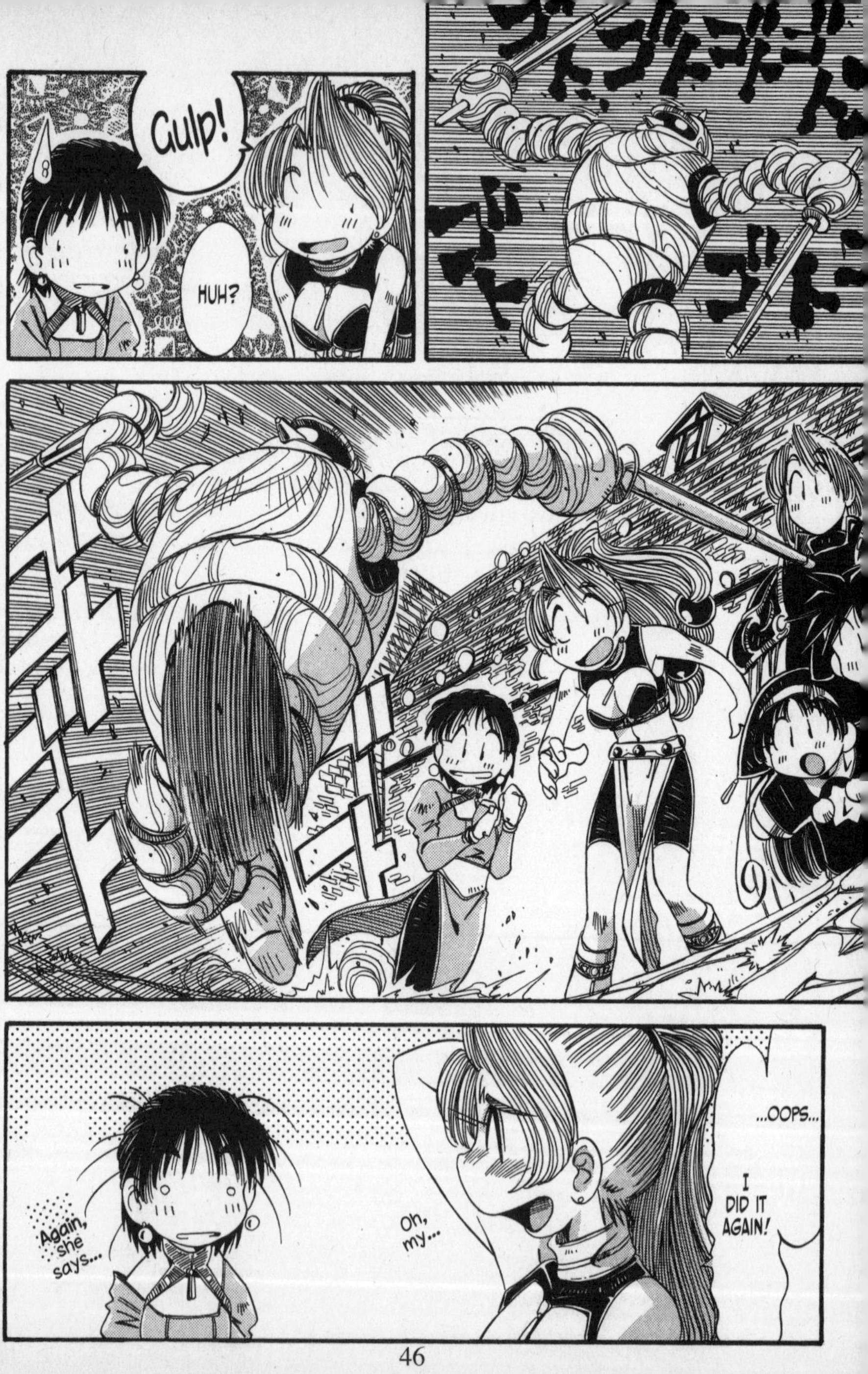
Gulp!
HUH?
...OOPS...
I DID IT AGAIN!
Oh, my...
Again, she says...

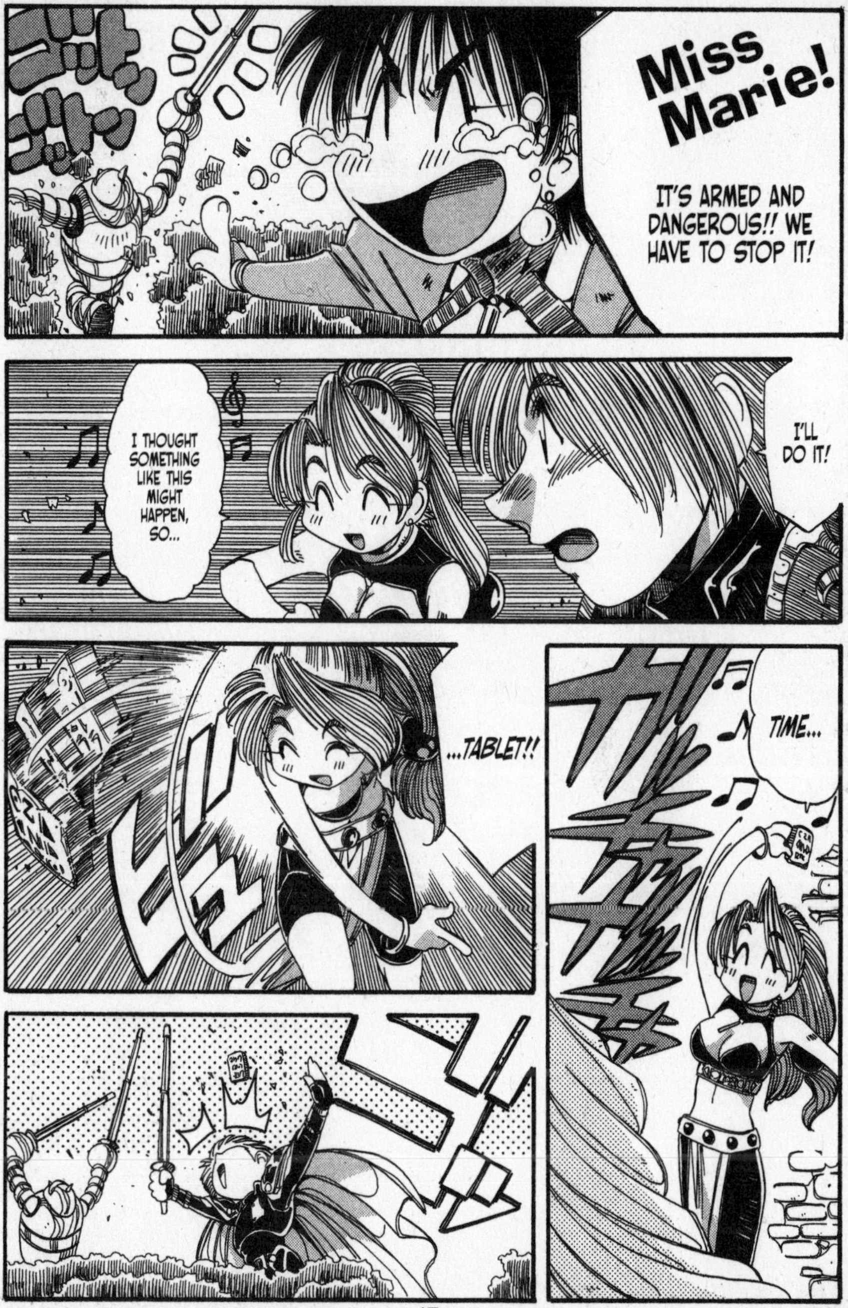

Miss Marie!
IT'S ARMED AND DANGEROUS!! WE HAVE TO STOP IT!
I'LL DO IT!
I THOUGHT SOMETHING LIKE THIS MIGHT HAPPEN, SO...
TIME...
...TABLET!!

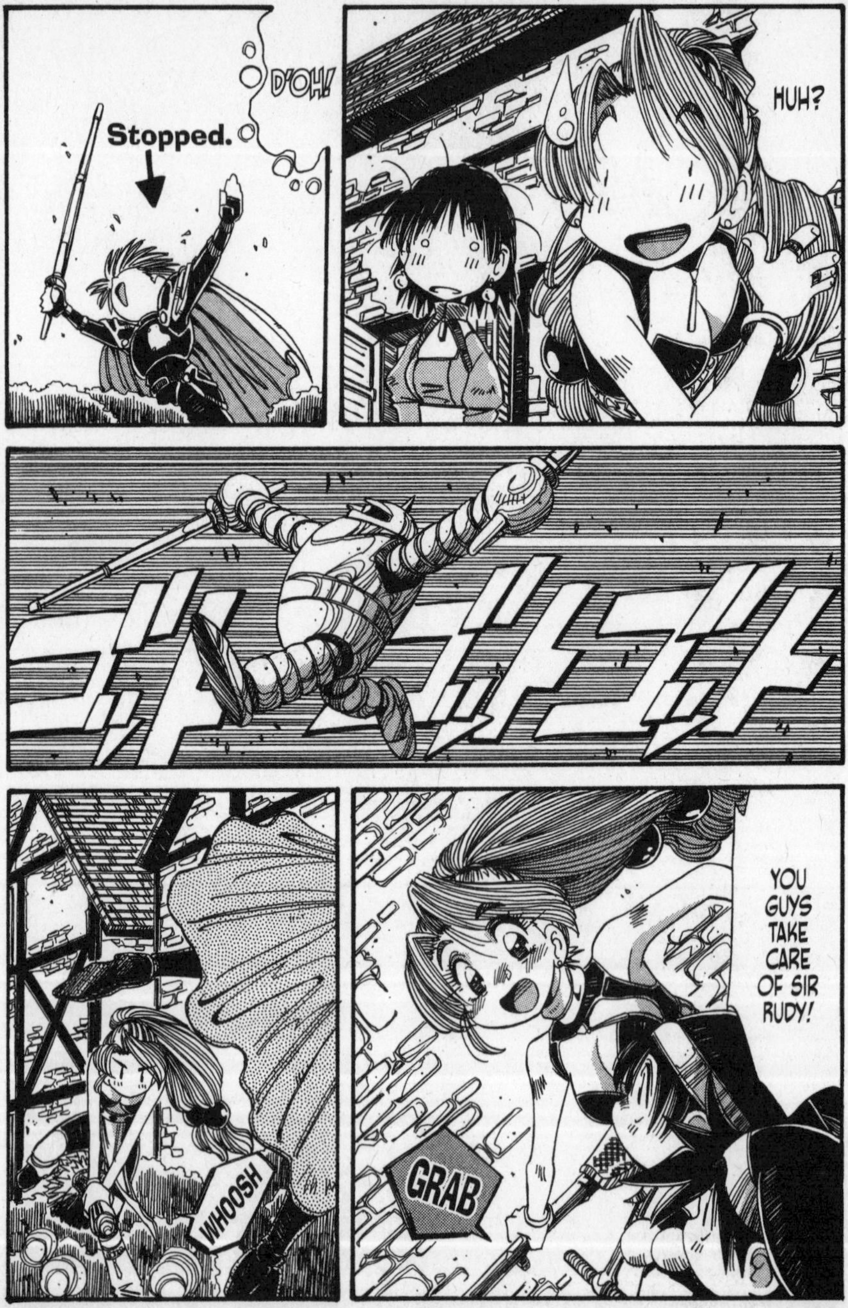
HUH?
D'OH!
Stopped.
YOU GUYS TAKE CARE OF SIR RUDY!
GRAB
WHOOSH

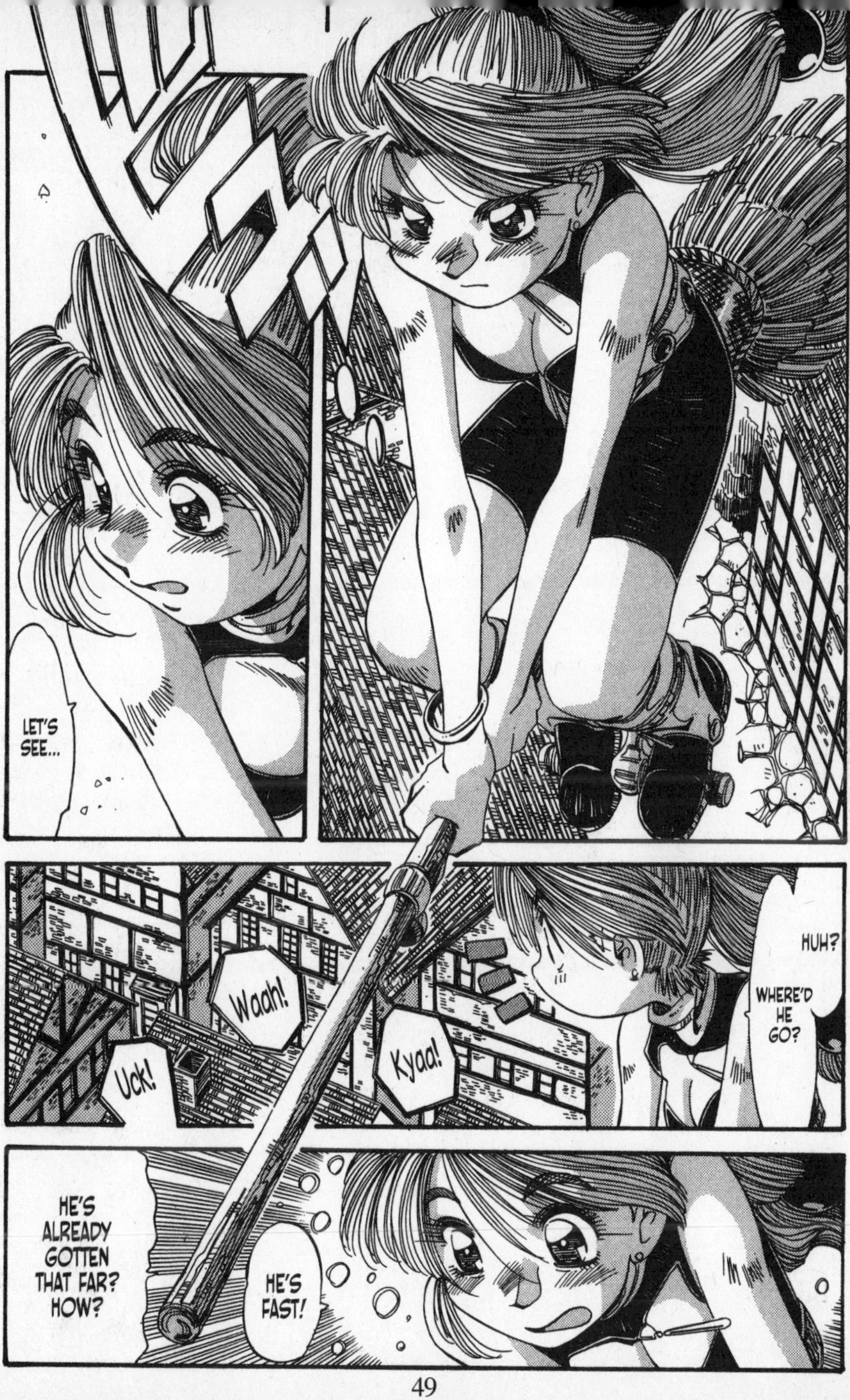
LET'S SEE...
HUH?
WHERE'D HE GO?
Kyaa!
Waah!
Uck!
HE'S FAST!
HE'S ALREADY GOTTEN THAT FAR? HOW?

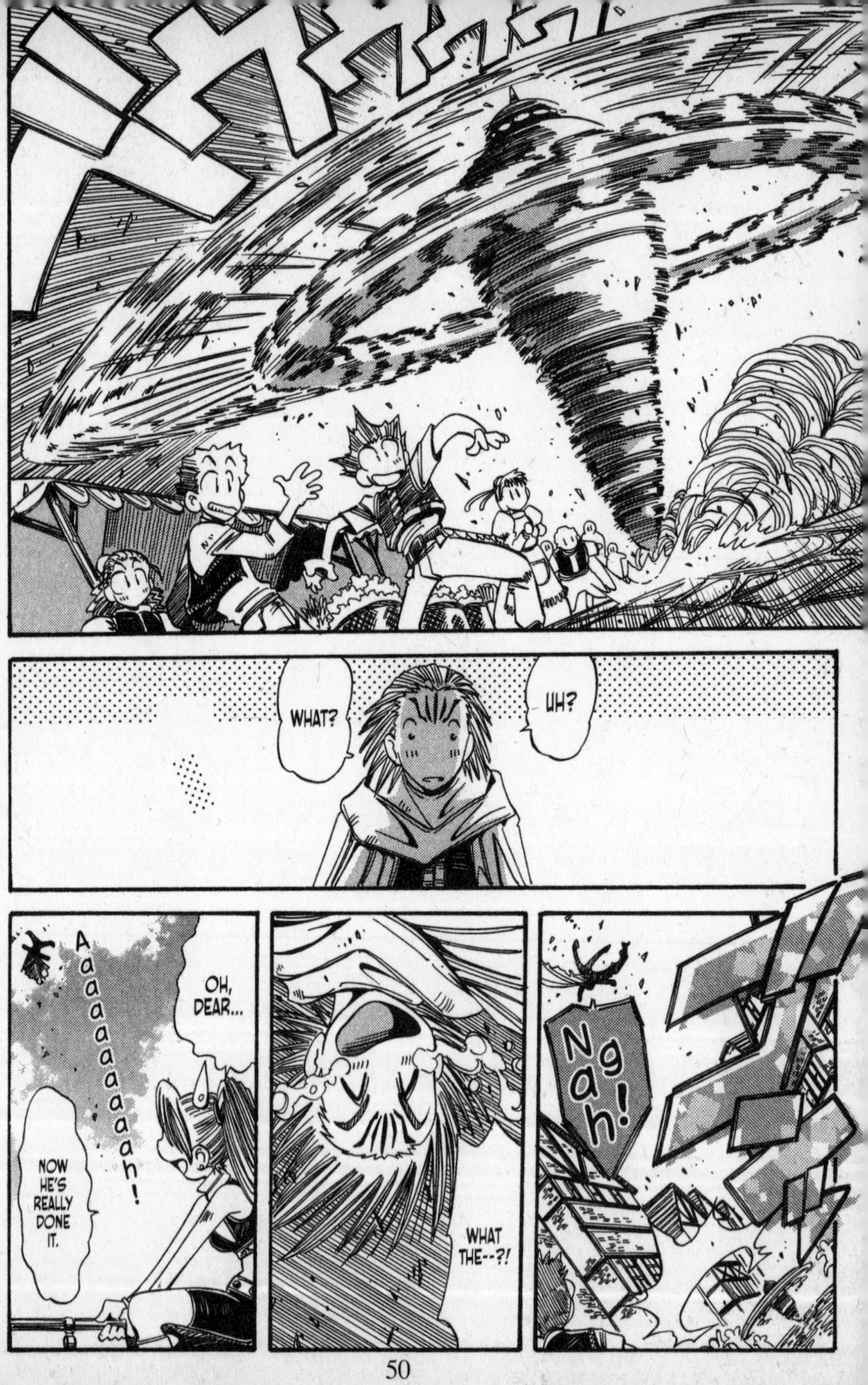
UH?
WHAT?
Ngah!
WHAT THE--?!
OH, DEAR...
Aaaaaaaaaah!
NOW HE'S REALLY DONE IT.

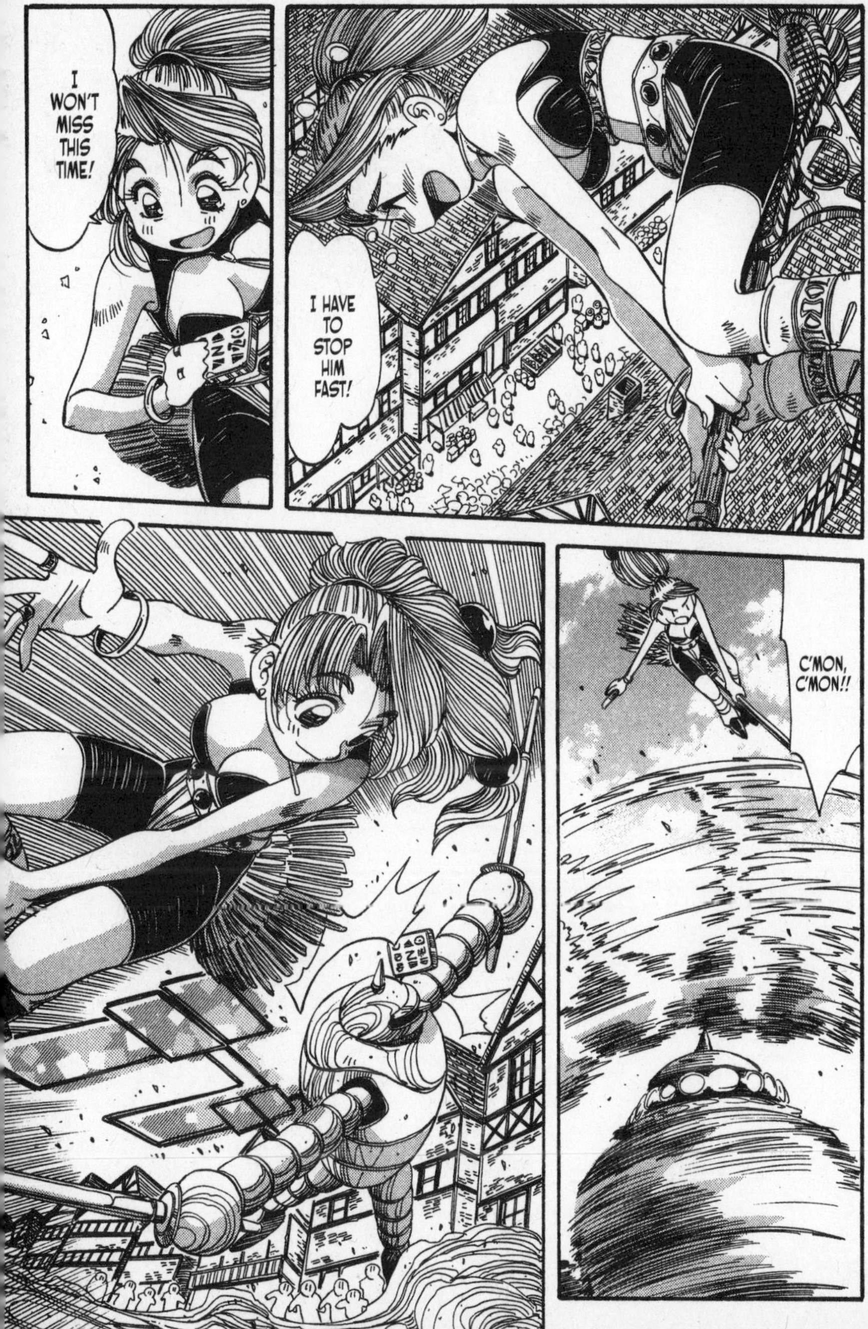

I HAVE TO STOP HIM FAST!
I WON'T MISS THIS TIME!
C'MON, C'MON!!

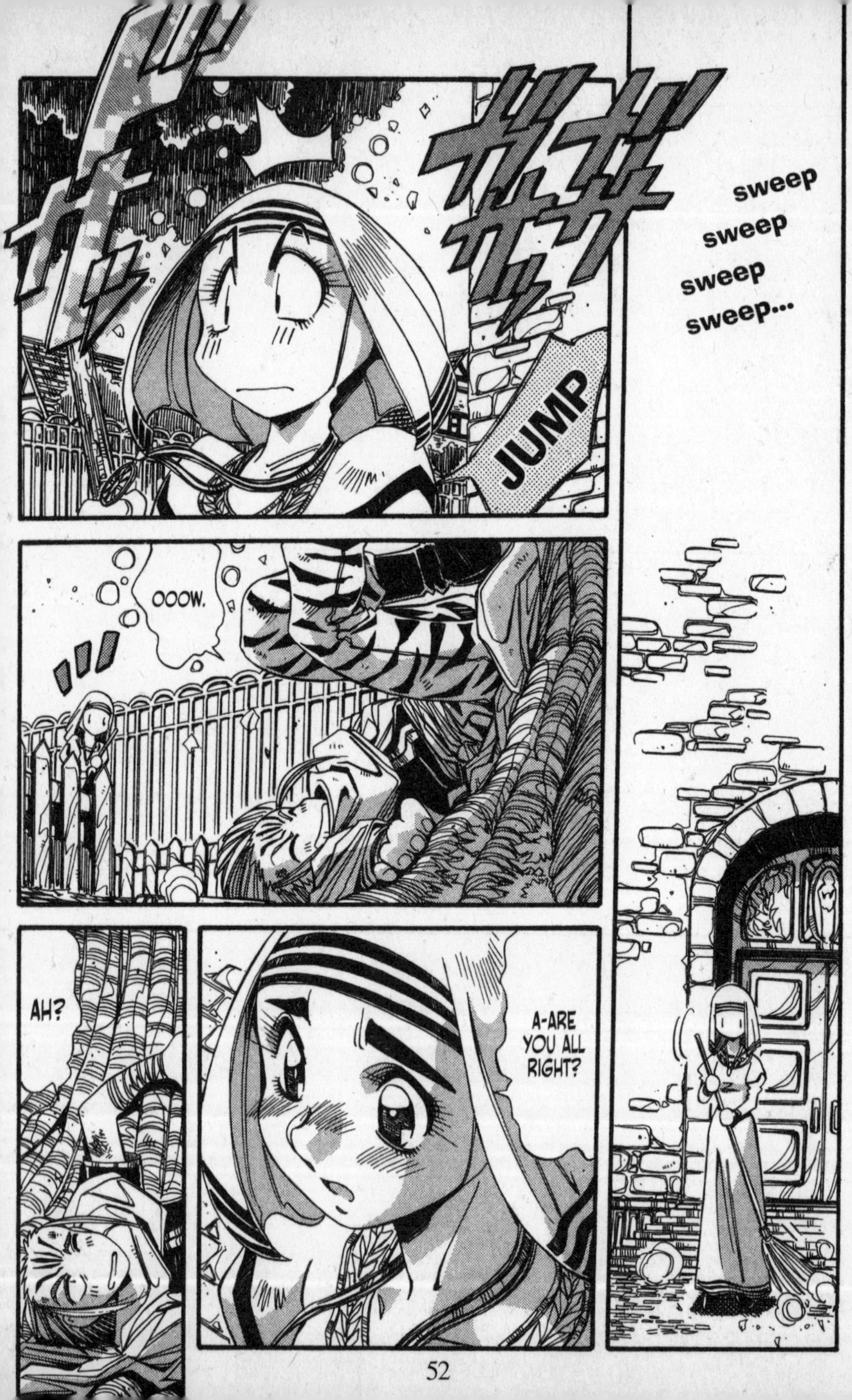
sweep
sweep
sweep
sweep...
JUMP
OOOW.
A-ARE YOU ALL RIGHT?
AH?

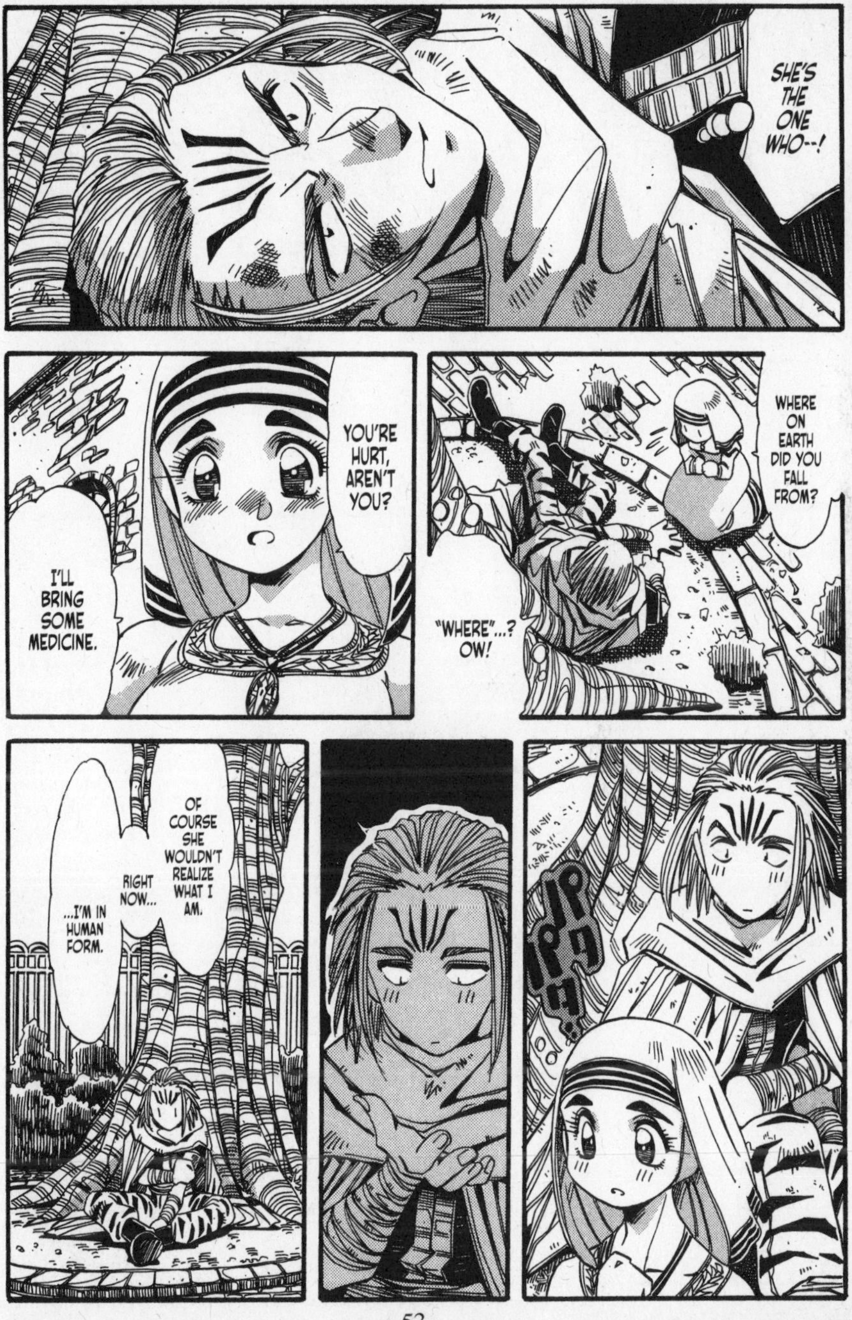
SHE'S THE ONE WHO--!
WHERE ON EARTH DID YOU FALL FROM?
"WHERE"...? OW!
YOU'RE HURT, AREN'T YOU?
I'LL BRING SOME MEDICINE.
OF COURSE SHE WOULDN'T REALIZE WHAT I AM.
RIGHT NOW...
...I'M IN HUMAN FORM.

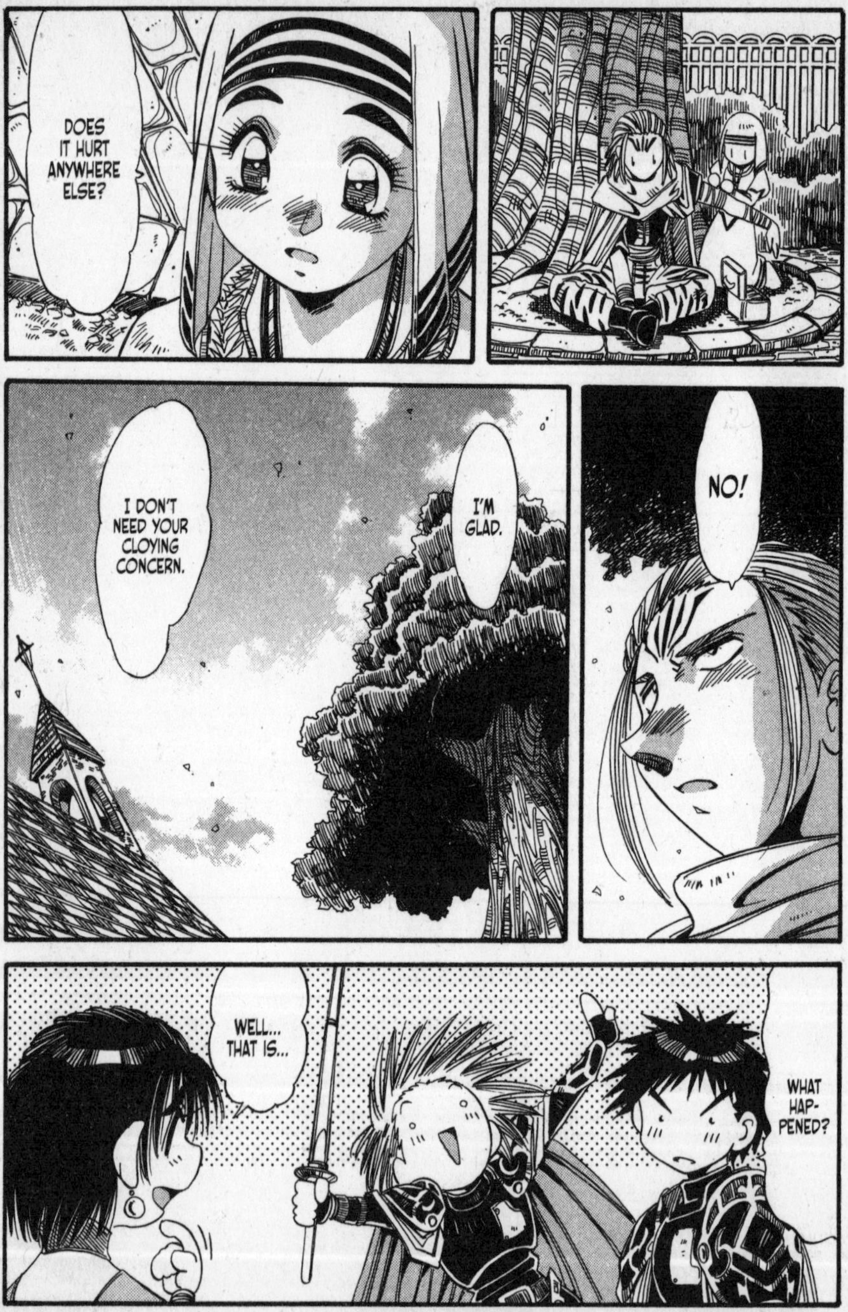
DOES IT HURT ANYWHERE ELSE?
NO!
I'M GLAD.
I DON'T NEED YOUR CLOYING CONCERN.
WHAT HAP-PENED?
WELL... THAT IS...

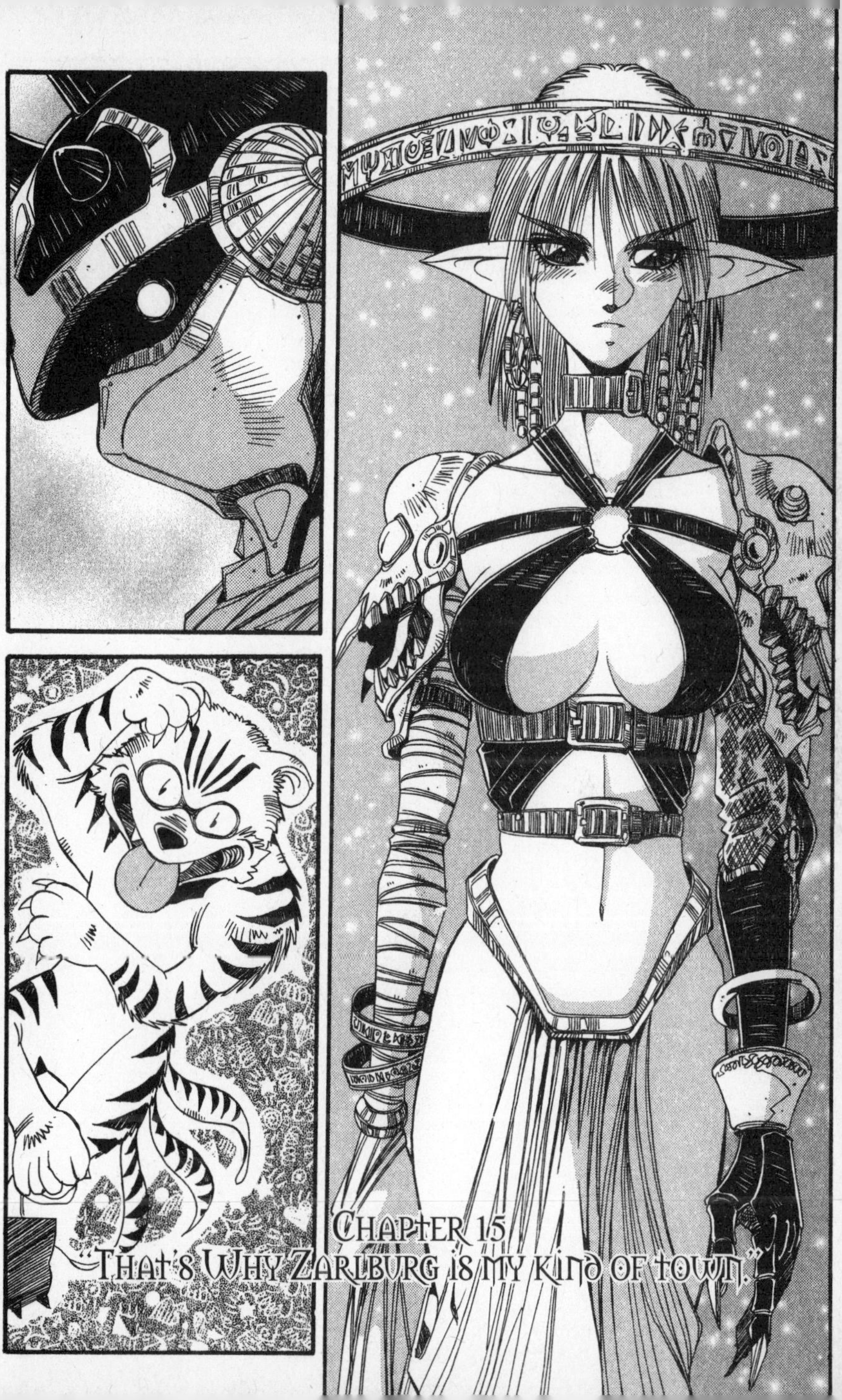

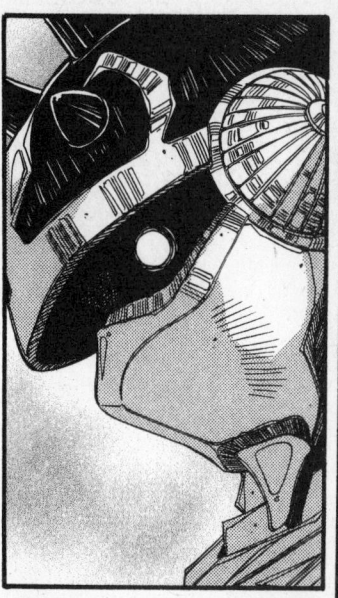

CHAPTER 15
"THAT'S WHY ZARLBURG IS MY KIND OF TOWN."

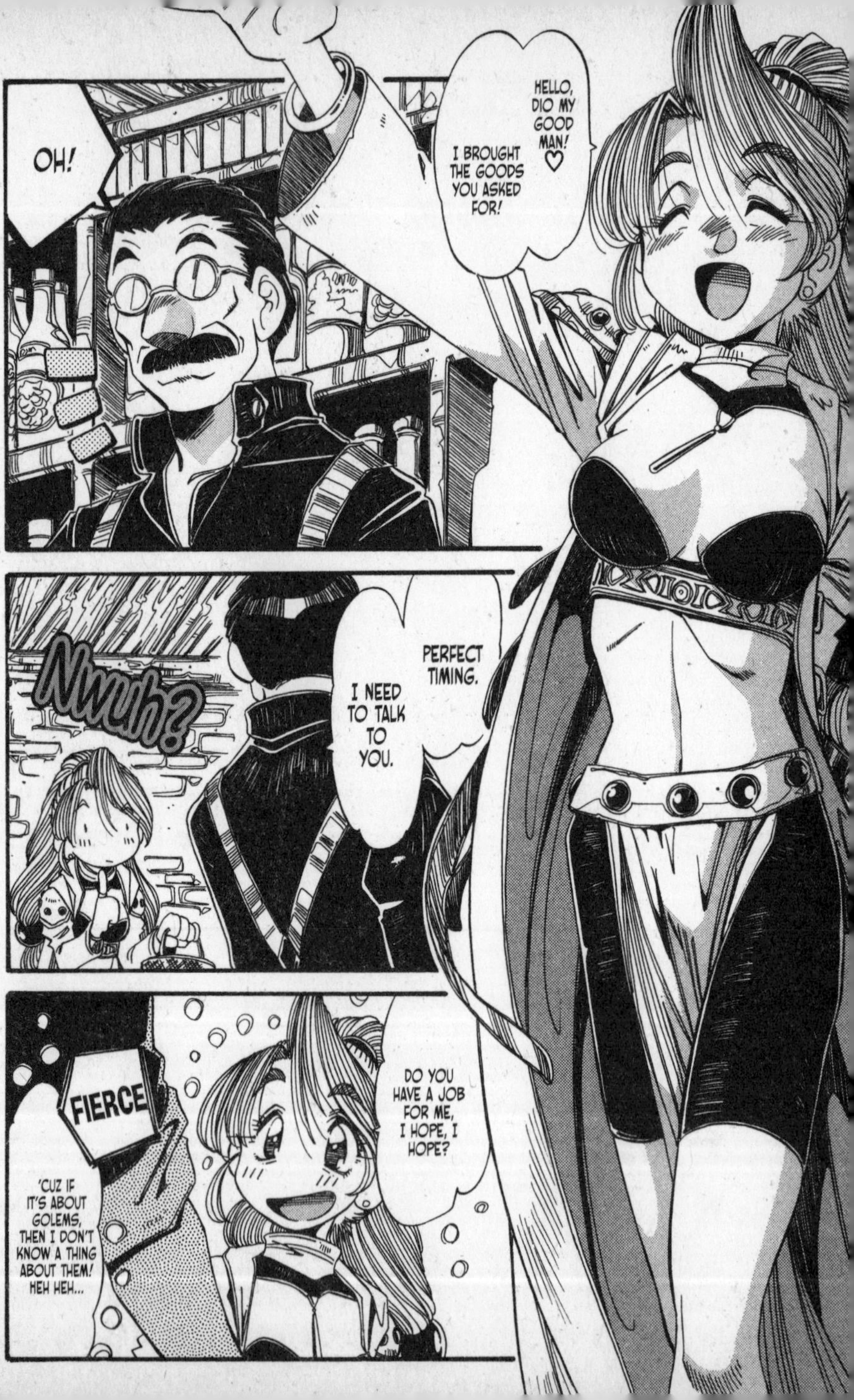
HELLO, DIO MY GOOD MAN! ♡
I BROUGHT THE GOODS YOU ASKED FOR!
OH!
PERFECT TIMING.
I NEED TO TALK TO YOU.
Nwuh?
DO YOU HAVE A JOB FOR ME, I HOPE, I HOPE?
FIERCE
'CUZ IF IT'S ABOUT GOLEMS, THEN I DON'T KNOW A THING ABOUT THEM! HEH HEH...

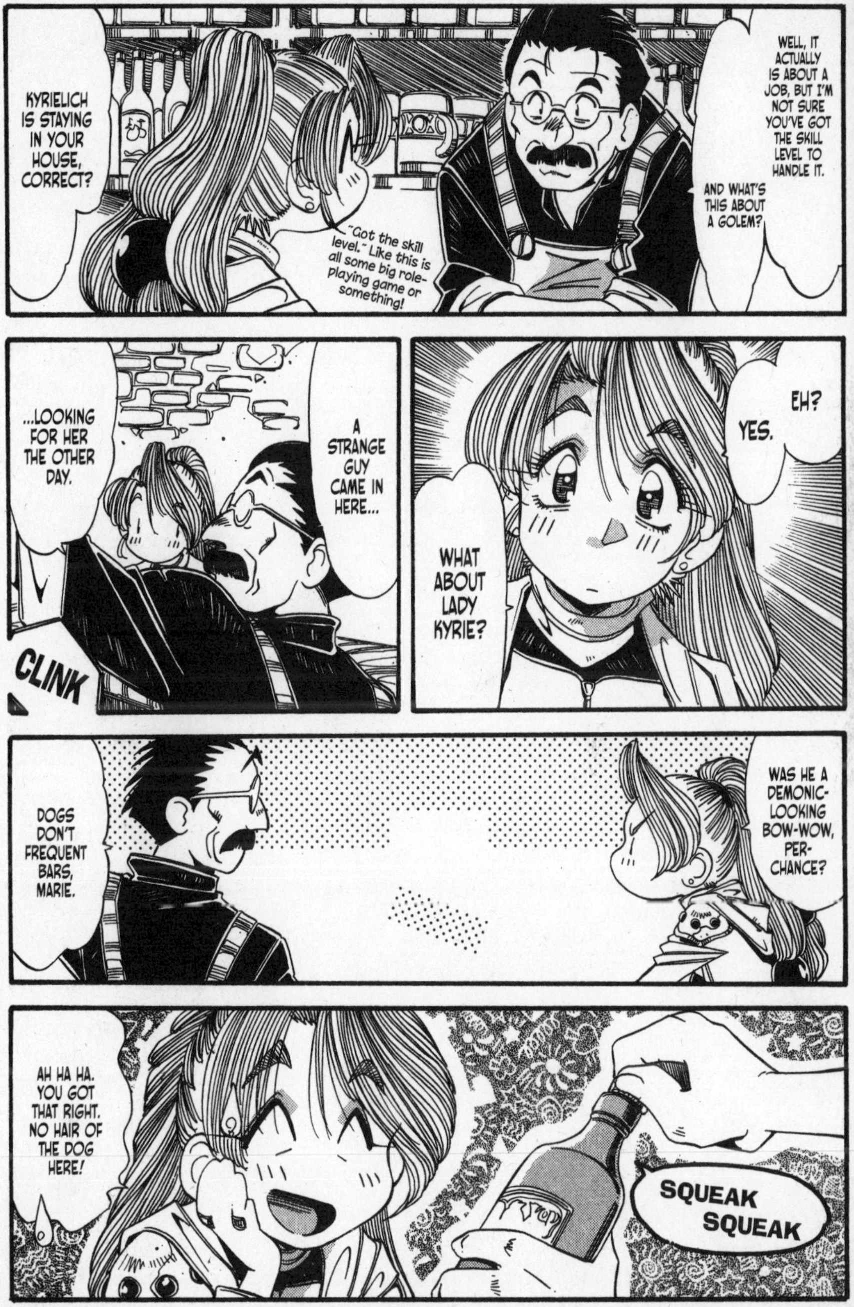
WELL, IT ACTUALLY IS ABOUT A JOB, BUT I'M NOT SURE YOU'VE GOT THE SKILL LEVEL TO HANDLE IT.
AND WHAT'S THIS ABOUT A GOLEM?
"Got the skill level." Like this is all some big role-playing game or something!
KYRIELICH IS STAYING IN YOUR HOUSE, CORRECT?
EH?
YES.
WHAT ABOUT LADY KYRIE?
A STRANGE GUY CAME IN HERE...
...LOOKING FOR HER THE OTHER DAY.
CLINK
WAS HE A DEMONIC-LOOKING BOW-WOW, PER-CHANCE?
DOGS DON'T FREQUENT BARS, MARIE.
SQUEAK SQUEAK
AH HA HA. YOU GOT THAT RIGHT. NO HAIR OF THE DOG HERE!

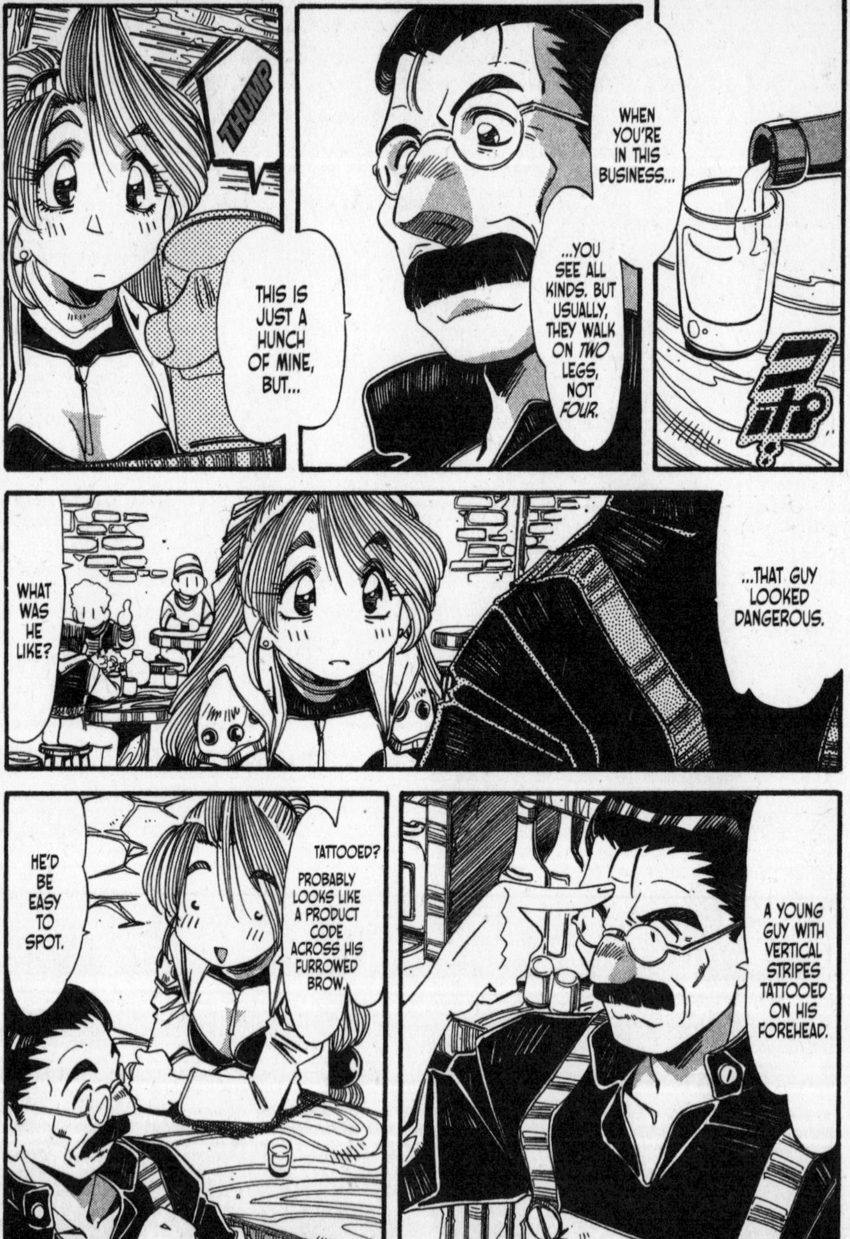

コポ
WHEN YOU'RE IN THIS BUSINESS...
...YOU SEE ALL KINDS. BUT USUALLY, THEY WALK ON *TWO* LEGS, NOT *FOUR.*
THUMP
THIS IS JUST A HUNCH OF MINE, BUT...
...THAT GUY LOOKED DANGEROUS.
WHAT WAS HE LIKE?
A YOUNG GUY WITH VERTICAL STRIPES TATTOOED ON HIS FOREHEAD.
TATTOOED? PROBABLY LOOKS LIKE A PRODUCT CODE ACROSS HIS FURROWED BROW.
HE'D BE EASY TO SPOT.

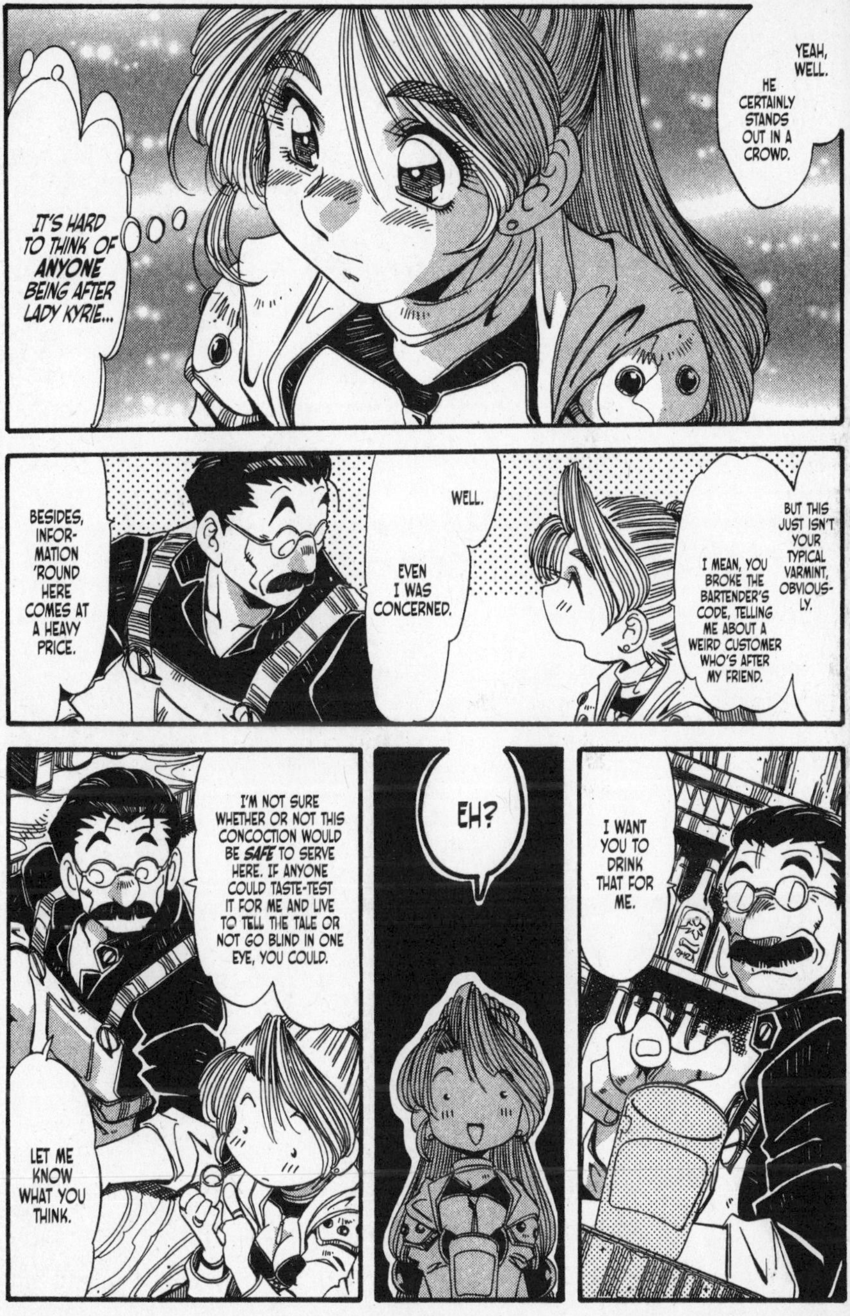
YEAH, WELL.
HE CERTAINLY STANDS OUT IN A CROWD.
IT'S HARD TO THINK OF ANYONE BEING AFTER LADY KYRIE...
BUT THIS JUST ISN'T YOUR TYPICAL VARMINT, OBVIOUSLY.
I MEAN, YOU BROKE THE BARTENDER'S CODE, TELLING ME ABOUT A WEIRD CUSTOMER WHO'S AFTER MY FRIEND.
WELL.
EVEN I WAS CONCERNED.
BESIDES, INFORMATION 'ROUND HERE COMES AT A HEAVY PRICE.
I WANT YOU TO DRINK THAT FOR ME.
EH?
I'M NOT SURE WHETHER OR NOT THIS CONCOCTION WOULD BE SAFE TO SERVE HERE. IF ANYONE COULD TASTE-TEST IT FOR ME AND LIVE TO TELL THE TALE OR NOT GO BLIND IN ONE EYE, YOU COULD.
LET ME KNOW WHAT YOU THINK.

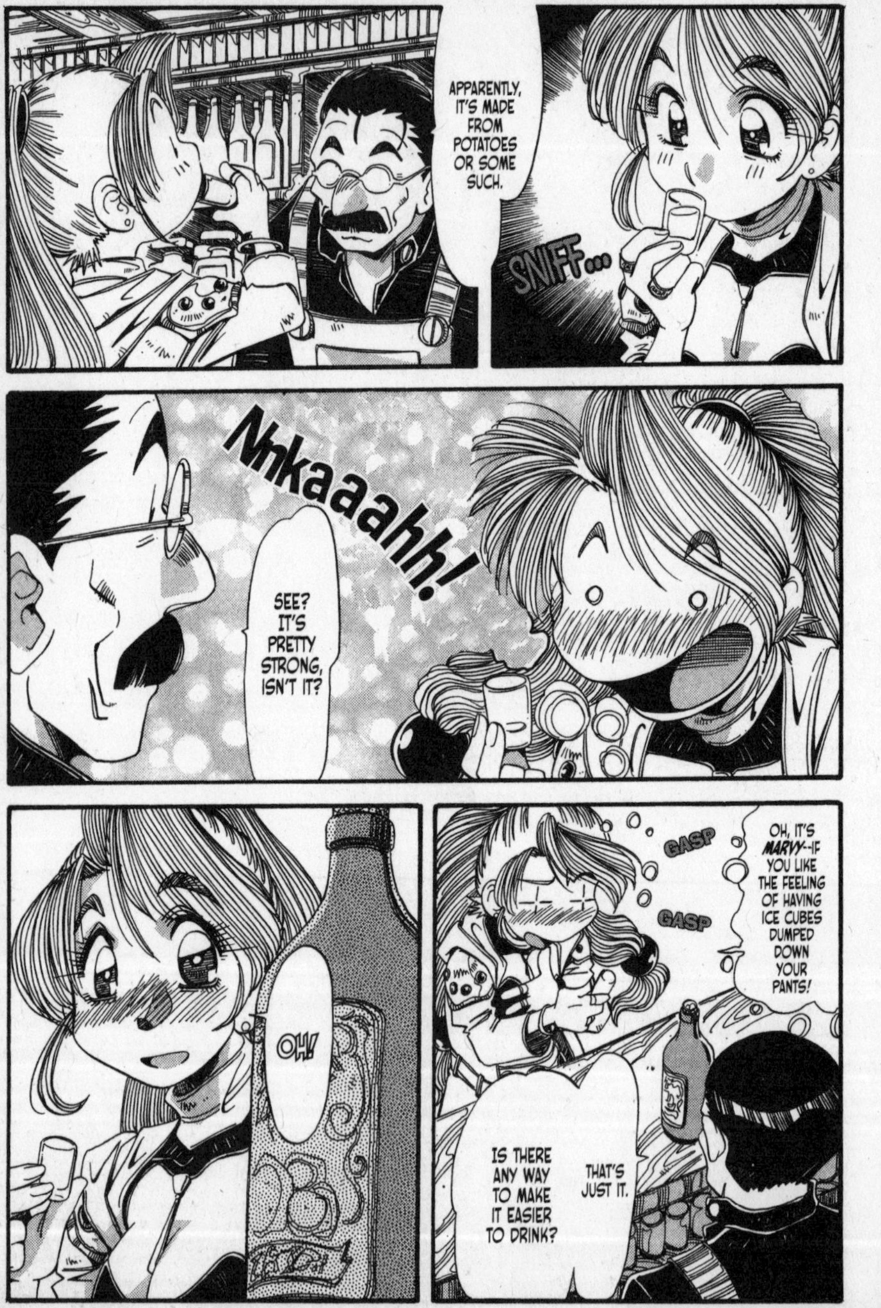
SNIFF...
APPARENTLY, IT'S MADE FROM POTATOES OR SOME SUCH.
Nhkaaahh!
SEE? IT'S PRETTY STRONG, ISN'T IT?
OH, IT'S *MARVY*--IF YOU LIKE THE FEELING OF HAVING ICE CUBES DUMPED DOWN YOUR PANTS!
GASP
GASP
THAT'S JUST IT.
IS THERE ANY WAY TO MAKE IT EASIER TO DRINK?
OH!

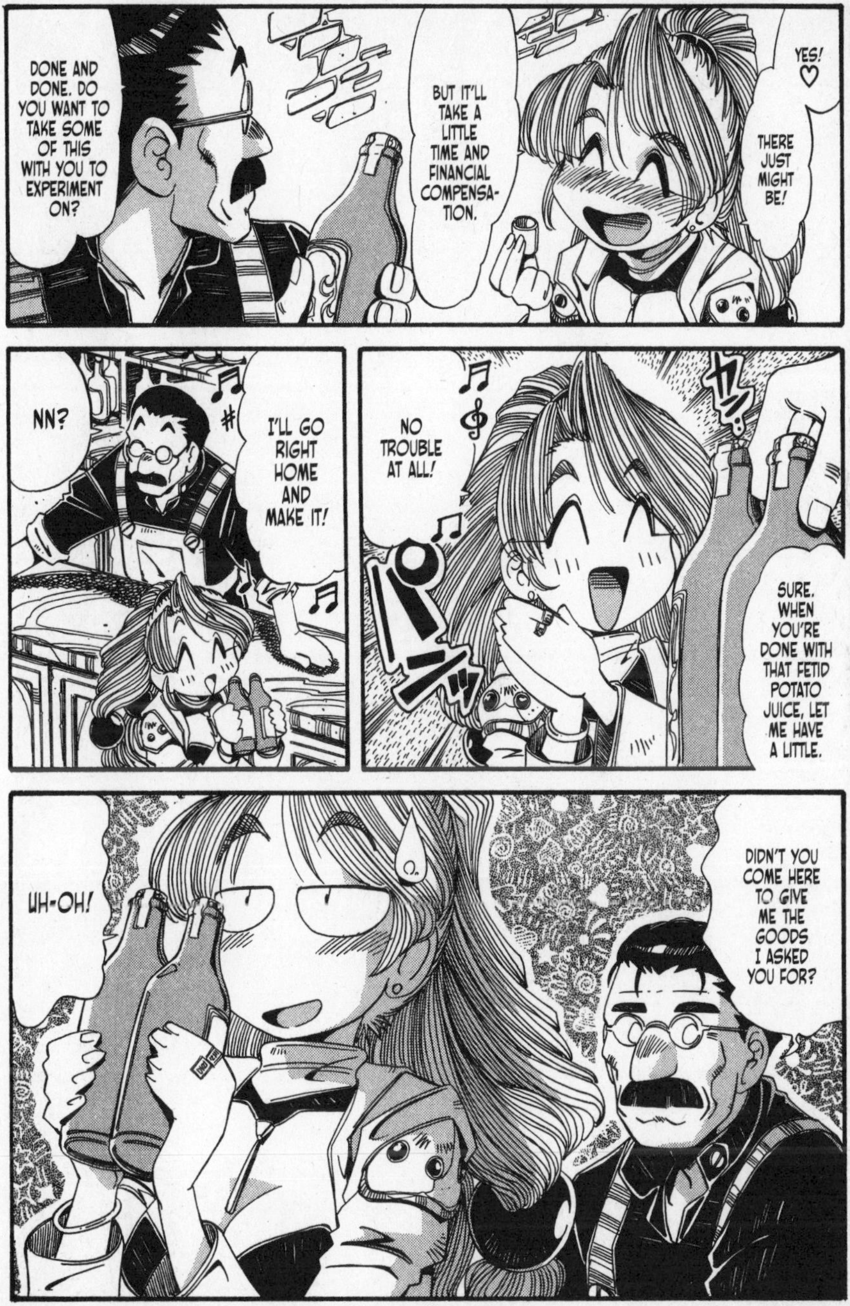
YES! ♡
THERE JUST MIGHT BE!
BUT IT'LL TAKE A LITTLE TIME AND FINANCIAL COMPENSA-TION.
DONE AND DONE. DO YOU WANT TO TAKE SOME OF THIS WITH YOU TO EXPERIMENT ON?
SURE. WHEN YOU'RE DONE WITH THAT FETID POTATO JUICE, LET ME HAVE A LITTLE.
NO TROUBLE AT ALL!
I'LL GO RIGHT HOME AND MAKE IT!
NN?
DIDN'T YOU COME HERE TO GIVE ME THE GOODS I ASKED YOU FOR?
UH-OH!

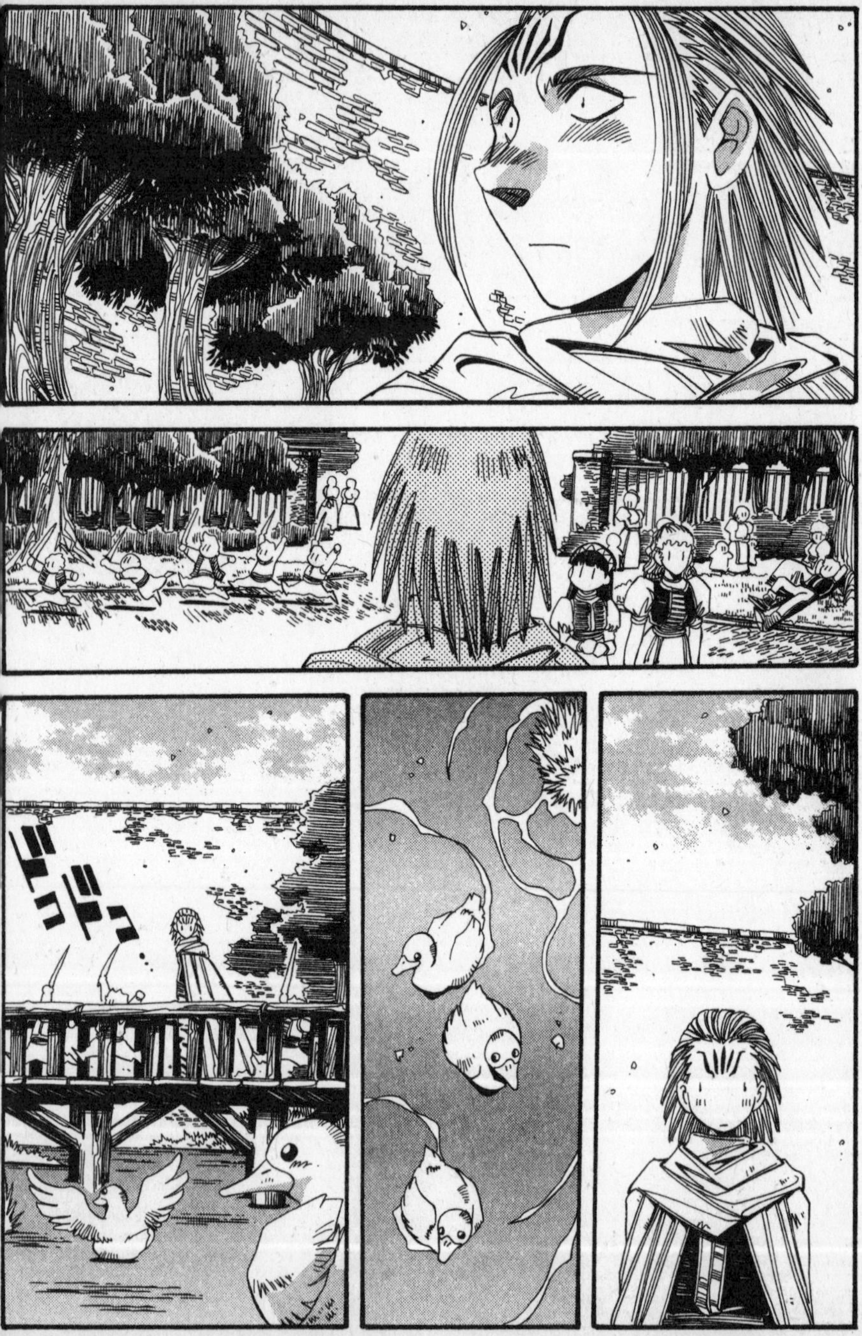
ドコドコ

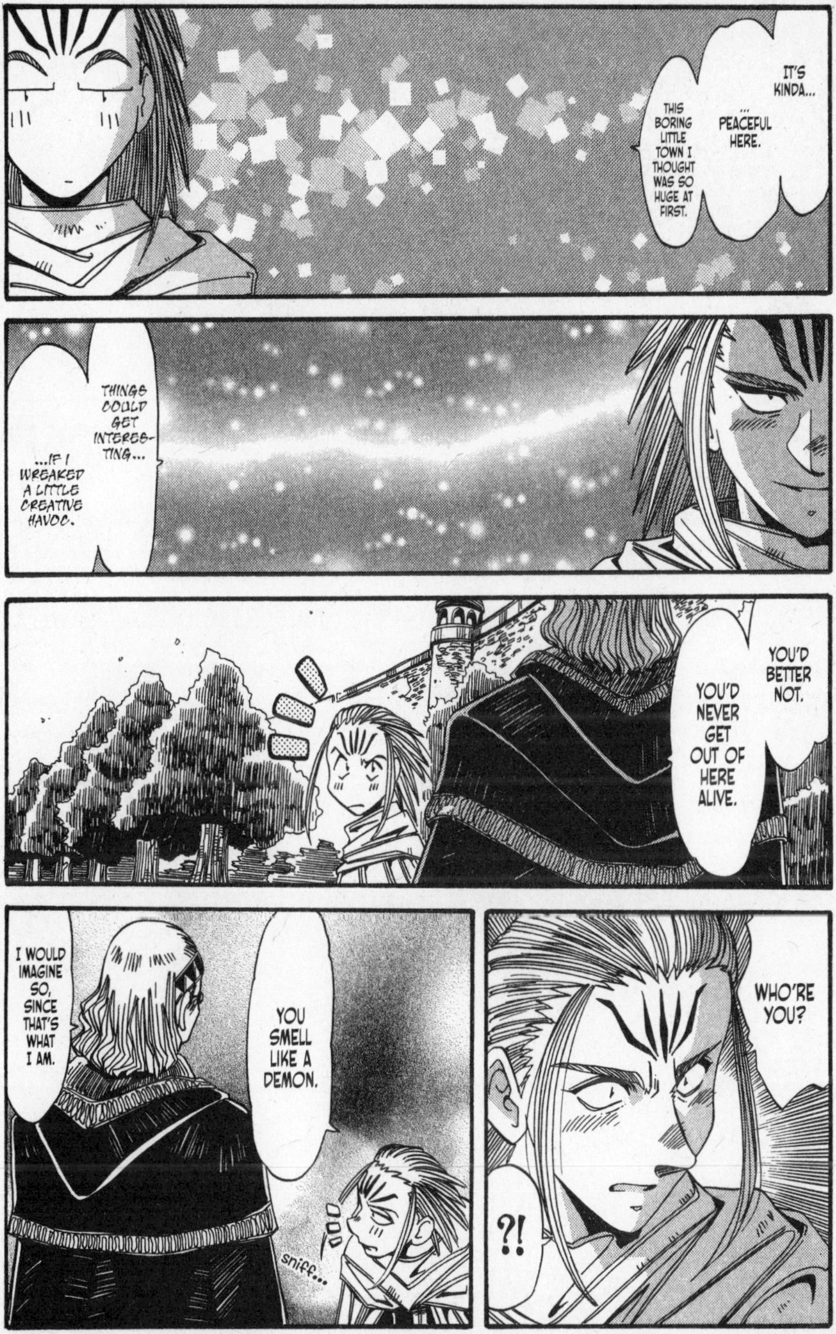
IT'S KINDA... ...PEACEFUL HERE.
THIS BORING LITTLE TOWN I THOUGHT WAS SO HUGE AT FIRST.
THINGS COULD GET INTERES-TING...
...IF I WREAKED A LITTLE CREATIVE HAVOC.
YOU'D BETTER NOT.
YOU'D NEVER GET OUT OF HERE ALIVE.
WHO'RE YOU?
?!
YOU SMELL LIKE A DEMON.
sniff...
I WOULD IMAGINE SO, SINCE THAT'S WHAT I AM.

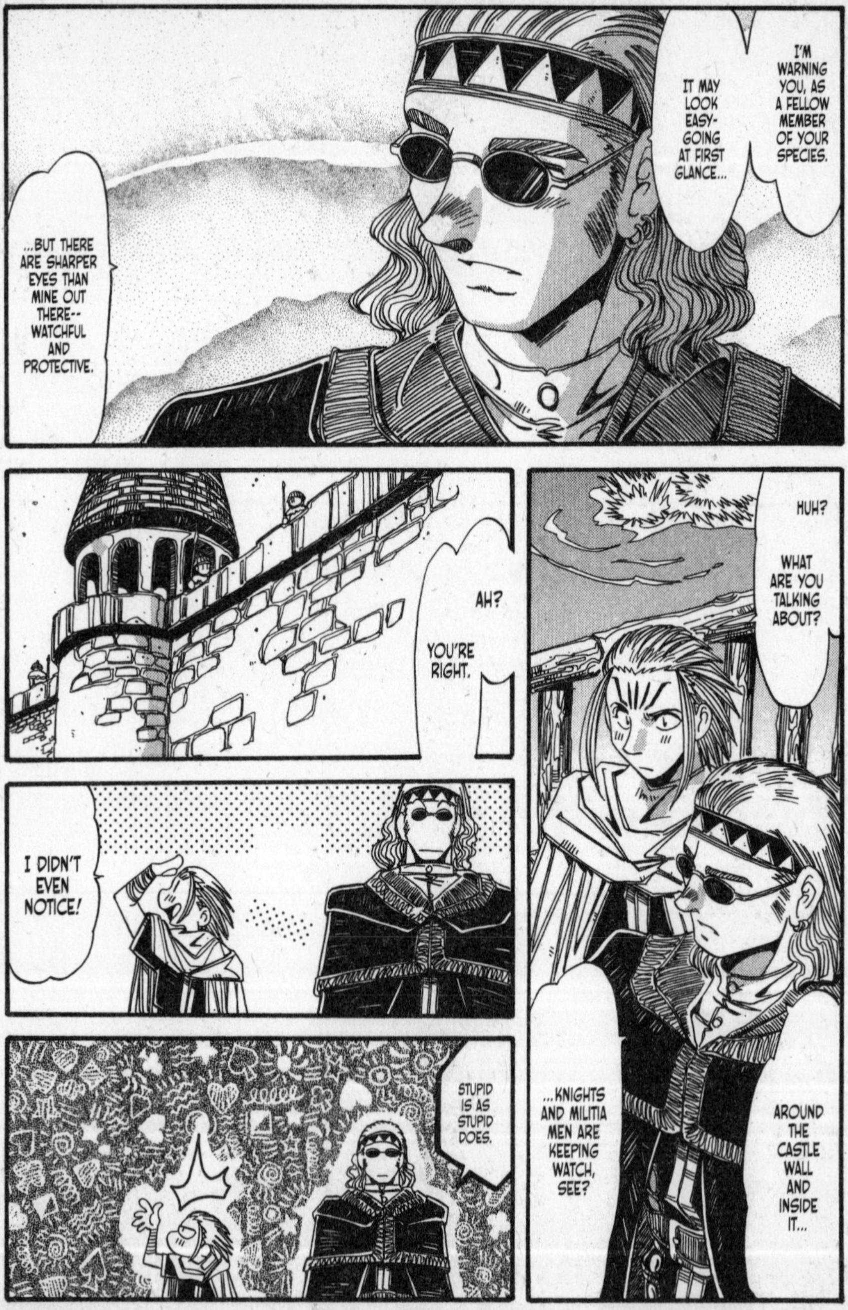
I'M WARNING YOU, AS A FELLOW MEMBER OF YOUR SPECIES.
IT MAY LOOK EASY-GOING AT FIRST GLANCE...
...BUT THERE ARE SHARPER EYES THAN MINE OUT THERE-- WATCHFUL AND PROTECTIVE.
HUH?
WHAT ARE YOU TALKING ABOUT?
AROUND THE CASTLE WALL AND INSIDE IT...
...KNIGHTS AND MILITIA MEN ARE KEEPING WATCH, SEE?
AH?
YOU'RE RIGHT.
I DIDN'T EVEN NOTICE!
STUPID IS AS STUPID DOES.

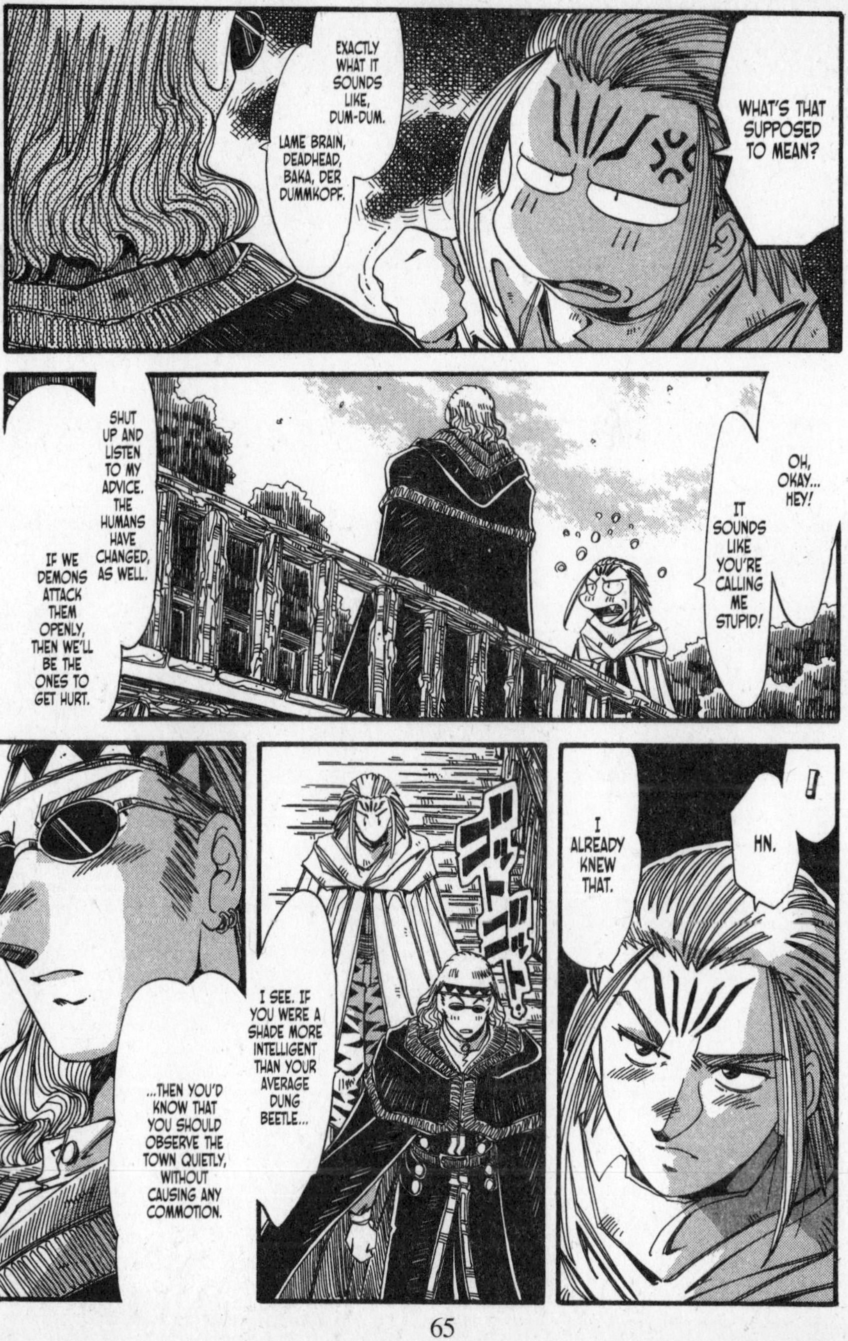
WHAT'S THAT SUPPOSED TO MEAN?
EXACTLY WHAT IT SOUNDS LIKE, DUM-DUM.
LAME BRAIN, DEADHEAD, BAKA, DER DUMMKOPF.
OH, OKAY... HEY!
IT SOUNDS LIKE YOU'RE CALLING ME STUPID!
SHUT UP AND LISTEN TO MY ADVICE. THE HUMANS HAVE CHANGED, AS WELL.
IF WE DEMONS ATTACK THEM OPENLY, THEN WE'LL BE THE ONES TO GET HURT.
!
HN.
I ALREADY KNEW THAT.
I SEE. IF YOU WERE A SHADE MORE INTELLIGENT THAN YOUR AVERAGE DUNG BEETLE...
...THEN YOU'D KNOW THAT YOU SHOULD OBSERVE THE TOWN QUIETLY, WITHOUT CAUSING ANY COMMOTION.

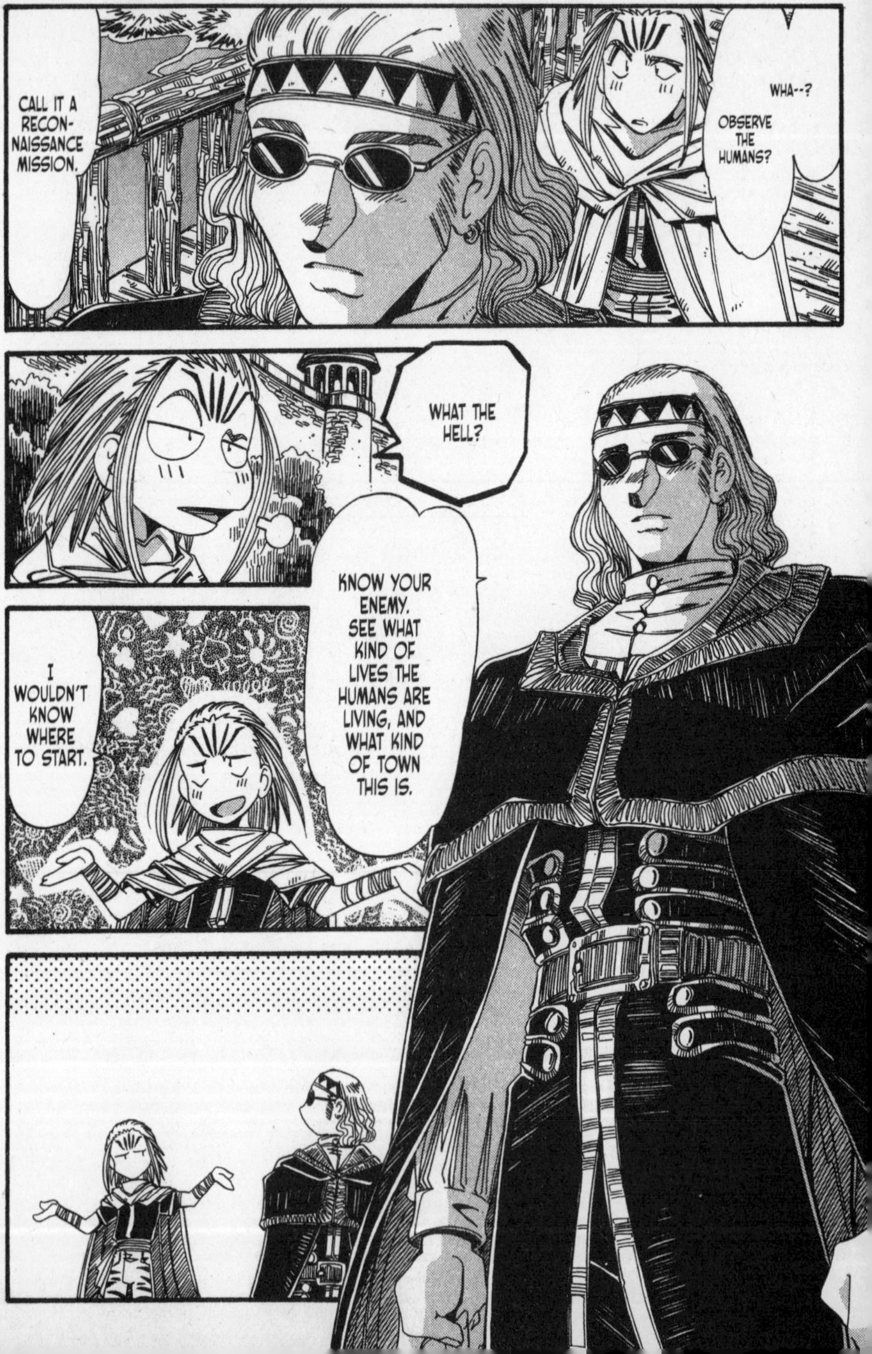
WHA--?
OBSERVE THE HUMANS?
CALL IT A RECON-NAISSANCE MISSION.
WHAT THE HELL?
KNOW YOUR ENEMY. SEE WHAT KIND OF LIVES THE HUMANS ARE LIVING, AND WHAT KIND OF TOWN THIS IS.
I WOULDN'T KNOW WHERE TO START.

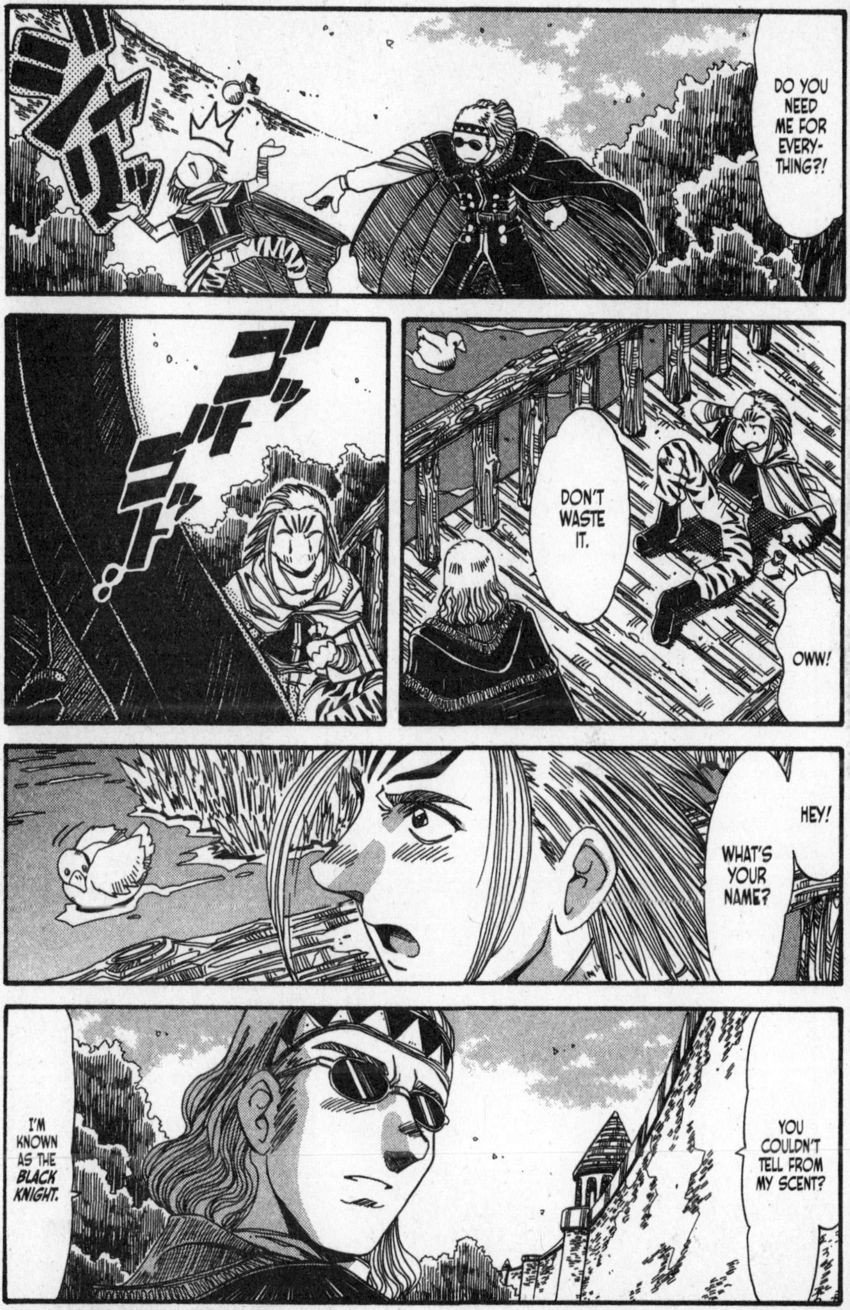
DO YOU NEED ME FOR EVERY-THING?!
DON'T WASTE IT.
OWW!
HEY!
WHAT'S YOUR NAME?
YOU COULDN'T TELL FROM MY SCENT?
I'M KNOWN AS THE *BLACK KNIGHT.*

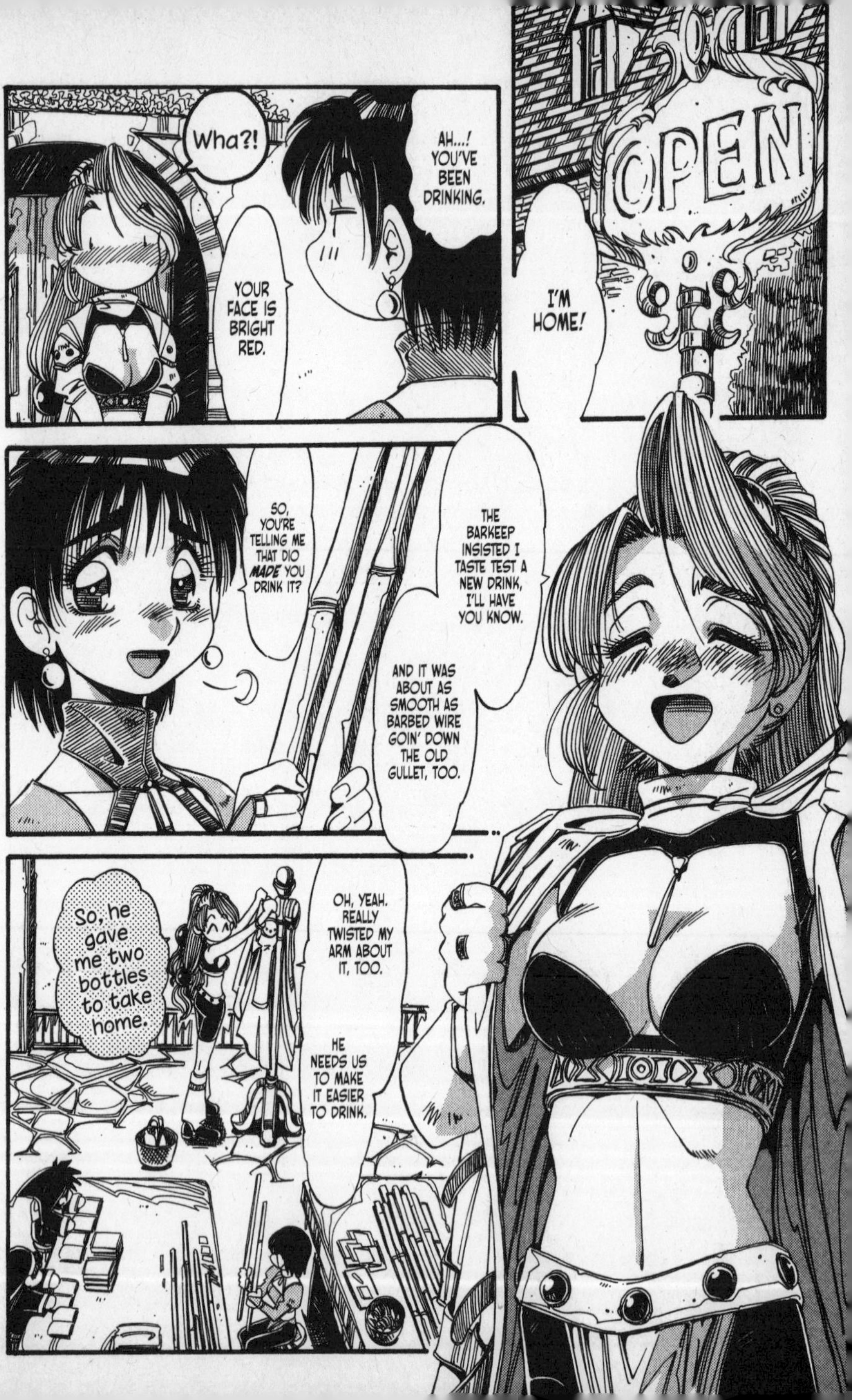
OPEN
I'M HOME!
AH...! YOU'VE BEEN DRINKING.
YOUR FACE IS BRIGHT RED.
Wha?!
THE BARKEEP INSISTED I TASTE TEST A NEW DRINK, I'LL HAVE YOU KNOW.
AND IT WAS ABOUT AS SMOOTH AS BARBED WIRE GOIN' DOWN THE OLD GULLET, TOO.
SO, YOU'RE TELLING ME THAT DIO *MADE* YOU DRINK IT?
OH, YEAH. REALLY TWISTED MY ARM ABOUT IT, TOO.
HE NEEDS US TO MAKE IT EASIER TO DRINK.
So, he gave me two bottles to take home.

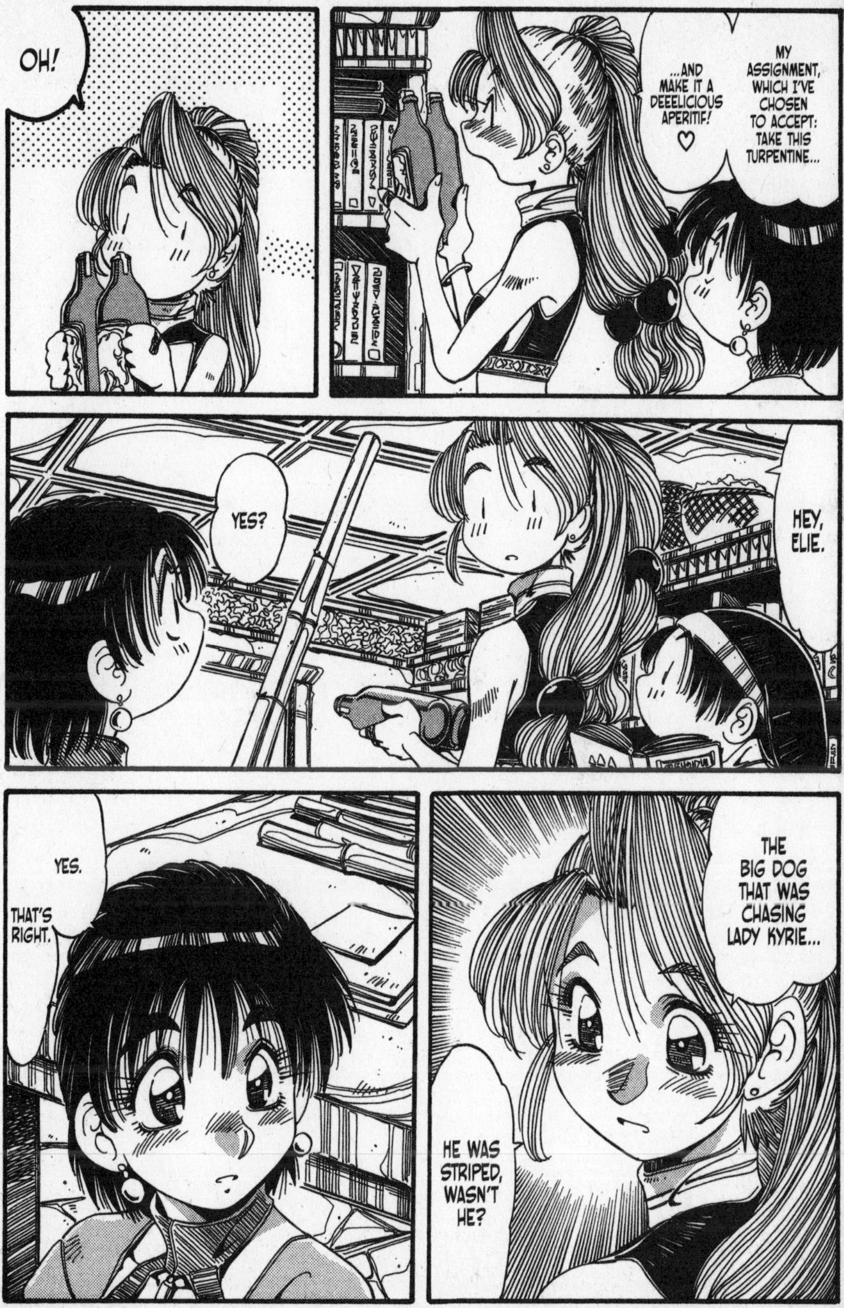
MY ASSIGNMENT, WHICH I'VE CHOSEN TO ACCEPT: TAKE THIS TURPENTINE...
...AND MAKE IT A DEEELICIOUS APERITIF! ♡
OH!
HEY, ELIE.
YES?
THE BIG DOG THAT WAS CHASING LADY KYRIE...
HE WAS STRIPED, WASN'T HE?
YES.
THAT'S RIGHT.

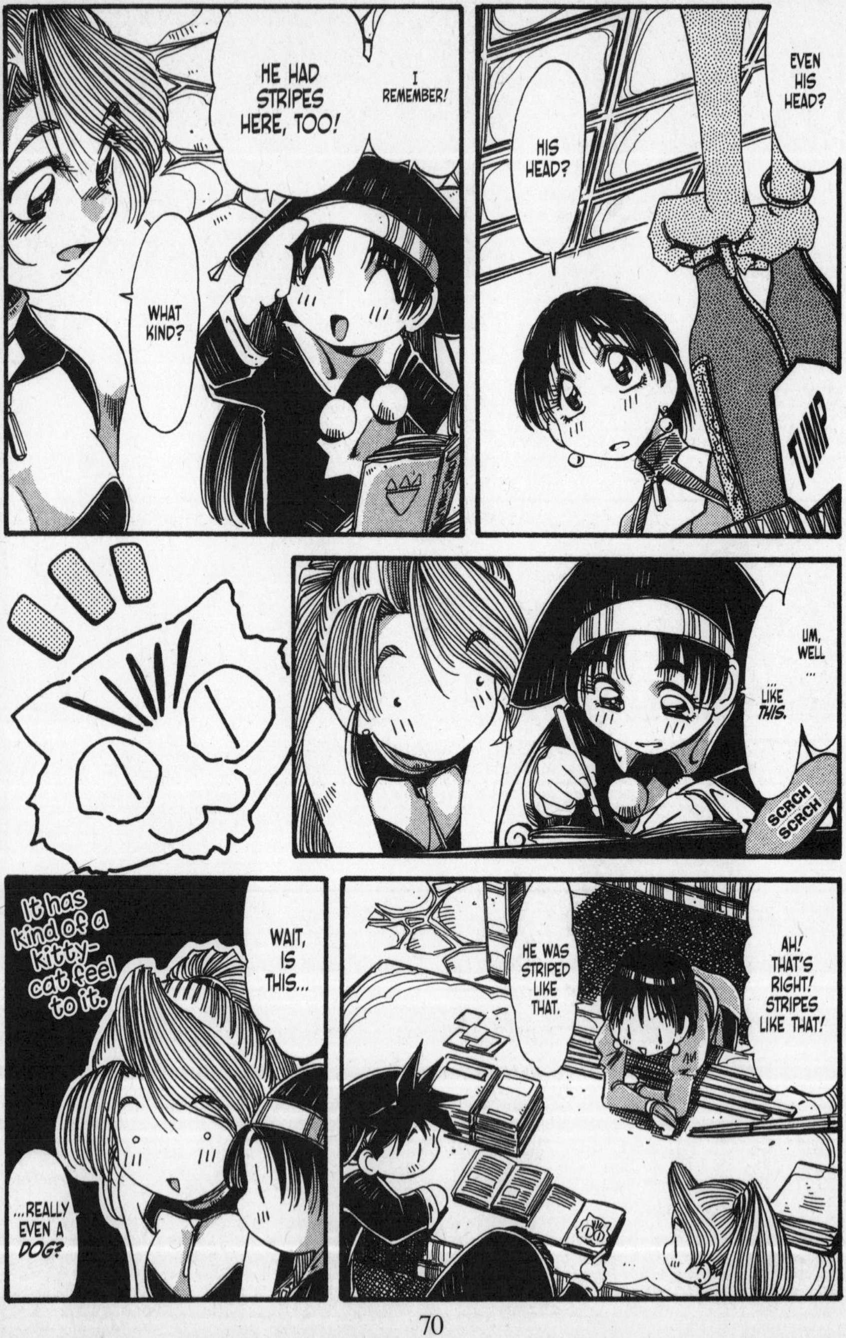
EVEN HIS HEAD?
HIS HEAD?
TUMP
I REMEMBER!
HE HAD STRIPES HERE, TOO!
...
WHAT KIND?
UM, WELL ...
... LIKE THIS.
SCRCH SCRCH
AH! THAT'S RIGHT! STRIPES LIKE THAT!
HE WAS STRIPED LIKE THAT.
...
WAIT, IS THIS...
It has kind of a kitty-cat feel to it.
...REALLY EVEN A DOG?

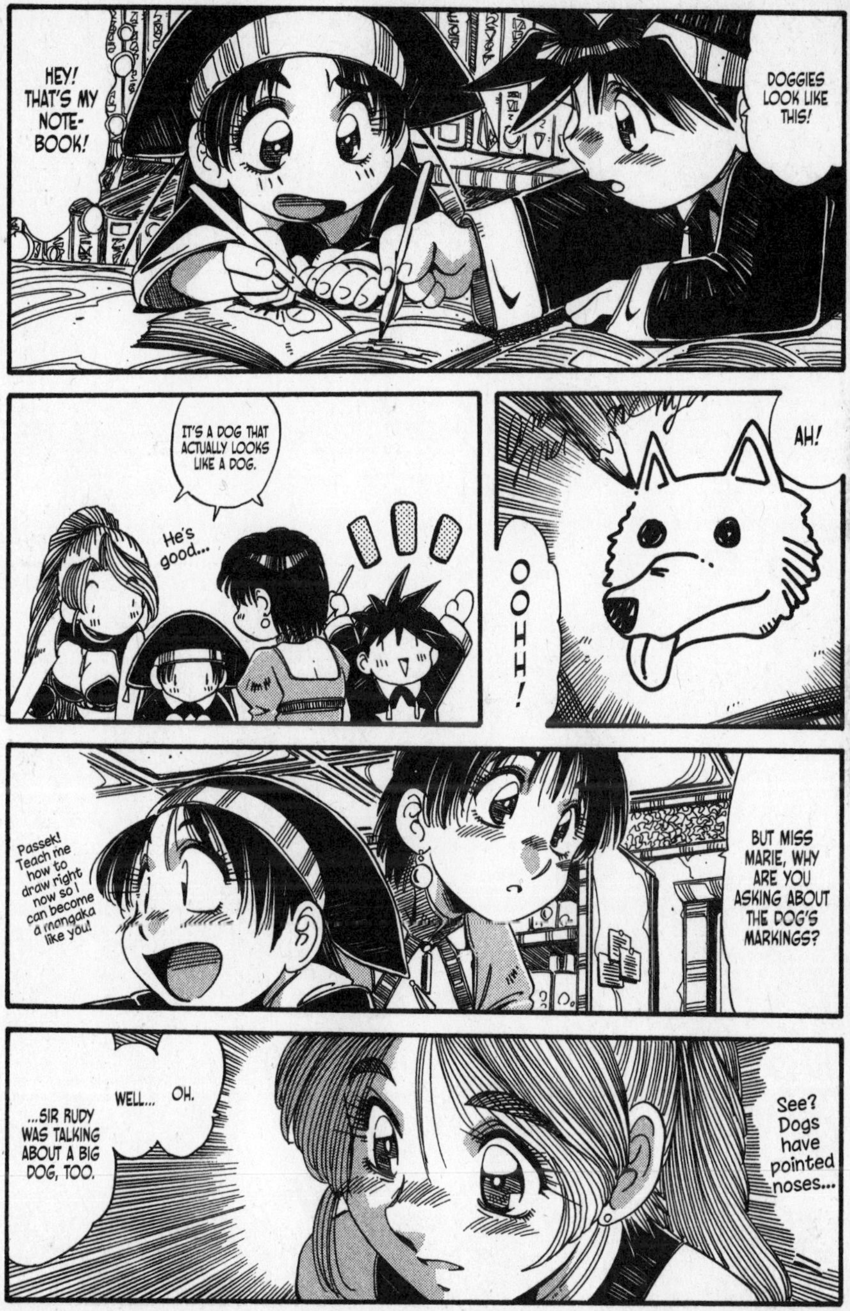
DOGGIES LOOK LIKE THIS!
HEY! THAT'S MY NOTEBOOK!
AH!
OOHH!
IT'S A DOG THAT ACTUALLY LOOKS LIKE A DOG.
He's good...
BUT MISS MARIE, WHY ARE YOU ASKING ABOUT THE DOG'S MARKINGS?
Passek! Teach me how to draw right now so I can become a mangaka like you!
See? Dogs have pointed noses...
OH.
WELL...
...SIR RUDY WAS TALKING ABOUT A BIG DOG, TOO.

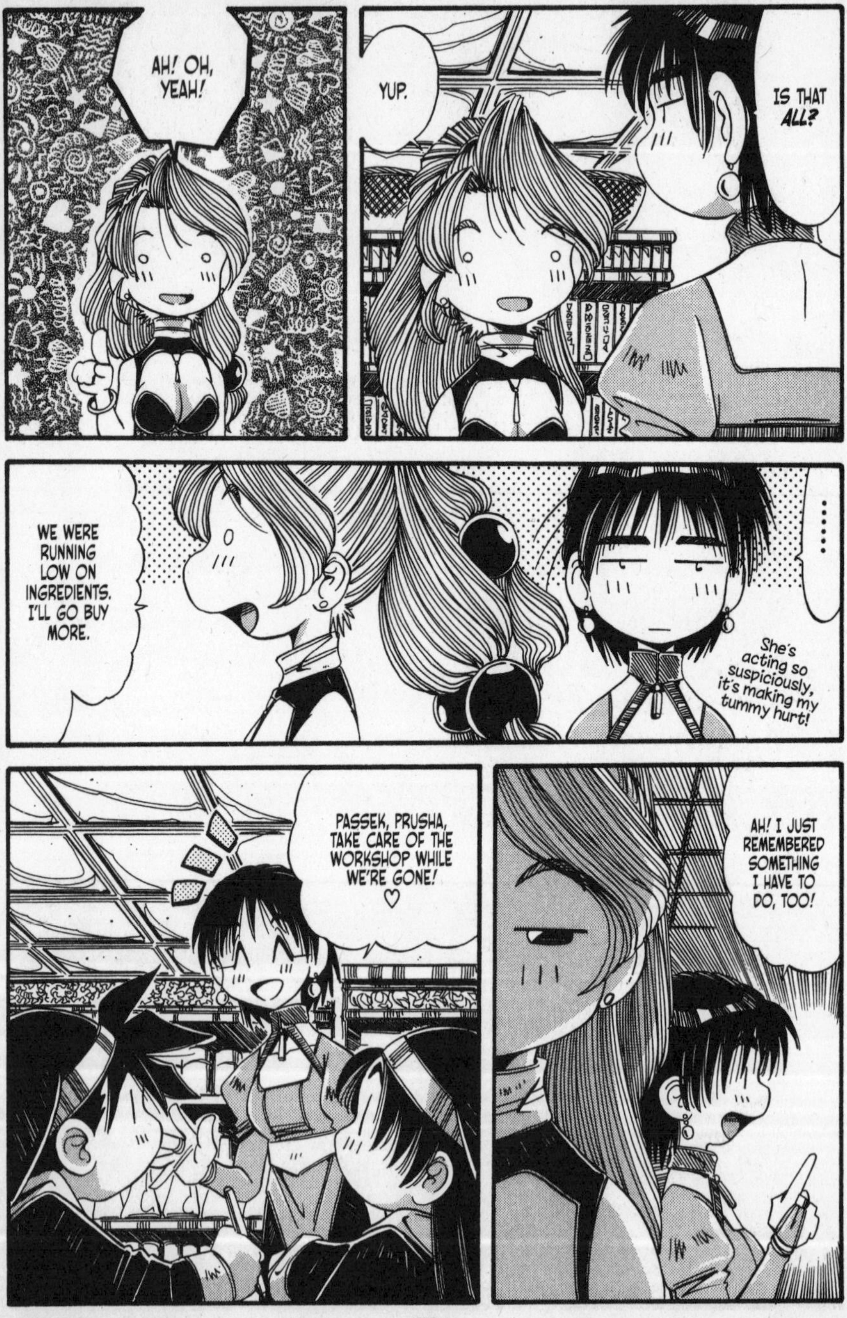
IS THAT ALL?
YUP.
AH! OH, YEAH!
......
She's acting so suspiciously, it's making my tummy hurt!
WE WERE RUNNING LOW ON INGREDIENTS. I'LL GO BUY MORE.
AH! I JUST REMEMBERED SOMETHING I HAVE TO DO, TOO!
PASSEK, PRUSHA, TAKE CARE OF THE WORKSHOP WHILE WE'RE GONE! ♡

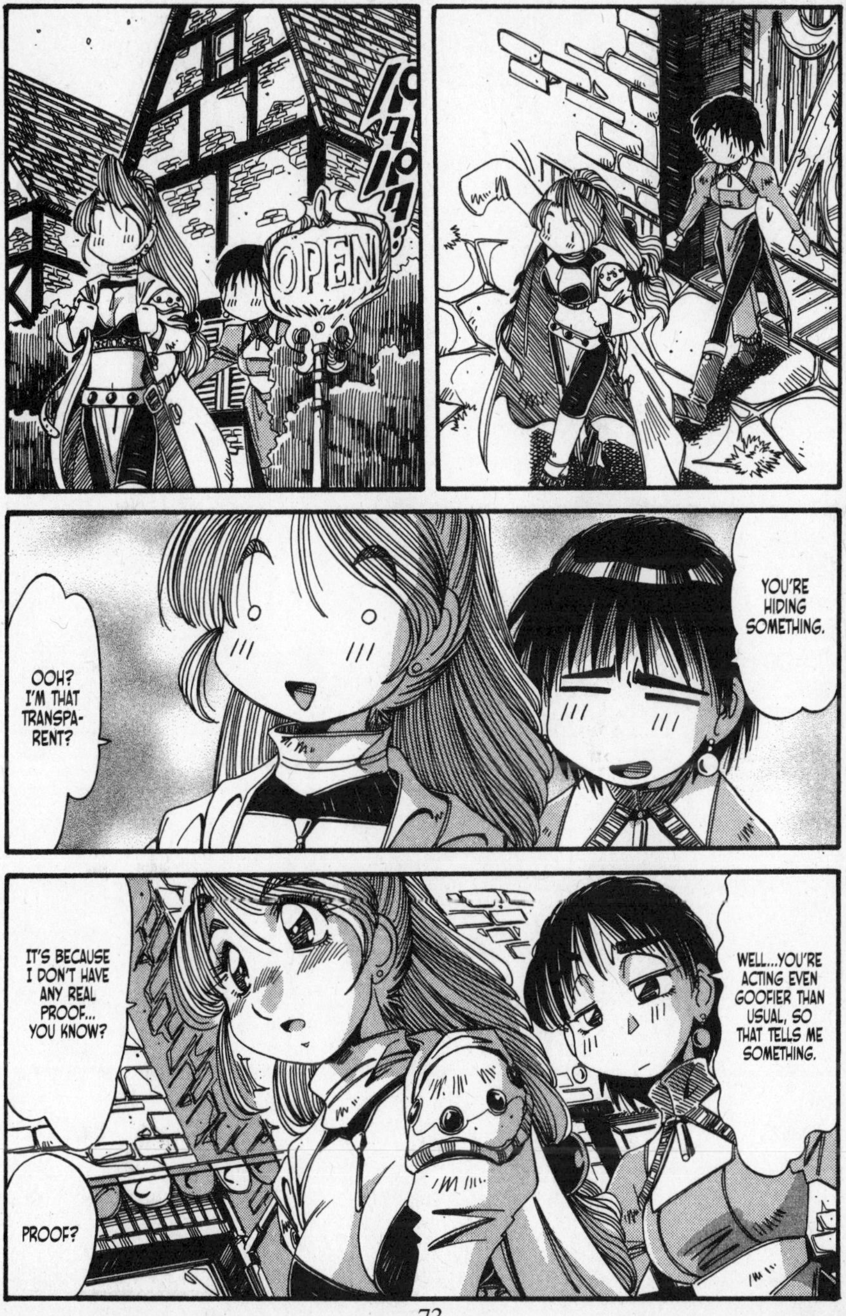
OPEN
YOU'RE HIDING SOMETHING.
OOH? I'M THAT TRANSPA-RENT?
WELL...YOU'RE ACTING EVEN GOOFIER THAN USUAL, SO THAT TELLS ME SOMETHING.
IT'S BECAUSE I DON'T HAVE ANY REAL PROOF... YOU KNOW?
PROOF?

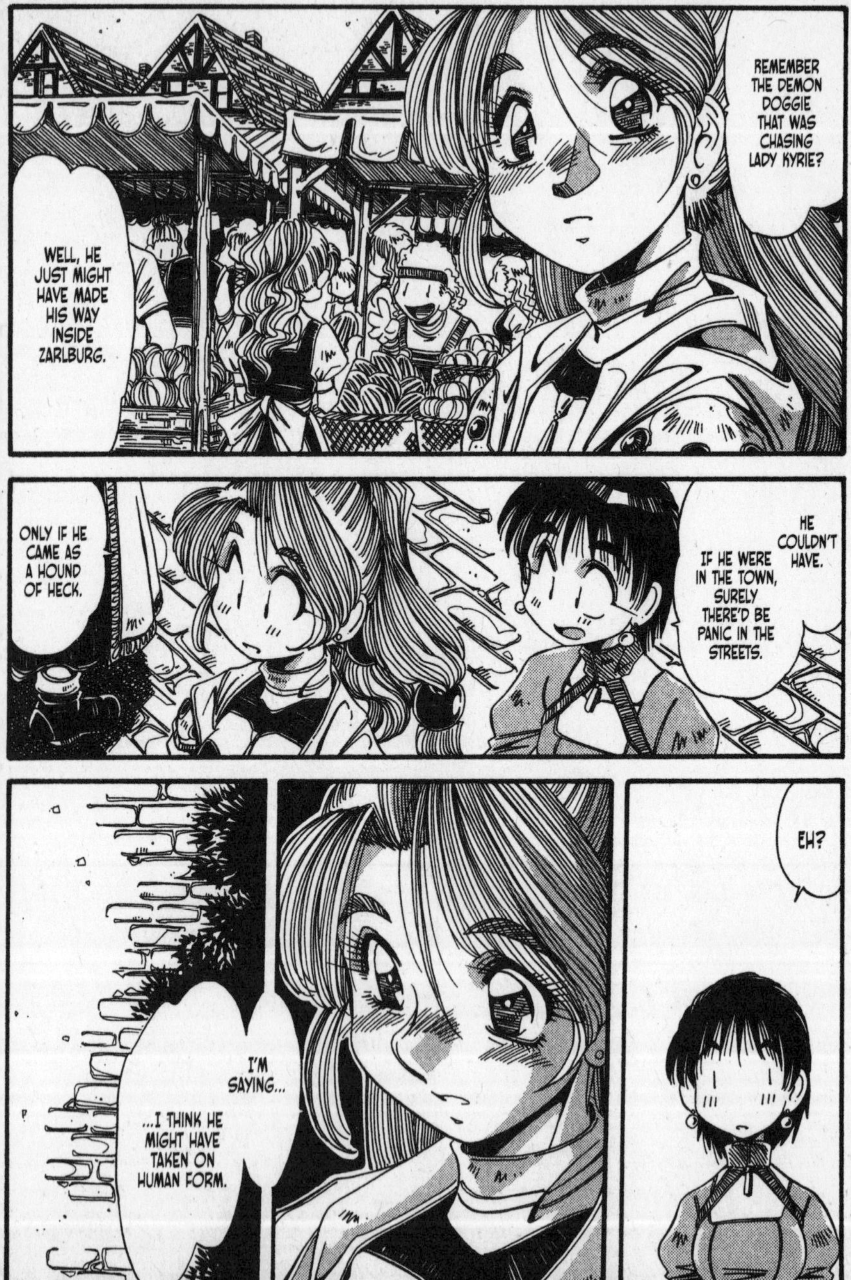
REMEMBER THE DEMON DOGGIE THAT WAS CHASING LADY KYRIE?
WELL, HE JUST MIGHT HAVE MADE HIS WAY INSIDE ZARLBURG.
HE COULDN'T HAVE.
IF HE WERE IN THE TOWN, SURELY THERE'D BE PANIC IN THE STREETS.
ONLY IF HE CAME AS A HOUND OF HECK.
EH?
I'M SAYING...
...I THINK HE MIGHT HAVE TAKEN ON HUMAN FORM.

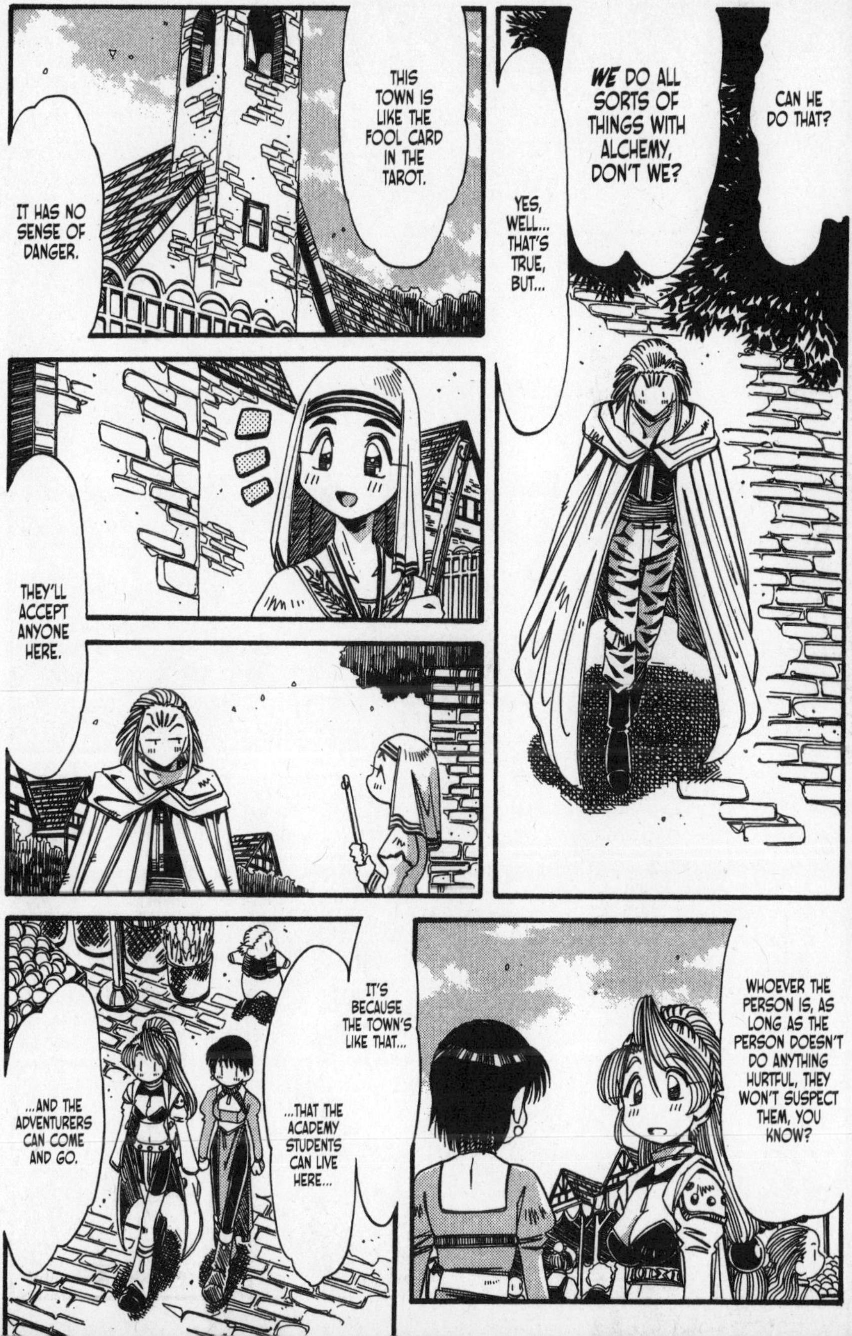
CAN HE DO THAT?
WE DO ALL SORTS OF THINGS WITH ALCHEMY, DON'T WE?
YES, WELL... THAT'S TRUE, BUT...
THIS TOWN IS LIKE THE FOOL CARD IN THE TAROT.
IT HAS NO SENSE OF DANGER.
THEY'LL ACCEPT ANYONE HERE.
WHOEVER THE PERSON IS, AS LONG AS THE PERSON DOESN'T DO ANYTHING HURTFUL, THEY WON'T SUSPECT THEM, YOU KNOW?
IT'S BECAUSE THE TOWN'S LIKE THAT...
...THAT THE ACADEMY STUDENTS CAN LIVE HERE...
...AND THE ADVENTURERS CAN COME AND GO.

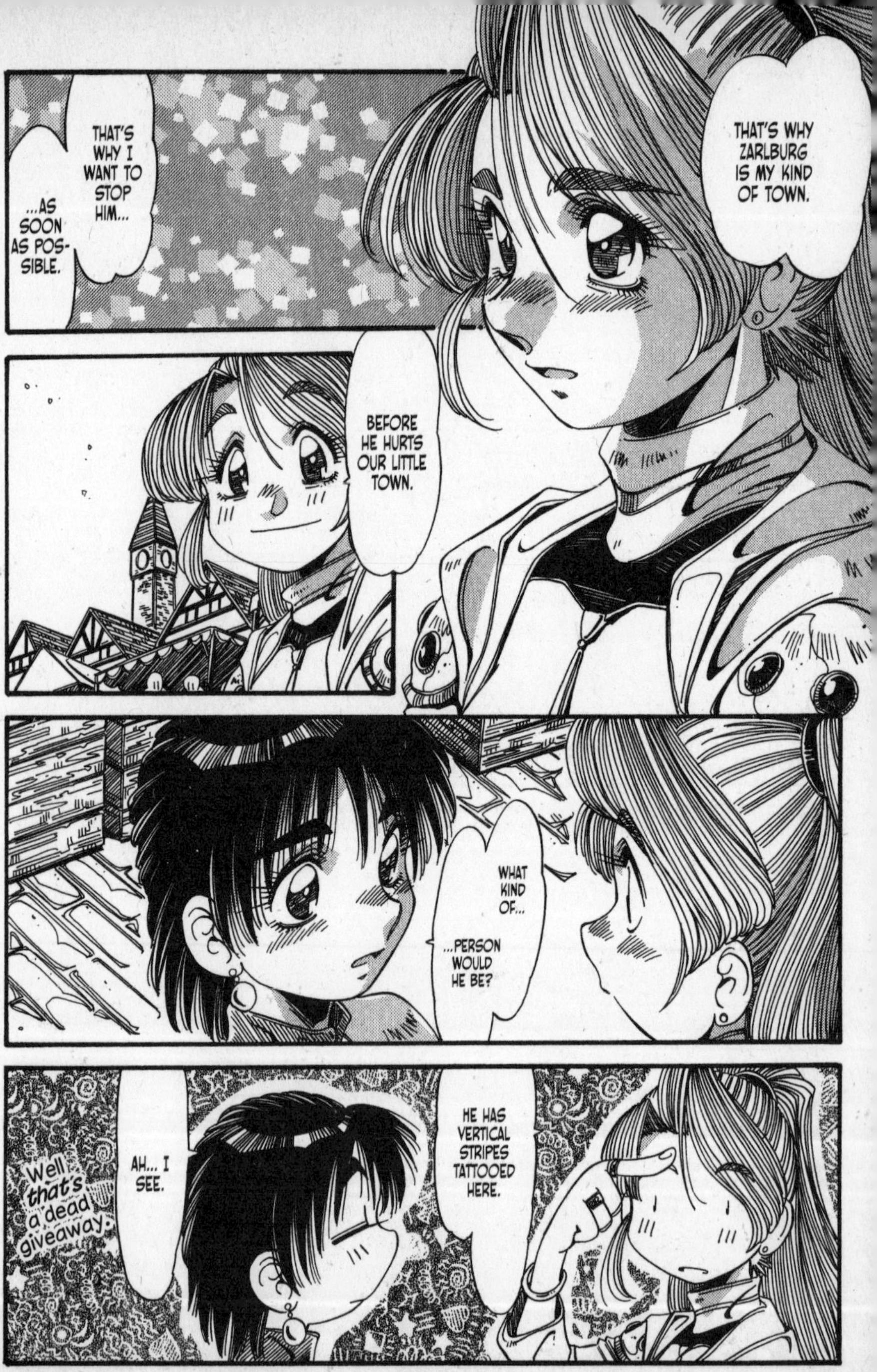
THAT'S WHY ZARLBURG IS MY KIND OF TOWN.
THAT'S WHY I WANT TO STOP HIM...
...AS SOON AS POS-SIBLE.
BEFORE HE HURTS OUR LITTLE TOWN.
WHAT KIND OF...
...PERSON WOULD HE BE?
HE HAS VERTICAL STRIPES TATTOOED HERE.
AH... I SEE.
Well *that's* a dead giveaway.

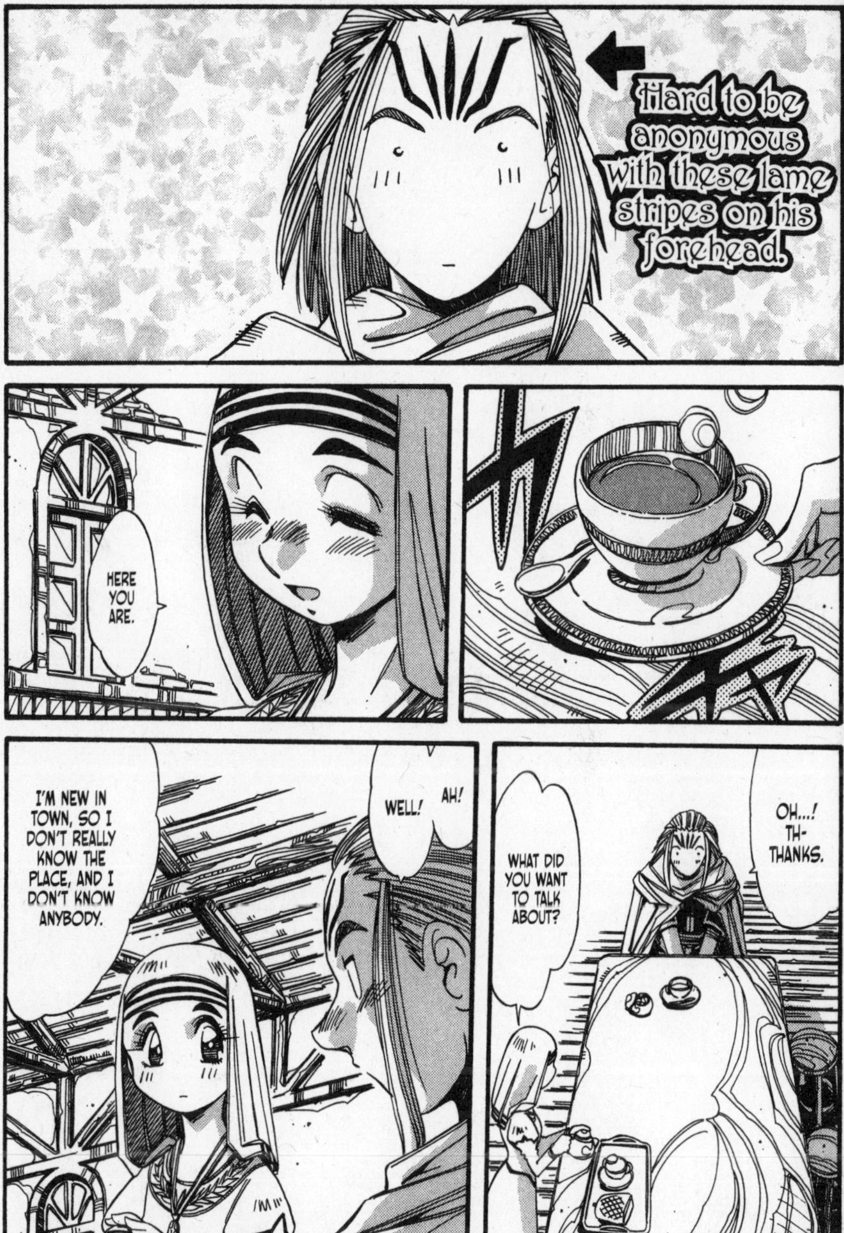
Hard to be anonymous with these lame stripes on his forehead.
HERE YOU ARE.
OH...! TH- THANKS.
WHAT DID YOU WANT TO TALK ABOUT?
AH!
WELL!
I'M NEW IN TOWN, SO I DON'T REALLY KNOW THE PLACE, AND I DON'T KNOW ANYBODY.

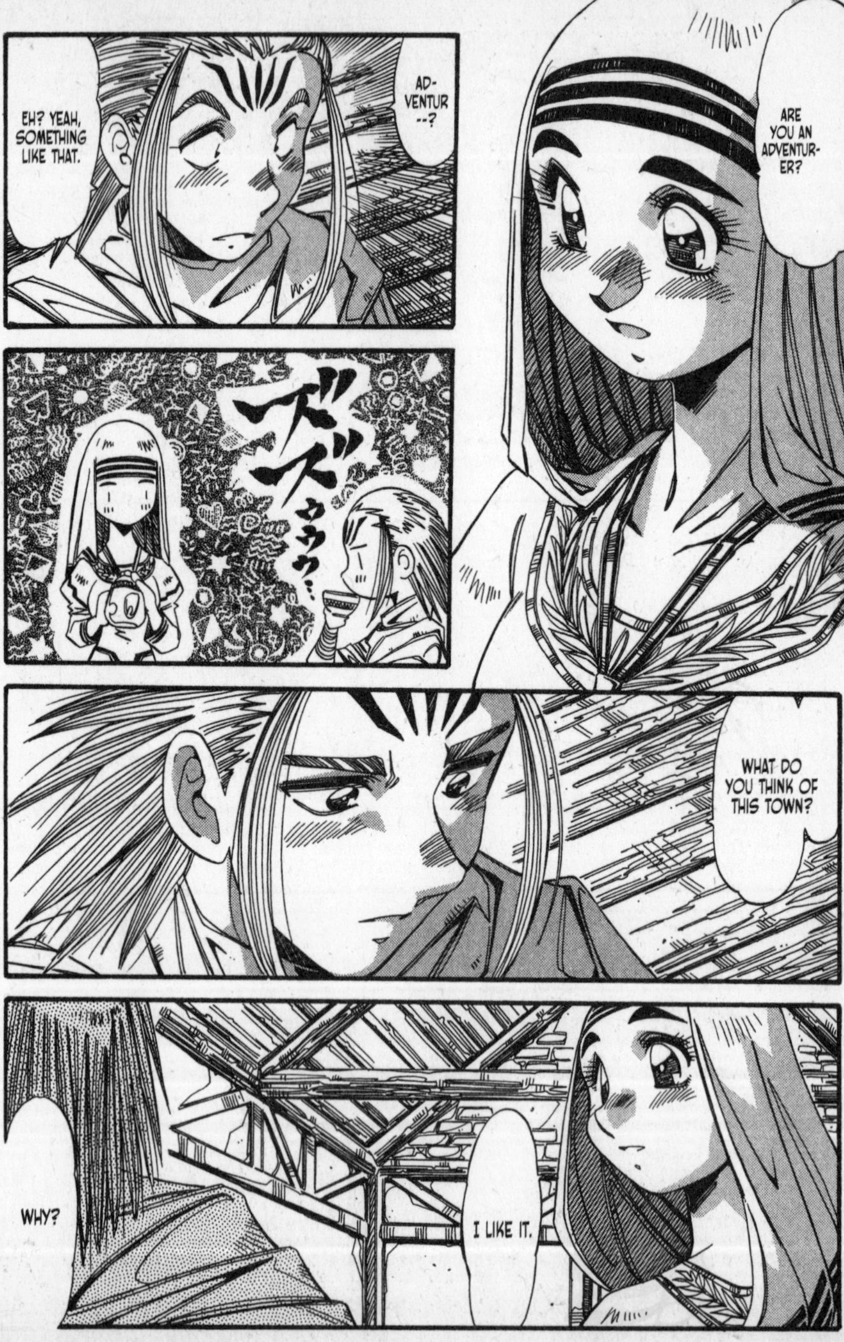
ARE YOU AN ADVENTURER?
ADVENTUR--?
EH? YEAH, SOMETHING LIKE THAT.
WHAT DO YOU THINK OF THIS TOWN?
I LIKE IT.
WHY?

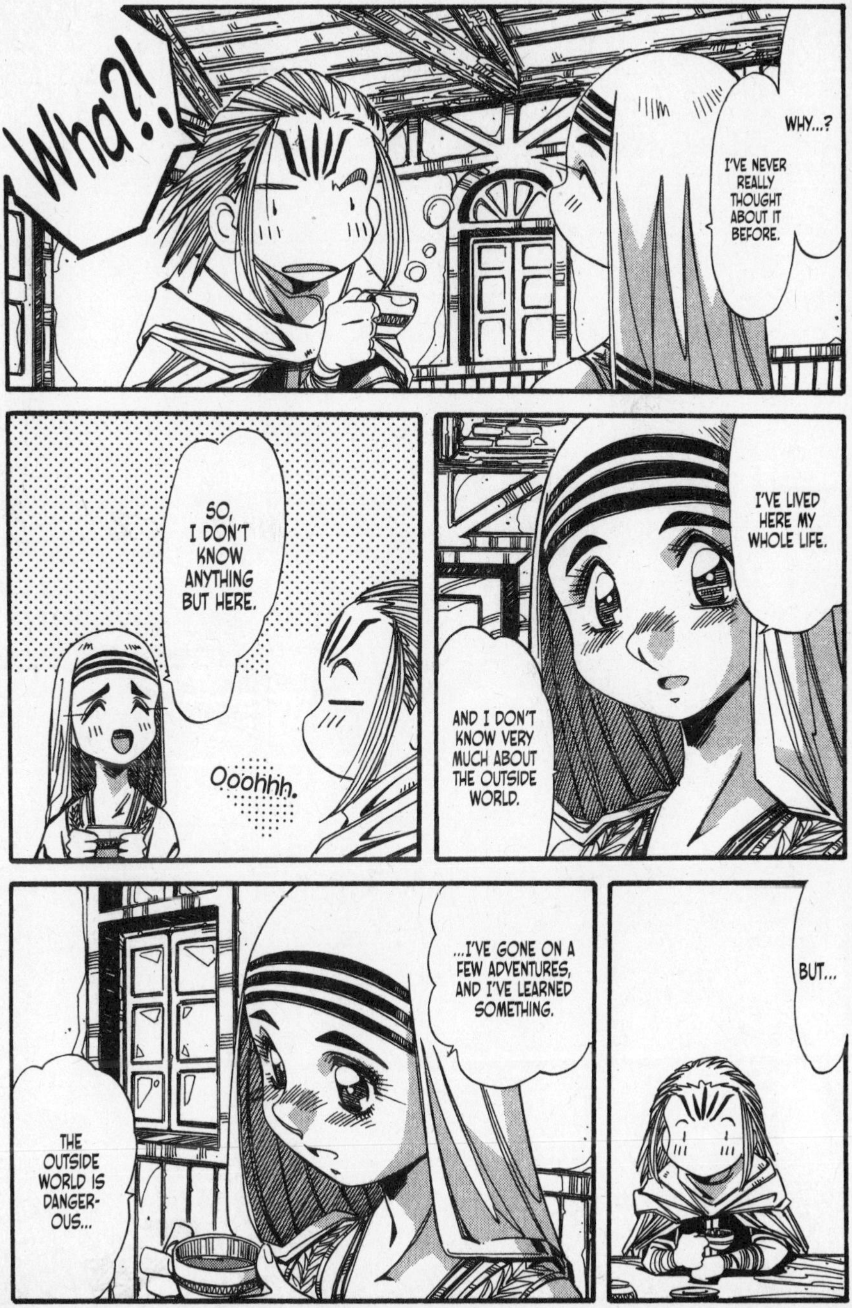
WHY...?
I'VE NEVER REALLY THOUGHT ABOUT IT BEFORE.
Wha?!
I'VE LIVED HERE MY WHOLE LIFE.
AND I DON'T KNOW VERY MUCH ABOUT THE OUTSIDE WORLD.
SO, I DON'T KNOW ANYTHING BUT HERE.
Ooohhh.
BUT...
...I'VE GONE ON A FEW ADVENTURES, AND I'VE LEARNED SOMETHING.
THE OUTSIDE WORLD IS DANGER-OUS...

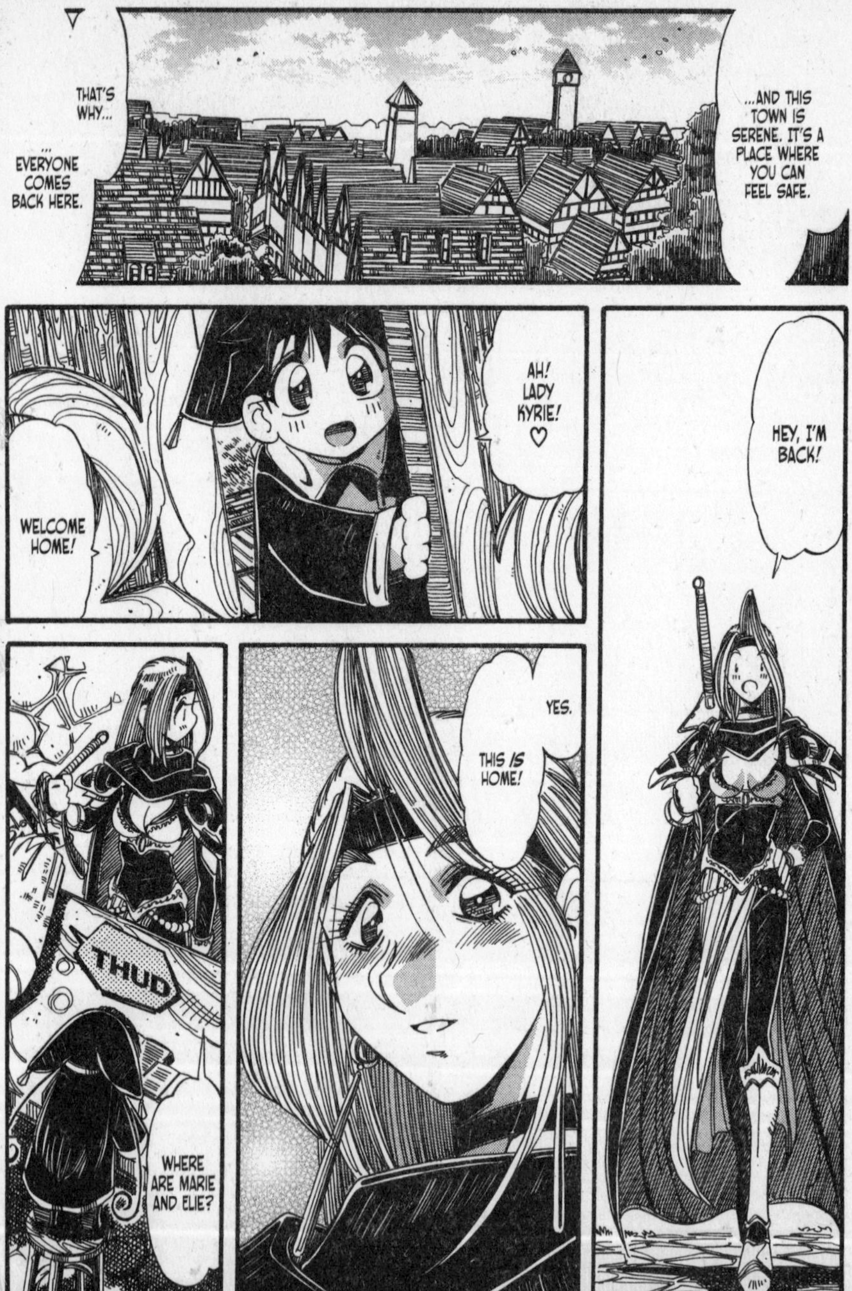
...AND THIS TOWN IS SERENE. IT'S A PLACE WHERE YOU CAN FEEL SAFE.
THAT'S WHY...
...EVERYONE COMES BACK HERE.
HEY, I'M BACK!
AH! LADY KYRIE! ♡
WELCOME HOME!
YES.
THIS *IS* HOME!
THUD
WHERE ARE MARIE AND ELIE?

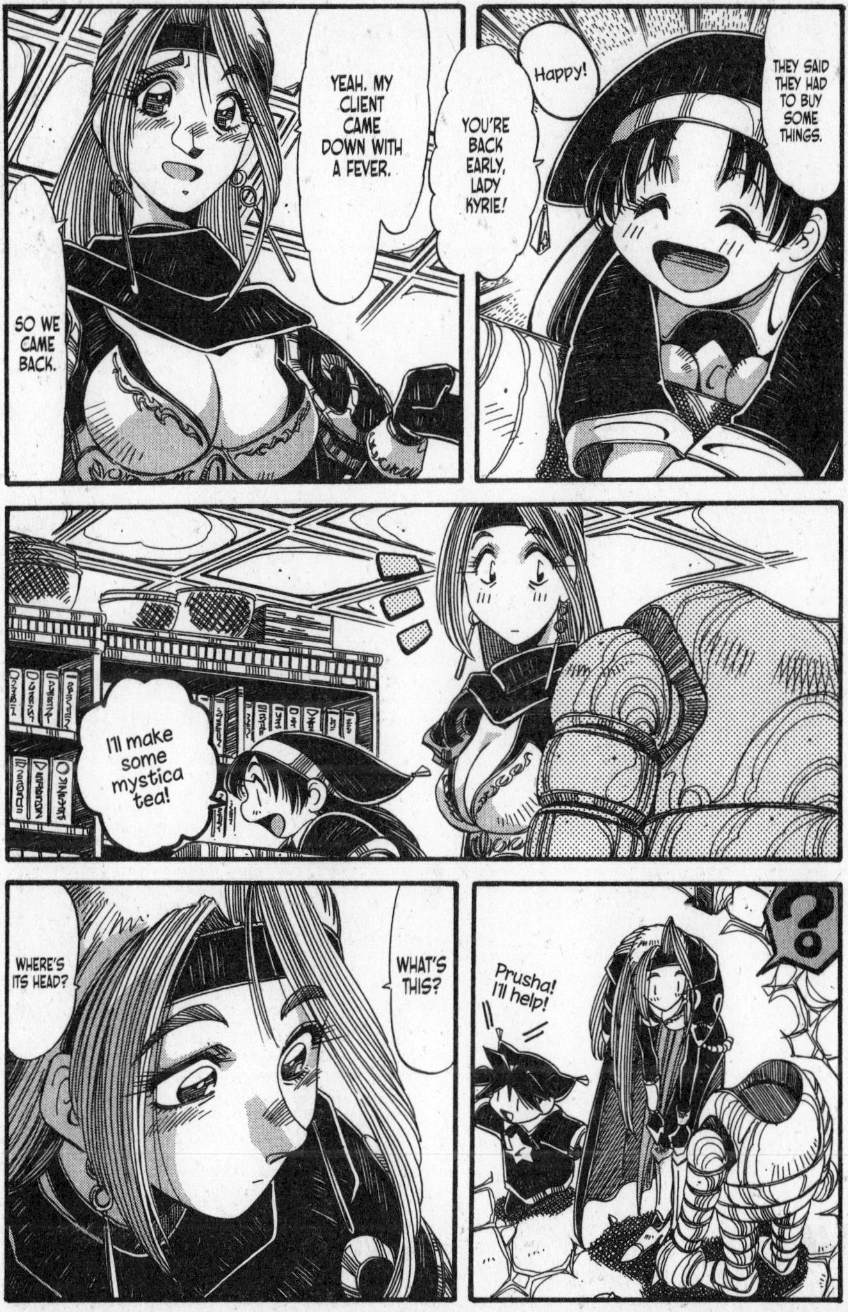
They said they had to buy some things.
Happy!
You're back early, Lady Kyrie!
Yeah. My client came down with a fever.
So we came back.
I'll make some mystica tea!
Prusha! I'll help!
What's this?
Where's its head?

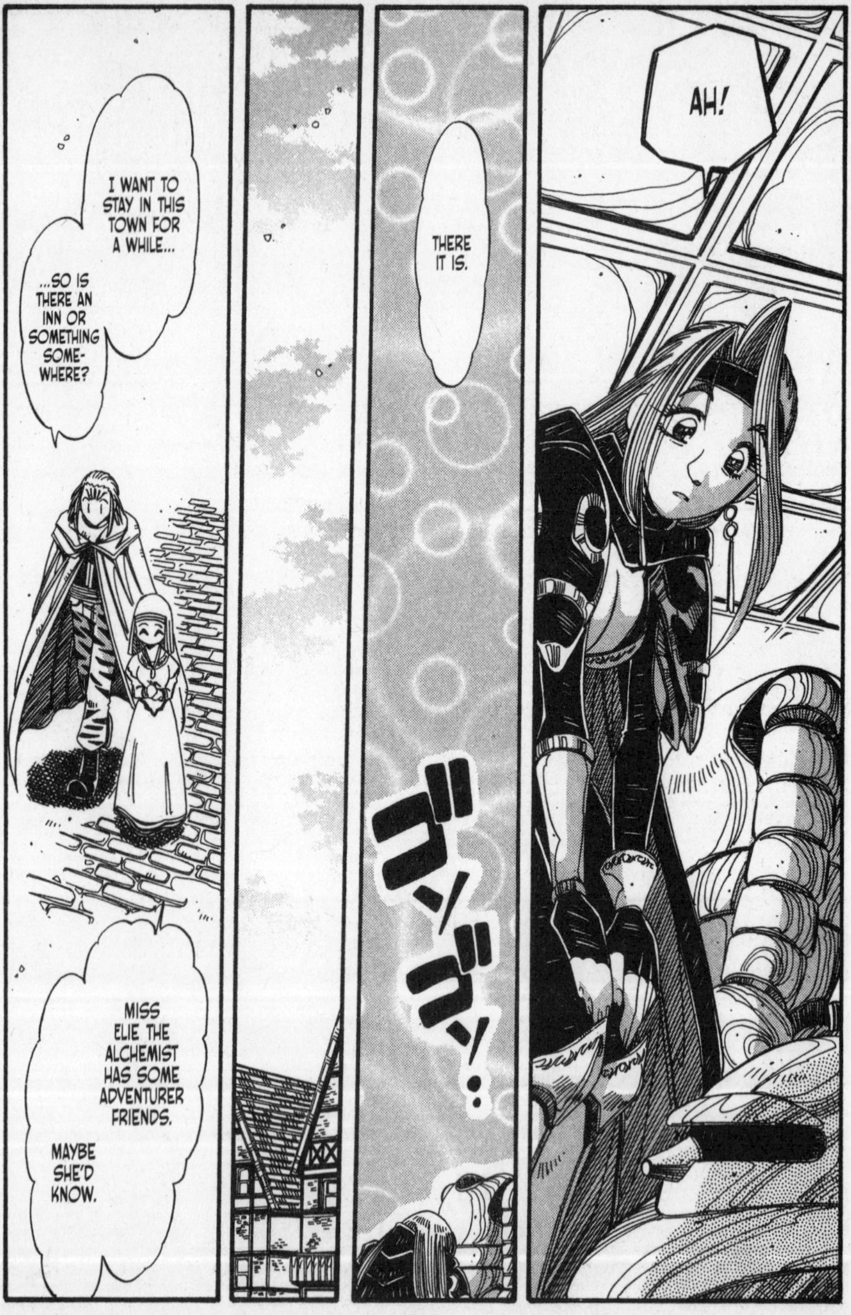
AH!
THERE IT IS.
I WANT TO STAY IN THIS TOWN FOR A WHILE...
...SO IS THERE AN INN OR SOMETHING SOME-WHERE?
MISS ELIE THE ALCHEMIST HAS SOME ADVENTURER FRIENDS.
MAYBE SHE'D KNOW.

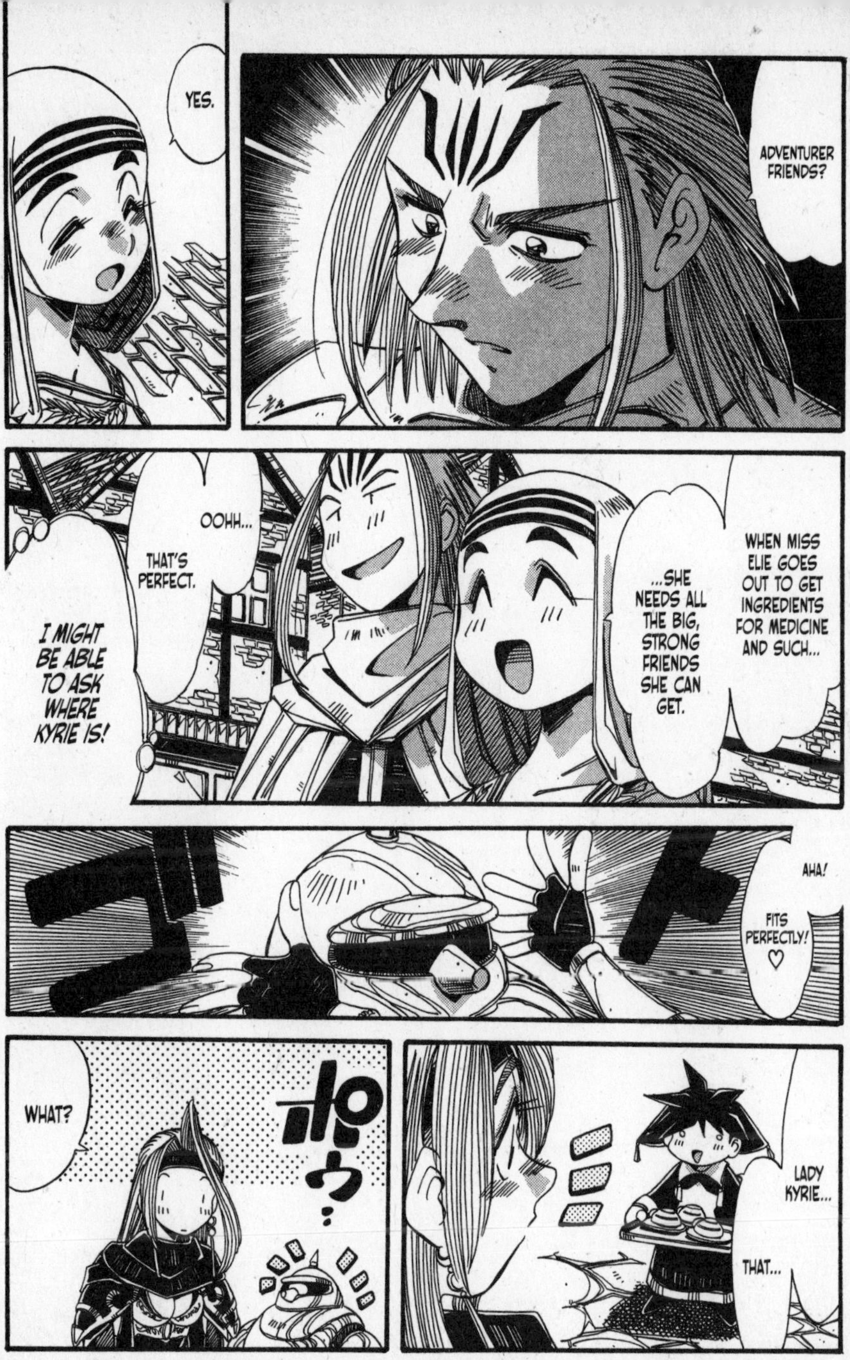
ADVENTURER FRIENDS?
YES.
WHEN MISS ELIE GOES OUT TO GET INGREDIENTS FOR MEDICINE AND SUCH...
...SHE NEEDS ALL THE BIG, STRONG FRIENDS SHE CAN GET.
OOHH...
THAT'S PERFECT.
I MIGHT BE ABLE TO ASK WHERE KYRIE IS!
AHA!
FITS PERFECTLY! ♡
LADY KYRIE...
THAT...
WHAT?
ポウ?

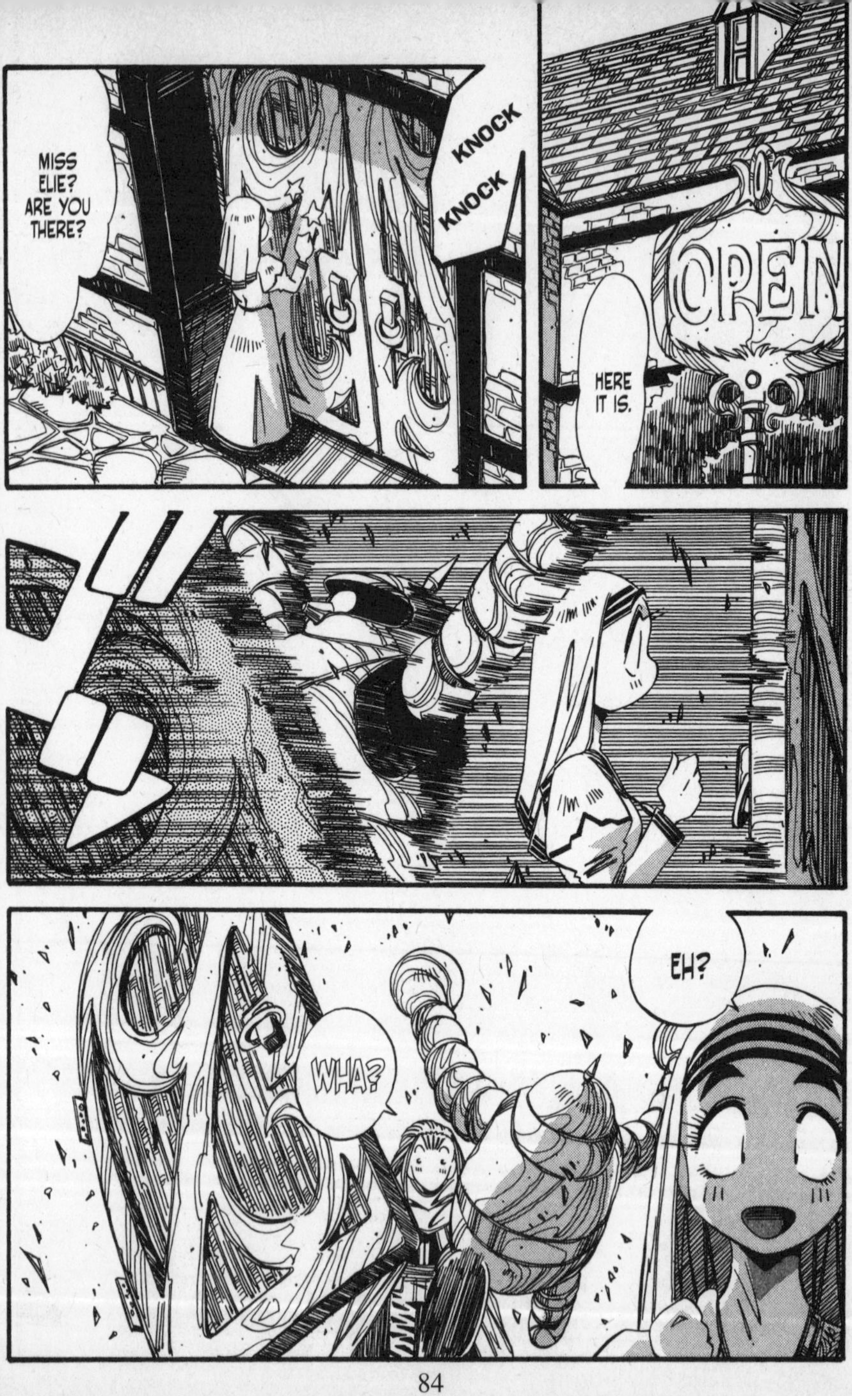
HERE IT IS.
KNOCK
KNOCK
MISS ELIE? ARE YOU THERE?
EH?
WHA?

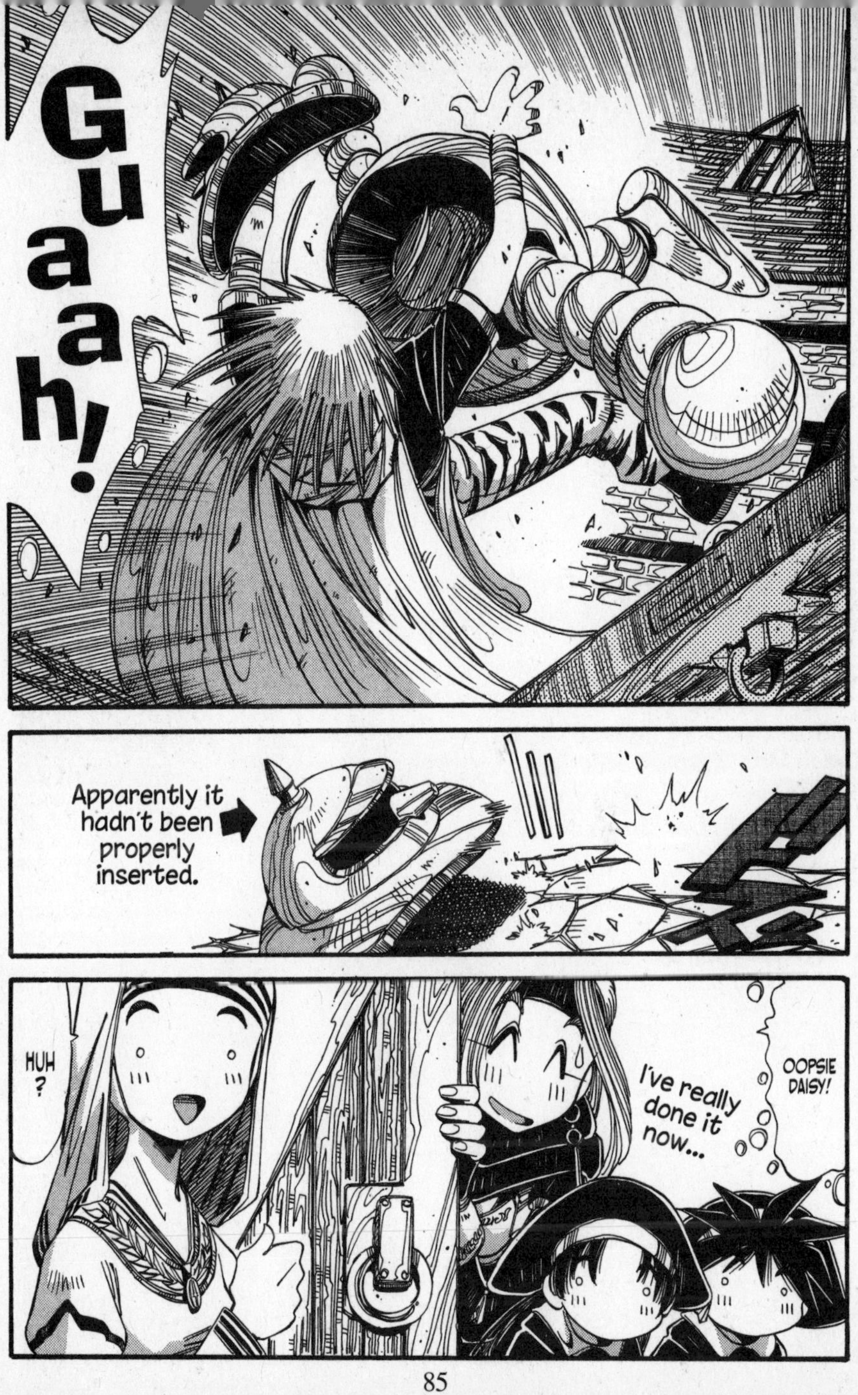
Guaaah!
Apparently it hadn't been properly inserted.
OOPSIE DAISY!
I've really done it now...
HUH ?

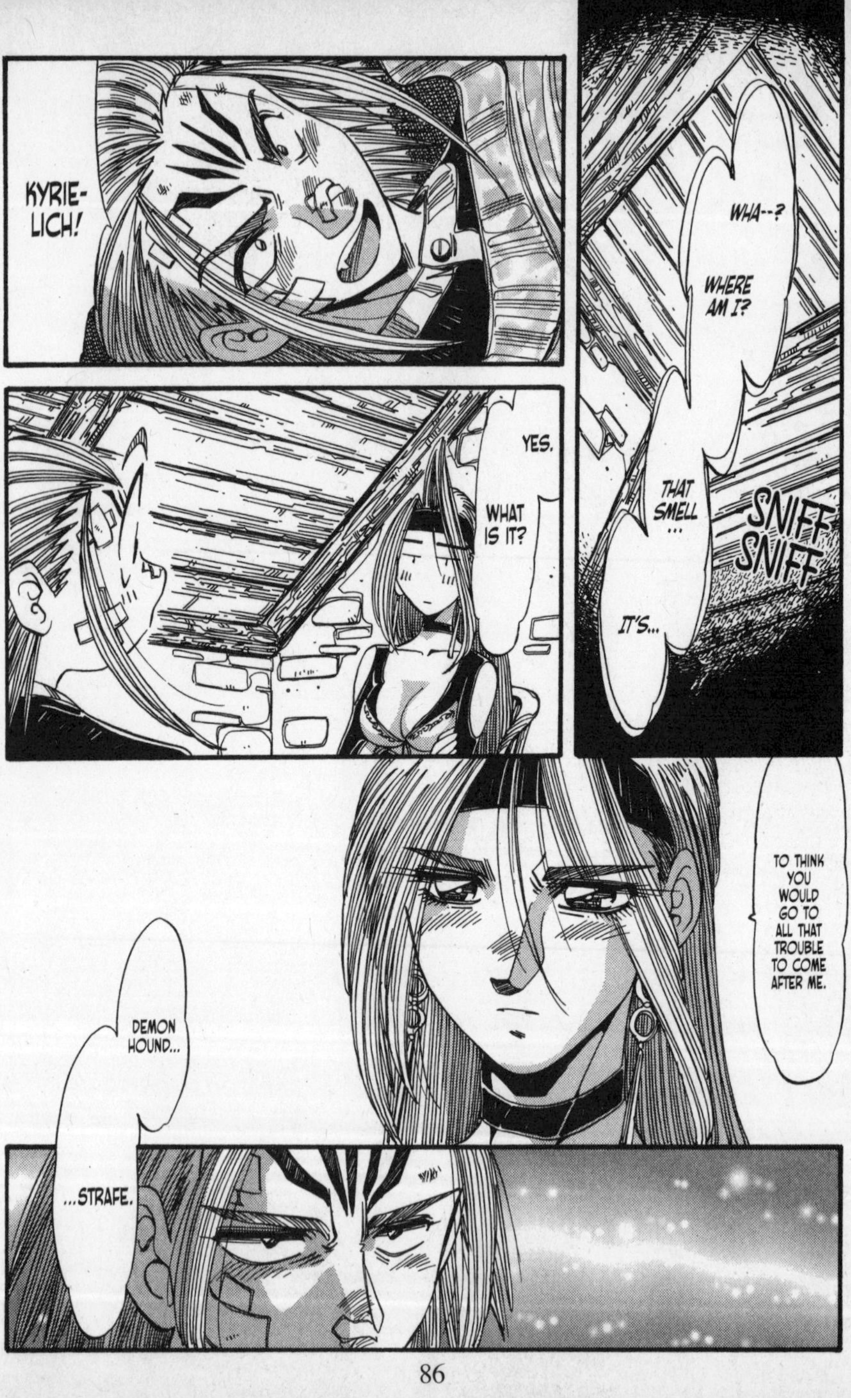
WHA--?
WHERE AM I?
THAT SMELL...
SNIFF SNIFF
IT'S...
KYRIE-LICH!
YES.
WHAT IS IT?
TO THINK YOU WOULD GO TO ALL THAT TROUBLE TO COME AFTER ME.
DEMON HOUND...
...STRAFE.

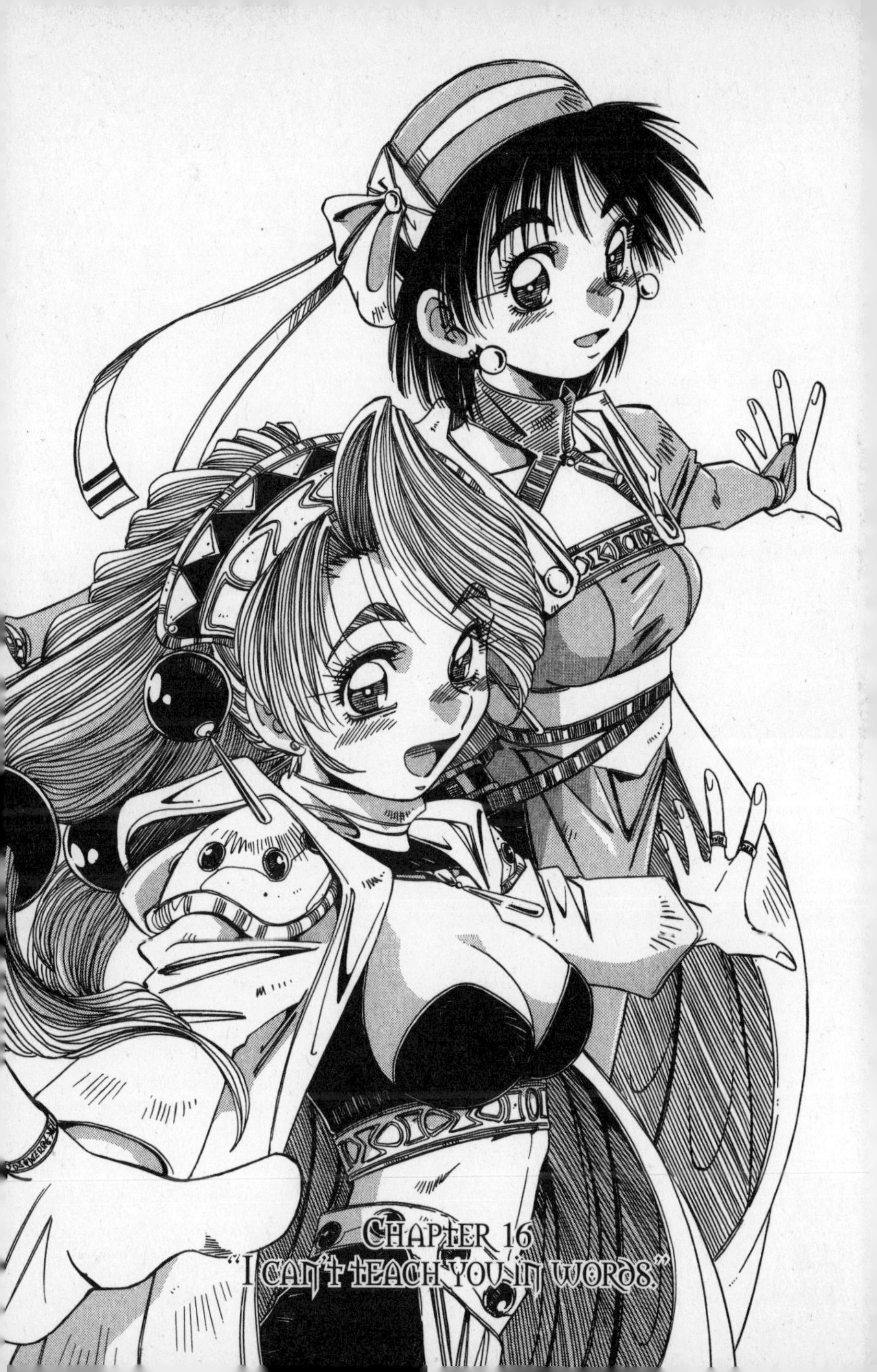
Chapter 16
"I can't teach you in words."

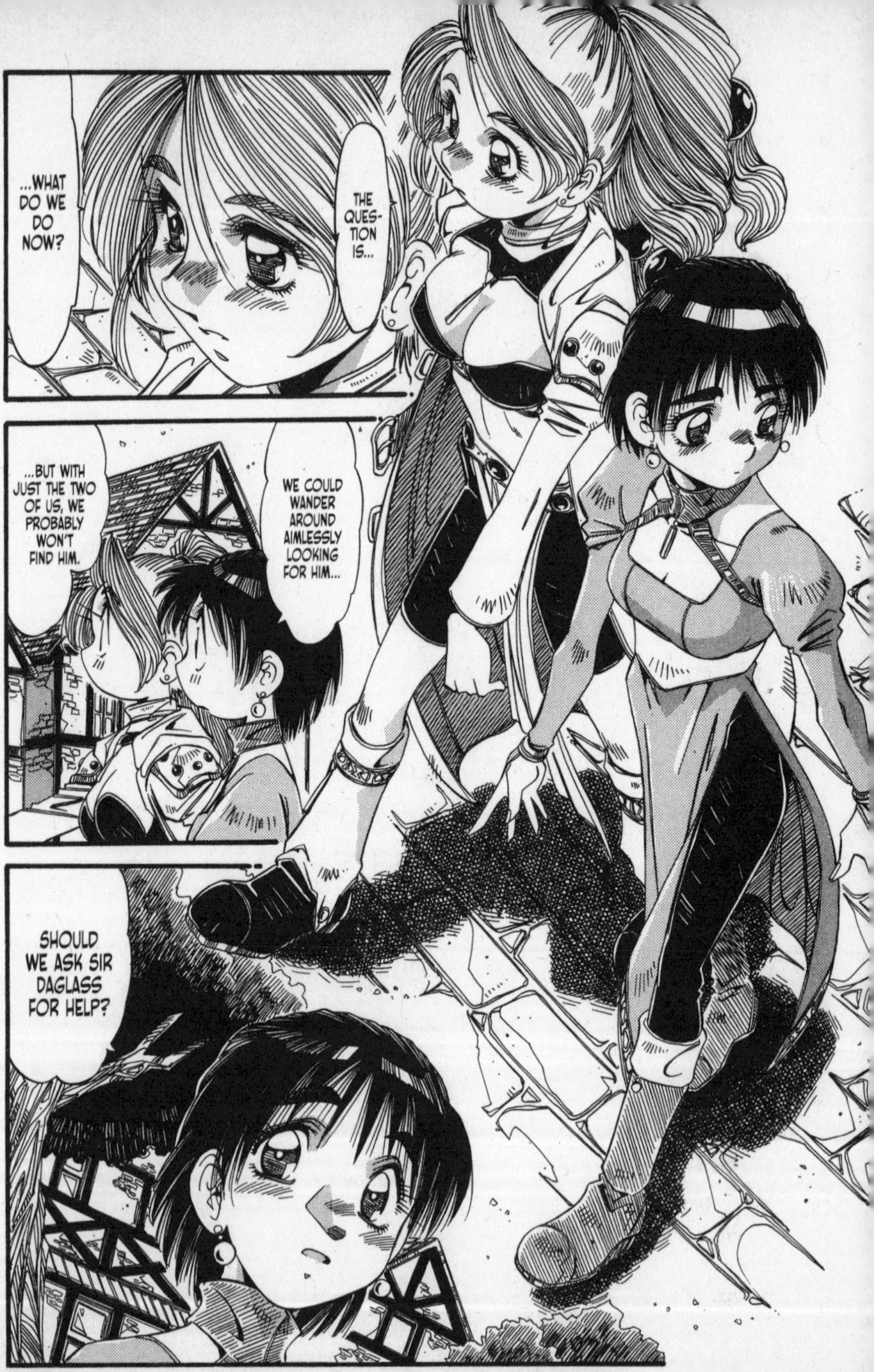
THE QUESTION IS...
...WHAT DO WE DO NOW?
WE COULD WANDER AROUND AIMLESSLY LOOKING FOR HIM...
...BUT WITH JUST THE TWO OF US, WE PROBABLY WON'T FIND HIM.
SHOULD WE ASK SIR DAGLASS FOR HELP?

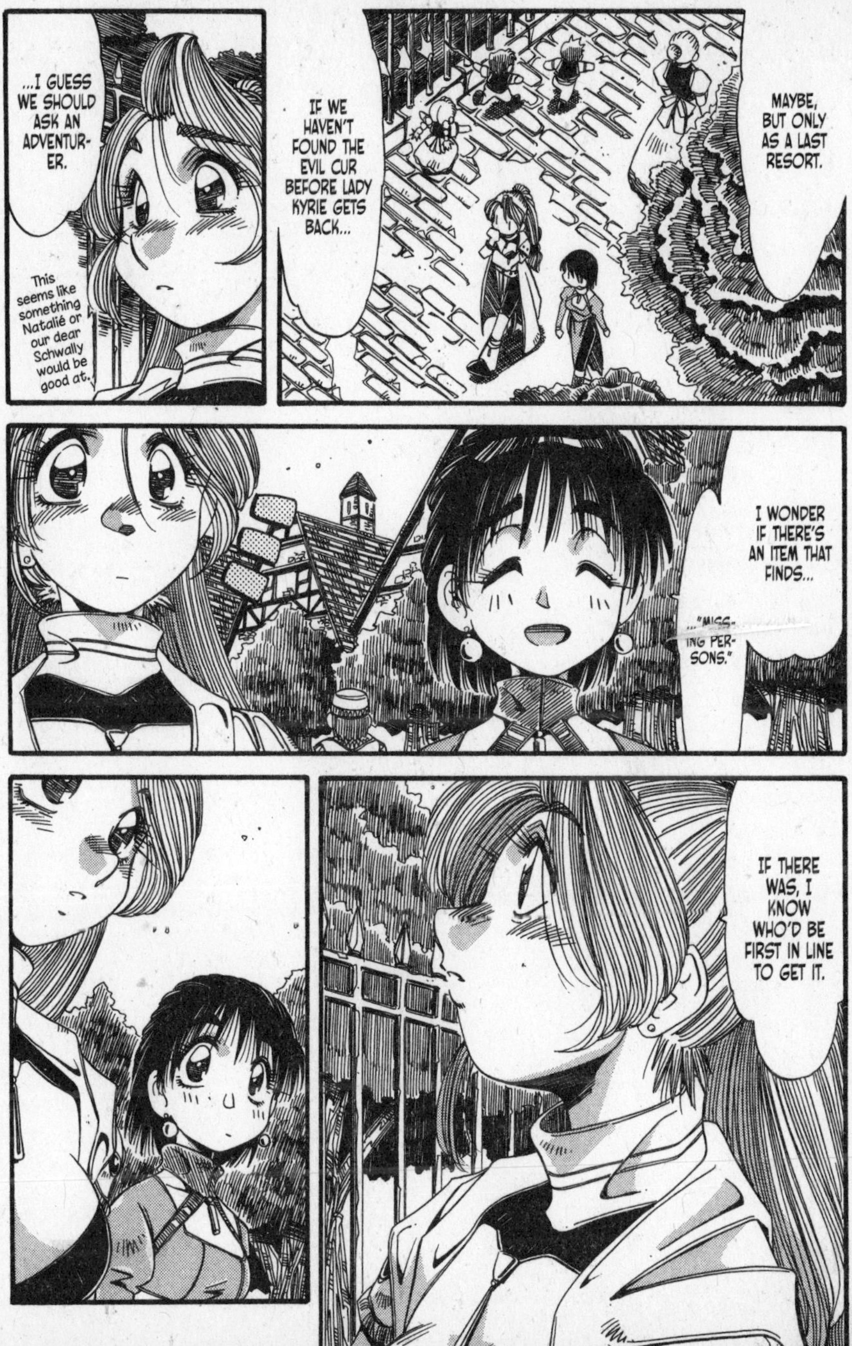
MAYBE, BUT ONLY AS A LAST RESORT.
IF WE HAVEN'T FOUND THE EVIL CUR BEFORE LADY KYRIE GETS BACK...
...I GUESS WE SHOULD ASK AN ADVENTURER.
This seems like something Natalié or our dear Schwally would be good at.
I WONDER IF THERE'S AN ITEM THAT FINDS...
..."MISSING PERSONS."
IF THERE WAS, I KNOW WHO'D BE FIRST IN LINE TO GET IT.

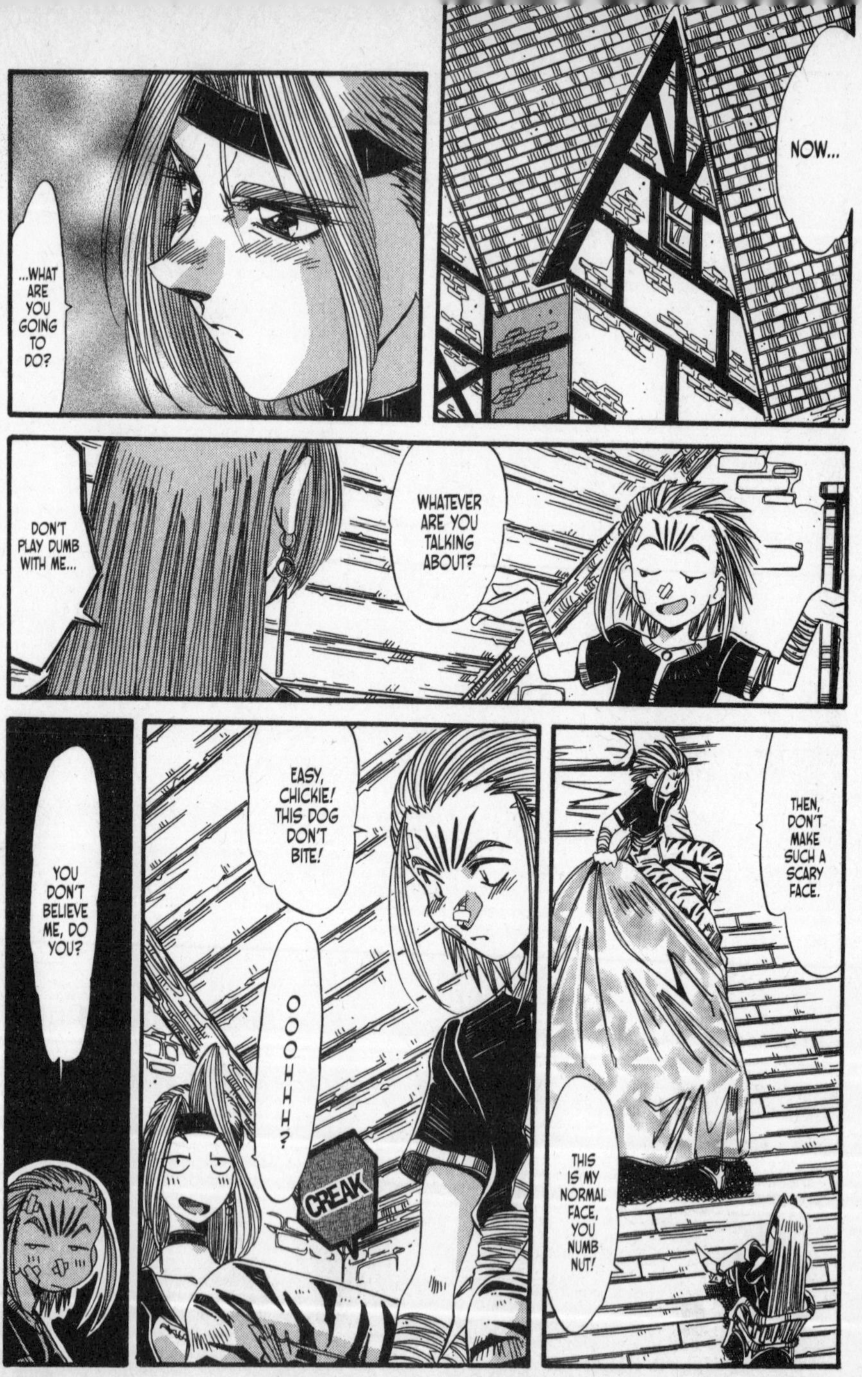
NOW...
...WHAT ARE YOU GOING TO DO?
WHATEVER ARE YOU TALKING ABOUT?
DON'T PLAY DUMB WITH ME...
THEN, DON'T MAKE SUCH A SCARY FACE.
THIS IS MY NORMAL FACE, YOU NUMB NUT!
EASY, CHICKIE! THIS DOG DON'T BITE!
OOOHHHH?
CREAK
YOU DON'T BELIEVE ME, DO YOU?

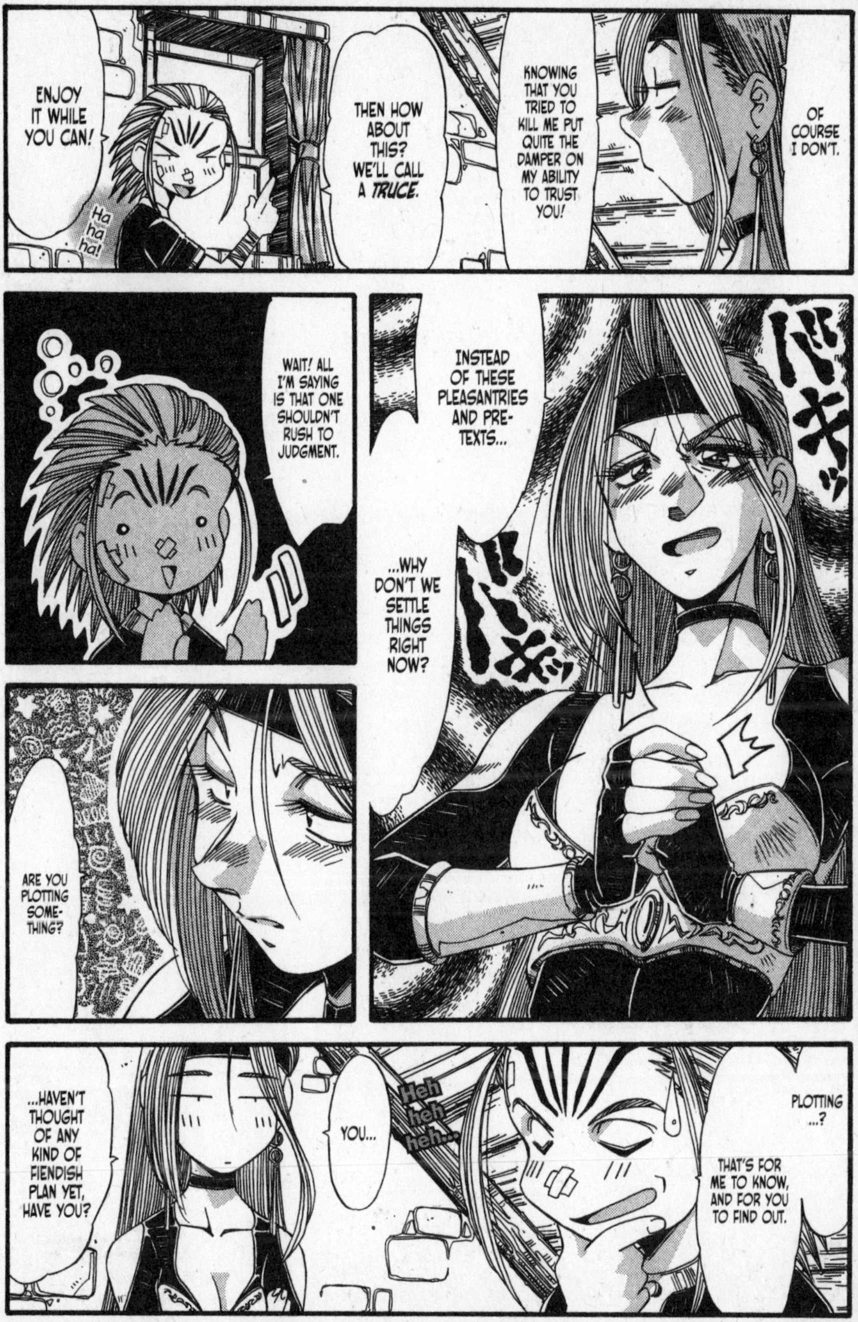
OF COURSE I DON'T.
KNOWING THAT YOU TRIED TO KILL ME PUT QUITE THE DAMPER ON MY ABILITY TO TRUST YOU!
THEN HOW ABOUT THIS? WE'LL CALL A *TRUCE*.
ENJOY IT WHILE YOU CAN!
Ha ha ha!
INSTEAD OF THESE PLEASANTRIES AND PRE-TEXTS...
...WHY DON'T WE SETTLE THINGS RIGHT NOW?
WAIT! ALL I'M SAYING IS THAT ONE SHOULDN'T RUSH TO JUDGMENT.
ARE YOU PLOTTING SOMETHING?
PLOTTING ...?
THAT'S FOR ME TO KNOW, AND FOR YOU TO FIND OUT.
Heh heh heh...
YOU...
...HAVEN'T THOUGHT OF ANY KIND OF FIENDISH PLAN YET, HAVE YOU?

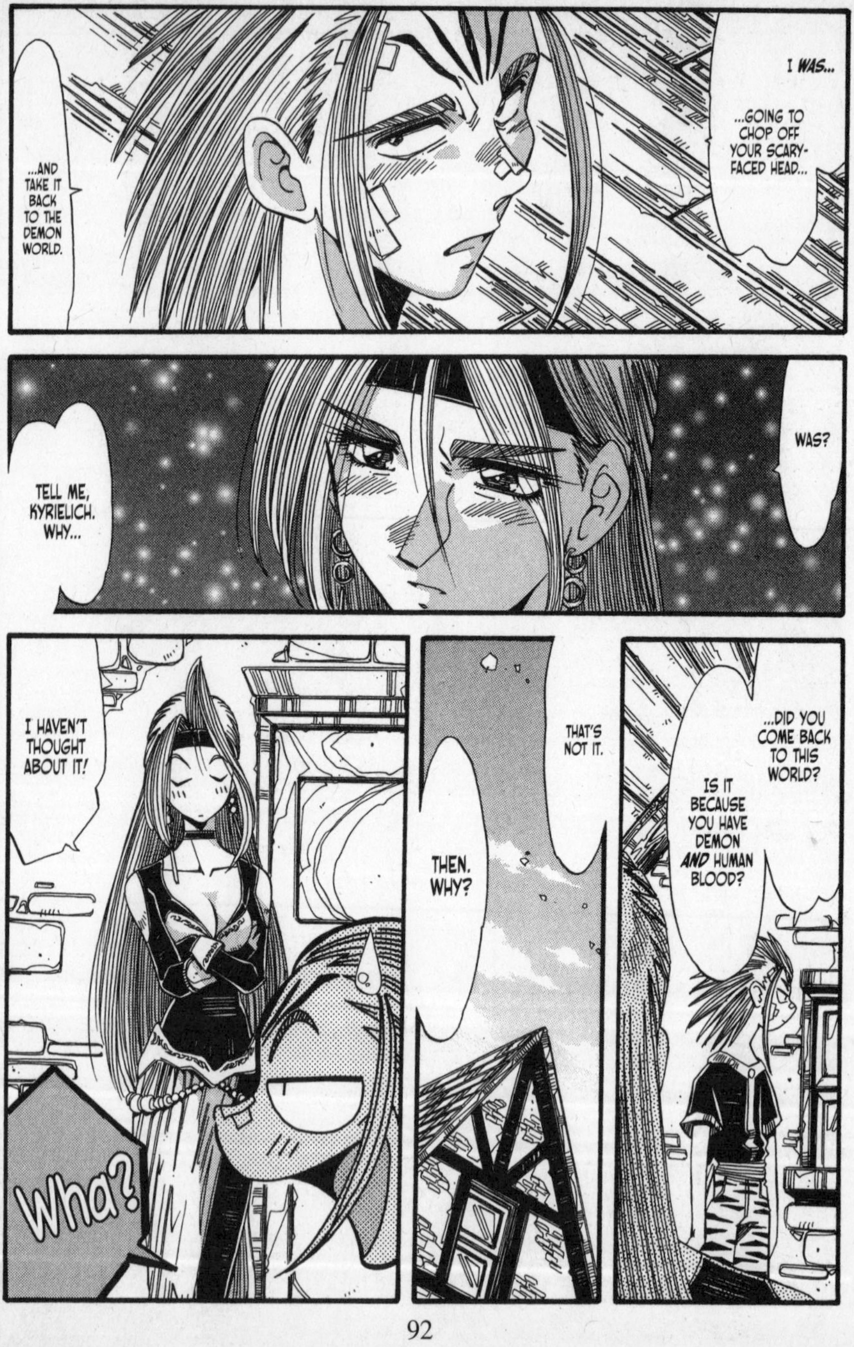
I *WAS*...
...GOING TO CHOP OFF YOUR SCARY-FACED HEAD...
...AND TAKE IT BACK TO THE DEMON WORLD.
WAS?
TELL ME, KYRIELICH. WHY...
...DID YOU COME BACK TO THIS WORLD?
IS IT BECAUSE YOU HAVE DEMON *AND* HUMAN BLOOD?
THAT'S NOT IT.
THEN. WHY?
I HAVEN'T THOUGHT ABOUT IT!
Wha?

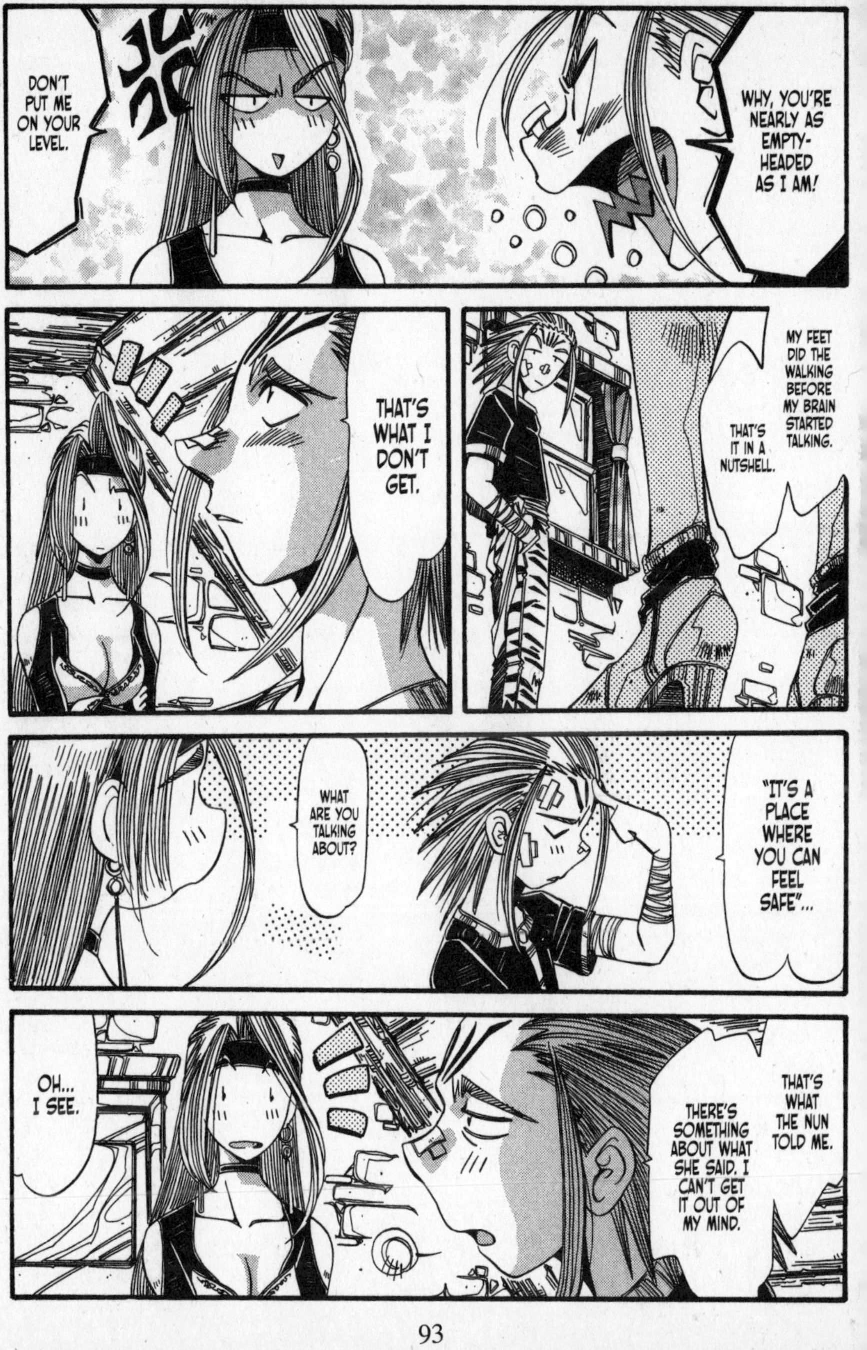
WHY, YOU'RE NEARLY AS EMPTY-HEADED AS I AM!
DON'T PUT ME ON YOUR LEVEL.
MY FEET DID THE WALKING BEFORE MY BRAIN STARTED TALKING.
THAT'S IT IN A NUTSHELL.
THAT'S WHAT I DON'T GET.
"IT'S A PLACE WHERE YOU CAN FEEL SAFE"...
WHAT ARE YOU TALKING ABOUT?
THAT'S WHAT THE NUN TOLD ME.
THERE'S SOMETHING ABOUT WHAT SHE SAID. I CAN'T GET IT OUT OF MY MIND.
OH... I SEE.

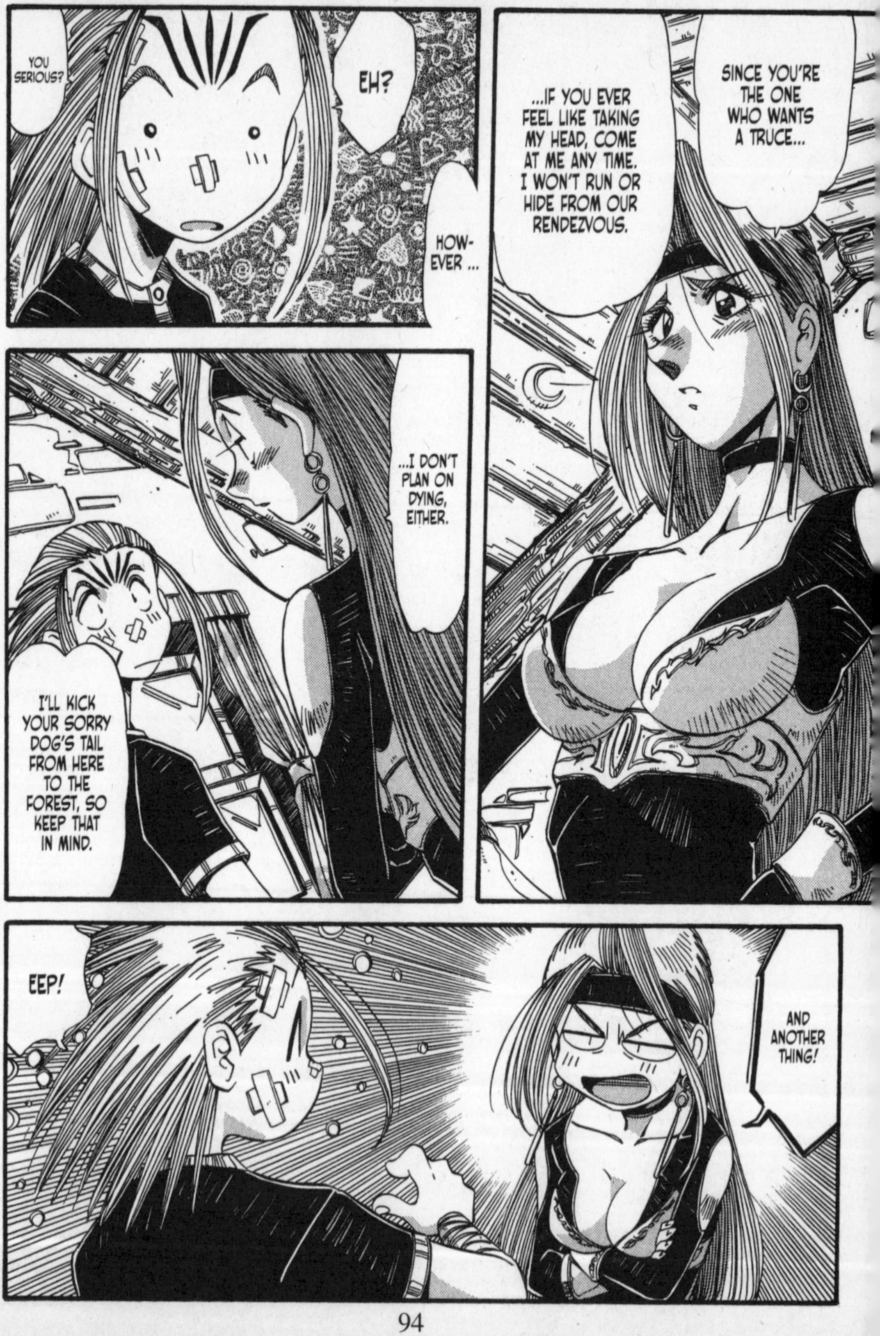
SINCE YOU'RE THE ONE WHO WANTS A TRUCE...
...IF YOU EVER FEEL LIKE TAKING MY HEAD, COME AT ME ANY TIME. I WON'T RUN OR HIDE FROM OUR RENDEZVOUS.
EH?
YOU SERIOUS?
HOW-EVER ...
...I DON'T PLAN ON DYING, EITHER.
I'LL KICK YOUR SORRY DOG'S TAIL FROM HERE TO THE FOREST, SO KEEP THAT IN MIND.
AND ANOTHER THING!
EEP!

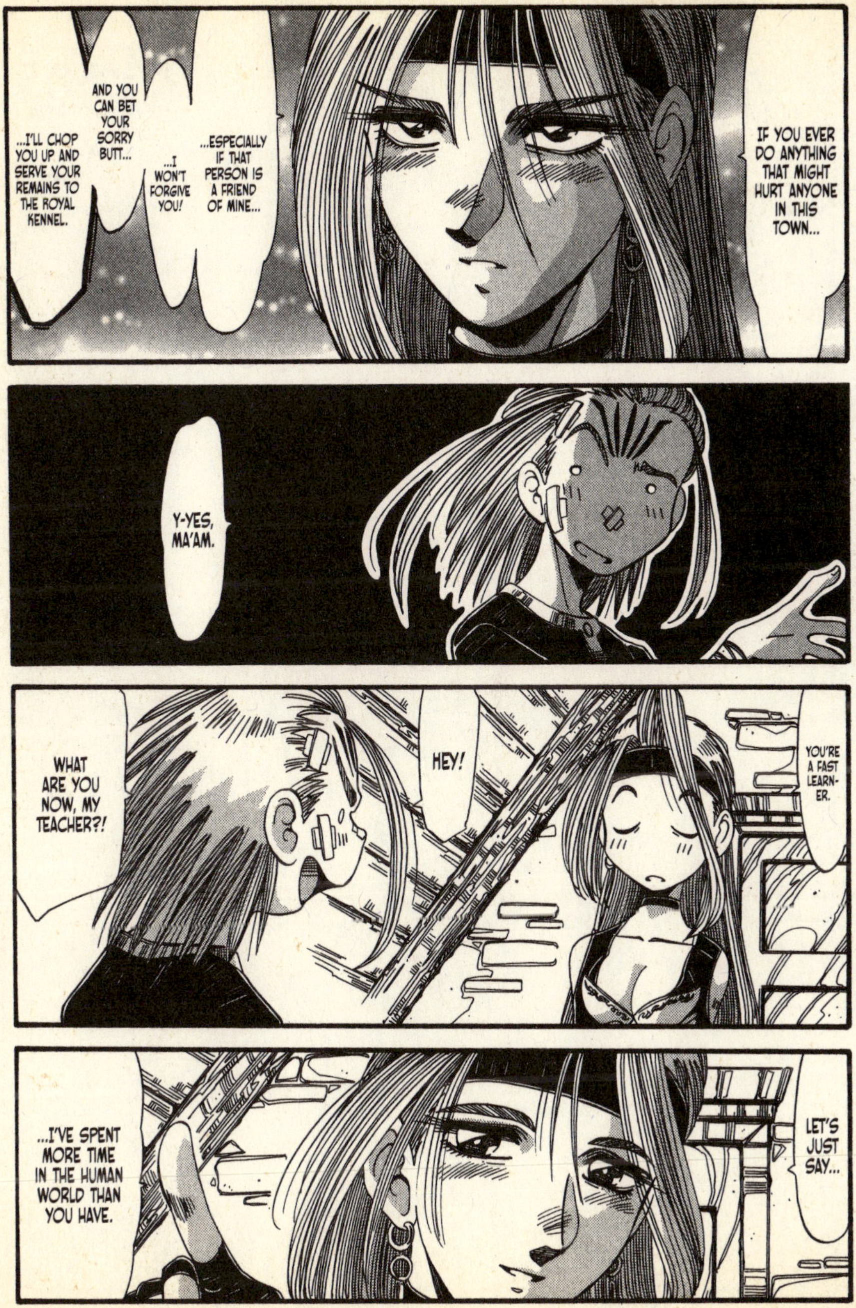
IF YOU EVER DO ANYTHING THAT MIGHT HURT ANYONE IN THIS TOWN...
...ESPECIALLY IF THAT PERSON IS A FRIEND OF MINE...
...I WON'T FORGIVE YOU!
AND YOU CAN BET YOUR SORRY BUTT...
...I'LL CHOP YOU UP AND SERVE YOUR REMAINS TO THE ROYAL KENNEL.
Y-YES, MA'AM.
YOU'RE A FAST LEARNER.
HEY!
WHAT ARE YOU NOW, MY TEACHER?!
LET'S JUST SAY...
...I'VE SPENT MORE TIME IN THE HUMAN WORLD THAN YOU HAVE.

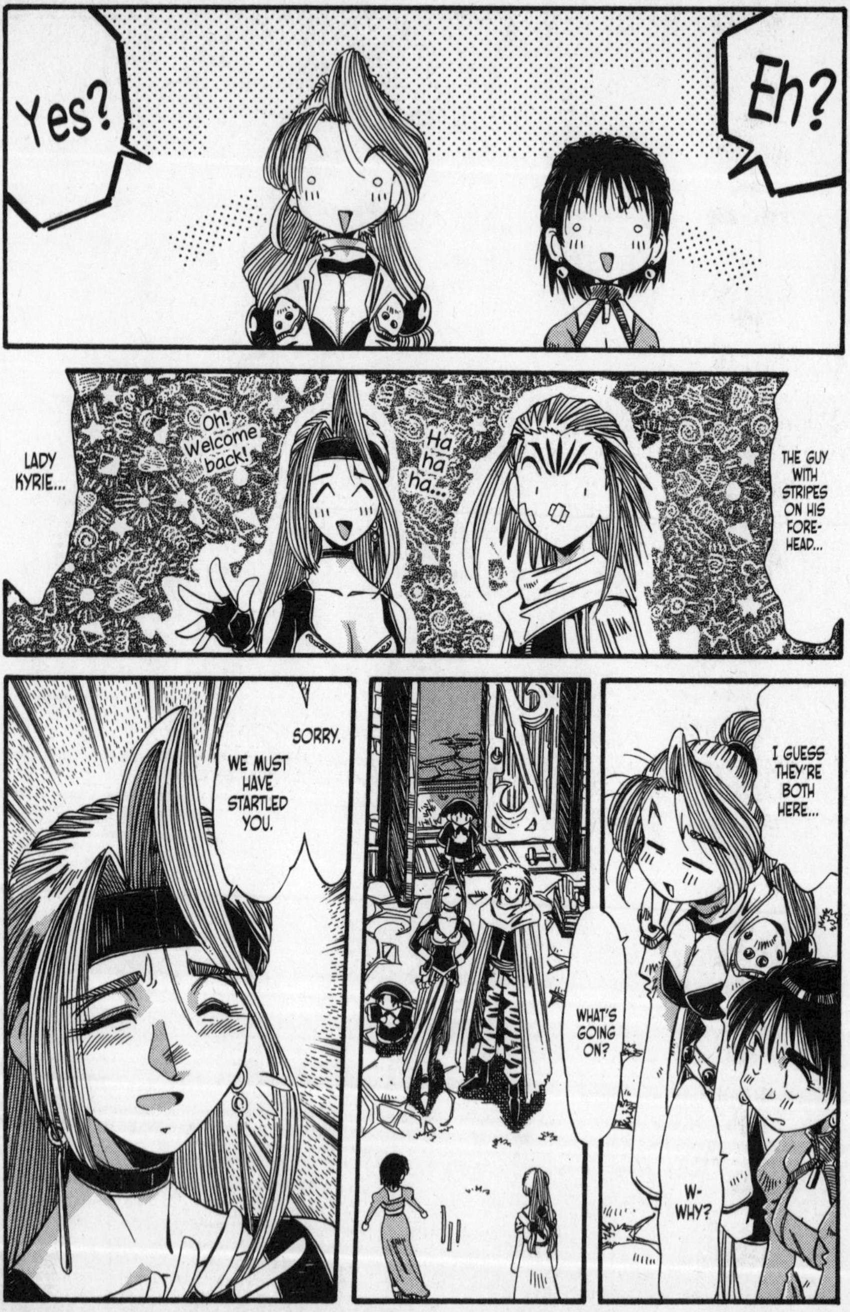
Eh?
Yes?
THE GUY WITH STRIPES ON HIS FOREHEAD...
Ha ha ha...
Oh! Welcome back!
LADY KYRIE...
I GUESS THEY'RE BOTH HERE...
W- WHY?
WHAT'S GOING ON?
SORRY.
WE MUST HAVE STARTLED YOU.

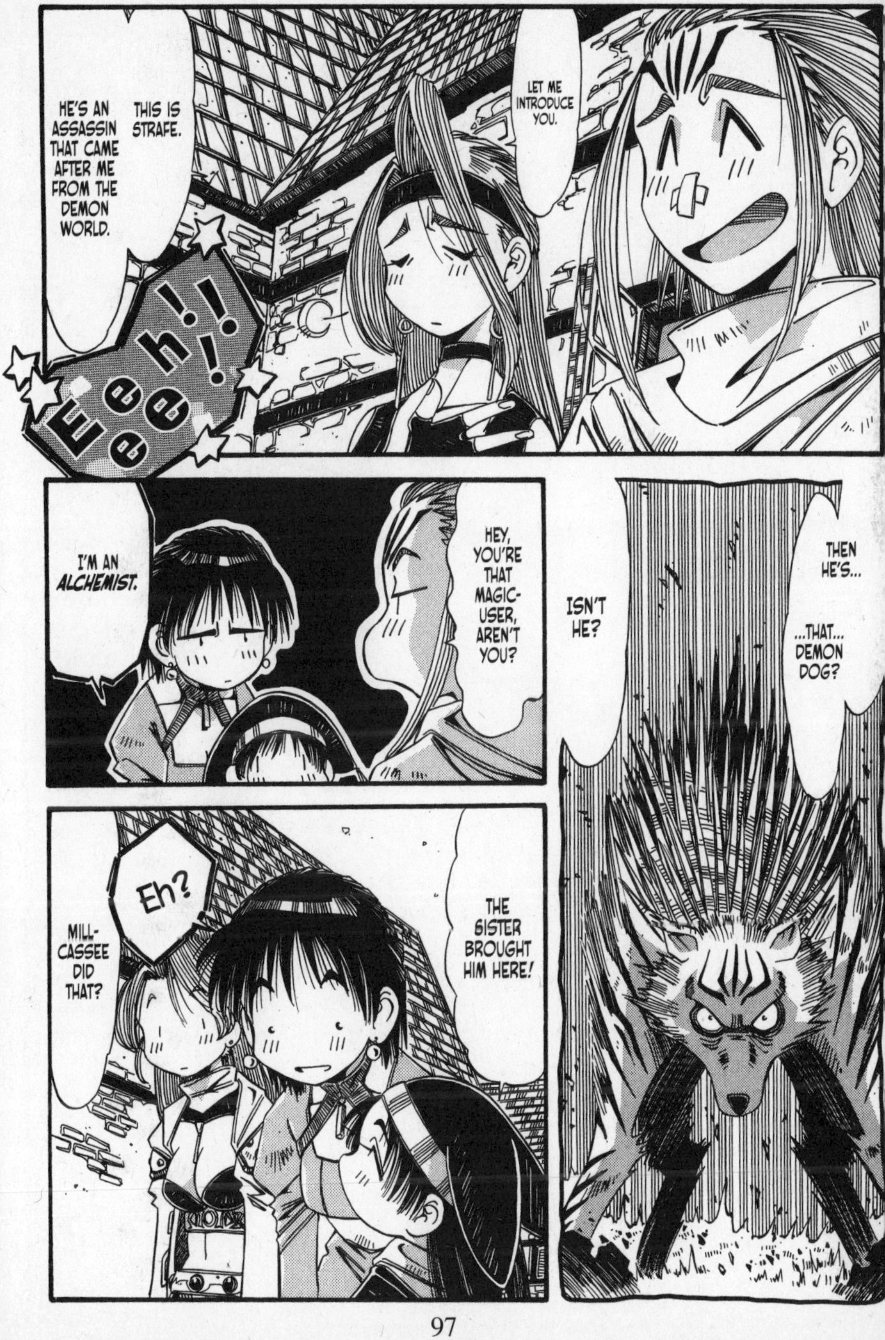
LET ME INTRODUCE YOU.
THIS IS STRAFE.
HE'S AN ASSASSIN THAT CAME AFTER ME FROM THE DEMON WORLD.
Eeeeh!!!
THEN HE'S...
...THAT... DEMON DOG?
ISN'T HE?
HEY, YOU'RE THAT MAGIC-USER, AREN'T YOU?
I'M AN *ALCHEMIST.*
THE SISTER BROUGHT HIM HERE!
Eh?
MILL-CASSEE DID THAT?

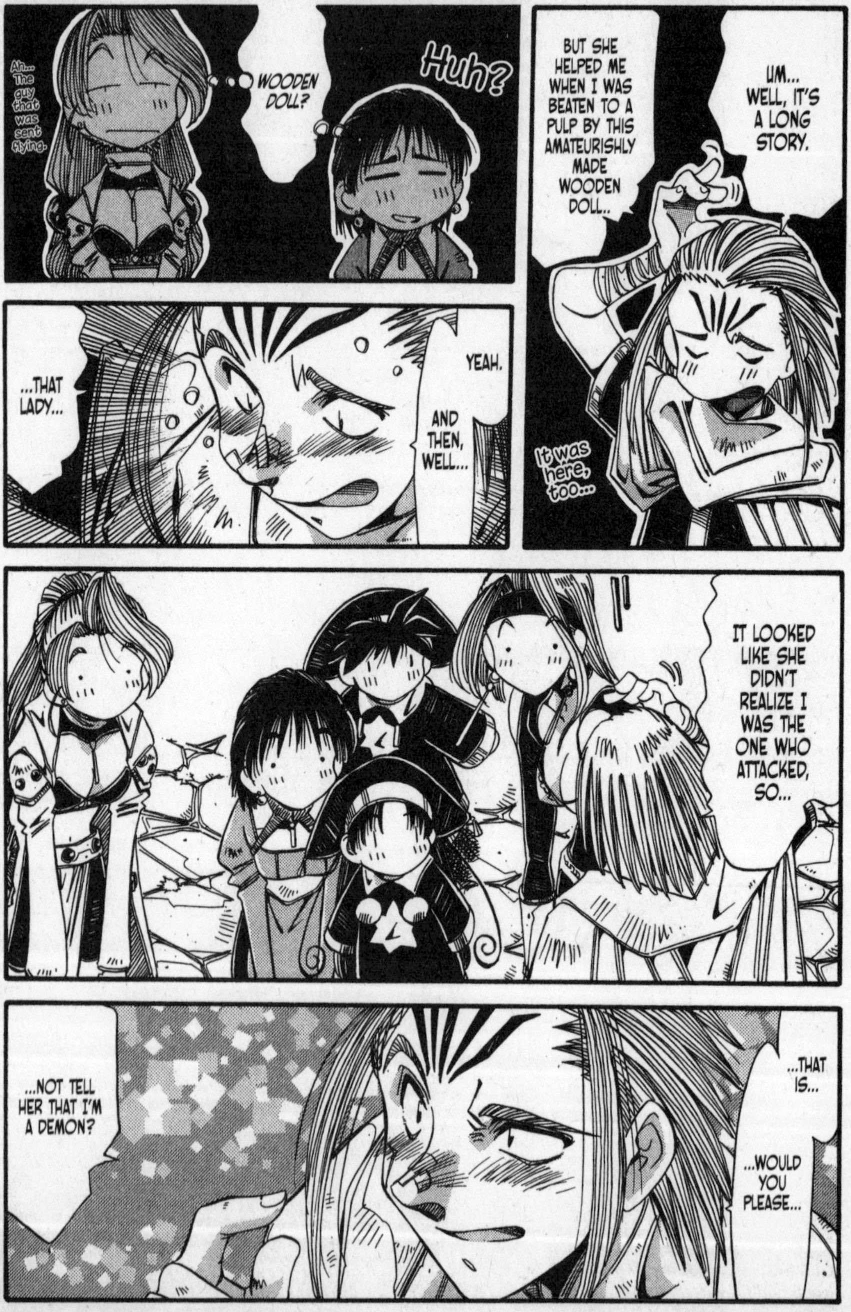
UM... WELL, IT'S A LONG STORY.
BUT SHE HELPED ME WHEN I WAS BEATEN TO A PULP BY THIS AMATEURISHLY MADE WOODEN DOLL..
It was here, too...
Huh?
WOODEN DOLL?
Ah... The guy that was sent flying.
YEAH.
AND THEN, WELL...
...THAT LADY...
IT LOOKED LIKE SHE DIDN'T REALIZE I WAS THE ONE WHO ATTACKED, SO...
...THAT IS...
...WOULD YOU PLEASE...
...NOT TELL HER THAT I'M A DEMON?

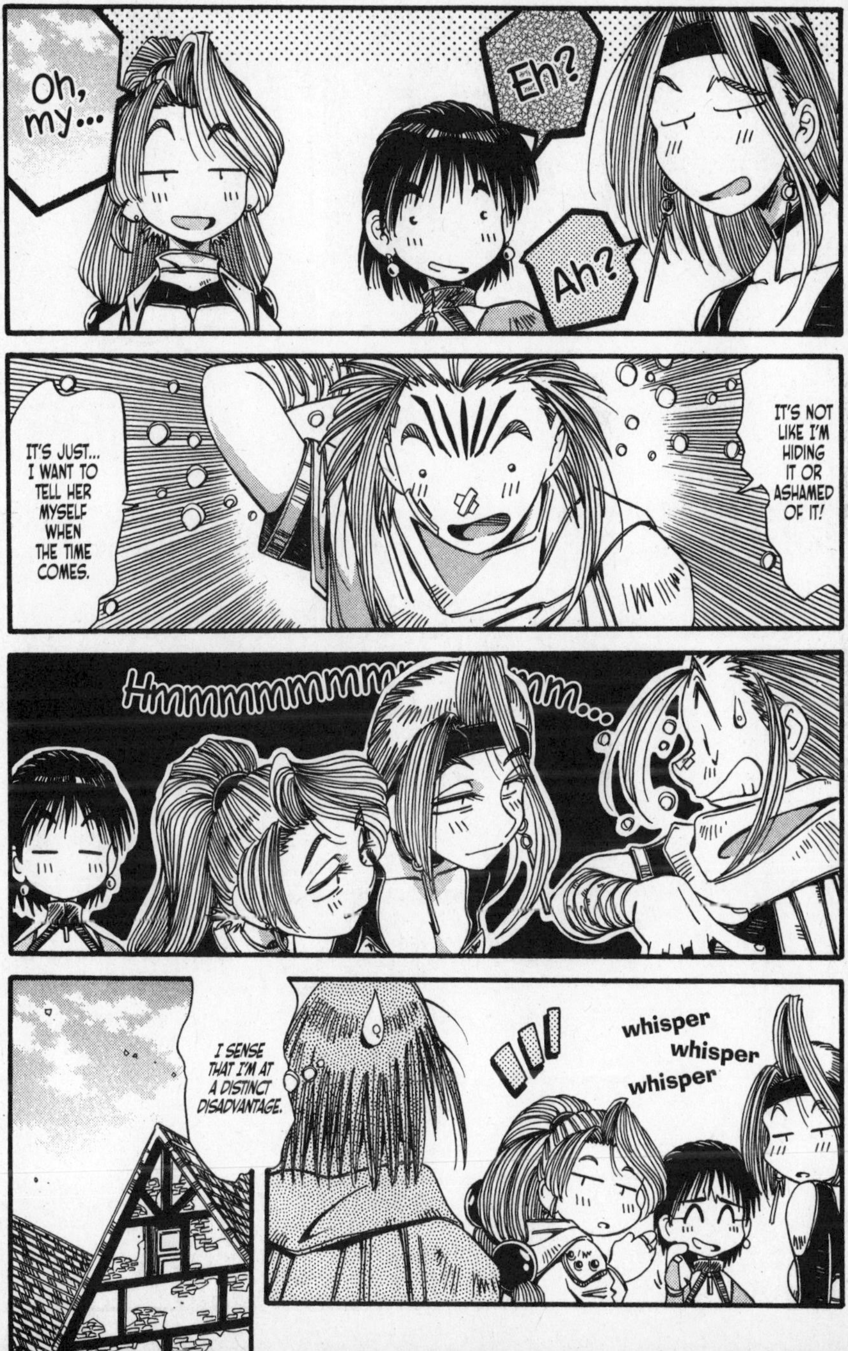
Eh?
Ah?
Oh, my...
IT'S NOT LIKE I'M HIDING IT OR ASHAMED OF IT!
IT'S JUST... I WANT TO TELL HER MYSELF WHEN THE TIME COMES.
Hmmmmmmmm mm...
whisper
whisper
whisper
I SENSE THAT I'M AT A DISTINCT DISADVANTAGE.

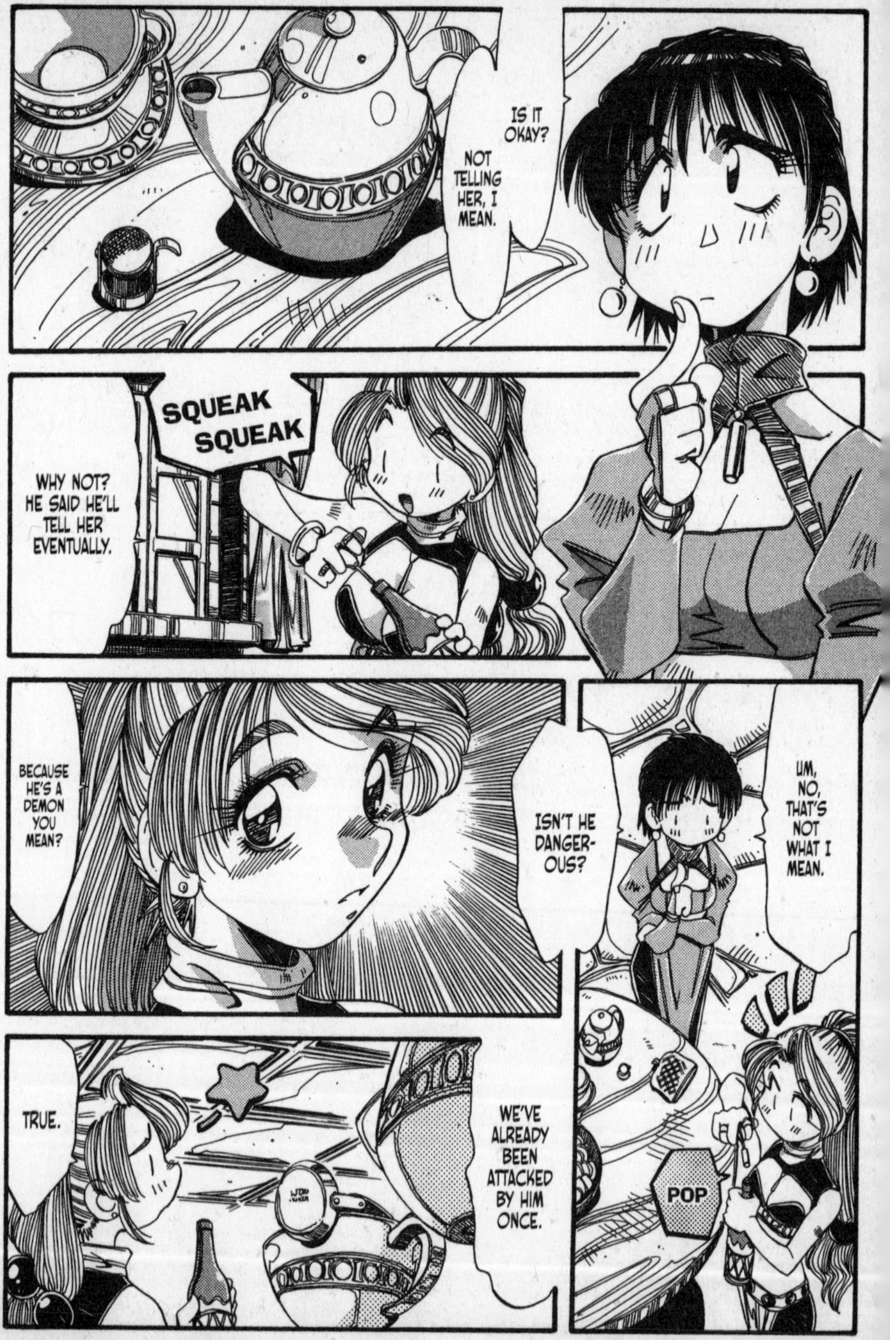
IS IT OKAY?
NOT TELLING HER, I MEAN.
SQUEAK SQUEAK
WHY NOT? HE SAID HE'LL TELL HER EVENTUALLY.
BECAUSE HE'S A DEMON YOU MEAN?
UM, NO, THAT'S NOT WHAT I MEAN.
ISN'T HE DANGER-OUS?
POP
WE'VE ALREADY BEEN ATTACKED BY HIM ONCE.
TRUE.

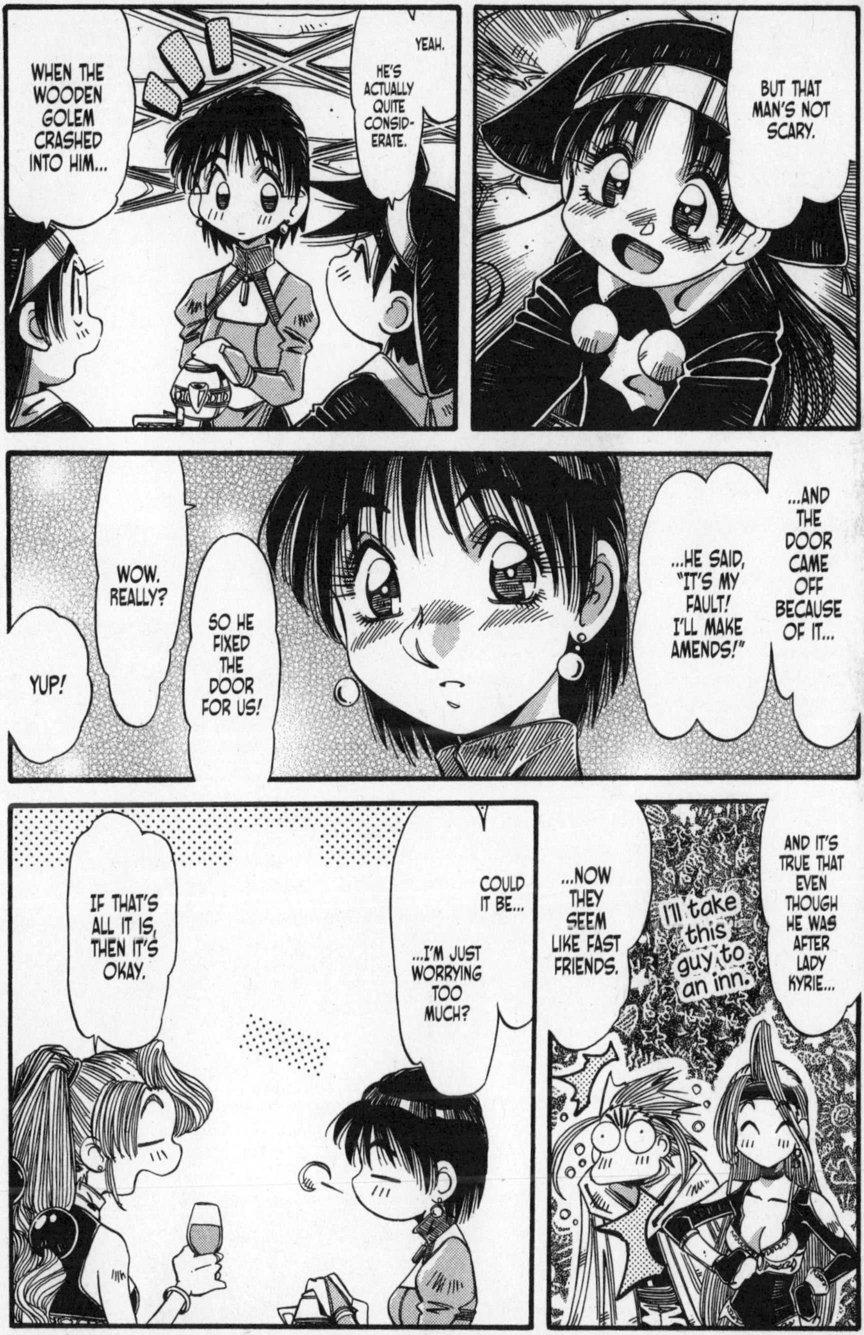
BUT THAT MAN'S NOT SCARY.
YEAH.
HE'S ACTUALLY QUITE CONSIDERATE.
WHEN THE WOODEN GOLEM CRASHED INTO HIM...
...AND THE DOOR CAME OFF BECAUSE OF IT...
...HE SAID, "IT'S MY FAULT! I'LL MAKE AMENDS!"
SO HE FIXED THE DOOR FOR US!
WOW. REALLY?
YUP!
AND IT'S TRUE THAT EVEN THOUGH HE WAS AFTER LADY KYRIE...
I'll take this guy to an inn.
...NOW THEY SEEM LIKE FAST FRIENDS.
COULD IT BE...
...I'M JUST WORRYING TOO MUCH?
IF THAT'S ALL IT IS, THEN IT'S OKAY.

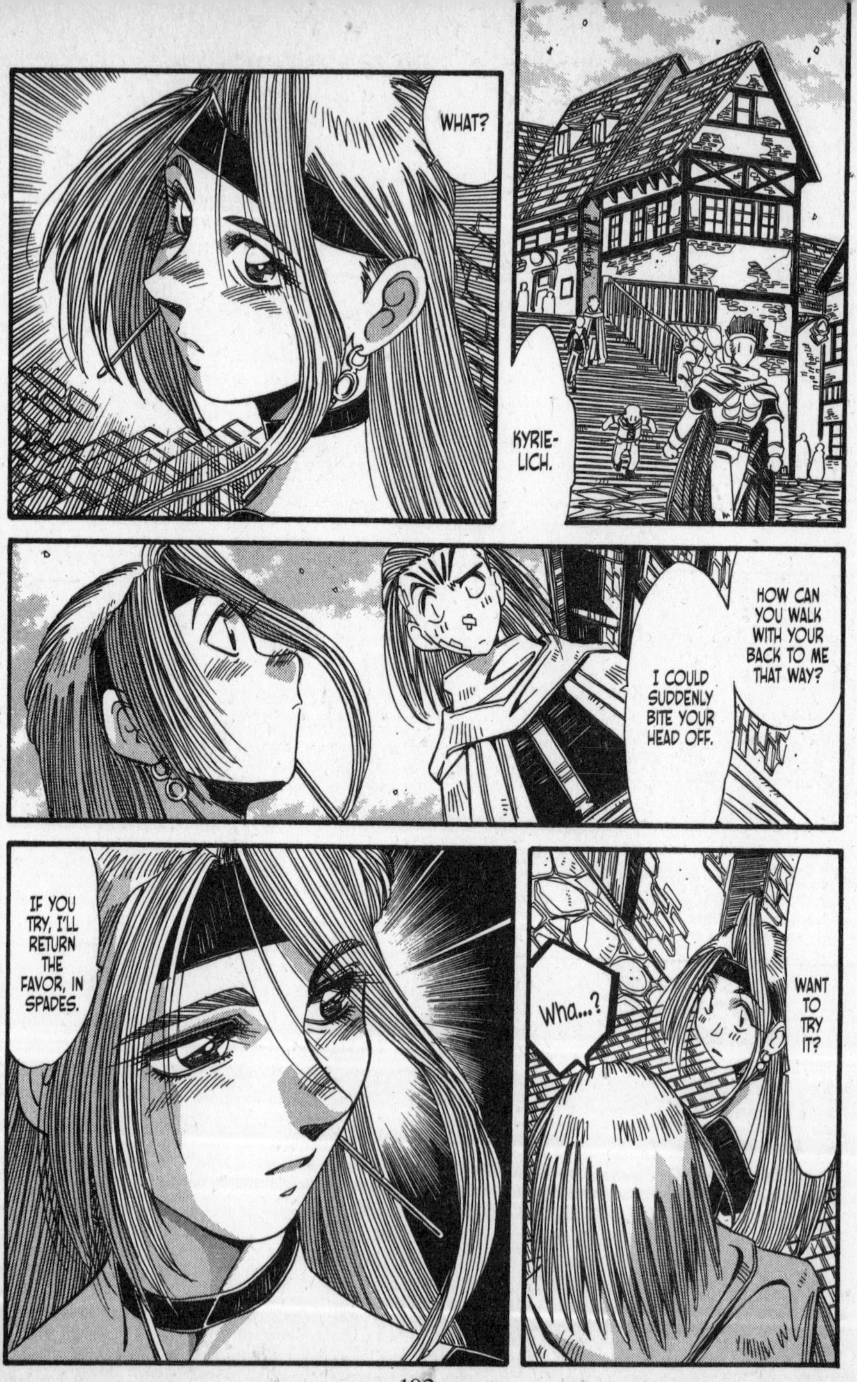
KYRIE-LICH.
WHAT?
HOW CAN YOU WALK WITH YOUR BACK TO ME THAT WAY?
I COULD SUDDENLY BITE YOUR HEAD OFF.
WANT TO TRY IT?
Wha...?
IF YOU TRY, I'LL RETURN THE FAVOR, IN SPADES.

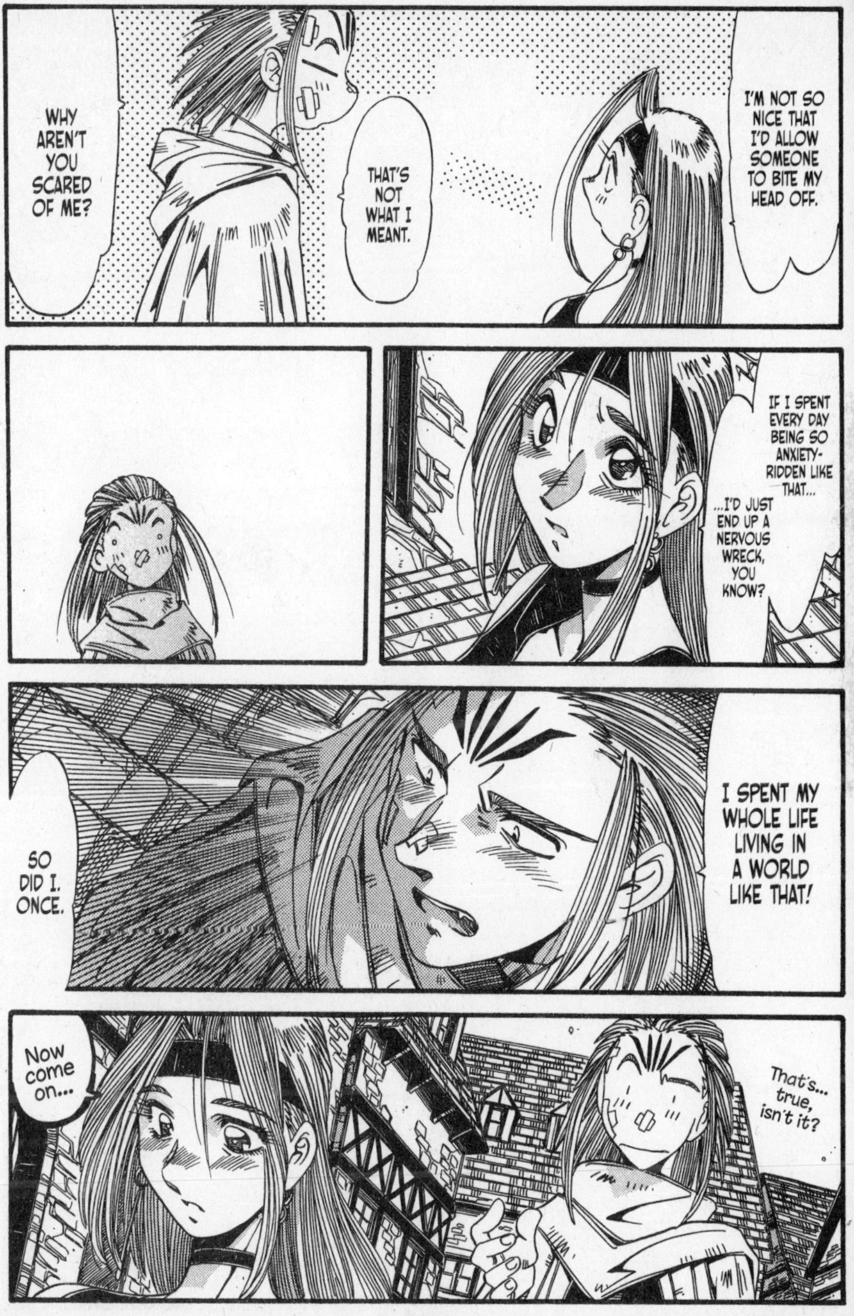
I'M NOT SO NICE THAT I'D ALLOW SOMEONE TO BITE MY HEAD OFF.
THAT'S NOT WHAT I MEANT.
WHY AREN'T YOU SCARED OF ME?
IF I SPENT EVERY DAY BEING SO ANXIETY-RIDDEN LIKE THAT...
...I'D JUST END UP A NERVOUS WRECK, YOU KNOW?
I SPENT MY WHOLE LIFE LIVING IN A WORLD LIKE THAT!
SO DID I. ONCE.
That's... true, isn't it?
Now come on...

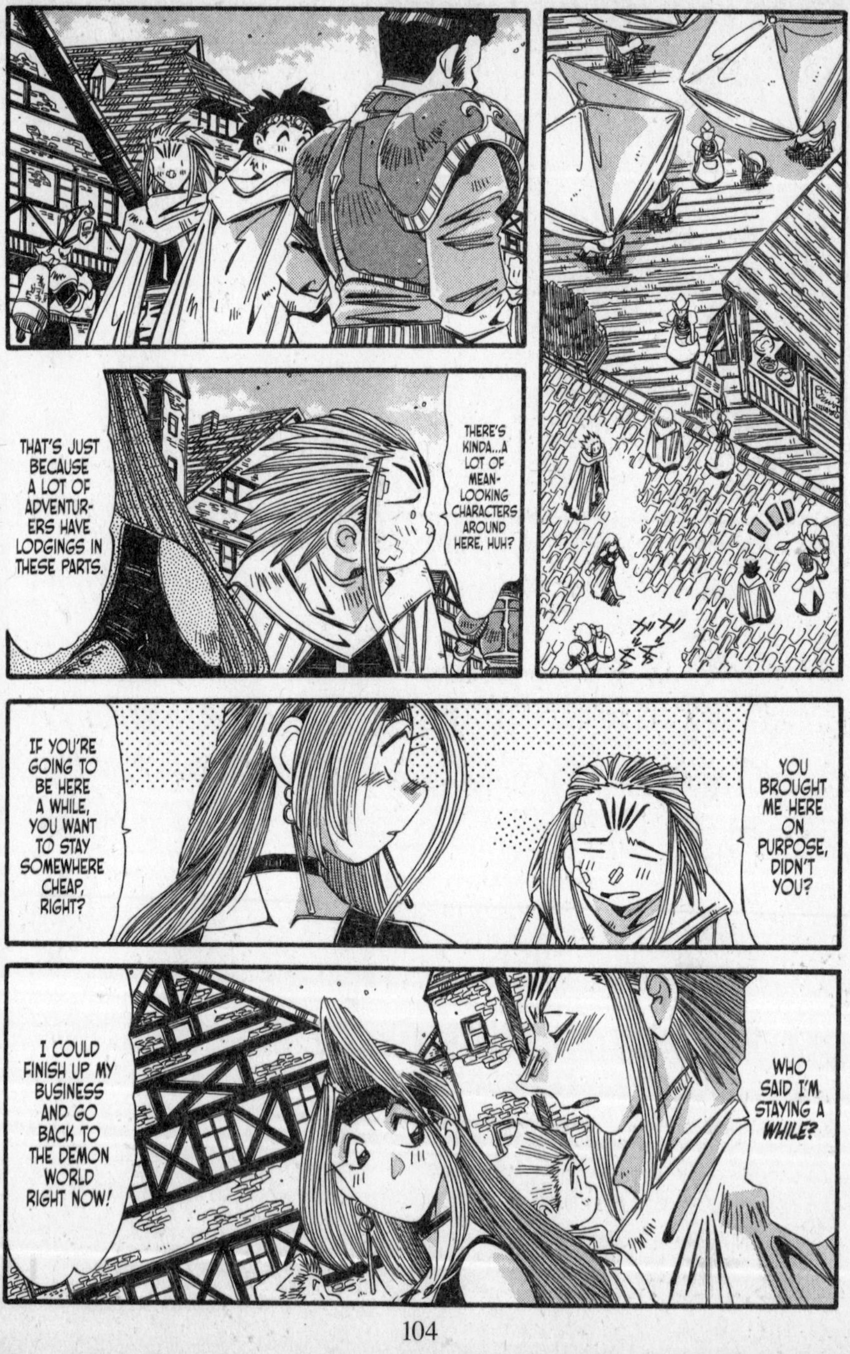
THERE'S KINDA...A LOT OF MEAN-LOOKING CHARACTERS AROUND HERE, HUH?
THAT'S JUST BECAUSE A LOT OF ADVENTURERS HAVE LODGINGS IN THESE PARTS.
YOU BROUGHT ME HERE ON PURPOSE, DIDN'T YOU?
IF YOU'RE GOING TO BE HERE A WHILE, YOU WANT TO STAY SOMEWHERE CHEAP, RIGHT?
WHO SAID I'M STAYING A *WHILE?*
I COULD FINISH UP MY BUSINESS AND GO BACK TO THE DEMON WORLD RIGHT NOW!

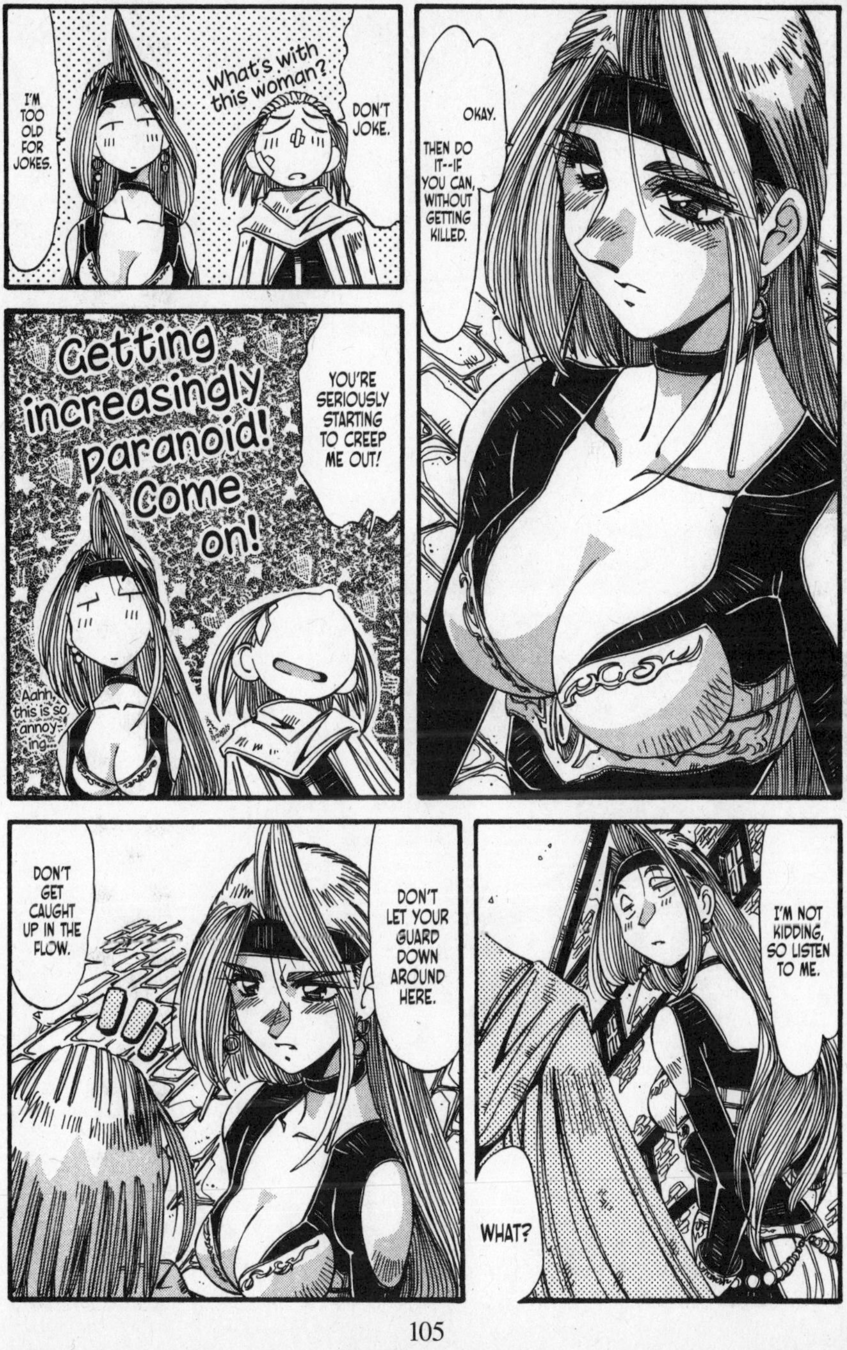
OKAY.
THEN DO IT--IF YOU CAN, WITHOUT GETTING KILLED.
DON'T JOKE.
What's with this woman?
I'M TOO OLD FOR JOKES.
YOU'RE SERIOUSLY STARTING TO CREEP ME OUT!
Getting increasingly paranoid! Come on!
Aahh, this is so annoying...
I'M NOT KIDDING, SO LISTEN TO ME.
WHAT?
DON'T LET YOUR GUARD DOWN AROUND HERE.
DON'T GET CAUGHT UP IN THE FLOW.

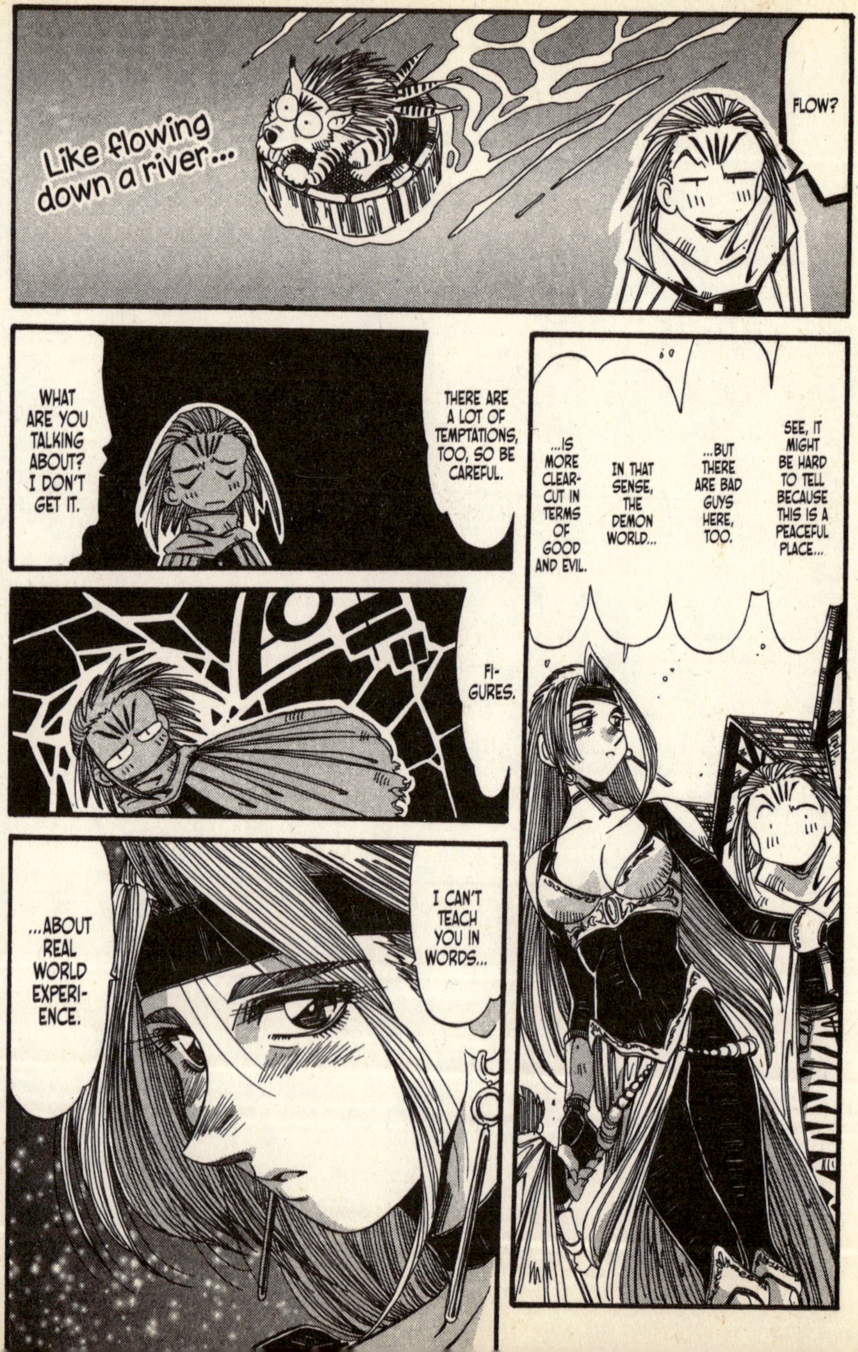
FLOW?
Like flowing down a river...
SEE, IT MIGHT BE HARD TO TELL BECAUSE THIS IS A PEACEFUL PLACE...
...BUT THERE ARE BAD GUYS HERE, TOO.
IN THAT SENSE, THE DEMON WORLD...
...IS MORE CLEAR-CUT IN TERMS OF GOOD AND EVIL.
THERE ARE A LOT OF TEMPTATIONS, TOO, SO BE CAREFUL.
WHAT ARE YOU TALKING ABOUT? I DON'T GET IT.
FI-GURES.
I CAN'T TEACH YOU IN WORDS...
...ABOUT REAL WORLD EXPERIENCE.

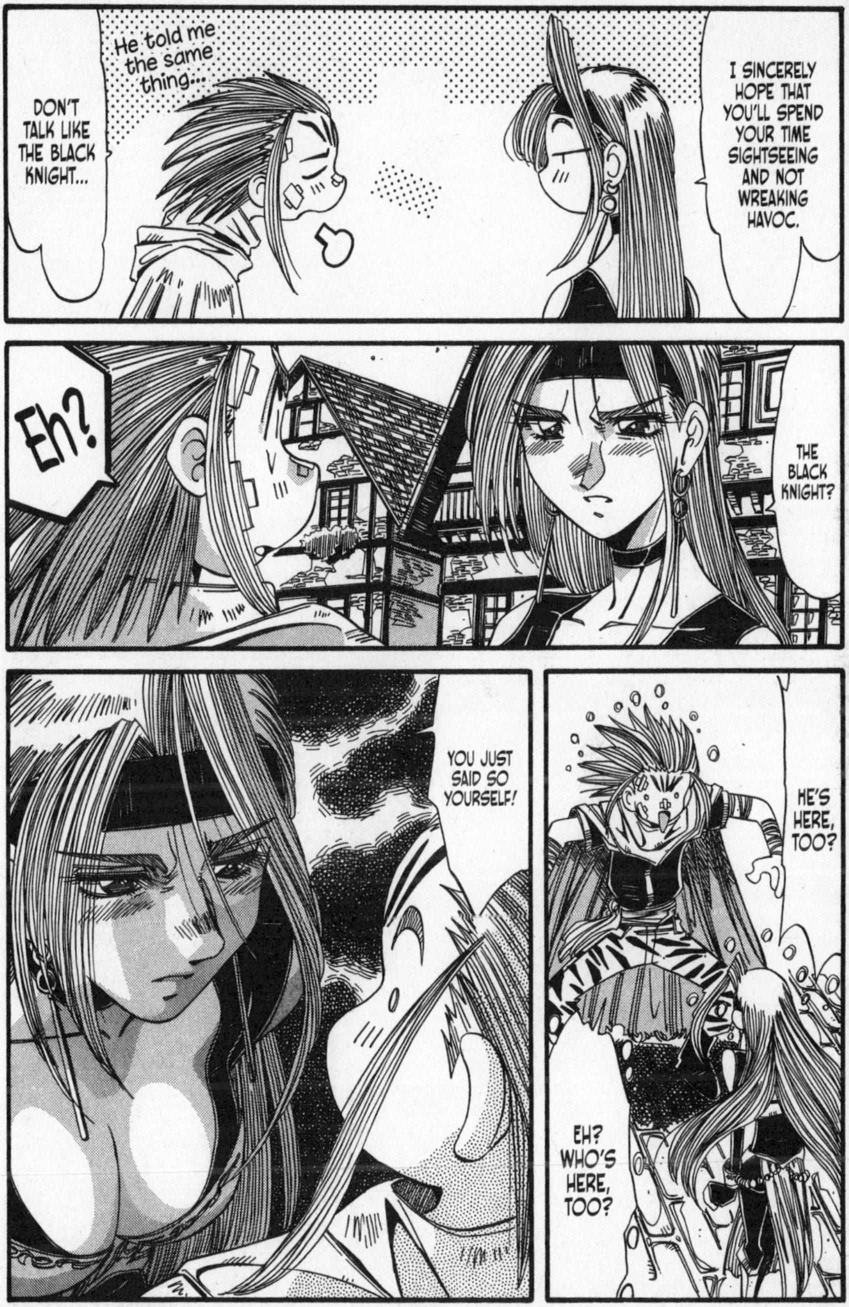
I SINCERELY HOPE THAT YOU'LL SPEND YOUR TIME SIGHTSEEING AND NOT WREAKING HAVOC.
He told me the same thing...
DON'T TALK LIKE THE BLACK KNIGHT...
THE BLACK KNIGHT?
Eh?
HE'S HERE, TOO?
EH? WHO'S HERE, TOO?
YOU JUST SAID SO YOURSELF!

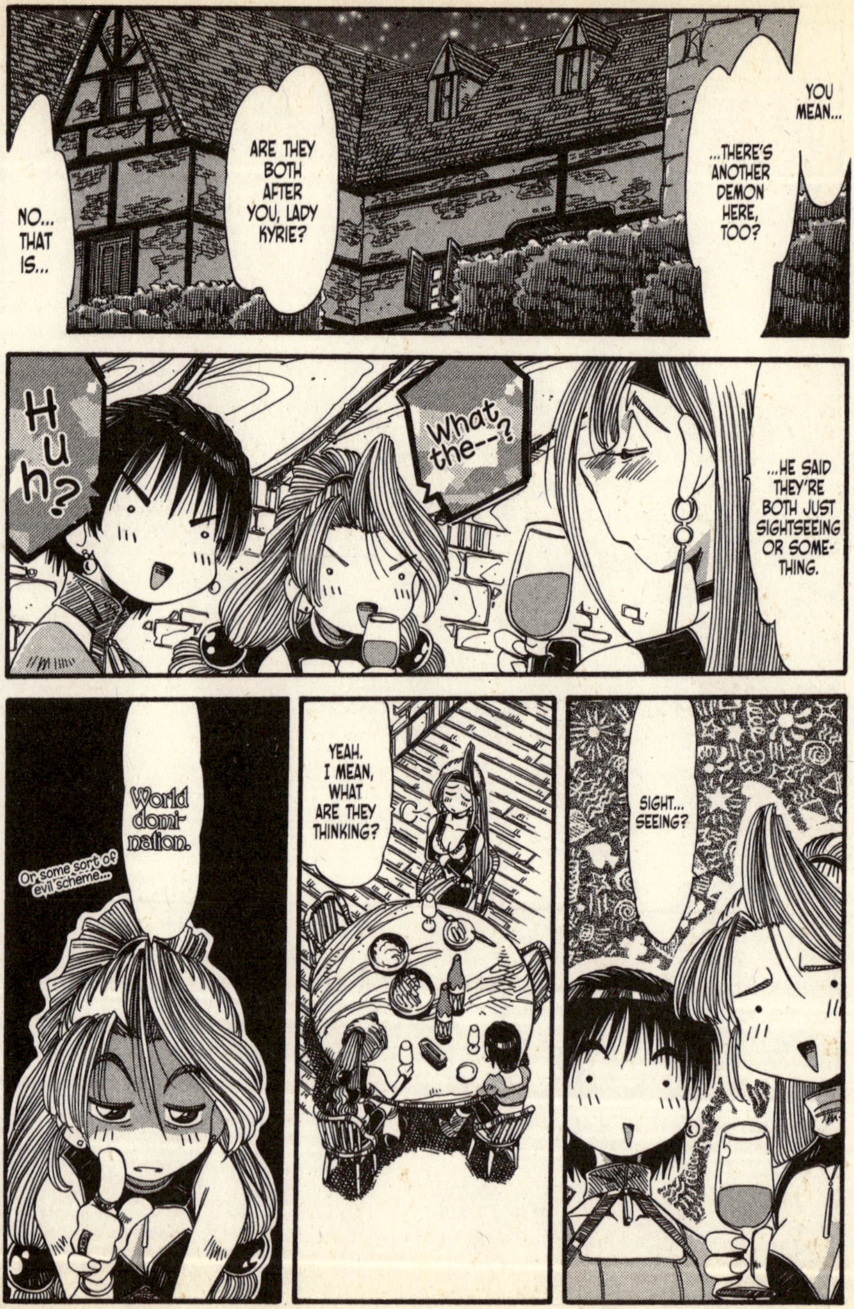
YOU MEAN...
...THERE'S ANOTHER DEMON HERE, TOO?
ARE THEY BOTH AFTER YOU, LADY KYRIE?
NO... THAT IS...
...HE SAID THEY'RE BOTH JUST SIGHTSEEING OR SOME-THING.
What the--?
Huh?
SIGHT... SEEING?
YEAH. I MEAN, WHAT ARE THEY THINKING?
World domi-nation.
Or some sort of evil scheme...

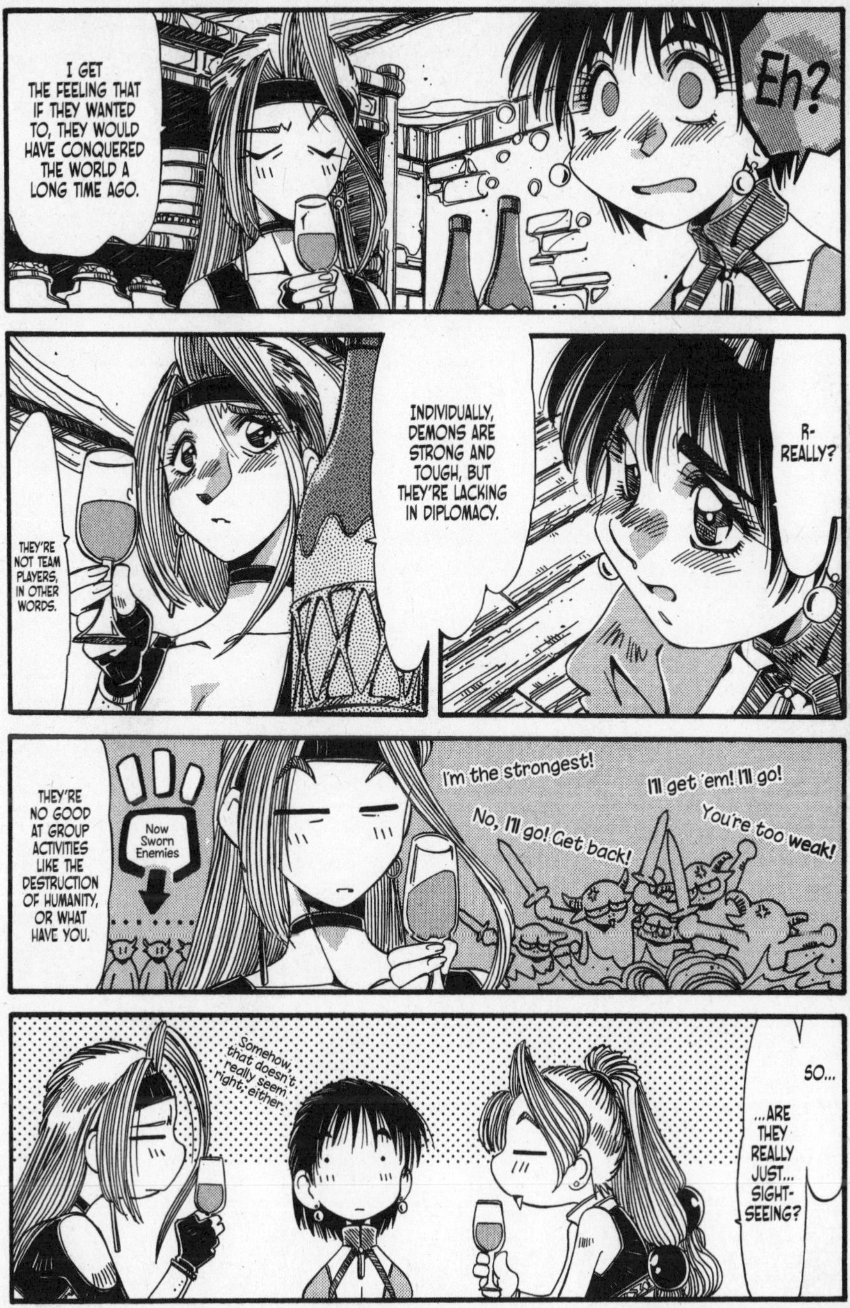
Eh?
I GET THE FEELING THAT IF THEY WANTED TO, THEY WOULD HAVE CONQUERED THE WORLD A LONG TIME AGO.
R-REALLY?
INDIVIDUALLY, DEMONS ARE STRONG AND TOUGH, BUT THEY'RE LACKING IN DIPLOMACY.
THEY'RE NOT TEAM PLAYERS, IN OTHER WORDS.
I'm the strongest!
I'll get 'em! I'll go!
No, I'll go! Get back!
You're too weak!
Now Sworn Enemies
THEY'RE NO GOOD AT GROUP ACTIVITIES LIKE THE DESTRUCTION OF HUMANITY, OR WHAT HAVE YOU.
SO...
...ARE THEY REALLY JUST... SIGHT-SEEING?
Somehow, that doesn't really seem right, either.

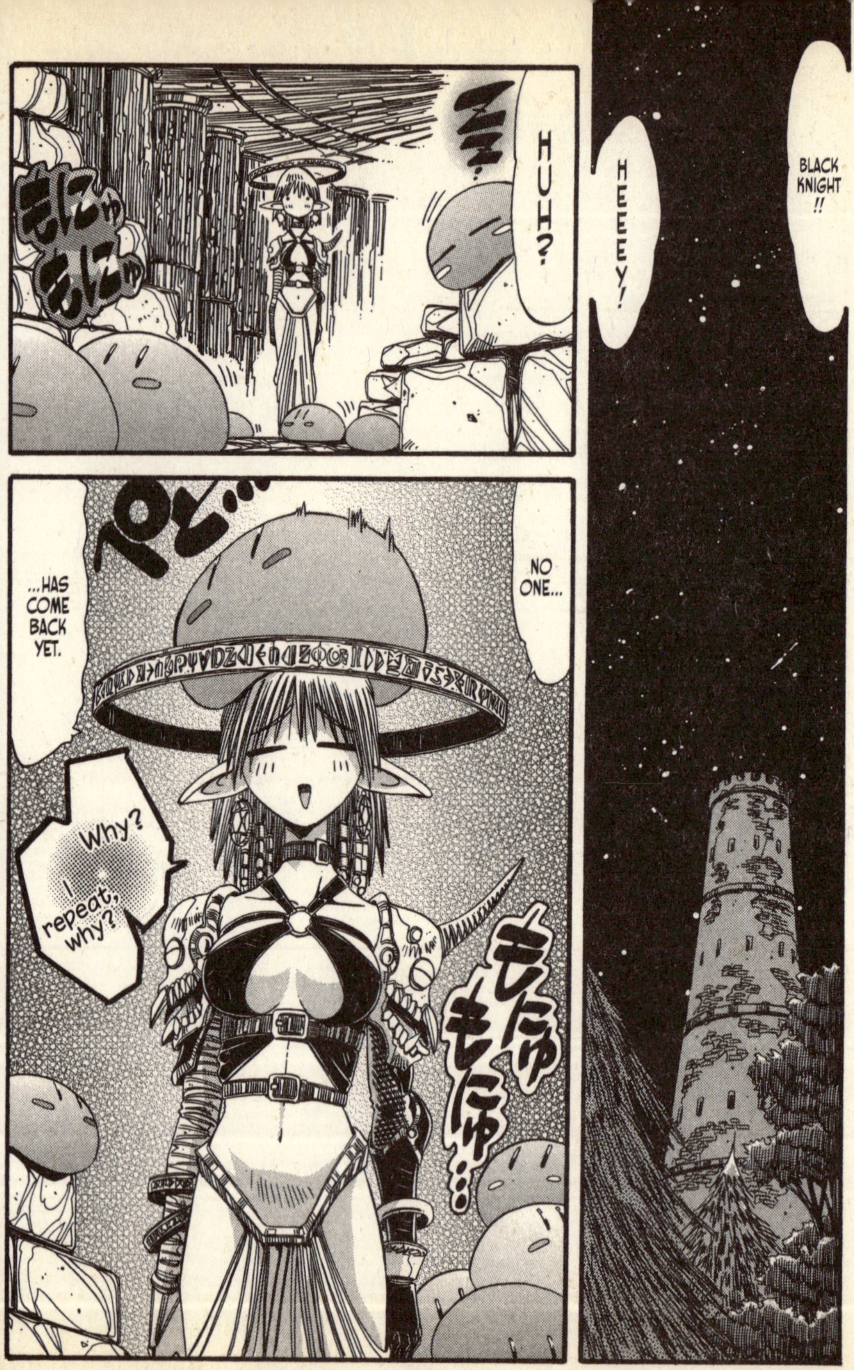
BLACK KNIGHT !!
HEEEEY!
HUH?
もにゅ もにゅ
NO ONE...
...HAS COME BACK YET.
Why? I repeat, why?
ぺと…
もにゅ もにゅ…

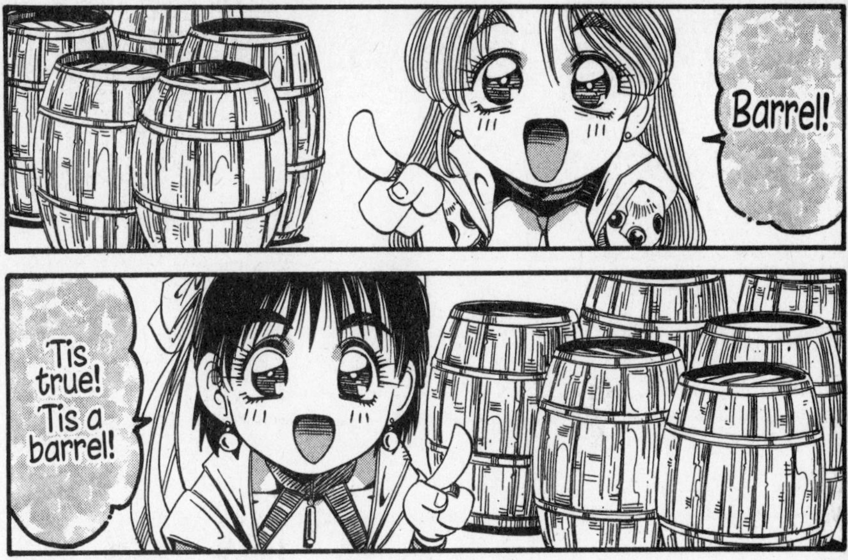
Barrel!
Tis true! Tis a barrel!

CHAPTER 17

"WHEN YOU CUT ME DOWN, IT HURT."

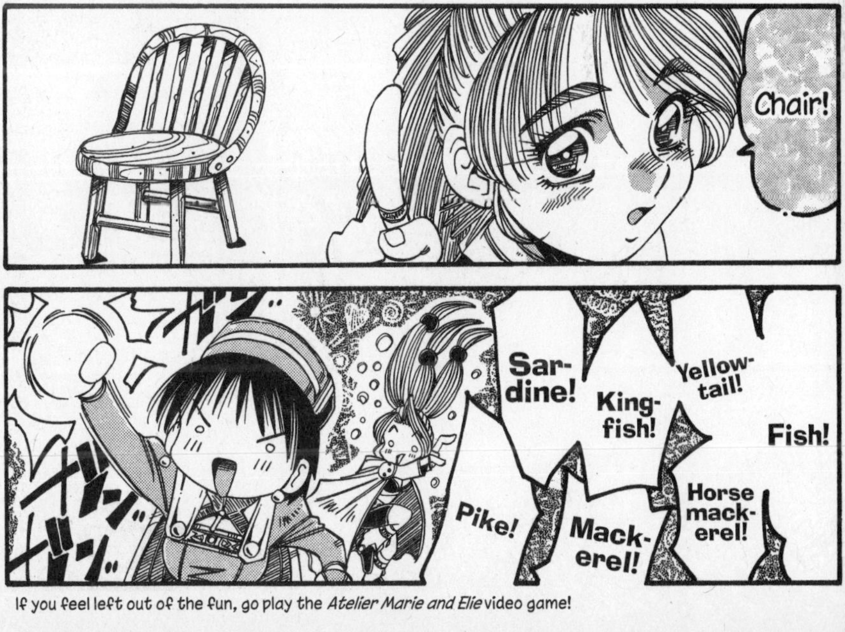
Chair!
Yellowtail!
Sardine!
Kingfish!
Fish!
Horse mackerel!
Mackerel!
Pike!

If you feel left out of the fun, go play the *Atelier Marie and Elie* video game!

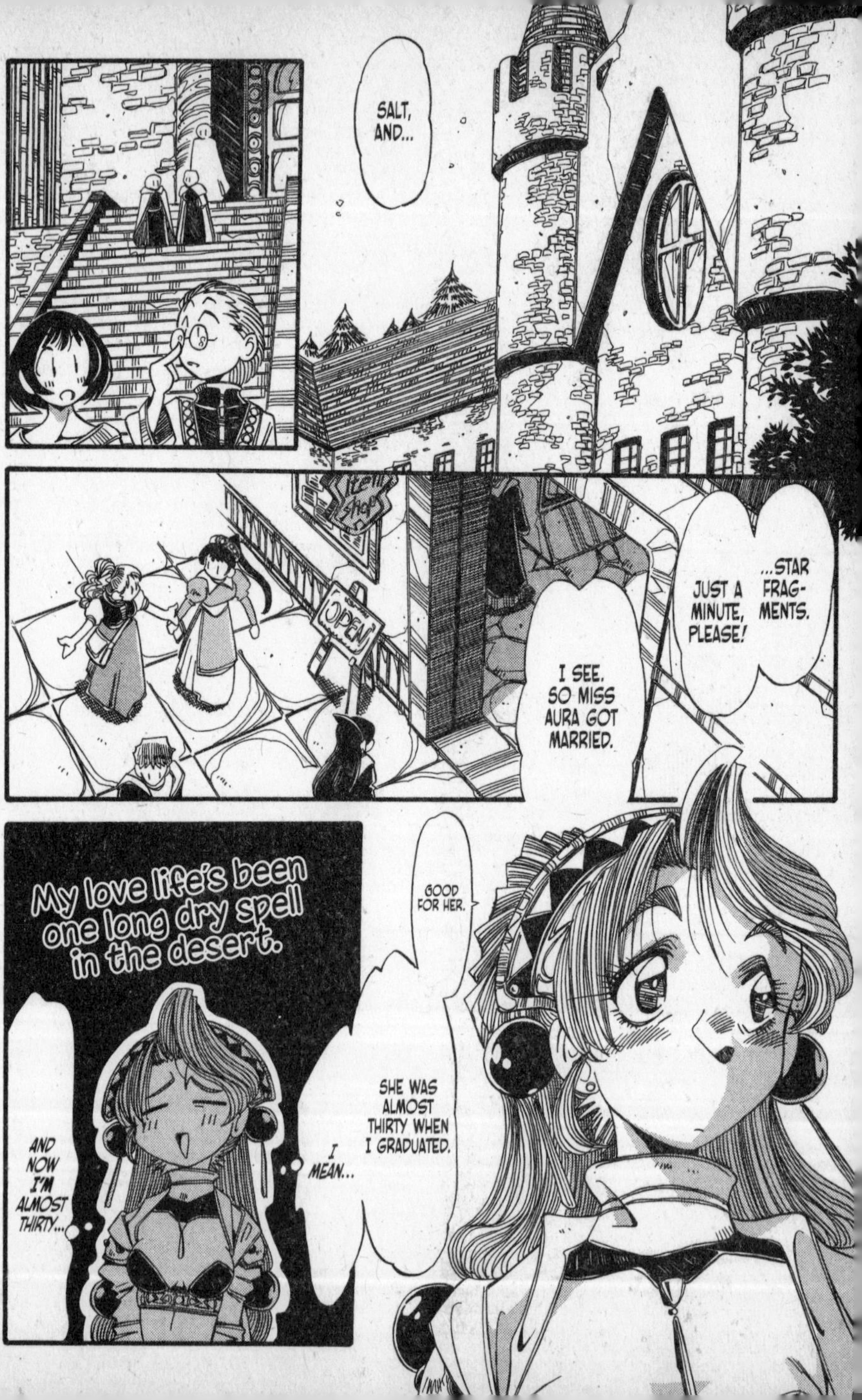
SALT, AND...
...STAR FRAG-MENTS.
JUST A MINUTE, PLEASE!
I SEE. SO MISS AURA GOT MARRIED.
GOOD FOR HER.
SHE WAS ALMOST THIRTY WHEN I GRADUATED.
I MEAN...
My love life's been one long dry spell in the desert.
AND NOW I'M ALMOST THIRTY...

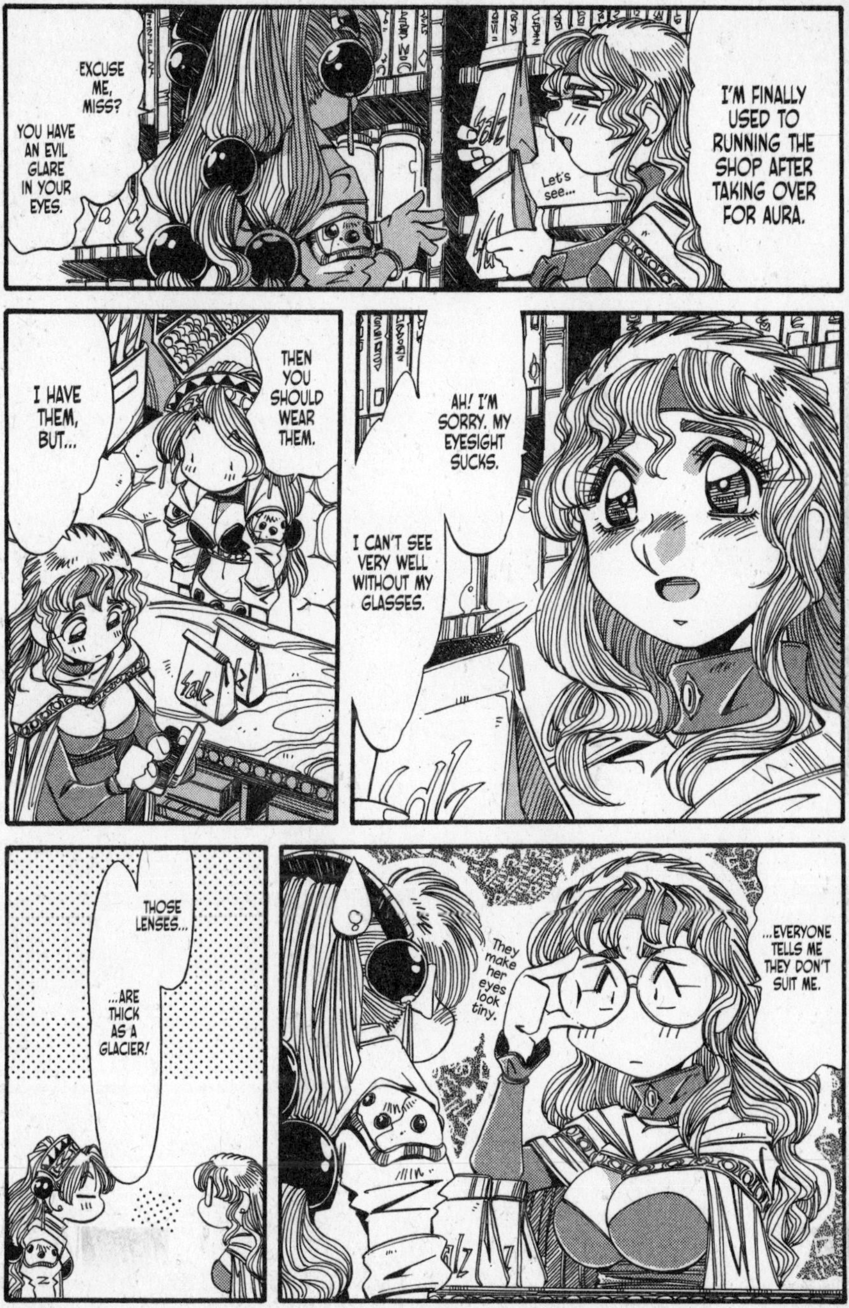
I'M FINALLY USED TO RUNNING THE SHOP AFTER TAKING OVER FOR AURA.
Let's see...
EXCUSE ME, MISS?
YOU HAVE AN EVIL GLARE IN YOUR EYES.
AH! I'M SORRY. MY EYESIGHT SUCKS.
I CAN'T SEE VERY WELL WITHOUT MY GLASSES.
THEN YOU SHOULD WEAR THEM.
I HAVE THEM, BUT...
...EVERYONE TELLS ME THEY DON'T SUIT ME.
They make her eyes look tiny.
THOSE LENSES...
...ARE THICK AS A GLACIER!

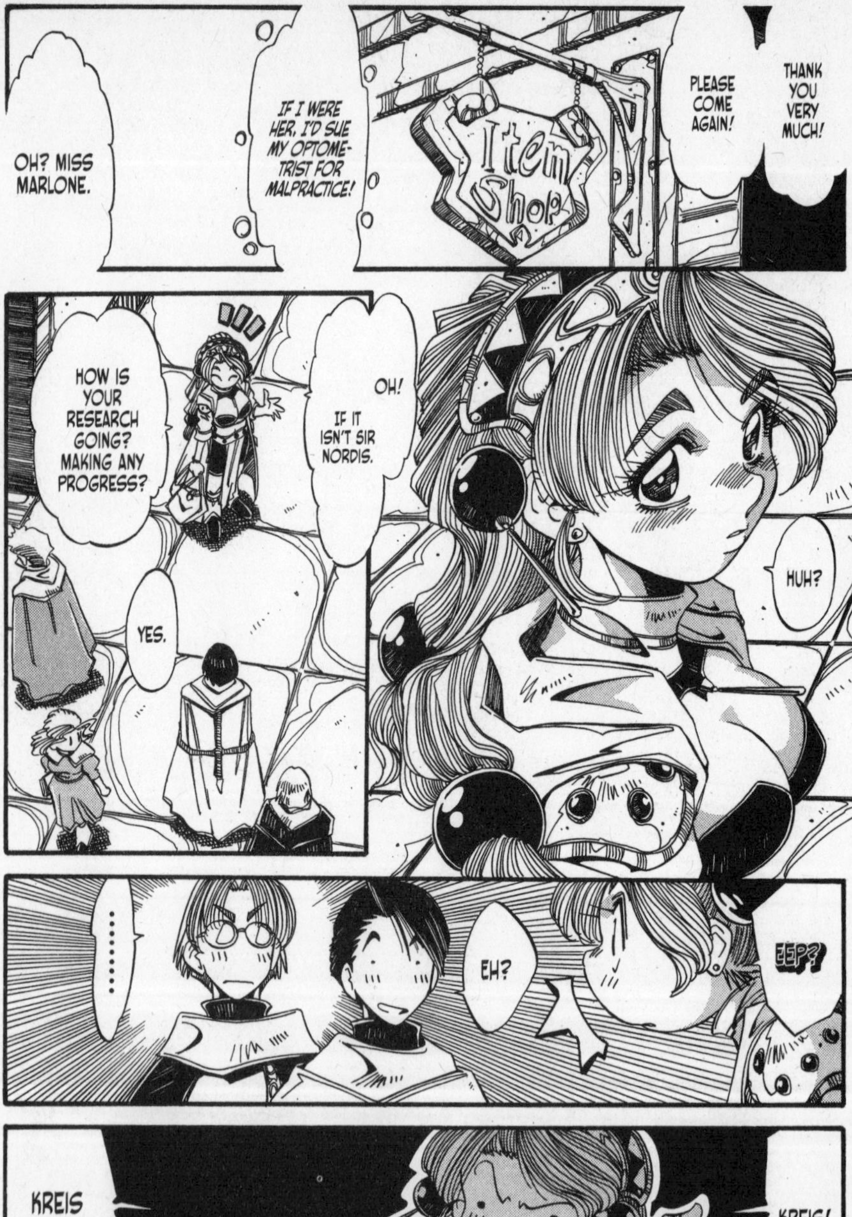
THANK YOU VERY MUCH!
PLEASE COME AGAIN!
Item Shop
IF I WERE HER, I'D SUE MY OPTOMETRIST FOR MALPRACTICE!
OH? MISS MARLONE.
HUH?
OH!
IF IT ISN'T SIR NORDIS.
HOW IS YOUR RESEARCH GOING? MAKING ANY PROGRESS?
YES.
EEP?
EH?
......
KREIS!
KREIS KUHL!

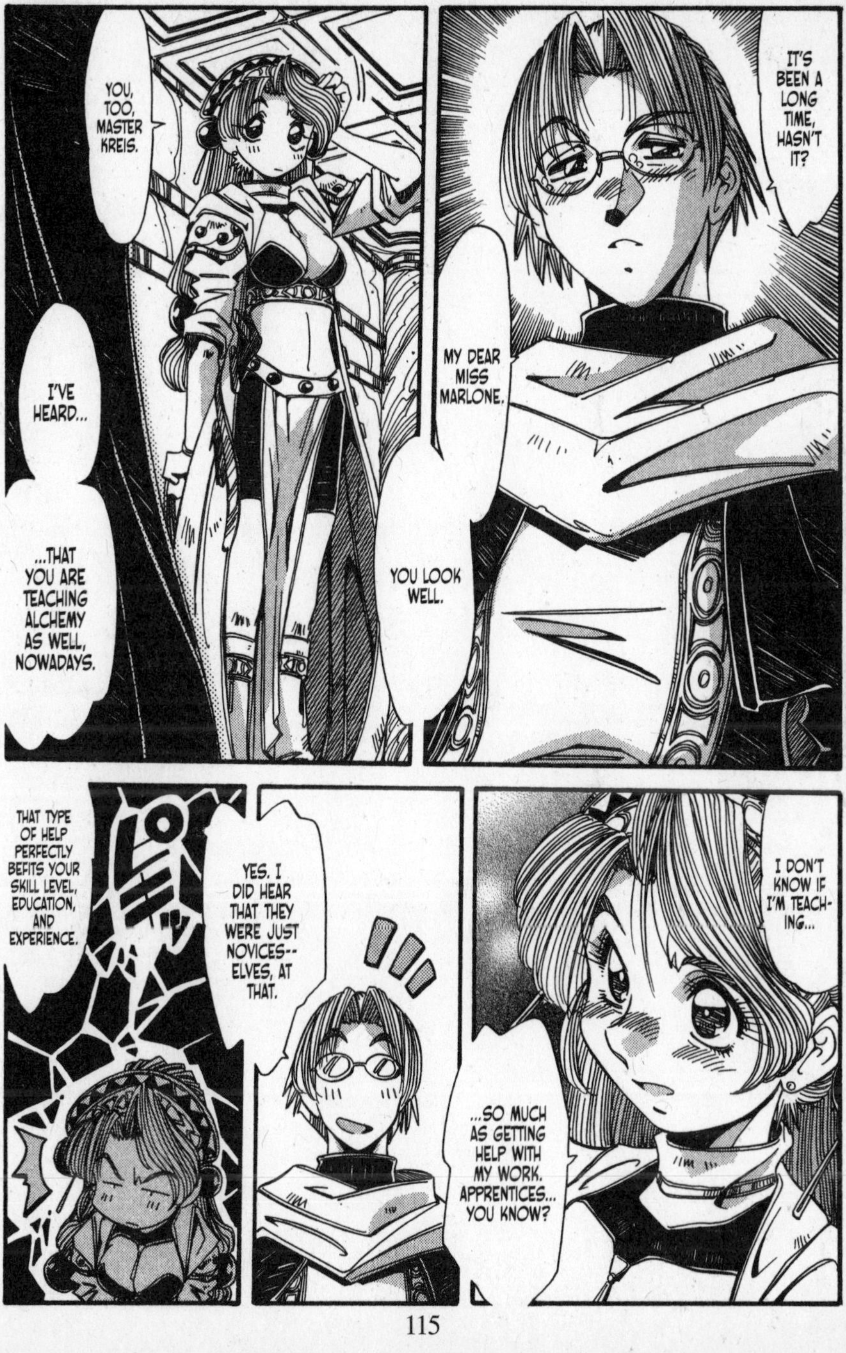
IT'S BEEN A LONG TIME, HASN'T IT?
MY DEAR MISS MARLONE.
YOU LOOK WELL.
YOU, TOO, MASTER KREIS.
I'VE HEARD...
...THAT YOU ARE TEACHING ALCHEMY AS WELL, NOWADAYS.
I DON'T KNOW IF I'M TEACH-ING...
...SO MUCH AS GETTING HELP WITH MY WORK. APPRENTICES... YOU KNOW?
YES. I DID HEAR THAT THEY WERE JUST NOVICES--ELVES, AT THAT.
THAT TYPE OF HELP PERFECTLY BEFITS YOUR SKILL LEVEL, EDUCATION, AND EXPERIENCE.

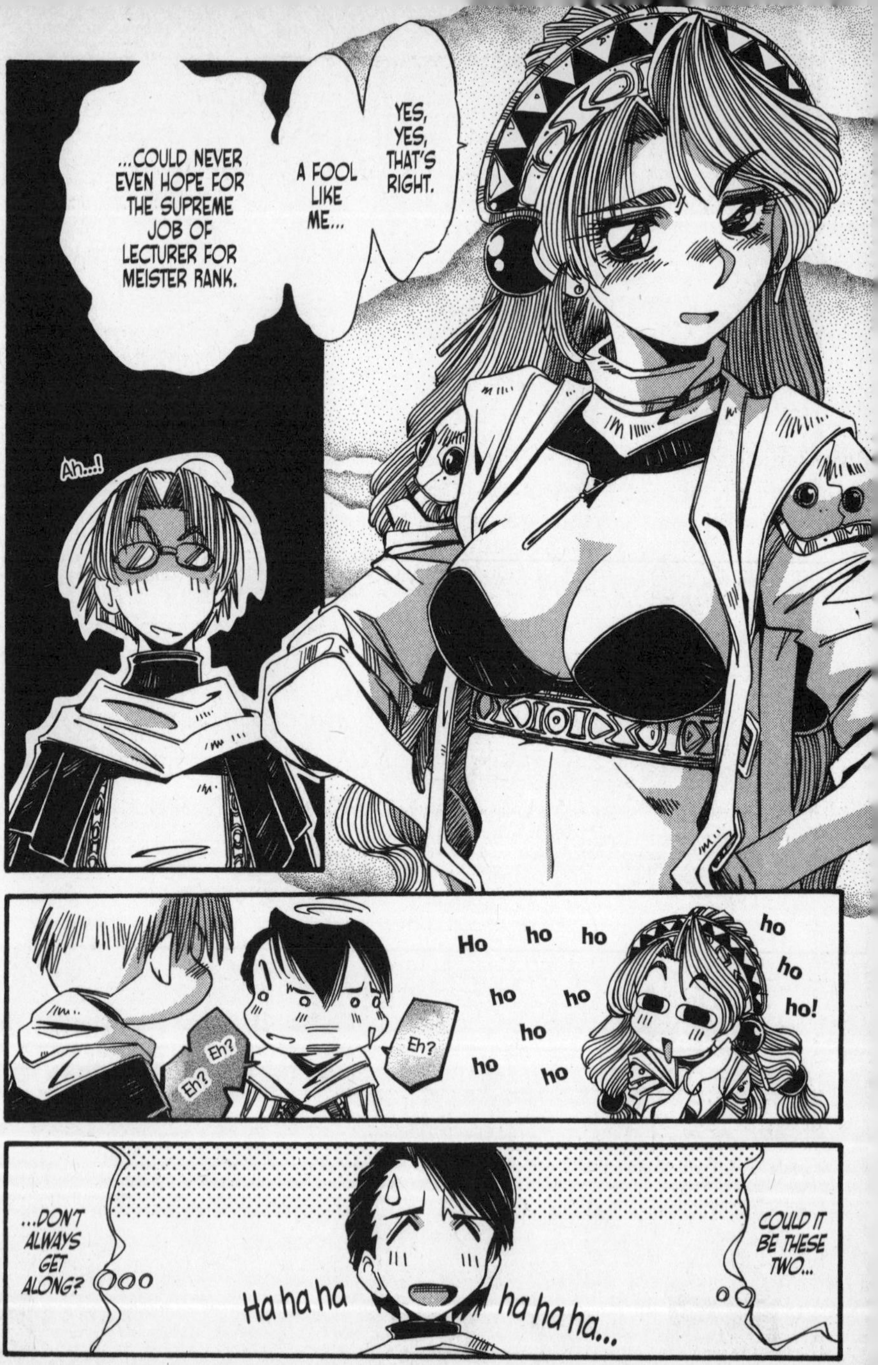
YES, YES, THAT'S RIGHT.
A FOOL LIKE ME...
...COULD NEVER EVEN HOPE FOR THE SUPREME JOB OF LECTURER FOR MEISTER RANK.
Ah...!
Ho ho ho ho ho ho ho ho ho ho ho ho!
Eh?
Eh? Eh?
COULD IT BE THESE TWO...
Ha ha ha ha ha ha...
...DON'T ALWAYS GET ALONG?

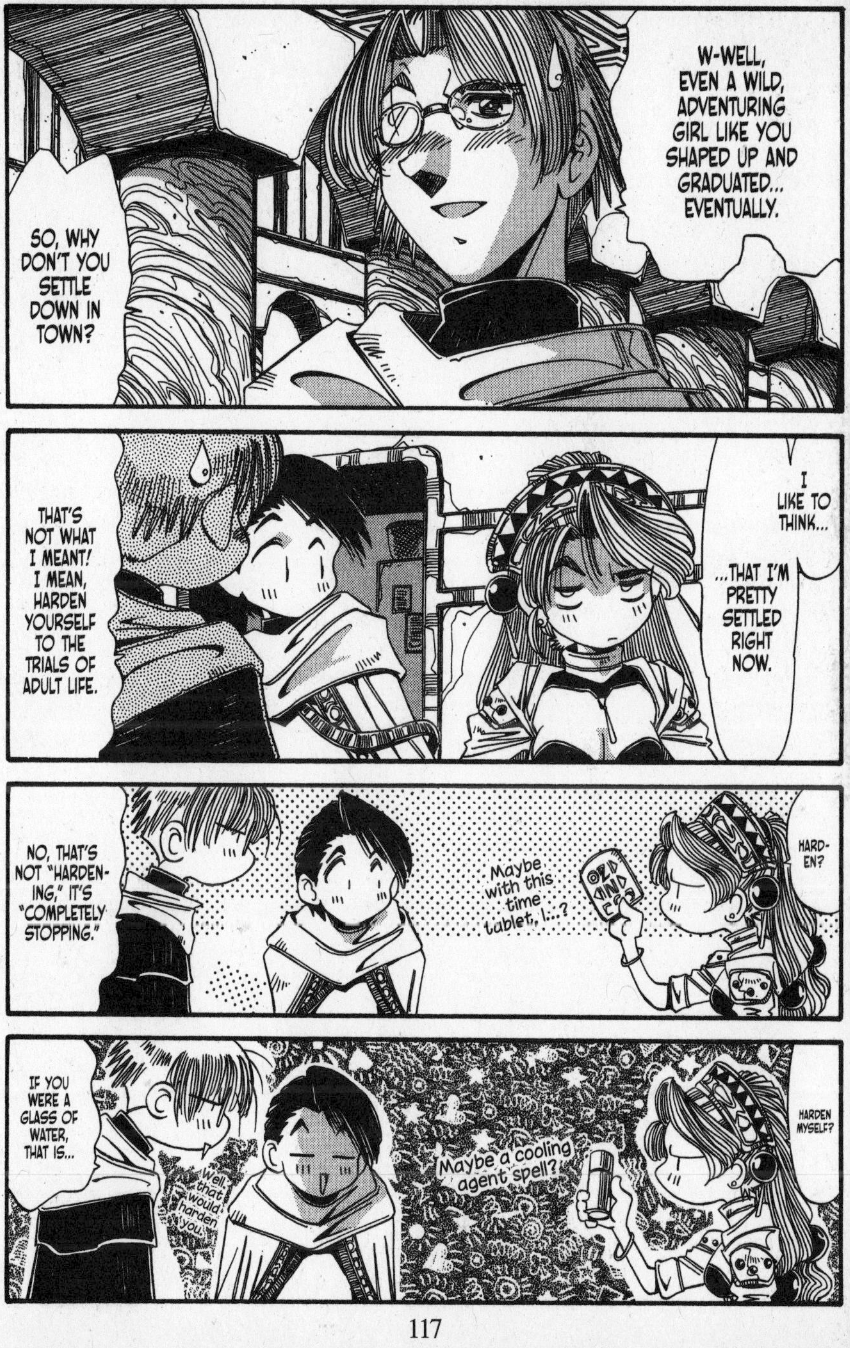
W-WELL, EVEN A WILD, ADVENTURING GIRL LIKE YOU SHAPED UP AND GRADUATED... EVENTUALLY.
SO, WHY DON'T YOU SETTLE DOWN IN TOWN?
I LIKE TO THINK...
...THAT I'M PRETTY SETTLED RIGHT NOW.
THAT'S NOT WHAT I MEANT! I MEAN, HARDEN YOURSELF TO THE TRIALS OF ADULT LIFE.
HARDEN?
Maybe with this time tablet, I...?
NO, THAT'S NOT "HARDENING," IT'S "COMPLETELY STOPPING."
HARDEN MYSELF?
Maybe a cooling agent spell?
Well, that would harden you.
IF YOU WERE A GLASS OF WATER, THAT IS...

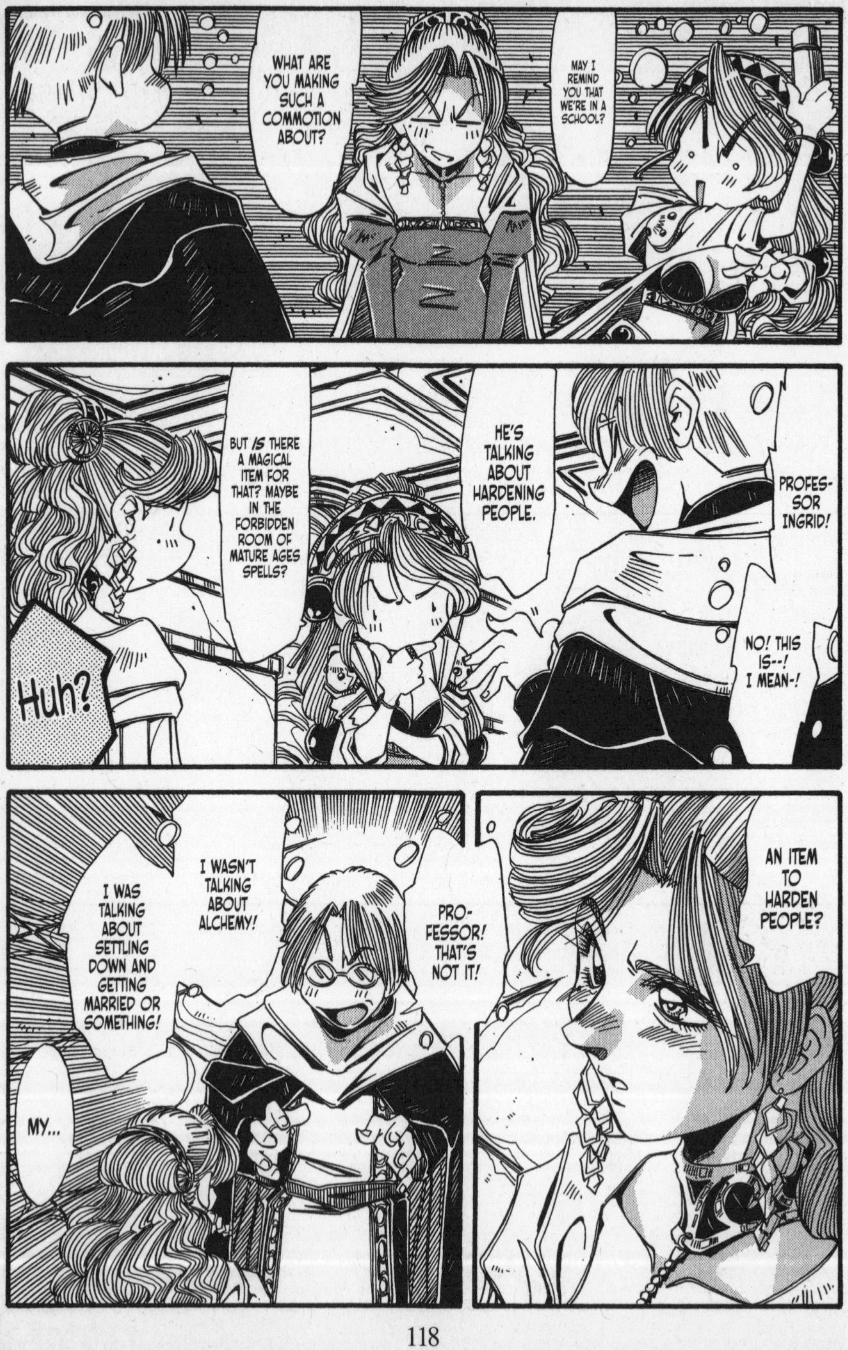
MAY I REMIND YOU THAT WE'RE IN A SCHOOL?
WHAT ARE YOU MAKING SUCH A COMMOTION ABOUT?
PROFES-SOR INGRID!
NO! THIS IS--! I MEAN-!
HE'S TALKING ABOUT HARDENING PEOPLE.
BUT *IS* THERE A MAGICAL ITEM FOR THAT? MAYBE IN THE FORBIDDEN ROOM OF MATURE AGES SPELLS?
Huh?
AN ITEM TO HARDEN PEOPLE?
PRO-FESSOR! THAT'S NOT IT!
I WASN'T TALKING ABOUT ALCHEMY!
I WAS TALKING ABOUT SETTLING DOWN AND GETTING MARRIED OR SOMETHING!
MY...

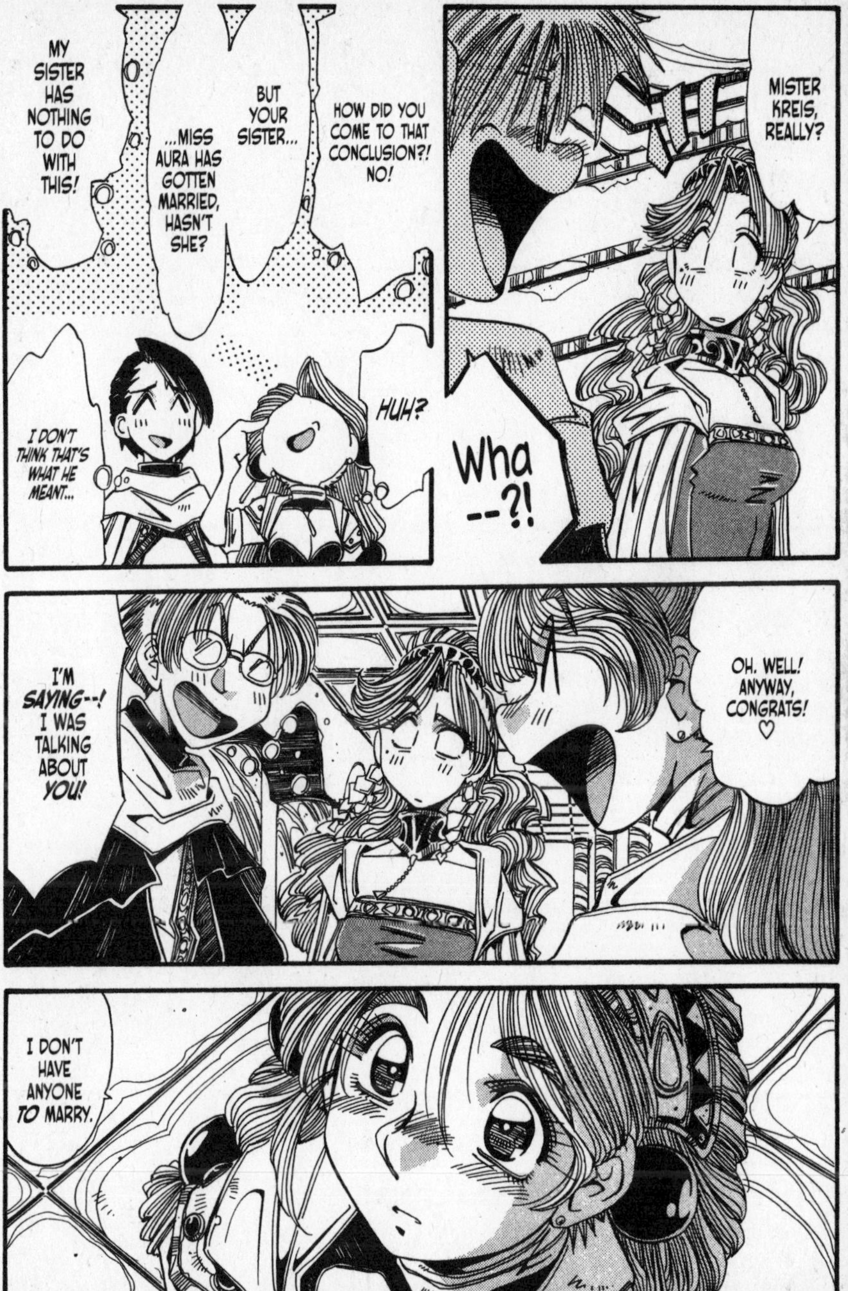
MISTER KREIS, REALLY?
Wha--?!
HOW DID YOU COME TO THAT CONCLUSION?! NO!
BUT YOUR SISTER...
...MISS AURA HAS GOTTEN MARRIED, HASN'T SHE?
MY SISTER HAS NOTHING TO DO WITH THIS!
HUH?
I DON'T THINK THAT'S WHAT HE MEANT...
OH. WELL! ANYWAY, CONGRATS! ♡
I'M SAYING--! I WAS TALKING ABOUT YOU!
I DON'T HAVE ANYONE TO MARRY.

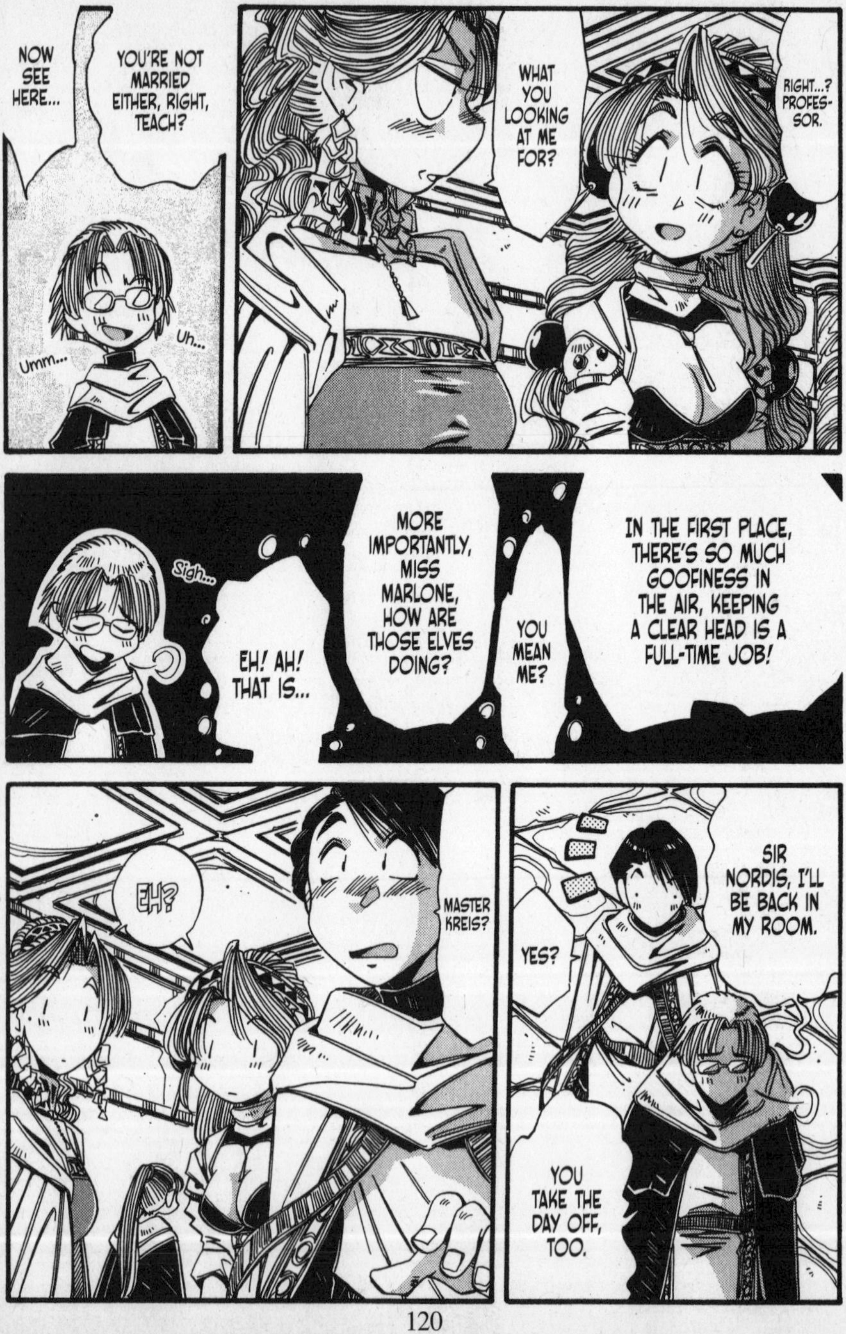
RIGHT...? PROFES-SOR.
WHAT YOU LOOKING AT ME FOR?
YOU'RE NOT MARRIED EITHER, RIGHT, TEACH?
NOW SEE HERE...
Uh...
Umm...
IN THE FIRST PLACE, THERE'S SO MUCH GOOFINESS IN THE AIR, KEEPING A CLEAR HEAD IS A FULL-TIME JOB!
YOU MEAN ME?
MORE IMPORTANTLY, MISS MARLONE, HOW ARE THOSE ELVES DOING?
Sigh...
EH! AH! THAT IS...
SIR NORDIS, I'LL BE BACK IN MY ROOM.
YES?
YOU TAKE THE DAY OFF, TOO.
MASTER KREIS?
EH?

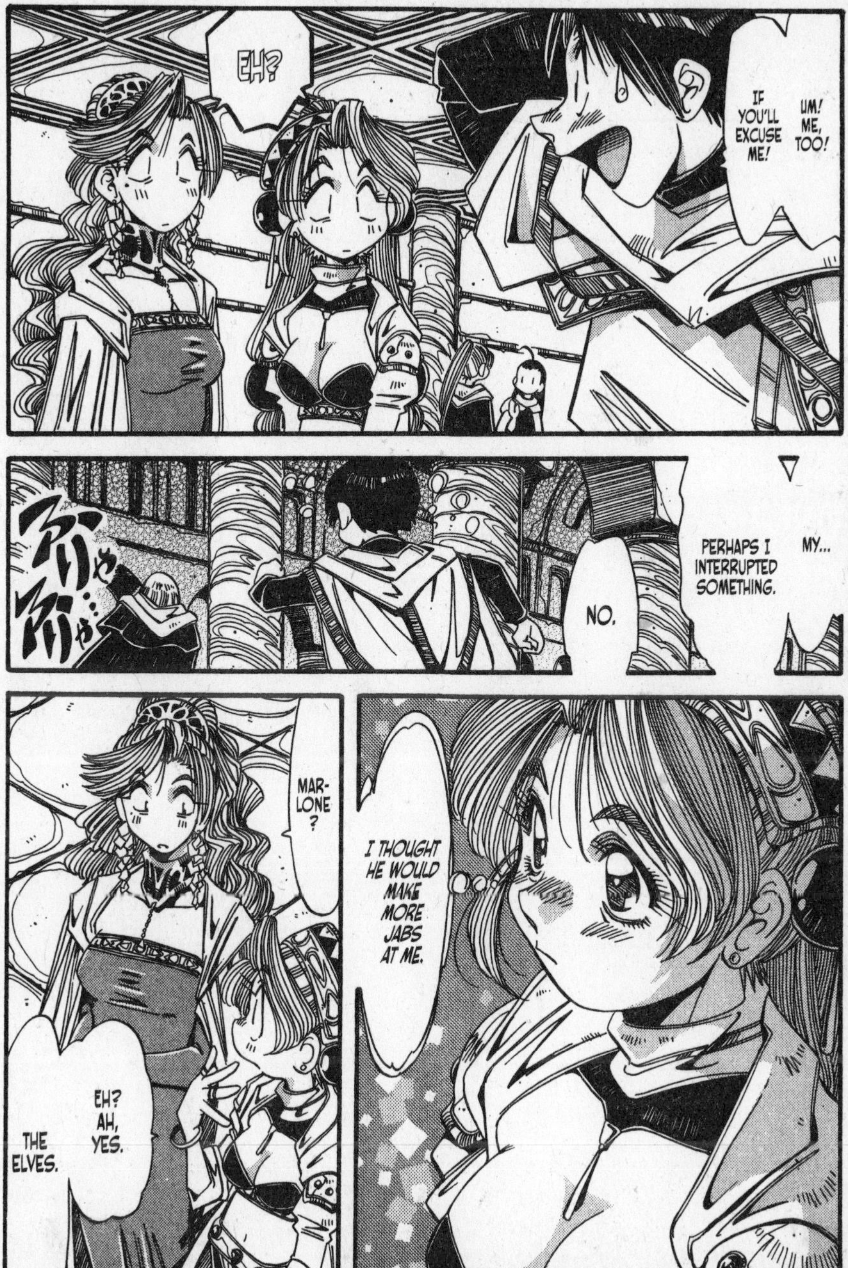
UM! ME, TOO!
IF YOU'LL EXCUSE ME!
EH?
MY...
PERHAPS I INTERRUPTED SOMETHING.
NO.
I THOUGHT HE WOULD MAKE MORE JABS AT ME.
MAR-LONE?
EH? AH, YES.
THE ELVES.

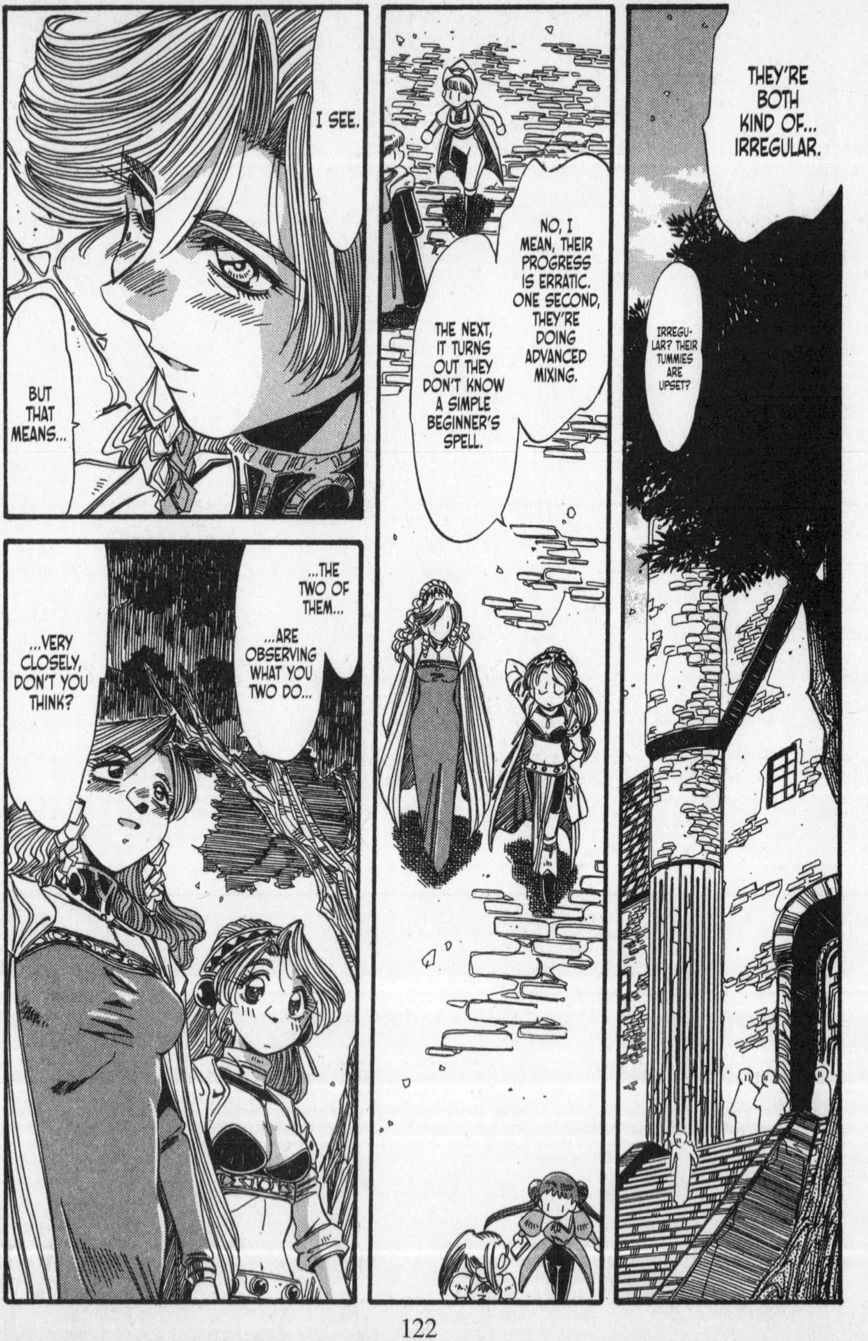
THEY'RE BOTH KIND OF... IRREGULAR.
IRREGU-LAR? THEIR TUMMIES ARE UPSET?
NO, I MEAN, THEIR PROGRESS IS ERRATIC. ONE SECOND, THEY'RE DOING ADVANCED MIXING.
THE NEXT, IT TURNS OUT THEY DON'T KNOW A SIMPLE BEGINNER'S SPELL.
I SEE.
BUT THAT MEANS...
...THE TWO OF THEM...
...ARE OBSERVING WHAT YOU TWO DO...
...VERY CLOSELY, DON'T YOU THINK?

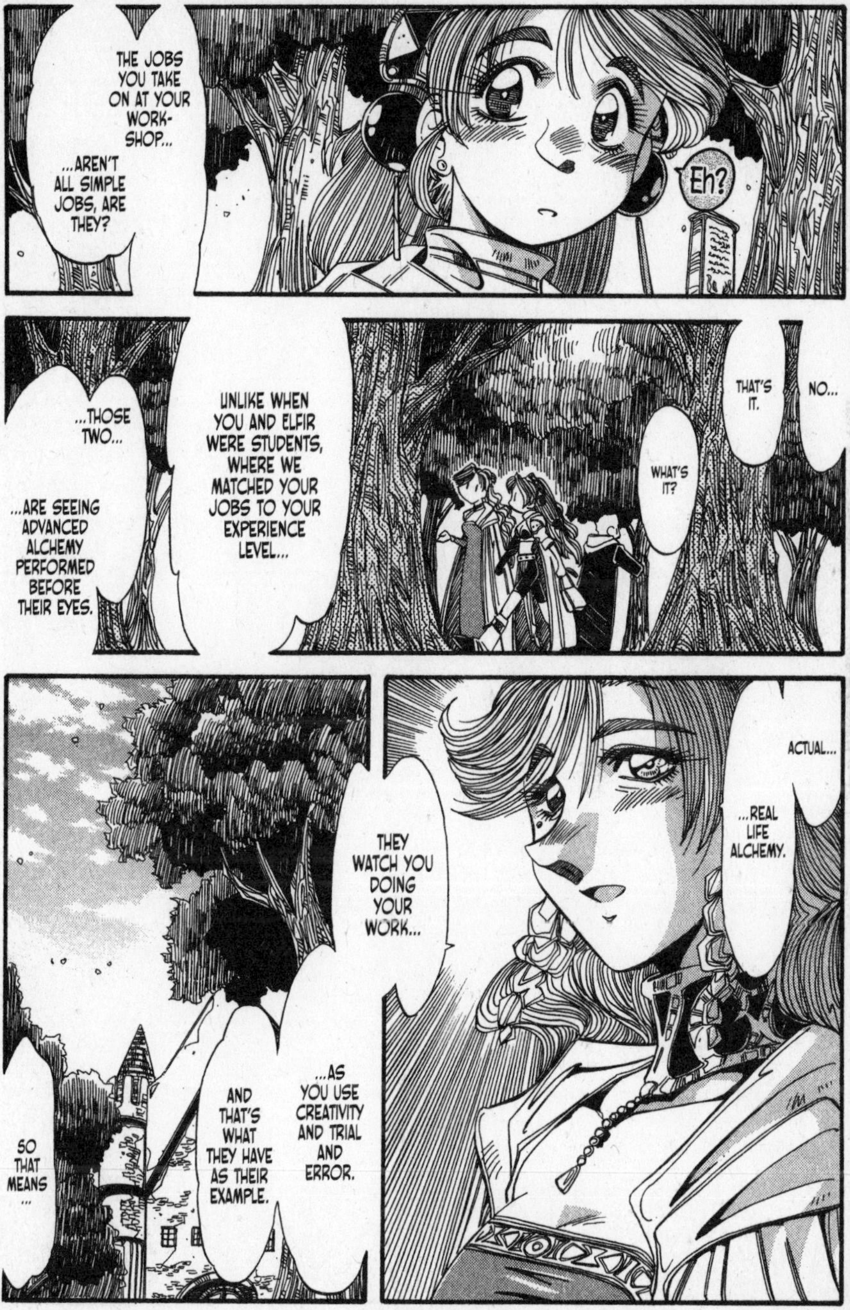
THE JOBS YOU TAKE ON AT YOUR WORK-SHOP...
...AREN'T ALL SIMPLE JOBS, ARE THEY?
Eh?
NO...
THAT'S IT.
WHAT'S IT?
UNLIKE WHEN YOU AND ELFIR WERE STUDENTS, WHERE WE MATCHED YOUR JOBS TO YOUR EXPERIENCE LEVEL...
...THOSE TWO...
...ARE SEEING ADVANCED ALCHEMY PERFORMED BEFORE THEIR EYES.
ACTUAL...
...REAL LIFE ALCHEMY.
THEY WATCH YOU DOING YOUR WORK...
...AS YOU USE CREATIVITY AND TRIAL AND ERROR.
AND THAT'S WHAT THEY HAVE AS THEIR EXAMPLE.
SO THAT MEANS ...

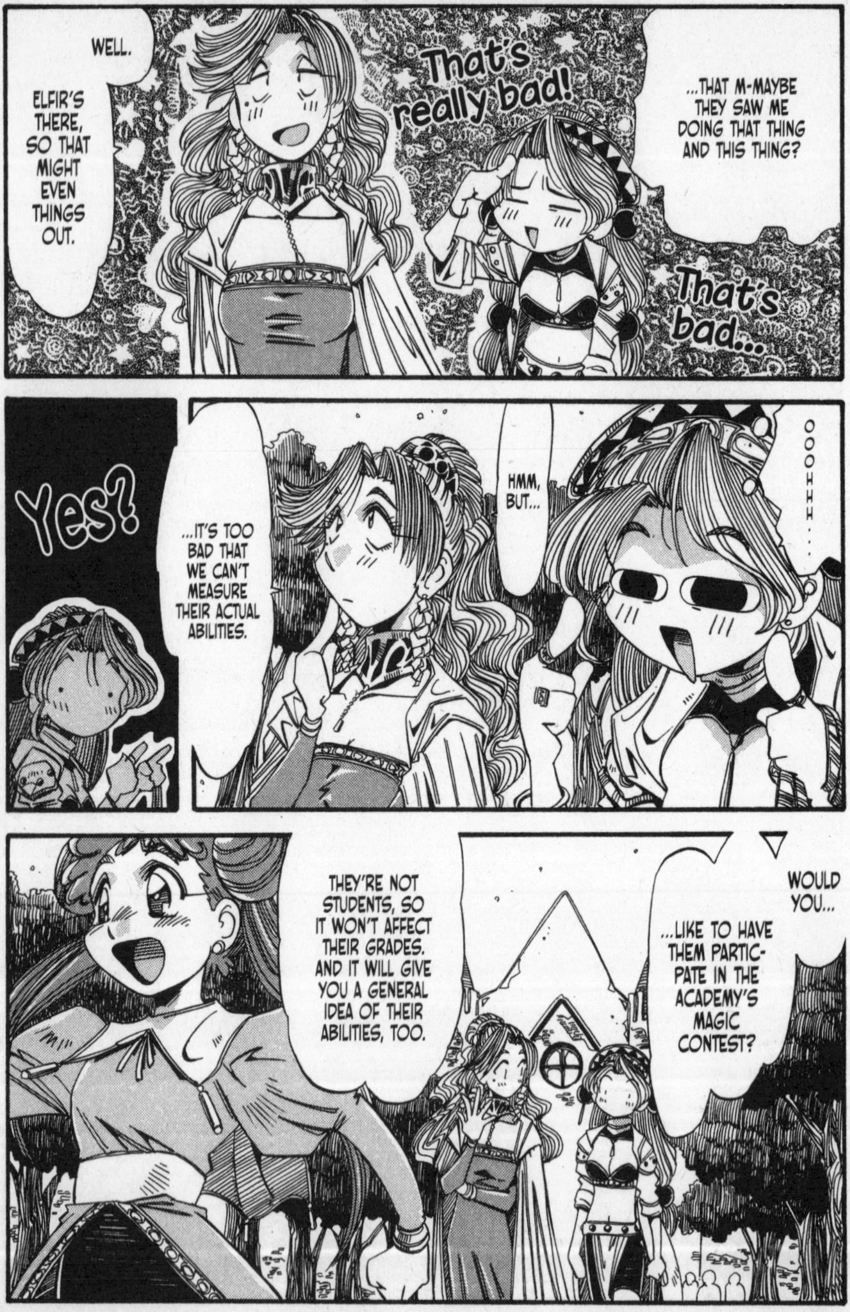
...THAT M-MAYBE THEY SAW ME DOING THAT THING AND THIS THING?
That's really bad!
That's bad...
WELL.
ELFIR'S THERE, SO THAT MIGHT EVEN THINGS OUT.
OOOHHH...
HMM, BUT...
...IT'S TOO BAD THAT WE CAN'T MEASURE THEIR ACTUAL ABILITIES.
Yes?
WOULD YOU...
...LIKE TO HAVE THEM PARTIC-PATE IN THE ACADEMY'S MAGIC CONTEST?
THEY'RE NOT STUDENTS, SO IT WON'T AFFECT THEIR GRADES. AND IT WILL GIVE YOU A GENERAL IDEA OF THEIR ABILITIES, TOO.

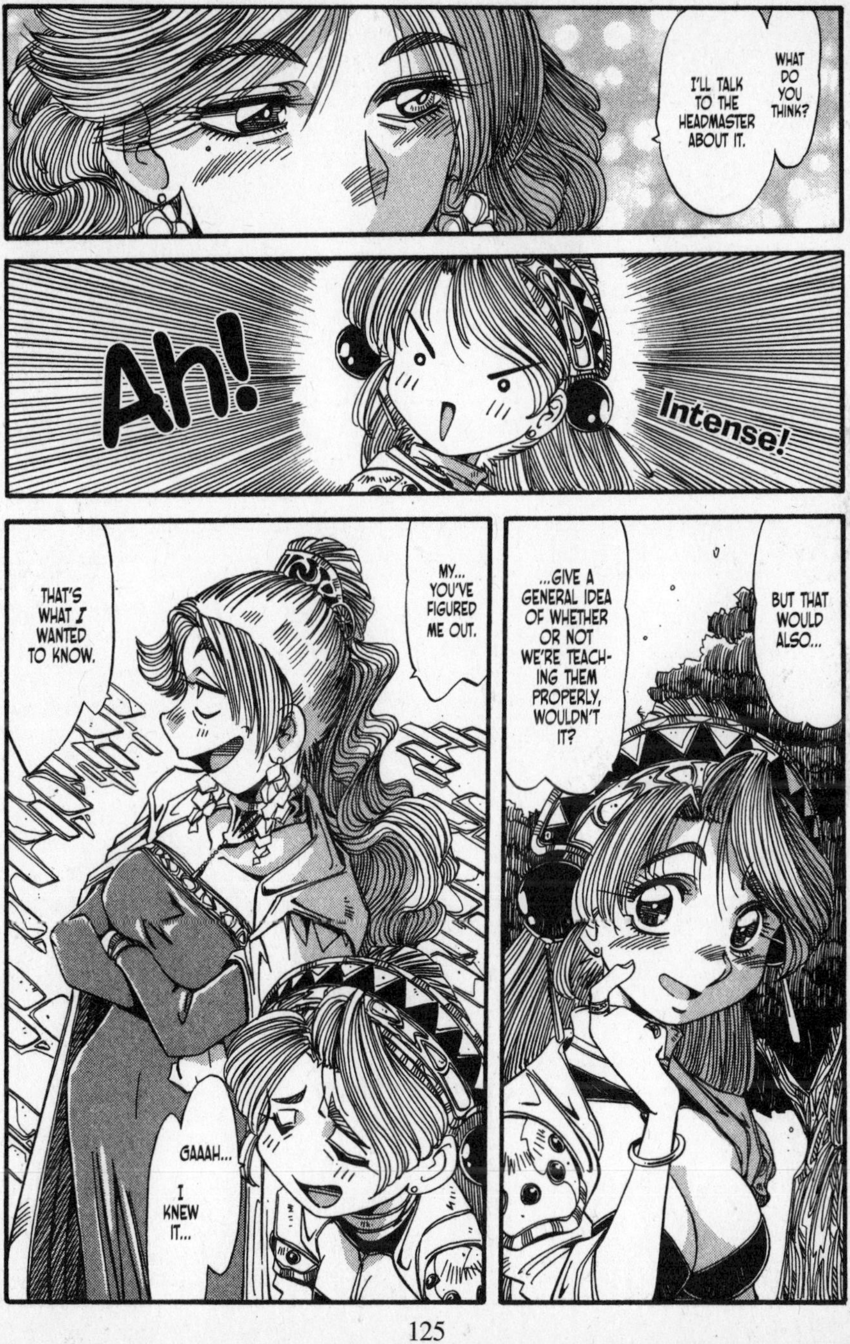
WHAT DO YOU THINK?
I'LL TALK TO THE HEADMASTER ABOUT IT.
Ah!
Intense!
BUT THAT WOULD ALSO...
...GIVE A GENERAL IDEA OF WHETHER OR NOT WE'RE TEACHING THEM PROPERLY, WOULDN'T IT?
MY... YOU'VE FIGURED ME OUT.
THAT'S WHAT *I* WANTED TO KNOW.
GAAAH...
I KNEW IT...

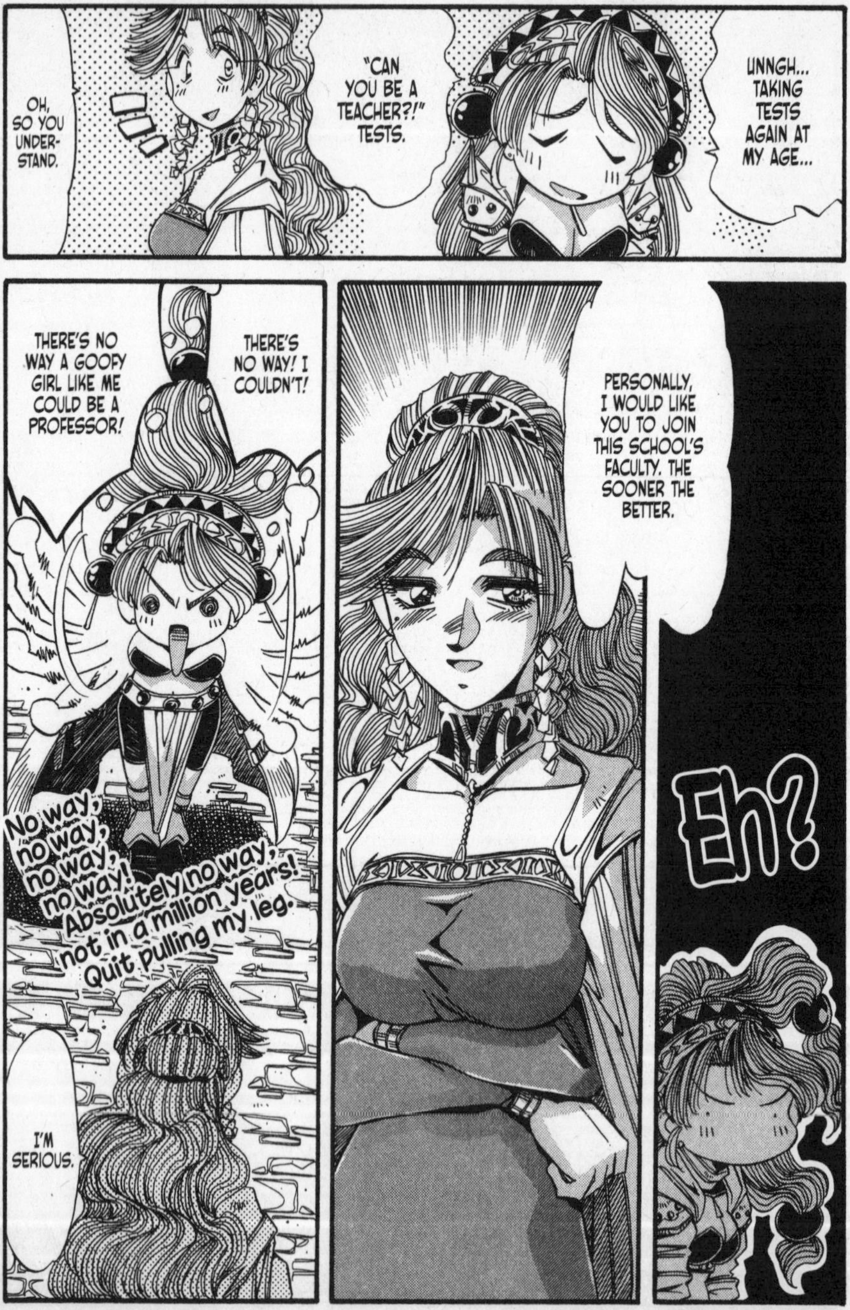
UNNGH... TAKING TESTS AGAIN AT MY AGE...
"CAN YOU BE A TEACHER?!" TESTS.
OH, SO YOU UNDER-STAND.
PERSONALLY, I WOULD LIKE YOU TO JOIN THIS SCHOOL'S FACULTY. THE SOONER THE BETTER.
Eh?
THERE'S NO WAY! I COULDN'T!
THERE'S NO WAY A GOOFY GIRL LIKE ME COULD BE A PROFESSOR!
No way, no way, no way, no way! Absolutely no way, not in a million years! Quit pulling my leg.
I'M SERIOUS.

Ah... Serious-ly?
BUT...
...IT HAS TO BE AFTER THE ELVES ARE FULL-FLEDGED ALCHEMISTS.
YOU CAN GIVE ME YOUR ANSWER AFTER THAT.
THINK ABOUT IT.
WEIRD TO HAVE HER SAY SOME-THING JUST...
...OUT OF THE BLUE LIKE THAT.

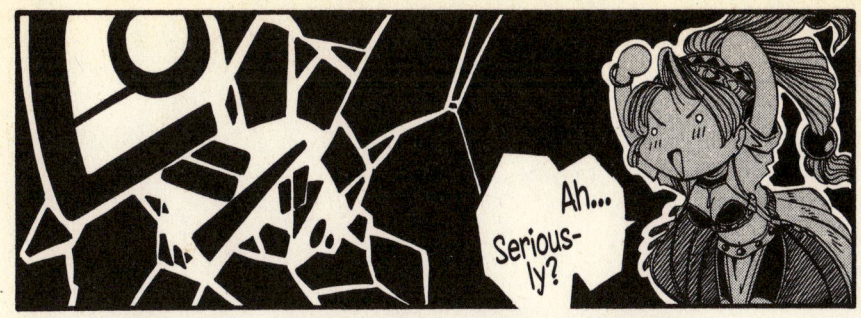

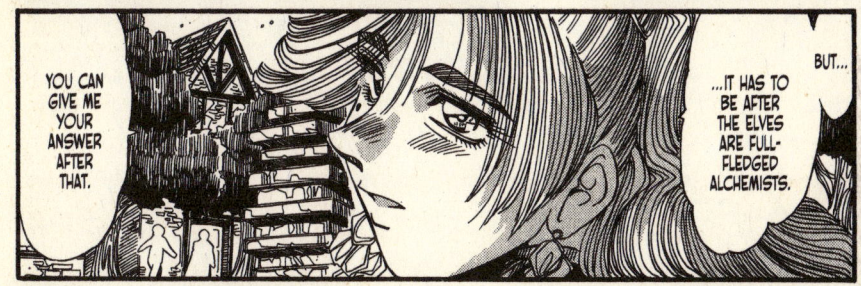

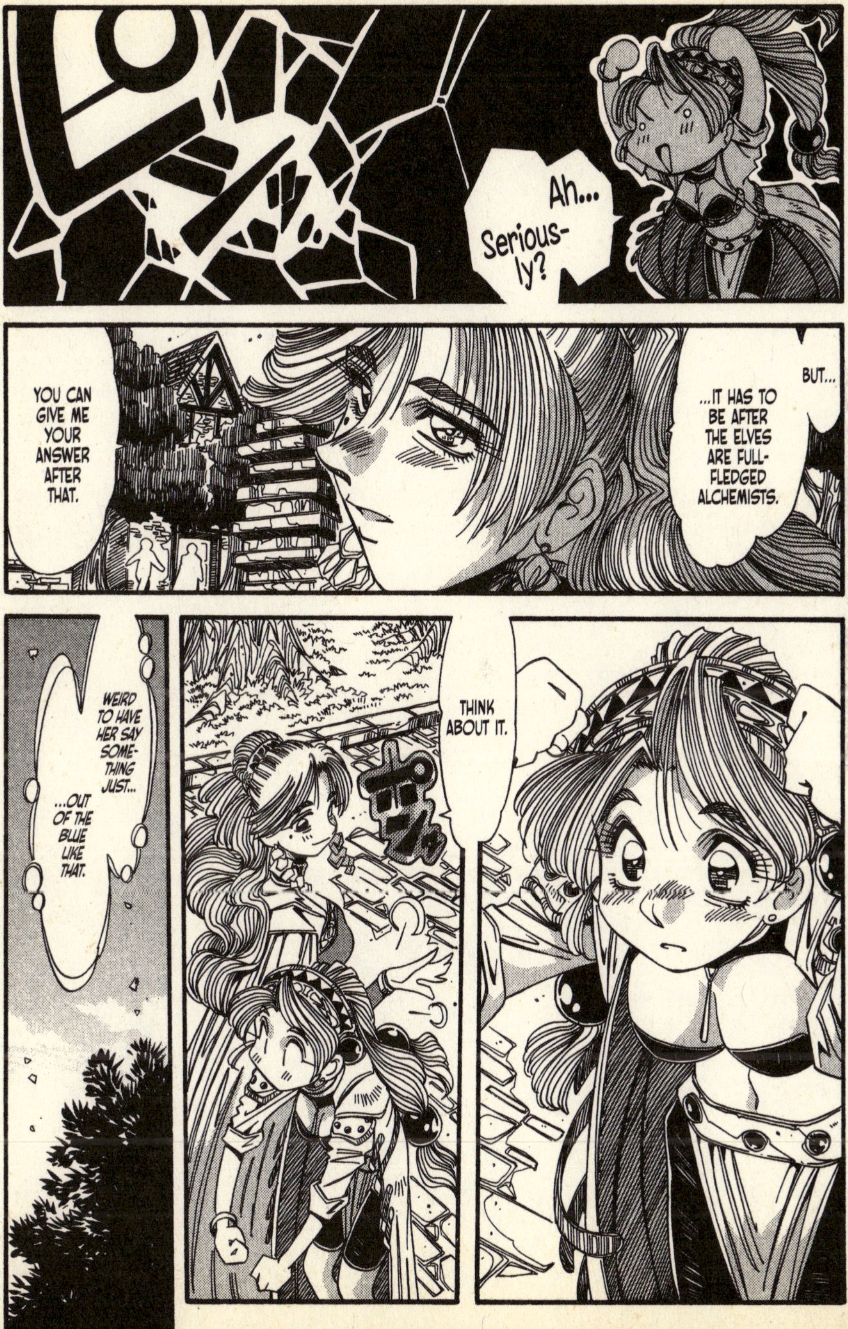

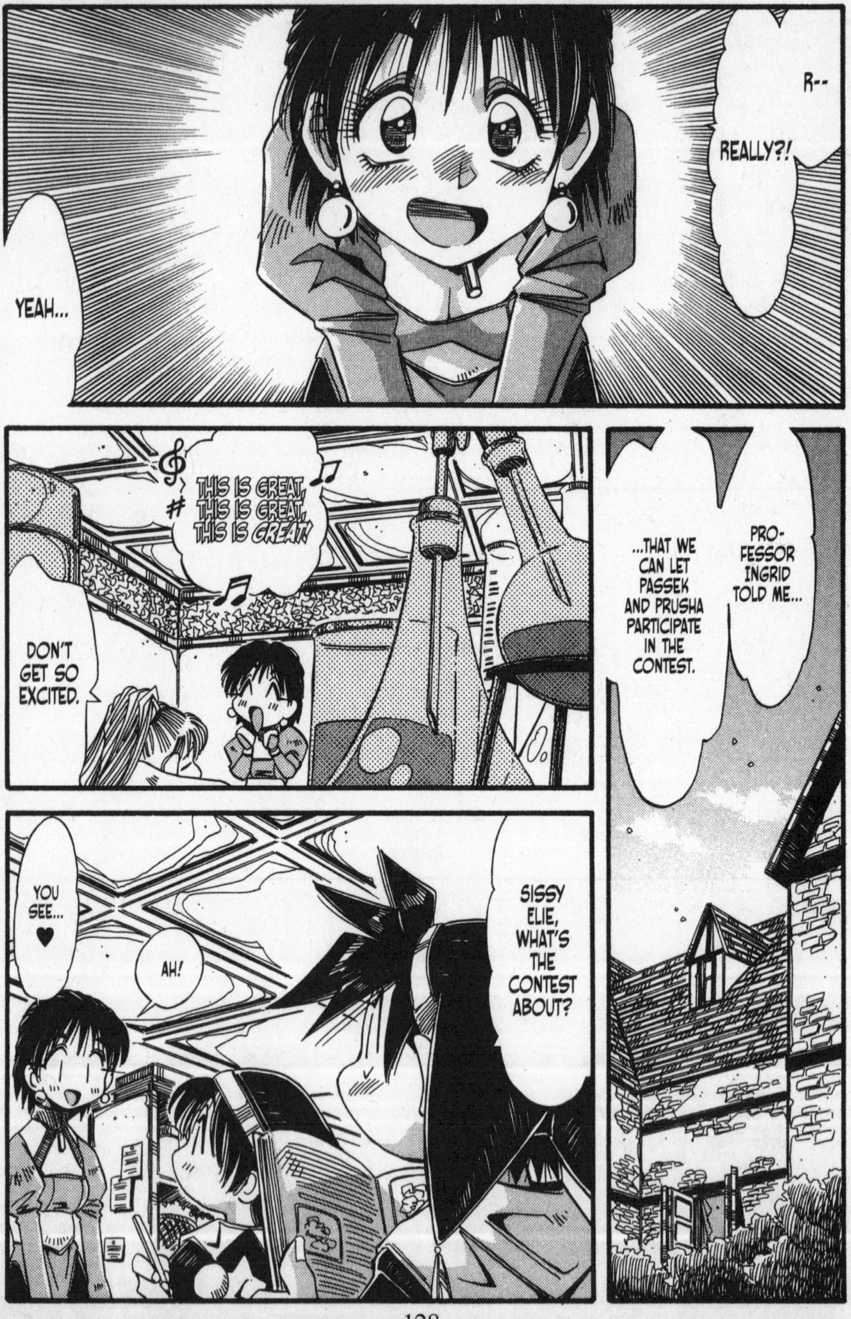
R--
REALLY?!
YEAH...
PROFESSOR INGRID TOLD ME...
...THAT WE CAN LET PASSEK AND PRUSHA PARTICIPATE IN THE CONTEST.
THIS IS GREAT, THIS IS GREAT, THIS IS GREAT!
DON'T GET SO EXCITED.
SISSY ELIE, WHAT'S THE CONTEST ABOUT?
AH!
YOU SEE... ♥

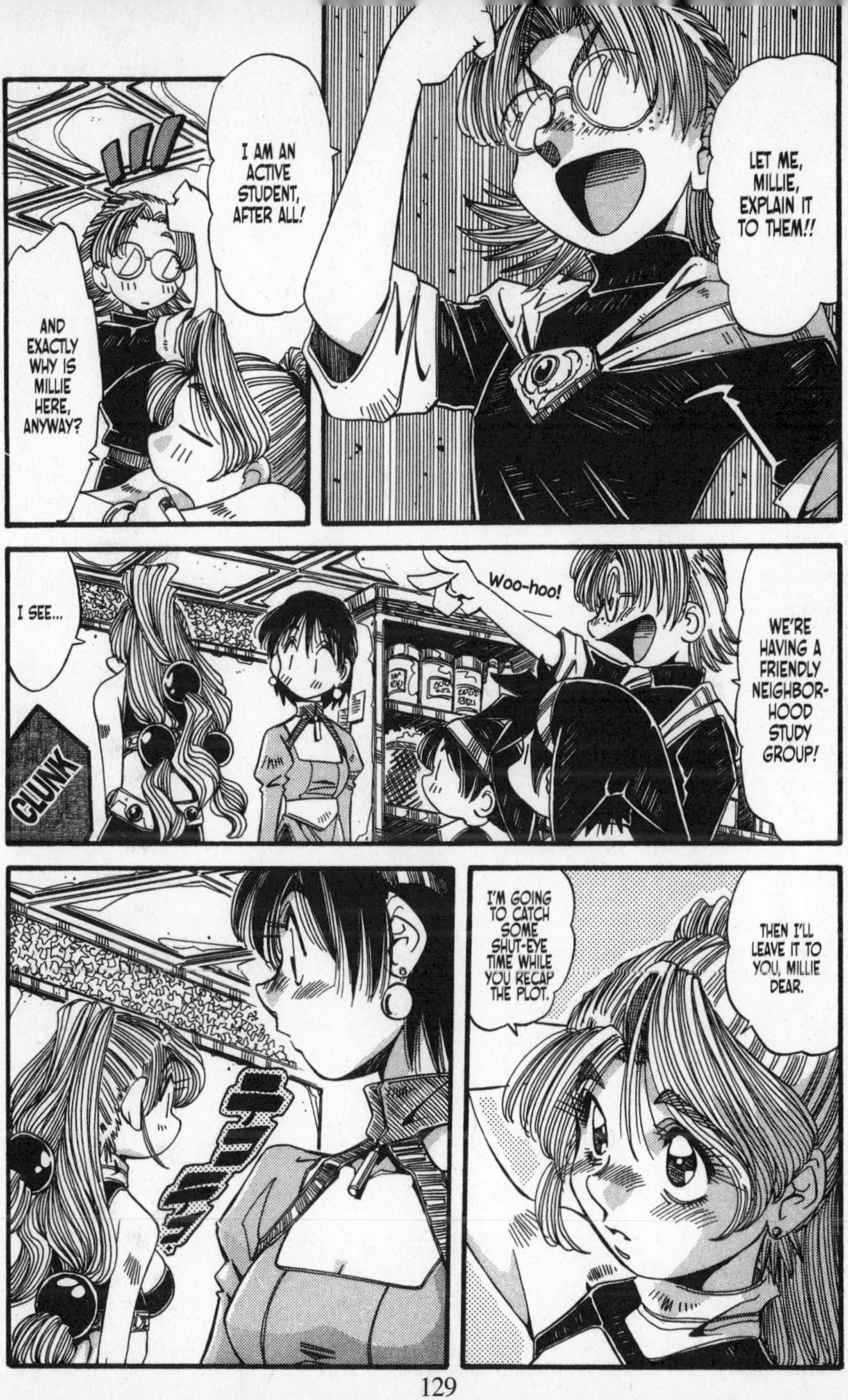
LET ME, MILLIE, EXPLAIN IT TO THEM!!
I AM AN ACTIVE STUDENT, AFTER ALL!
AND EXACTLY WHY IS MILLIE HERE, ANYWAY?
WE'RE HAVING A FRIENDLY NEIGHBOR-HOOD STUDY GROUP!
Woo-hoo!
I SEE...
CLUNK
THEN I'LL LEAVE IT TO YOU, MILLIE DEAR.
I'M GOING TO CATCH SOME SHUT-EYE TIME WHILE YOU RECAP THE PLOT.

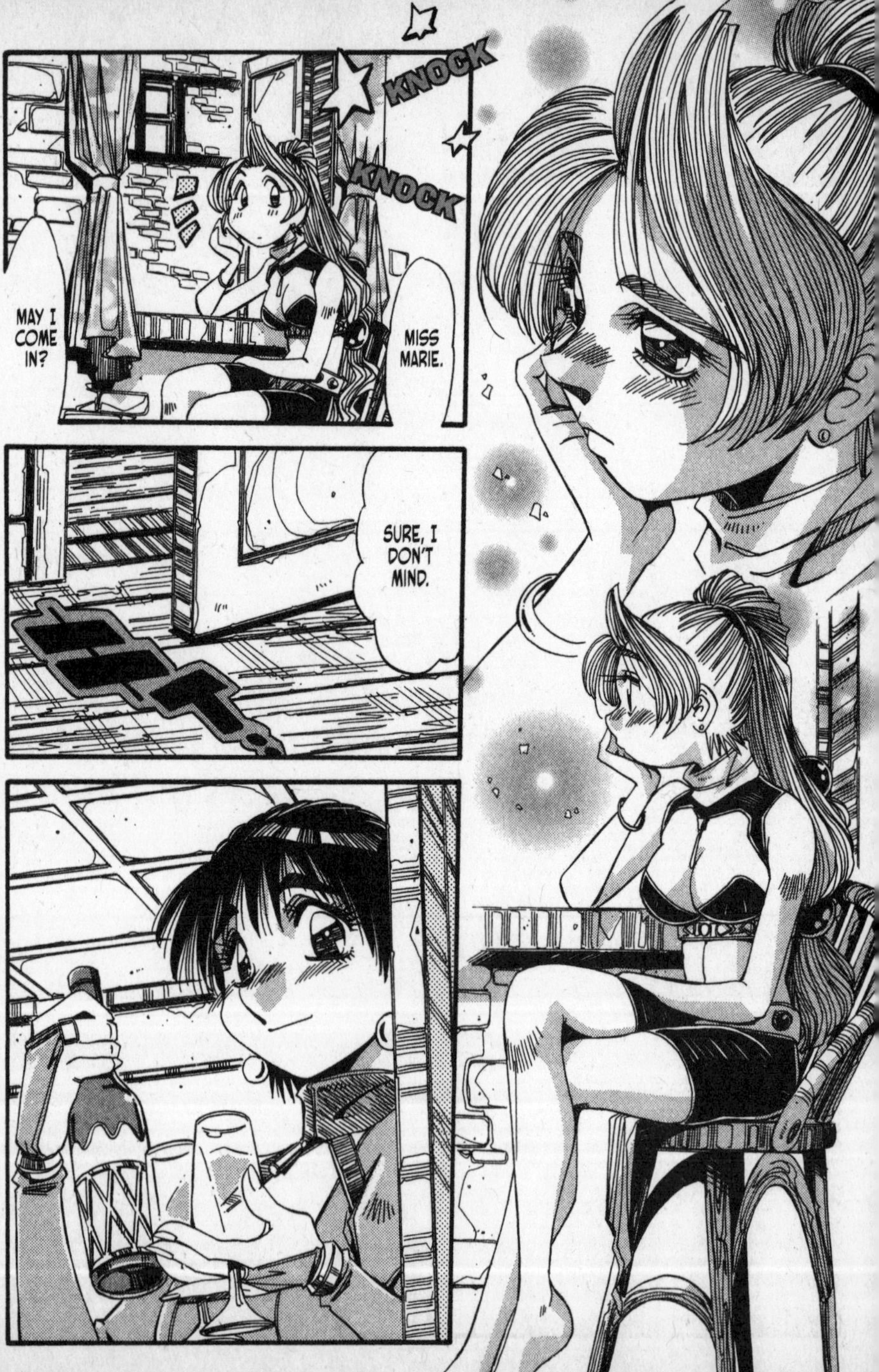
KNOCK
KNOCK
MISS MARIE.
MAY I COME IN?
SURE, I DON'T MIND.

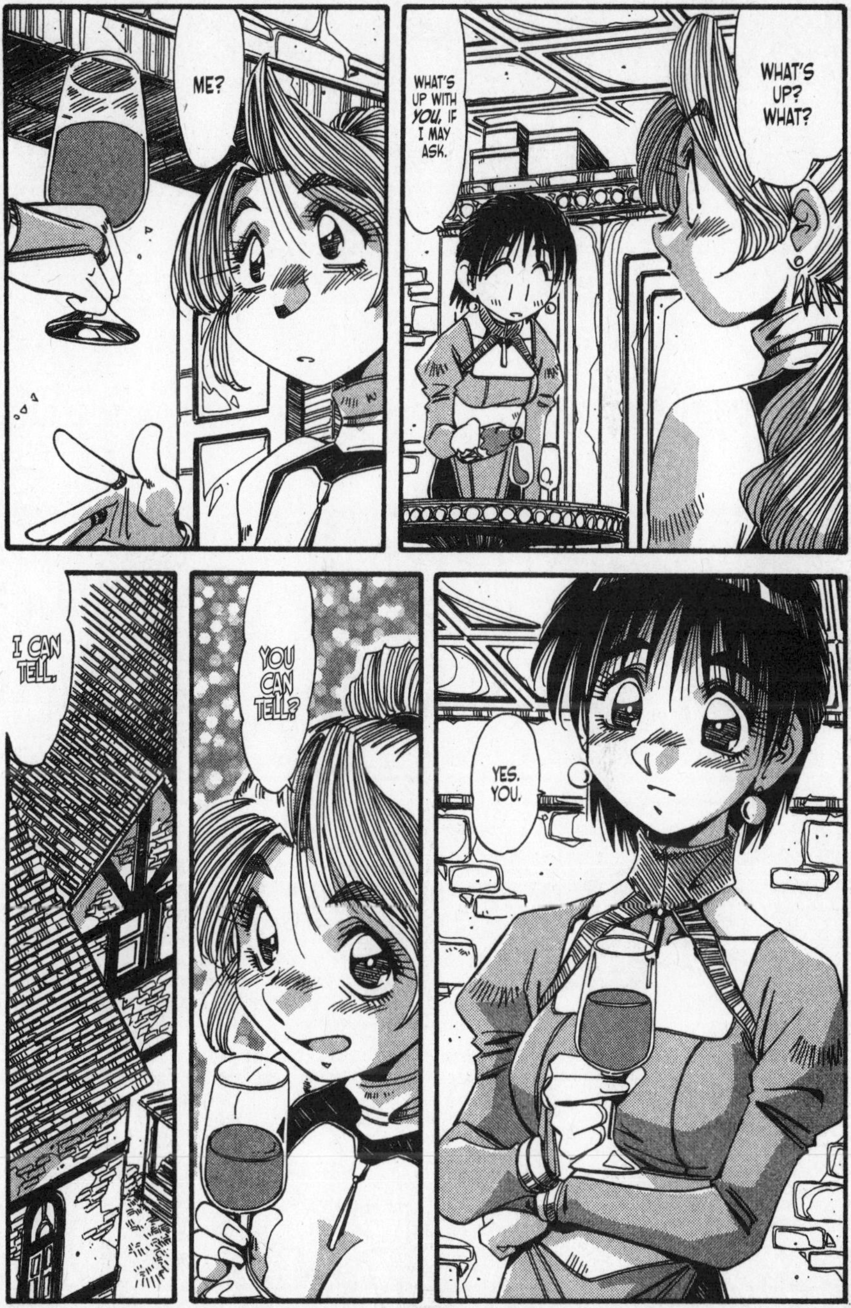
WHAT'S UP? WHAT?
WHAT'S UP WITH *YOU,* IF I MAY ASK.
ME?
YES. YOU.
YOU CAN TELL?
I CAN TELL.

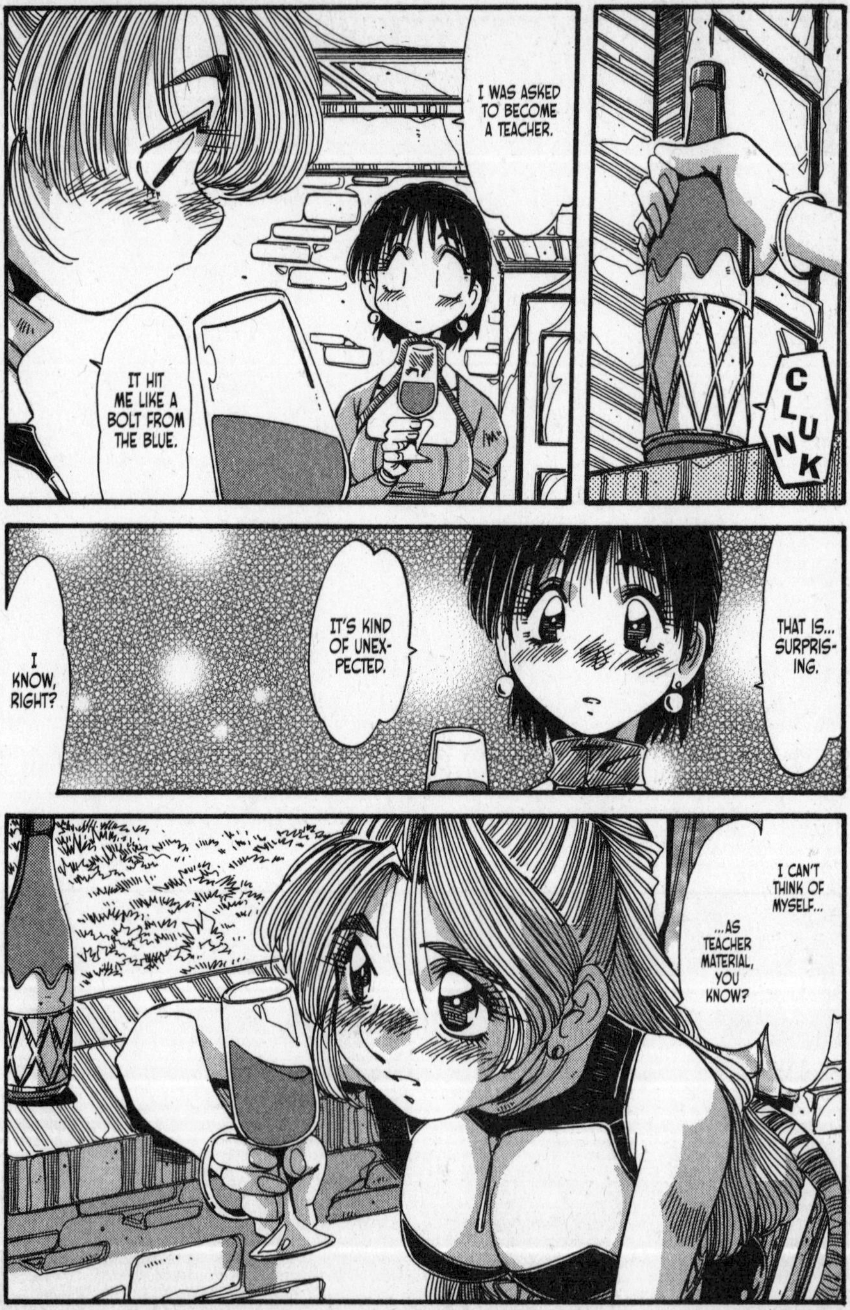
CLUNK
I WAS ASKED TO BECOME A TEACHER.
IT HIT ME LIKE A BOLT FROM THE BLUE.
THAT IS... SURPRIS-ING.
IT'S KIND OF UNEX-PECTED.
I KNOW, RIGHT?
I CAN'T THINK OF MYSELF...
...AS TEACHER MATERIAL, YOU KNOW?

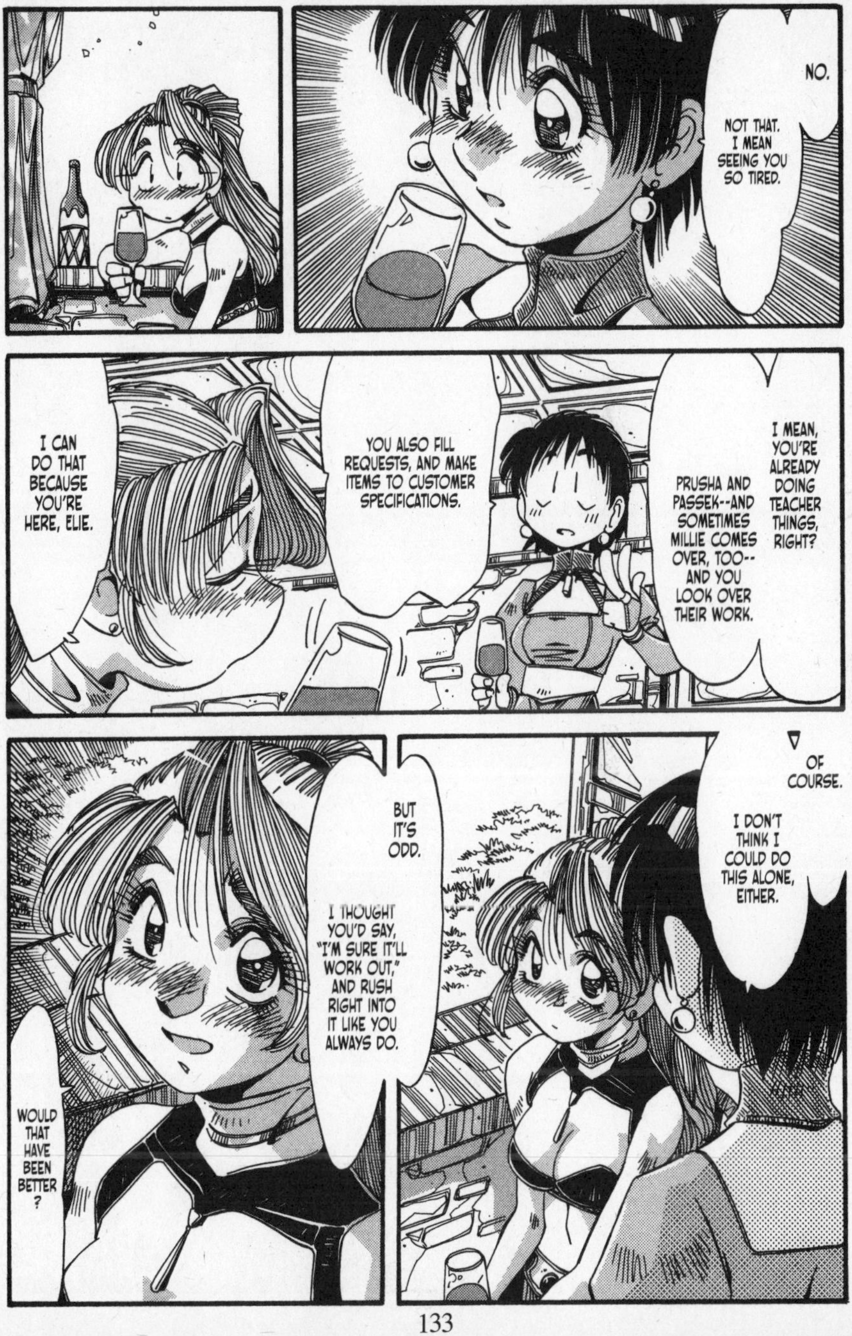
NO.
NOT THAT. I MEAN SEEING YOU SO TIRED.
I MEAN, YOU'RE ALREADY DOING TEACHER THINGS, RIGHT?
PRUSHA AND PASSEK--AND SOMETIMES MILLIE COMES OVER, TOO--AND YOU LOOK OVER THEIR WORK.
YOU ALSO FILL REQUESTS, AND MAKE ITEMS TO CUSTOMER SPECIFICATIONS.
I CAN DO THAT BECAUSE YOU'RE HERE, ELIE.
OF COURSE.
I DON'T THINK I COULD DO THIS ALONE, EITHER.
BUT IT'S ODD.
I THOUGHT YOU'D SAY, "I'M SURE IT'LL WORK OUT," AND RUSH RIGHT INTO IT LIKE YOU ALWAYS DO.
WOULD THAT HAVE BEEN BETTER?

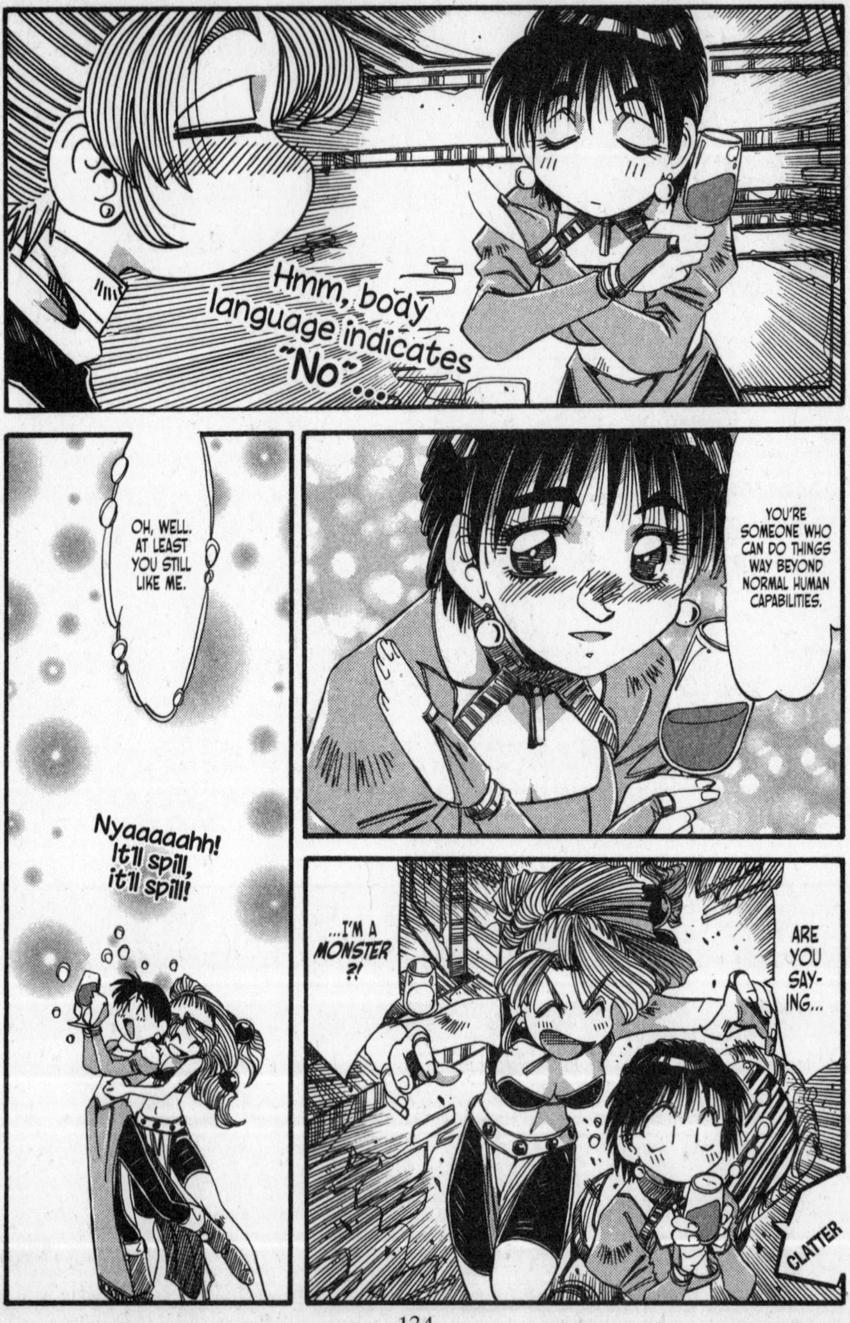
Hmm, body language indicates "No"...
YOU'RE SOMEONE WHO CAN DO THINGS WAY BEYOND NORMAL HUMAN CAPABILITIES.
ARE YOU SAY-ING...
...I'M A *MONSTER* ?!
CLATTER
OH, WELL. AT LEAST YOU STILL LIKE ME.
Nyaaaaahh! It'll spill, it'll spill!

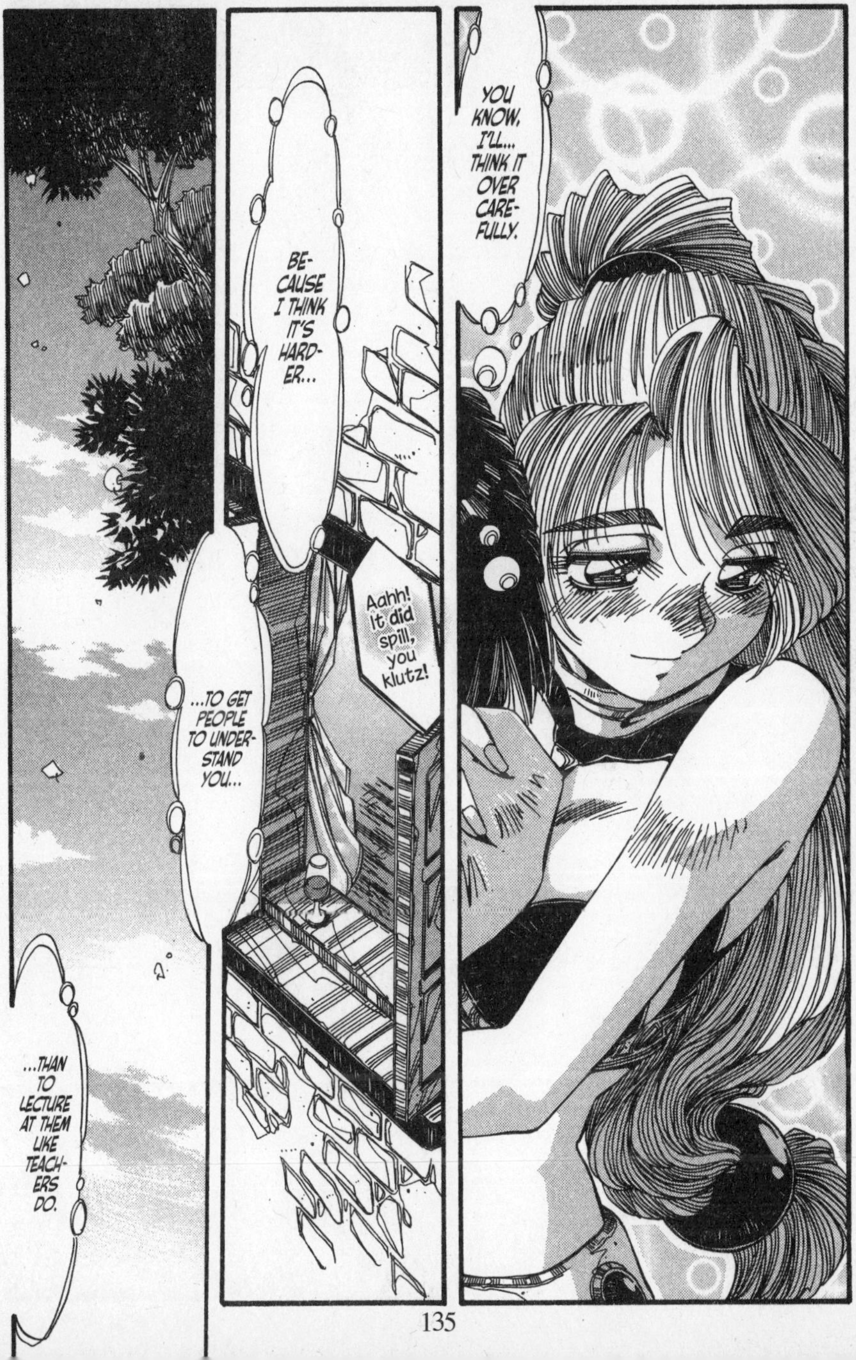
YOU KNOW, I'LL... THINK IT OVER CARE-FULLY.
BE-CAUSE I THINK IT'S HARD-ER...
Aahh! It did spill, you klutz!
...TO GET PEOPLE TO UNDER-STAND YOU...
...THAN TO LECTURE AT THEM LIKE TEACH-ERS DO.

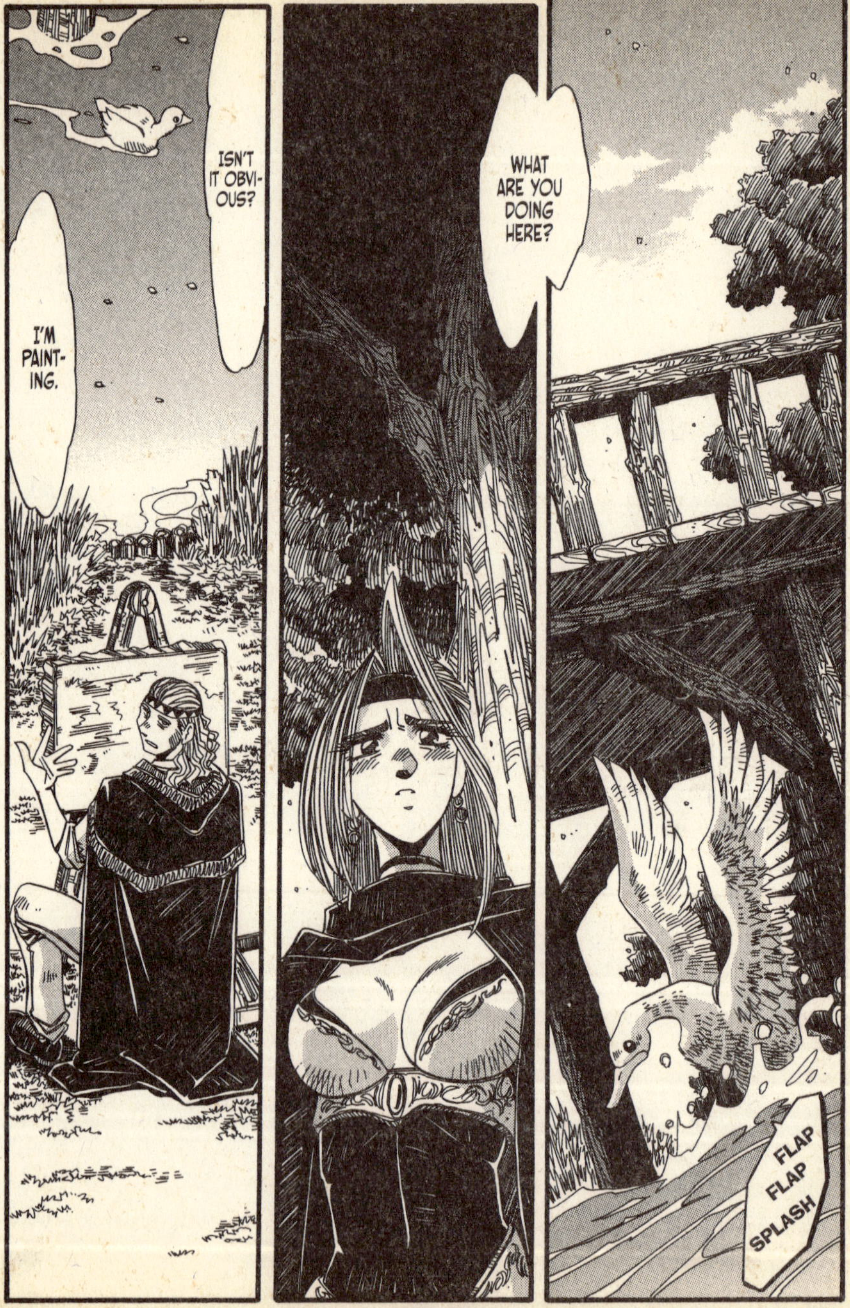
WHAT ARE YOU DOING HERE?
FLAP FLAP SPLASH
ISN'T IT OBVI-OUS?
I'M PAINT-ING.

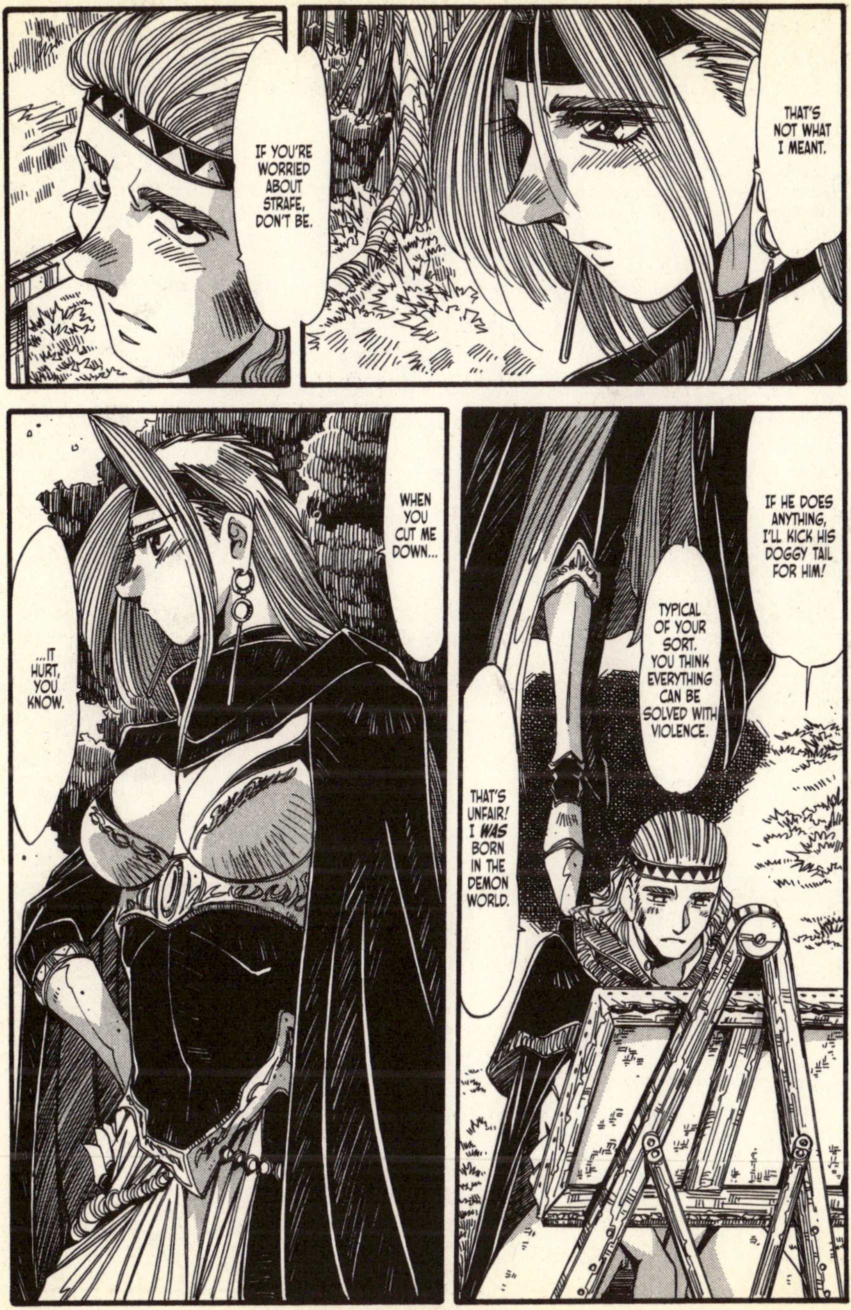
THAT'S NOT WHAT I MEANT.
IF YOU'RE WORRIED ABOUT STRAFE, DON'T BE.
IF HE DOES ANYTHING, I'LL KICK HIS DOGGY TAIL FOR HIM!
TYPICAL OF YOUR SORT. YOU THINK EVERYTHING CAN BE SOLVED WITH VIOLENCE.
THAT'S UNFAIR! I ***WAS*** BORN IN THE DEMON WORLD.
WHEN YOU CUT ME DOWN...
...IT HURT, YOU KNOW.

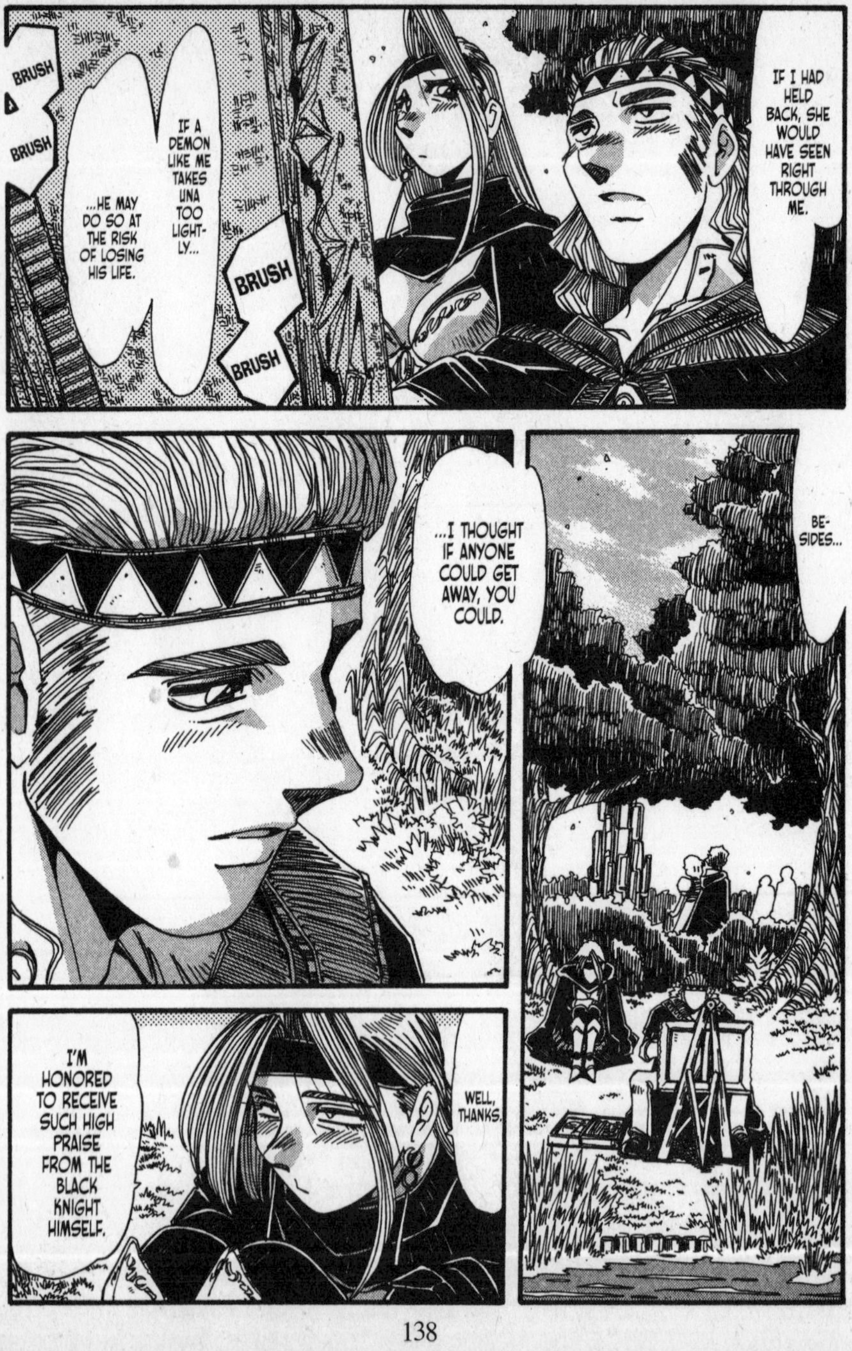
IF I HAD HELD BACK, SHE WOULD HAVE SEEN RIGHT THROUGH ME.
BRUSH
BRUSH
IF A DEMON LIKE ME TAKES UNA TOO LIGHTLY...
...HE MAY DO SO AT THE RISK OF LOSING HIS LIFE.
BRUSH
BRUSH
BE-SIDES...
...I THOUGHT IF ANYONE COULD GET AWAY, YOU COULD.
WELL, THANKS.
I'M HONORED TO RECEIVE SUCH HIGH PRAISE FROM THE BLACK KNIGHT HIMSELF.

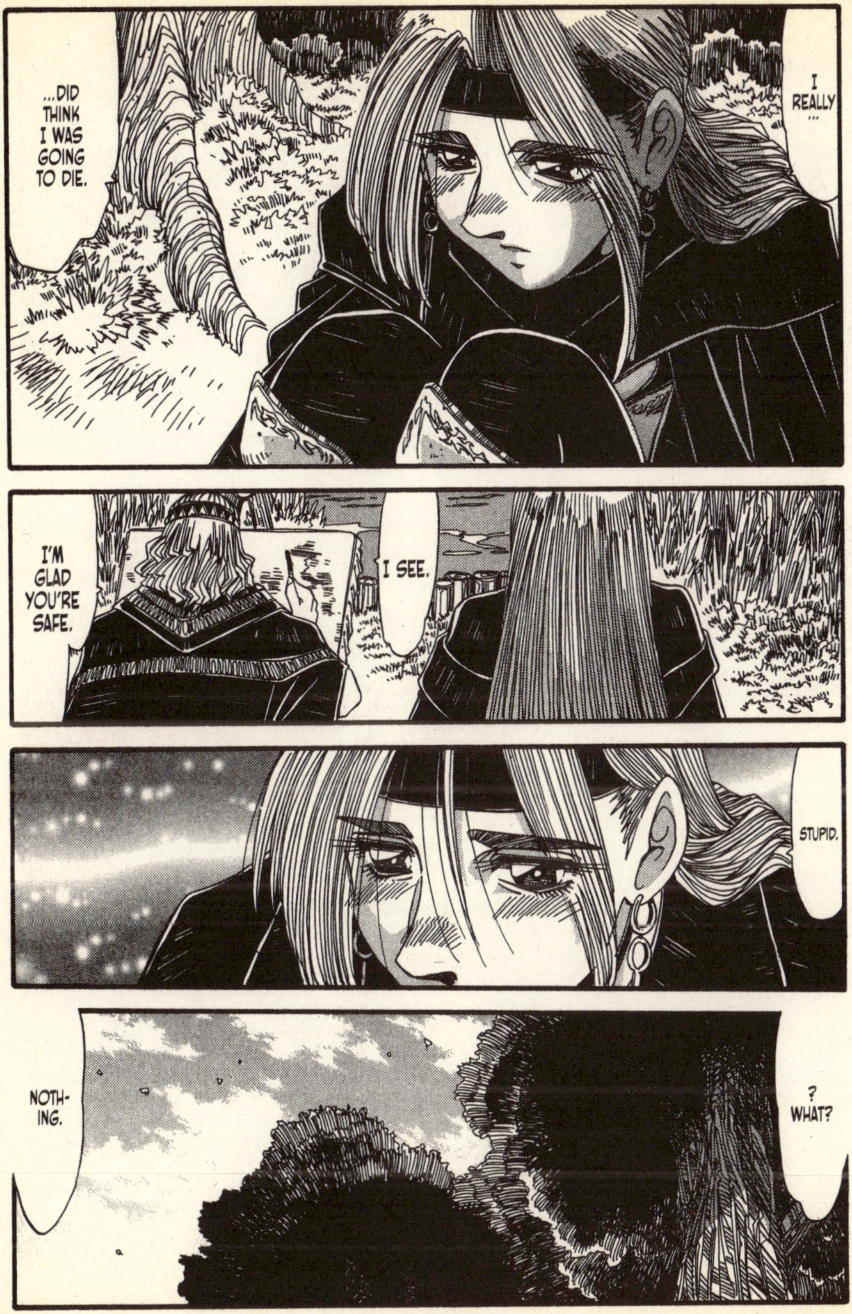
I REALLY...
...DID THINK I WAS GOING TO DIE.
I SEE.
I'M GLAD YOU'RE SAFE.
STUPID.
? WHAT?
NOTH-ING.

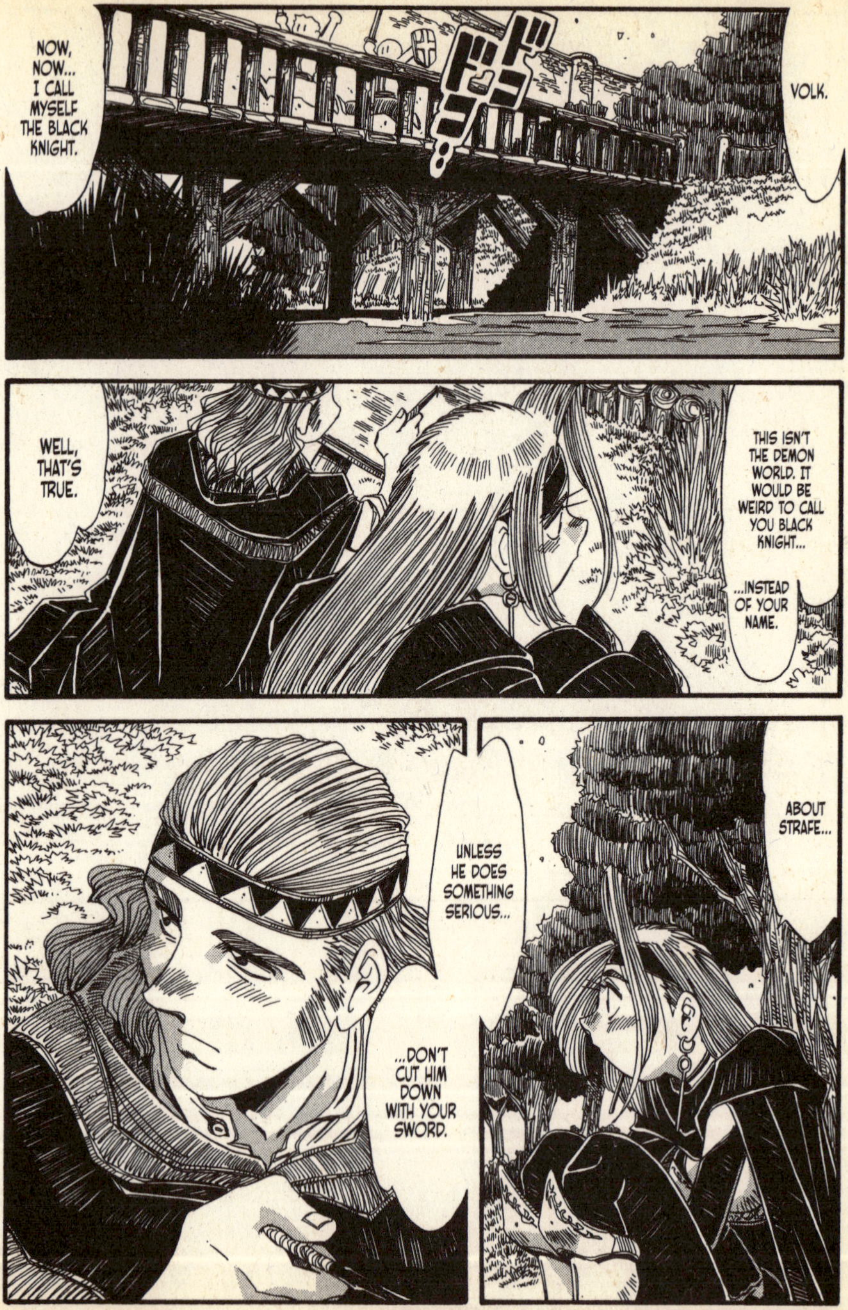
VOLK.
NOW, NOW... I CALL MYSELF THE BLACK KNIGHT.
THIS ISN'T THE DEMON WORLD. IT WOULD BE WEIRD TO CALL YOU BLACK KNIGHT...
...INSTEAD OF YOUR NAME.
WELL, THAT'S TRUE.
ABOUT STRAFE...
UNLESS HE DOES SOMETHING SERIOUS...
...DON'T CUT HIM DOWN WITH YOUR SWORD.

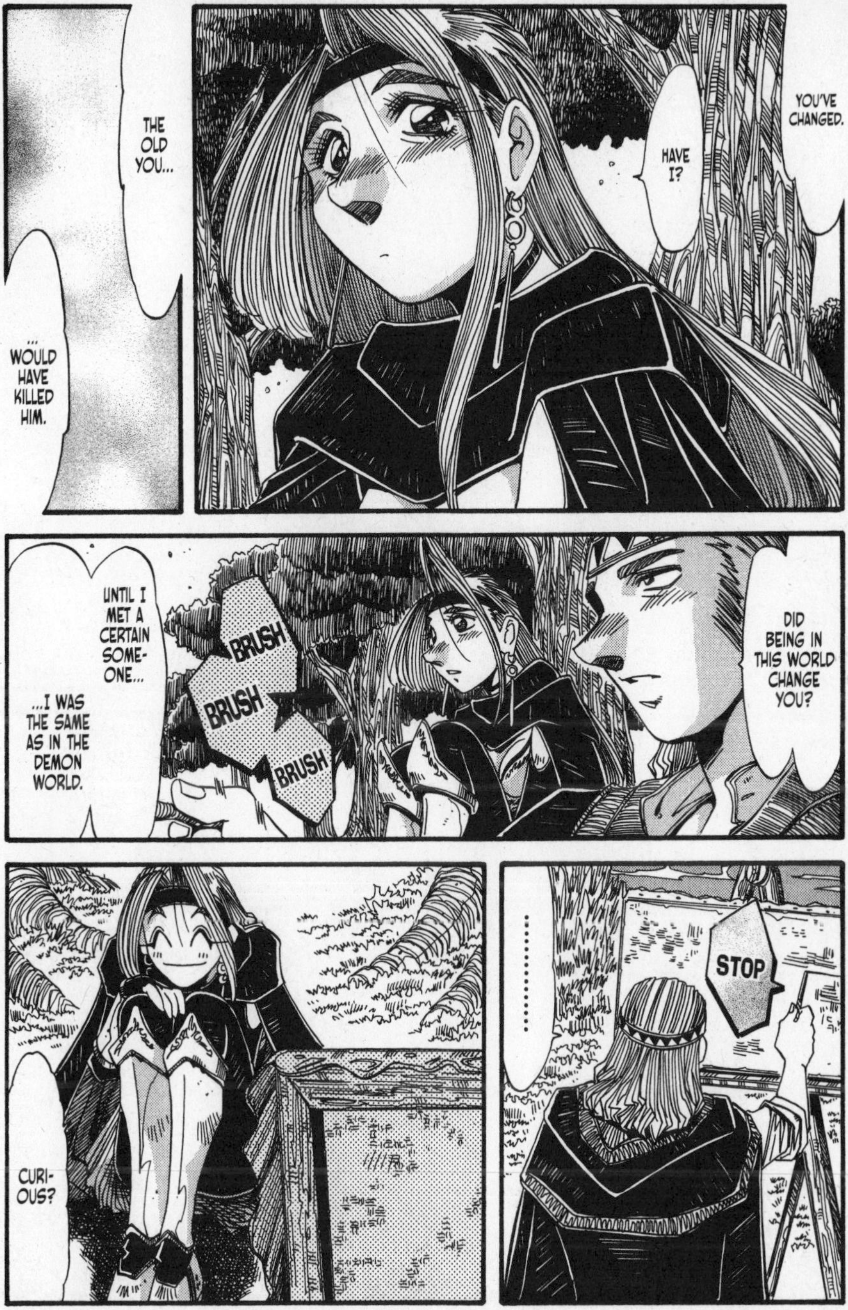
YOU'VE CHANGED.
HAVE I?
THE OLD YOU...
...WOULD HAVE KILLED HIM.
DID BEING IN THIS WORLD CHANGE YOU?
BRUSH
BRUSH
BRUSH
UNTIL I MET A CERTAIN SOME-ONE...
...I WAS THE SAME AS IN THE DEMON WORLD.
STOP
......
CURI-OUS?

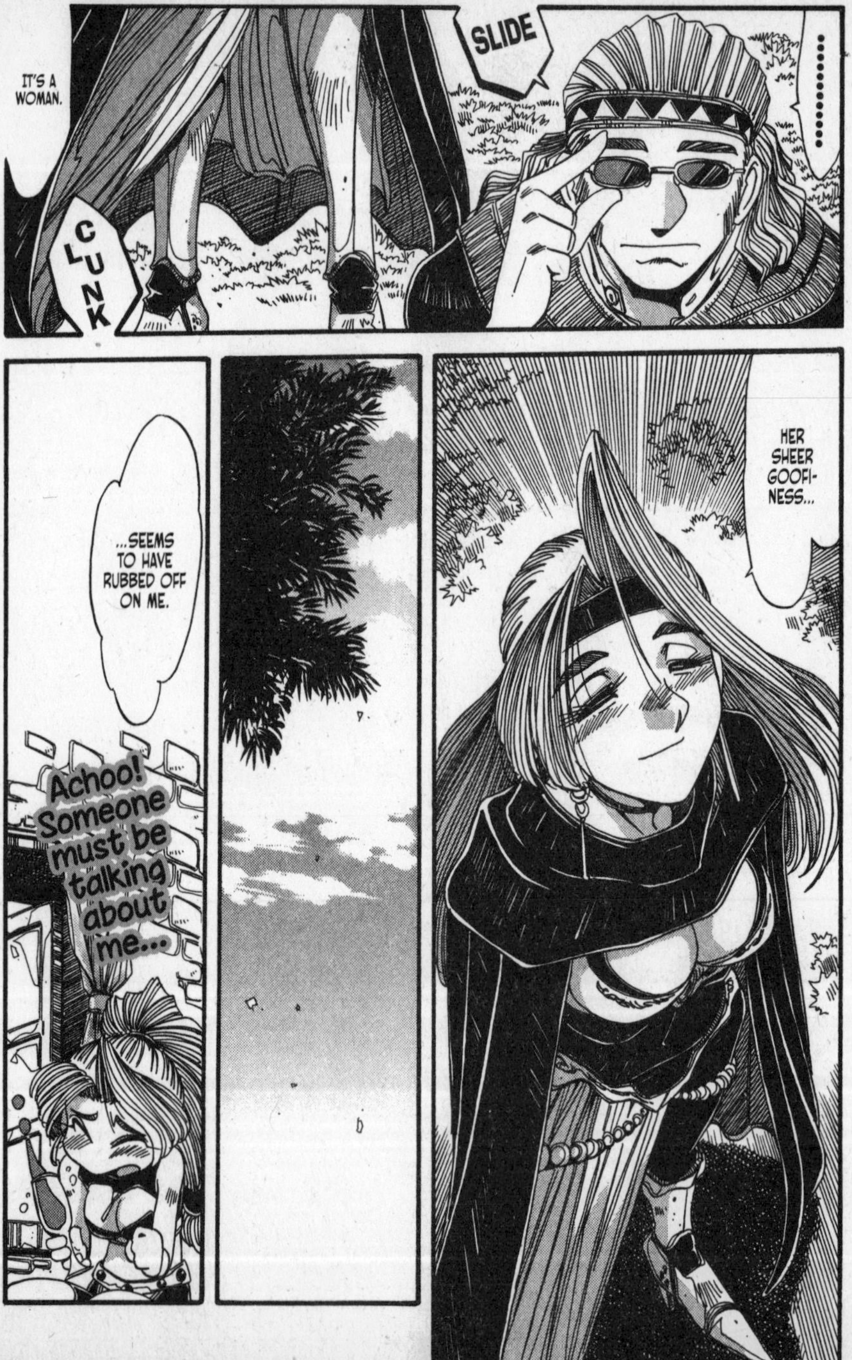
SLIDE
......
IT'S A WOMAN.
CLUNK
HER SHEER GOOFINESS...
...SEEMS TO HAVE RUBBED OFF ON ME.
Achoo! Someone must be talking about me...

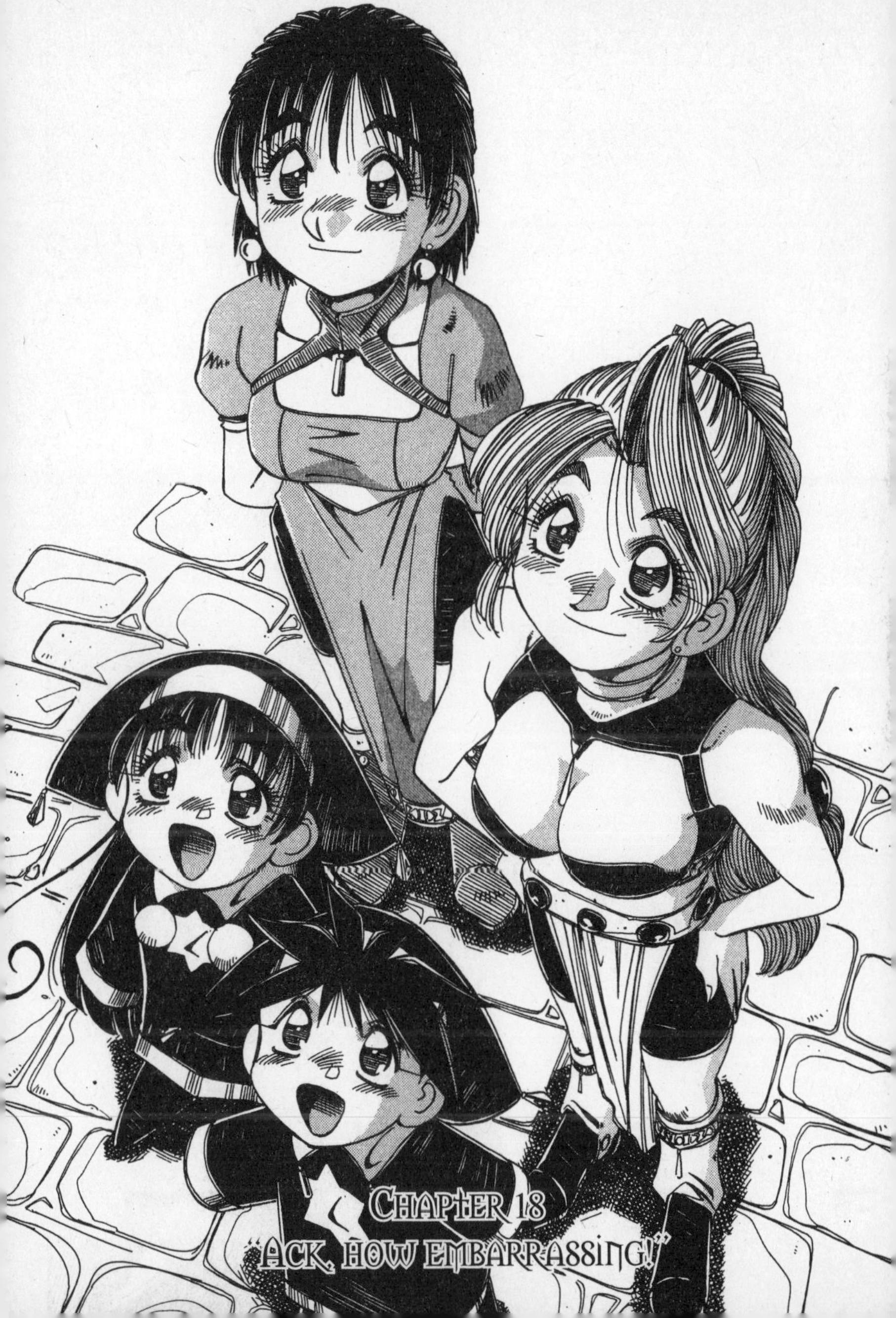
Chapter 18
"Ack, How Embarrassing!"

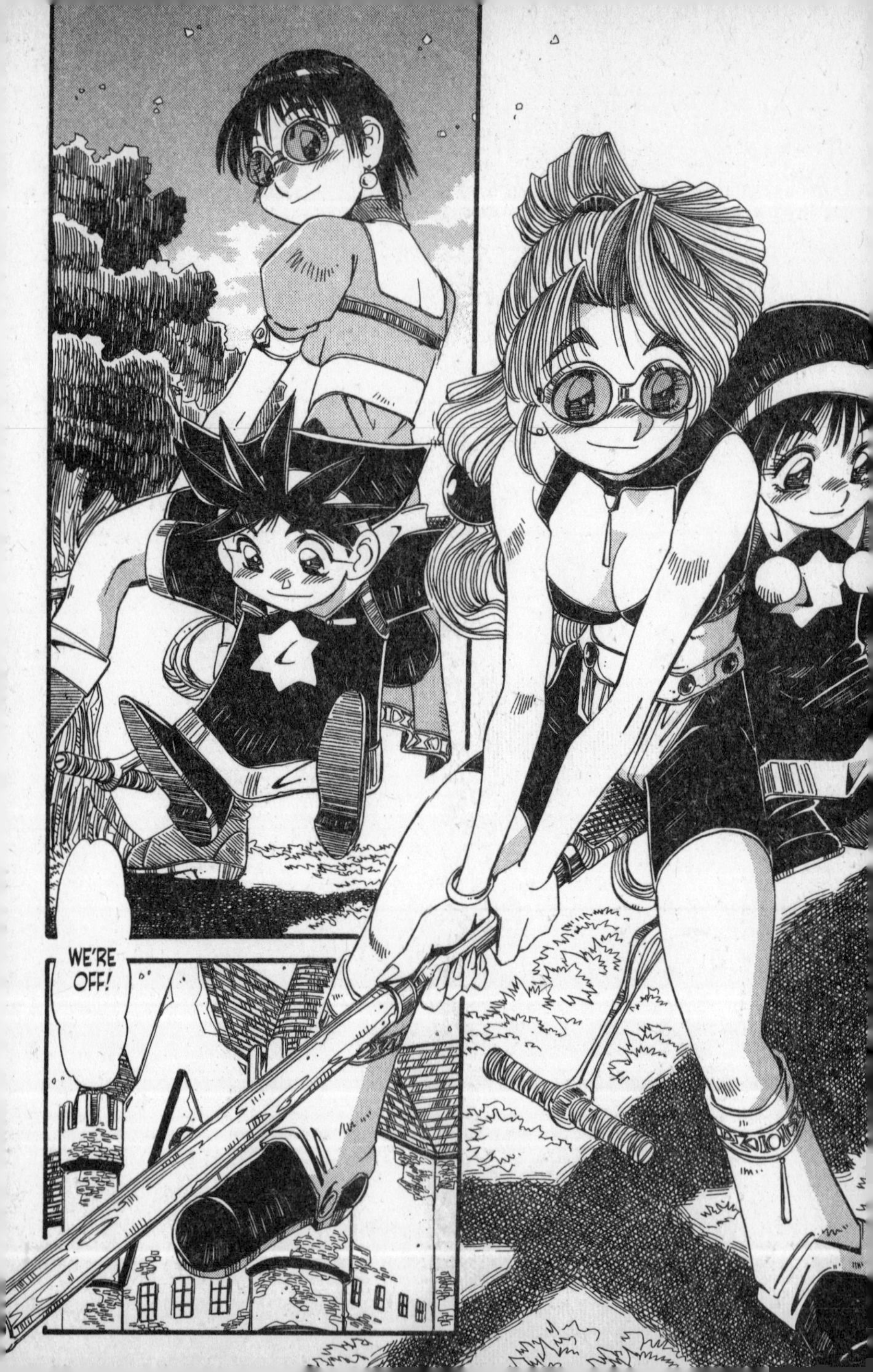
WE'RE OFF!

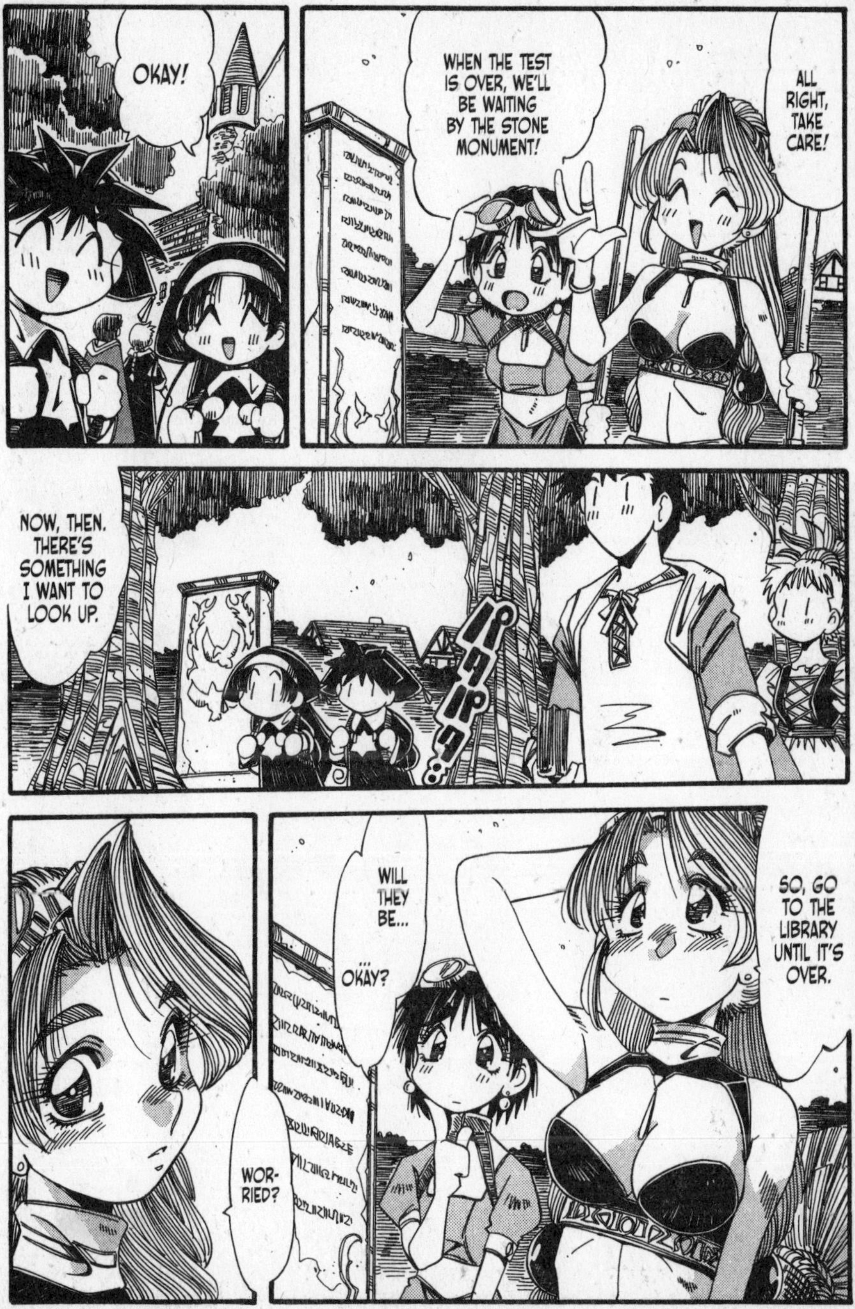
ALL RIGHT, TAKE CARE!
WHEN THE TEST IS OVER, WE'LL BE WAITING BY THE STONE MONUMENT!
OKAY!
NOW, THEN. THERE'S SOMETHING I WANT TO LOOK UP.
SO, GO TO THE LIBRARY UNTIL IT'S OVER.
WILL THEY BE...
...OKAY?
WOR-RIED?

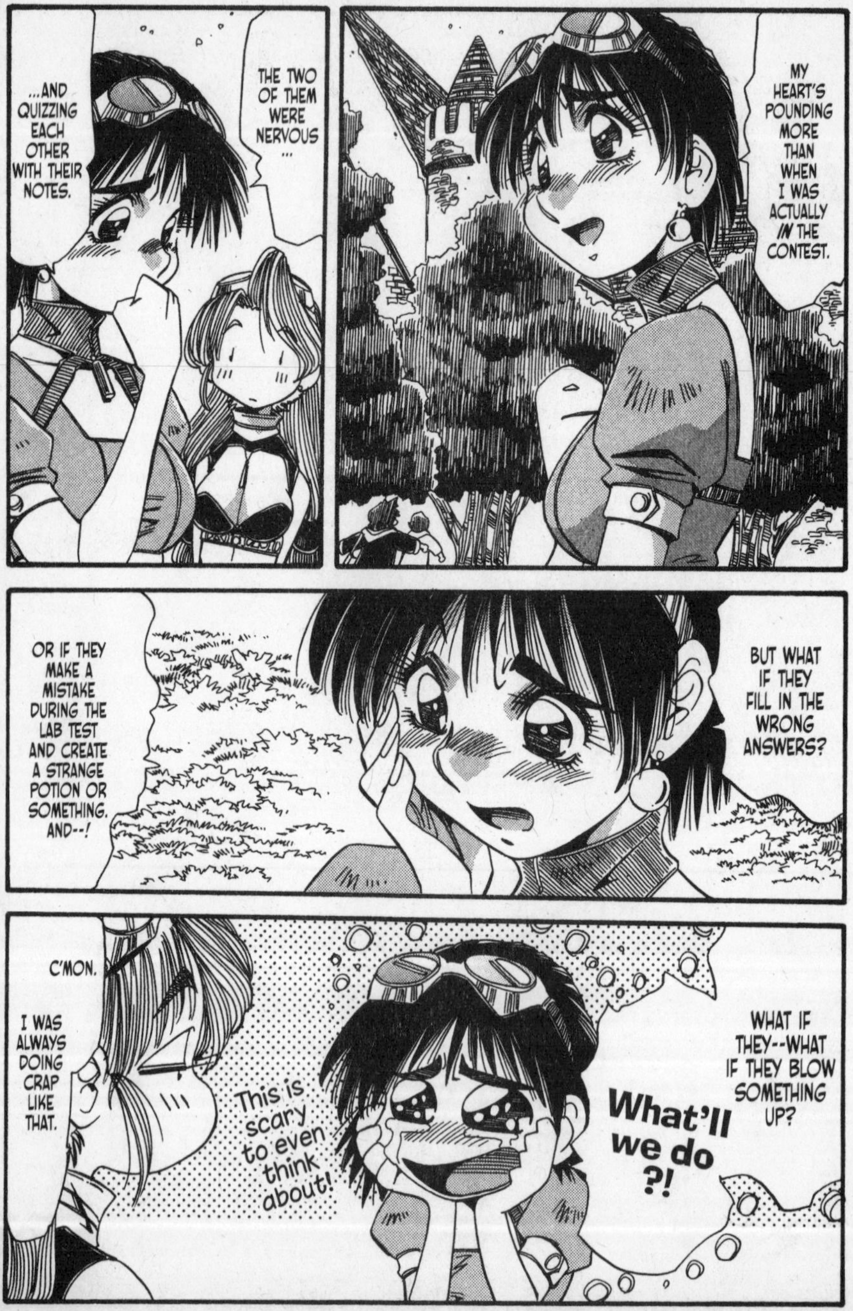
MY HEART'S POUNDING MORE THAN WHEN I WAS ACTUALLY *IN* THE CONTEST.
THE TWO OF THEM WERE NERVOUS ...
...AND QUIZZING EACH OTHER WITH THEIR NOTES.
BUT WHAT IF THEY FILL IN THE WRONG ANSWERS?
OR IF THEY MAKE A MISTAKE DURING THE LAB TEST AND CREATE A STRANGE POTION OR SOMETHING. AND--!
WHAT IF THEY--WHAT IF THEY BLOW SOMETHING UP?
What'll we do ?!
This is scary to even think about!
C'MON.
I WAS ALWAYS DOING CRAP LIKE THAT.

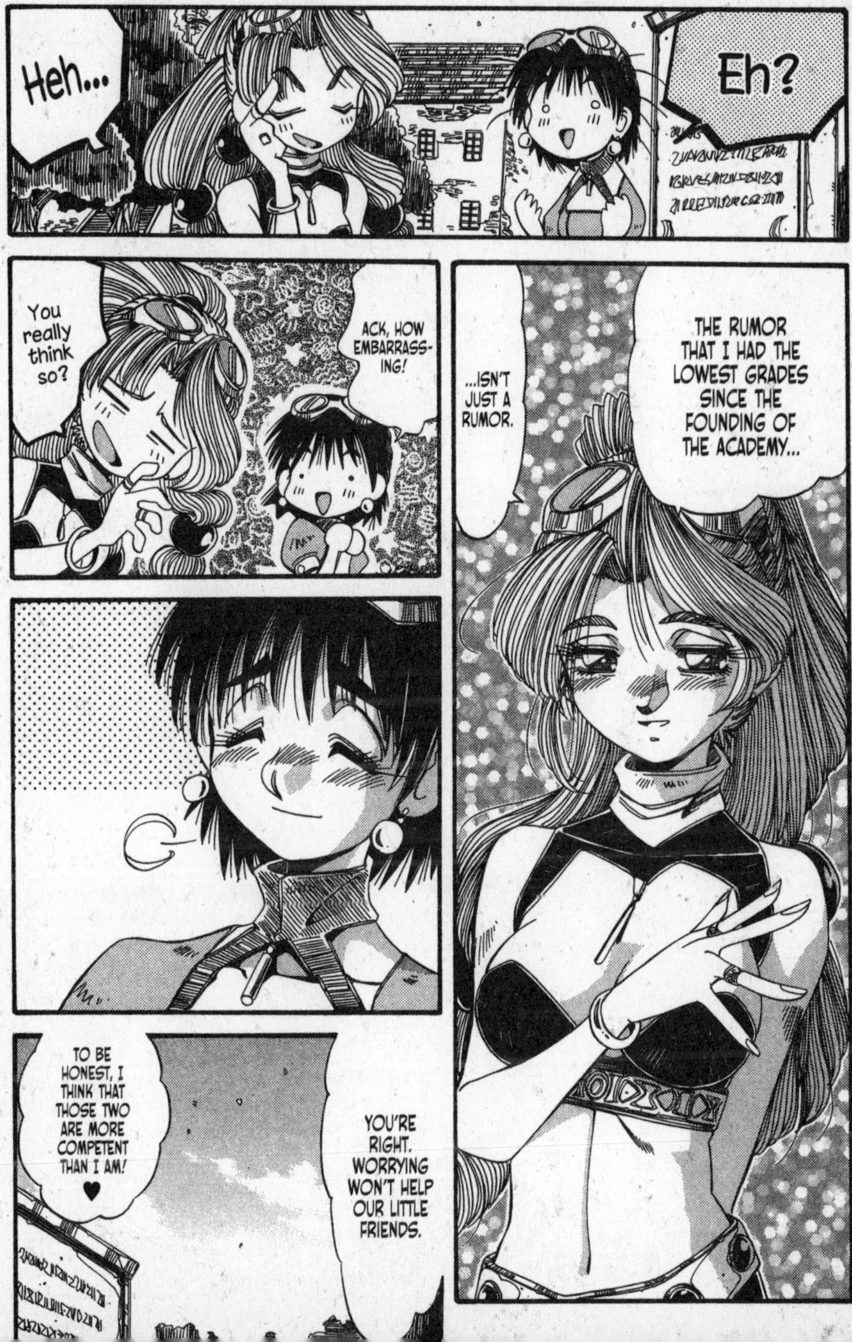
Eh?
Heh...
THE RUMOR THAT I HAD THE LOWEST GRADES SINCE THE FOUNDING OF THE ACADEMY...
...ISN'T JUST A RUMOR.
ACK, HOW EMBARRASS-ING!
You really think so?
YOU'RE RIGHT. WORRYING WON'T HELP OUR LITTLE FRIENDS.
TO BE HONEST, I THINK THAT THOSE TWO ARE MORE COMPETENT THAN I AM! ♥

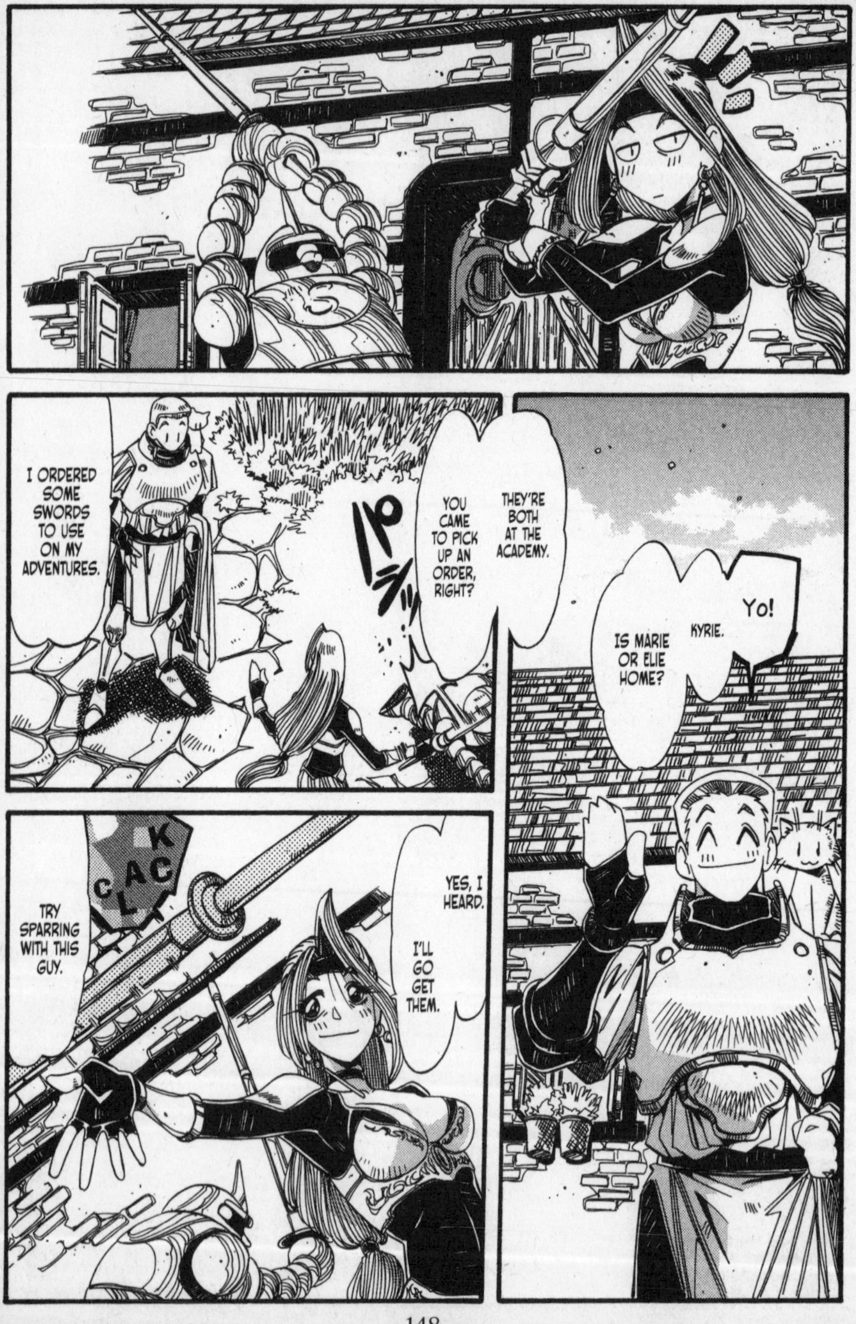
Yo!
KYRIE.
IS MARIE OR ELIE HOME?
THEY'RE BOTH AT THE ACADEMY.
YOU CAME TO PICK UP AN ORDER, RIGHT?
I ORDERED SOME SWORDS TO USE ON MY ADVENTURES.
YES, I HEARD.
I'LL GO GET THEM.
CLACK
TRY SPARRING WITH THIS GUY.

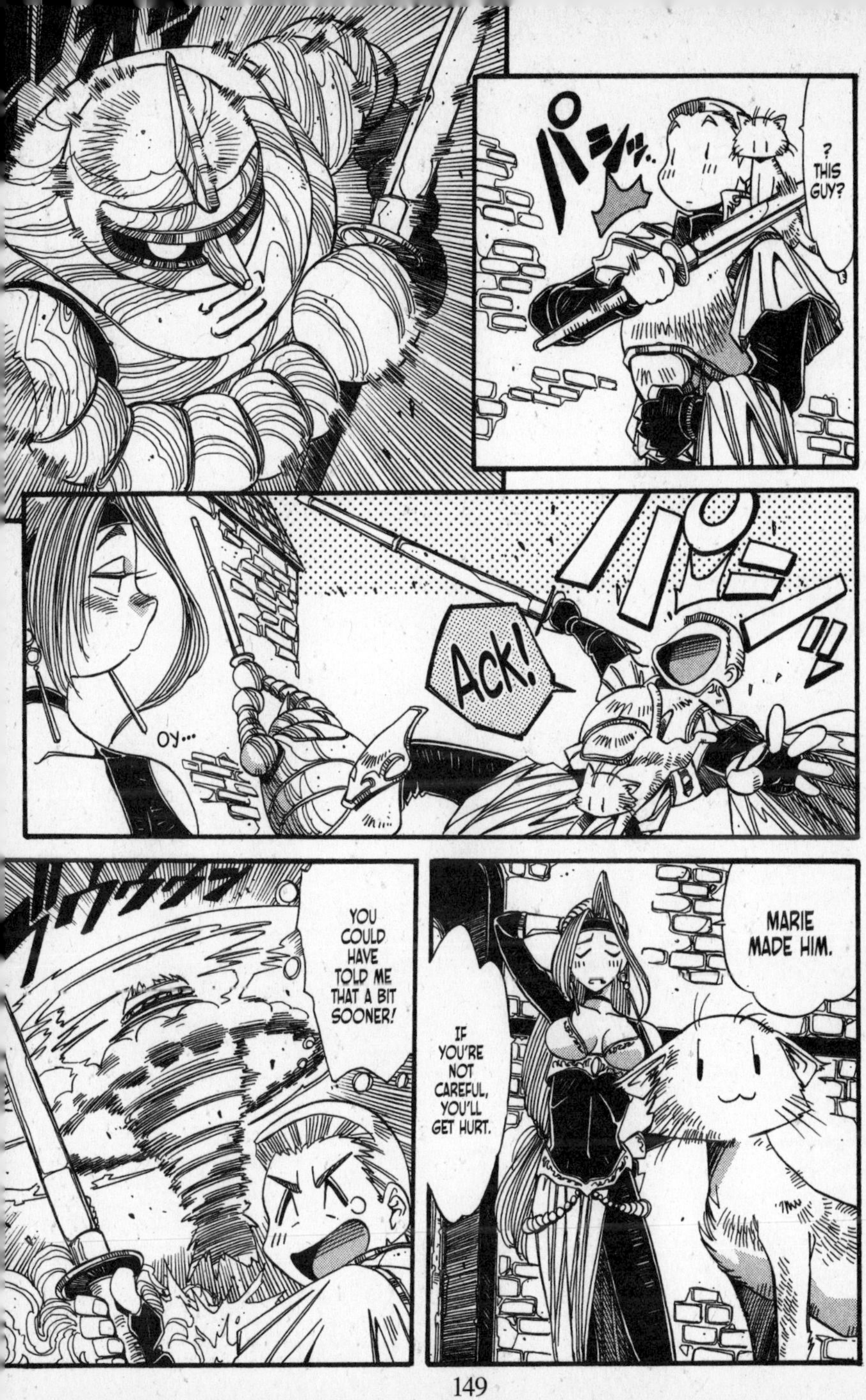
? THIS GUY?
ACK!
OY...
MARIE MADE HIM.
IF YOU'RE NOT CAREFUL, YOU'LL GET HURT.
YOU COULD HAVE TOLD ME THAT A BIT SOONER!

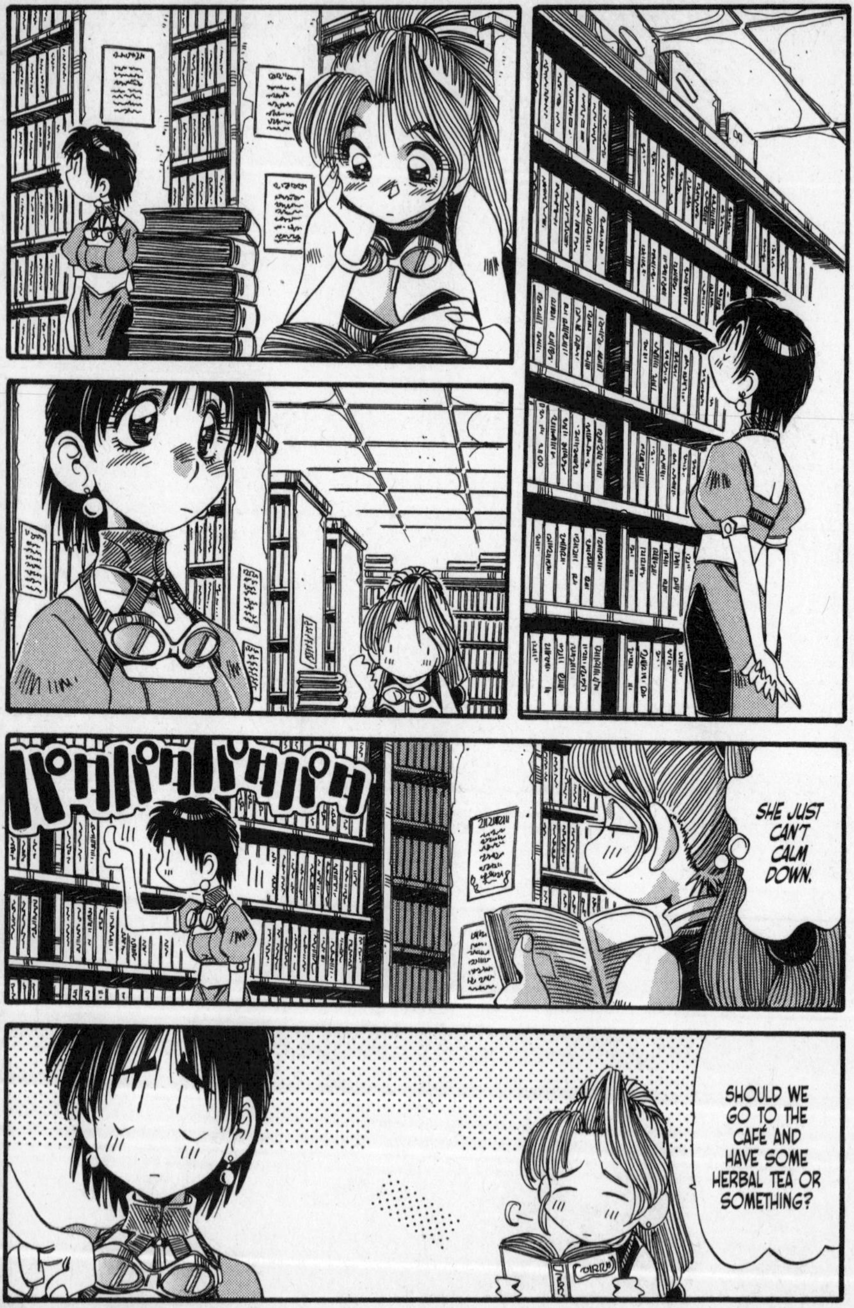
SHE JUST CAN'T CALM DOWN.
SHOULD WE GO TO THE CAFÉ AND HAVE SOME HERBAL TEA OR SOMETHING?

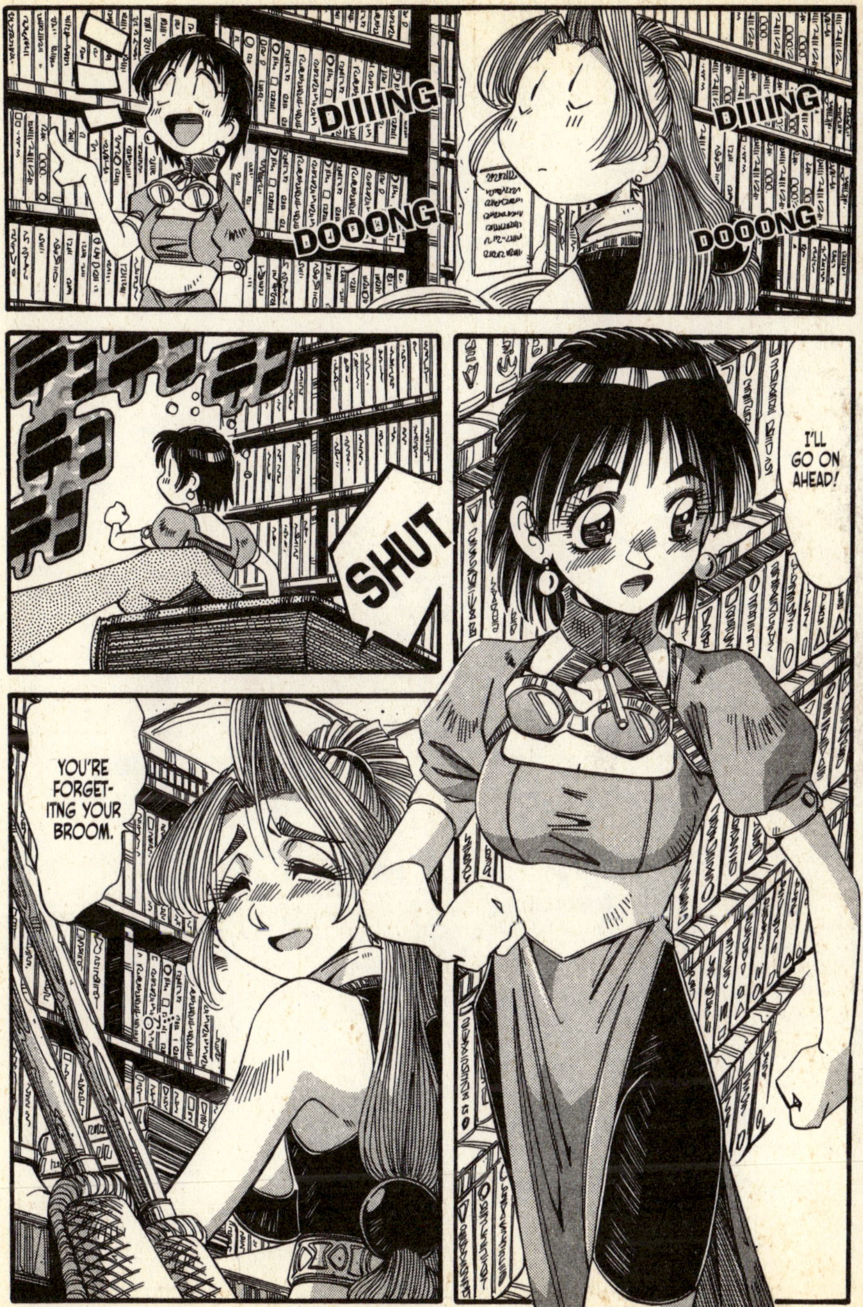
DIIIING
DOOONG
DIIIING
DOOONG
I'LL GO ON AHEAD!
SHUT
YOU'RE FORGET-ITNG YOUR BROOM.

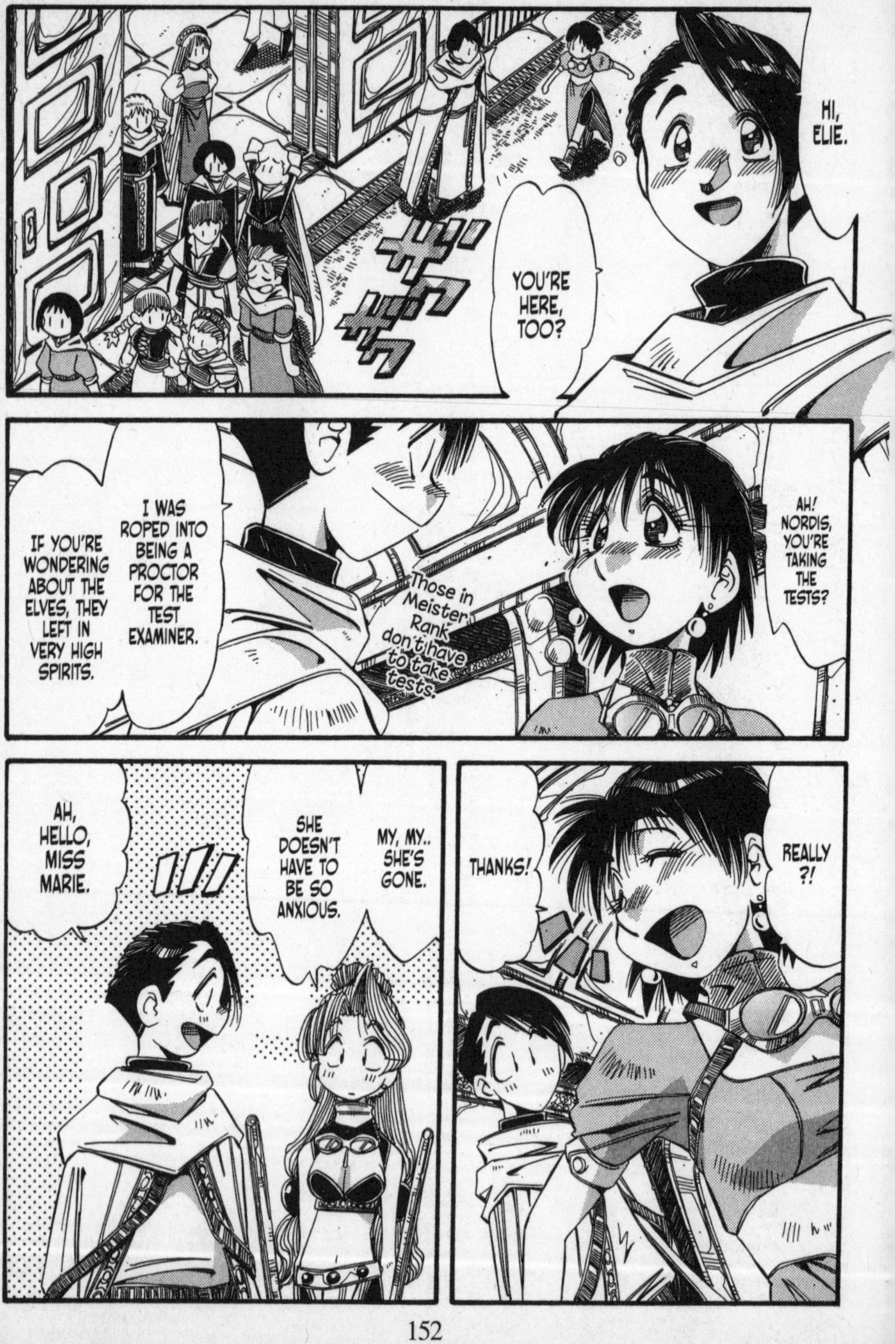
HI, ELIE.
YOU'RE HERE, TOO?
AH! NORDIS, YOU'RE TAKING THE TESTS?
Those in Meister Rank don't have to take tests.
I WAS ROPED INTO BEING A PROCTOR FOR THE TEST EXAMINER.
IF YOU'RE WONDERING ABOUT THE ELVES, THEY LEFT IN VERY HIGH SPIRITS.
REALLY?!
THANKS!
MY, MY.. SHE'S GONE.
SHE DOESN'T HAVE TO BE SO ANXIOUS.
AH, HELLO, MISS MARIE.

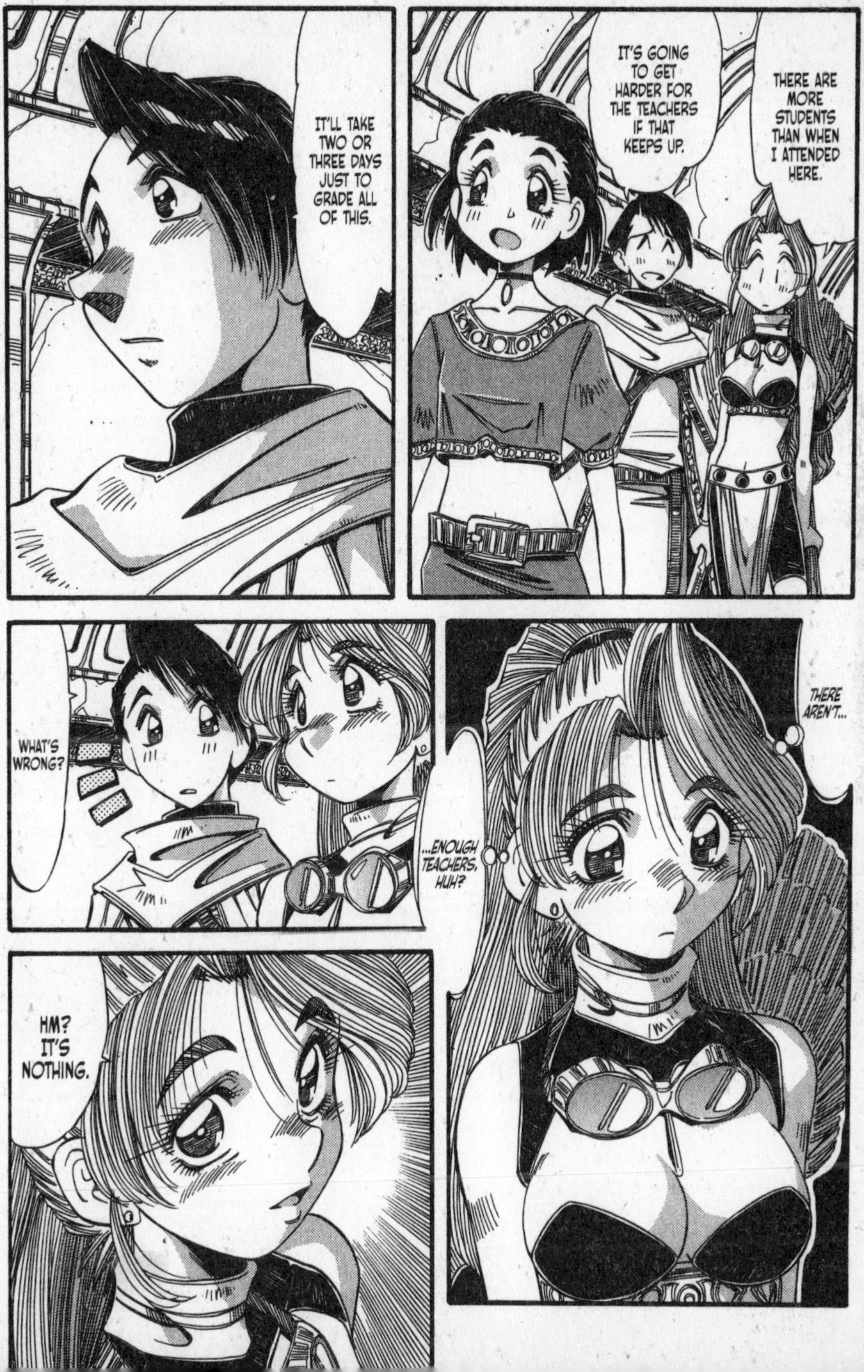
THERE ARE MORE STUDENTS THAN WHEN I ATTENDED HERE.
IT'S GOING TO GET HARDER FOR THE TEACHERS IF THAT KEEPS UP.
IT'LL TAKE TWO OR THREE DAYS JUST TO GRADE ALL OF THIS.
THERE AREN'T...
...ENOUGH TEACHERS, HUH?
WHAT'S WRONG?
HM? IT'S NOTHING.

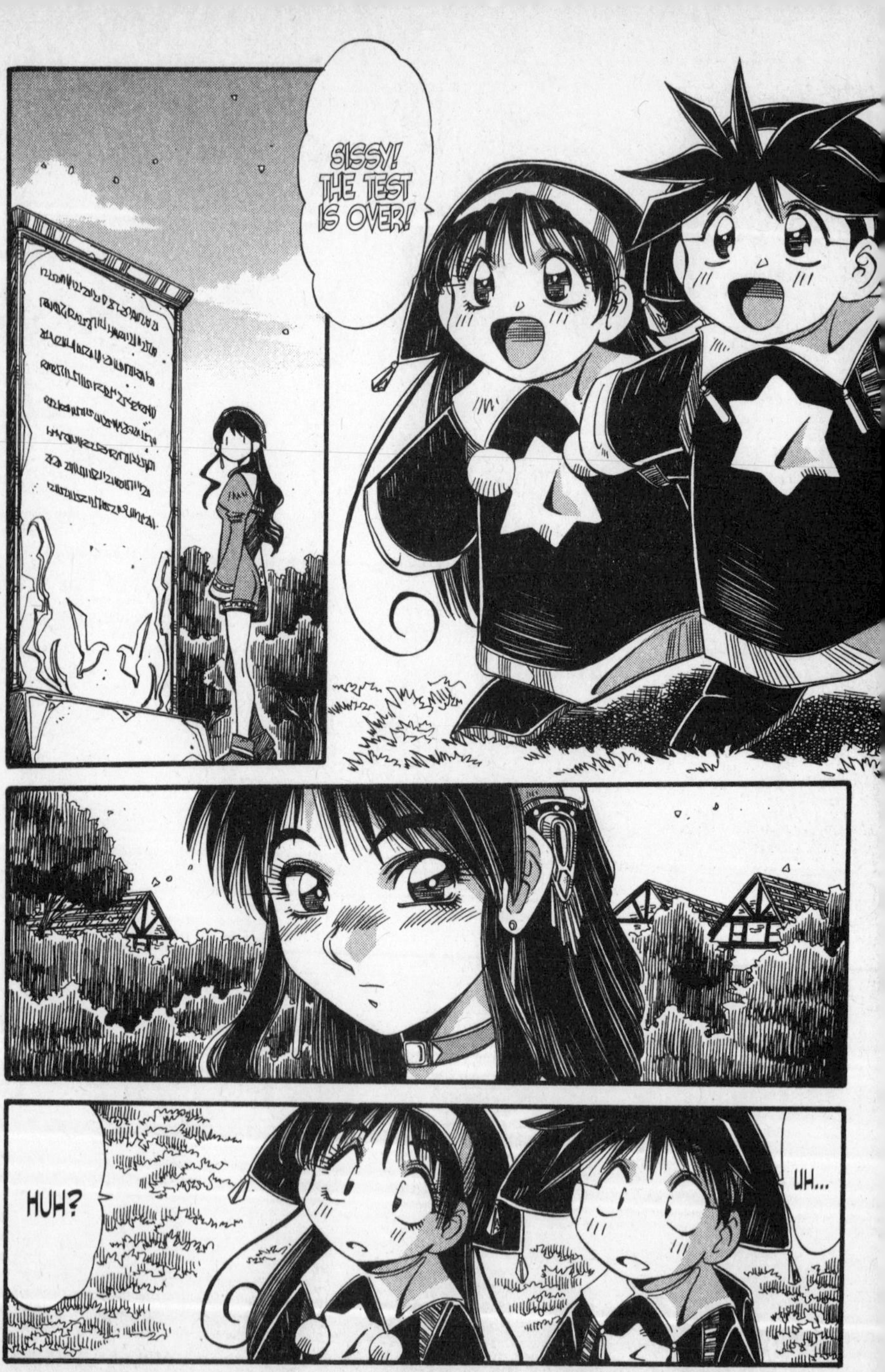
SISSY! THE TEST IS OVER!
UH...
HUH?

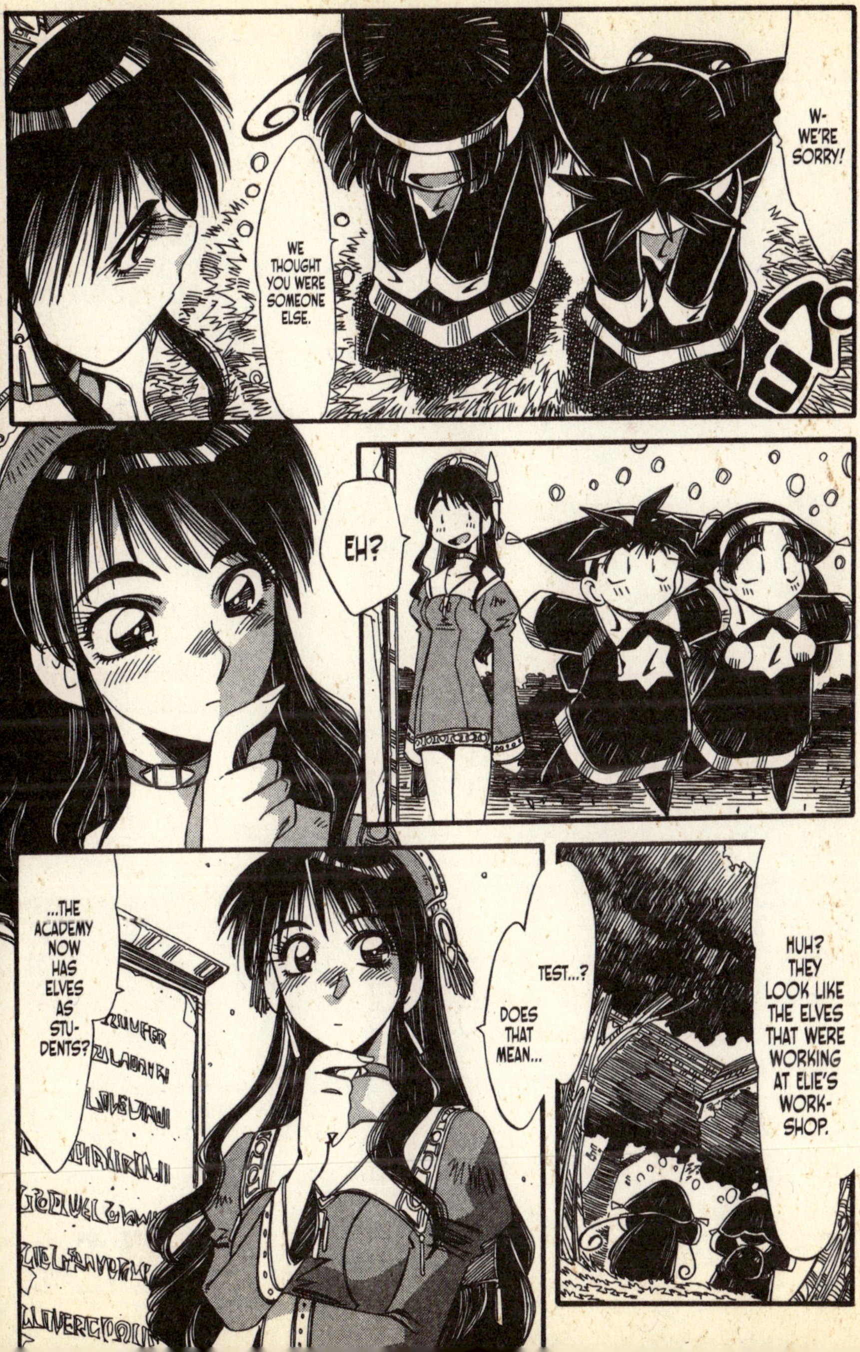
W- WE'RE SORRY!
WE THOUGHT YOU WERE SOMEONE ELSE.
EH?
HUH? THEY LOOK LIKE THE ELVES THAT WERE WORKING AT ELIE'S WORK- SHOP.
TEST...?
DOES THAT MEAN...
...THE ACADEMY NOW HAS ELVES AS STU- DENTS?

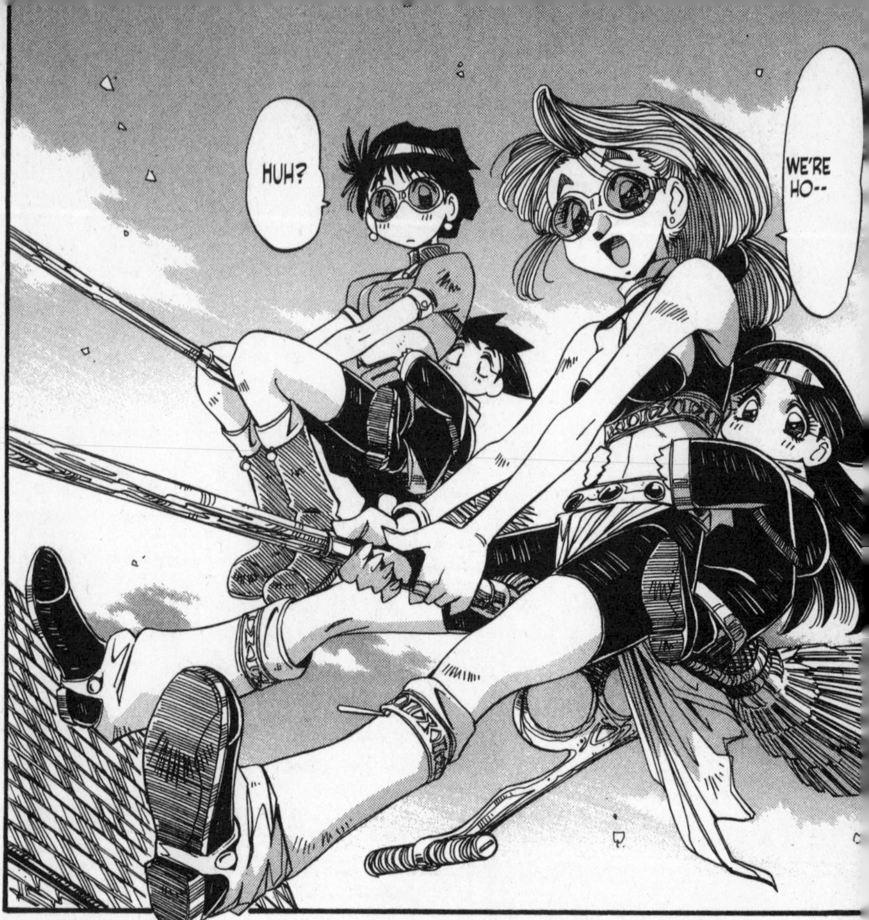
WE'RE HO--
HUH?

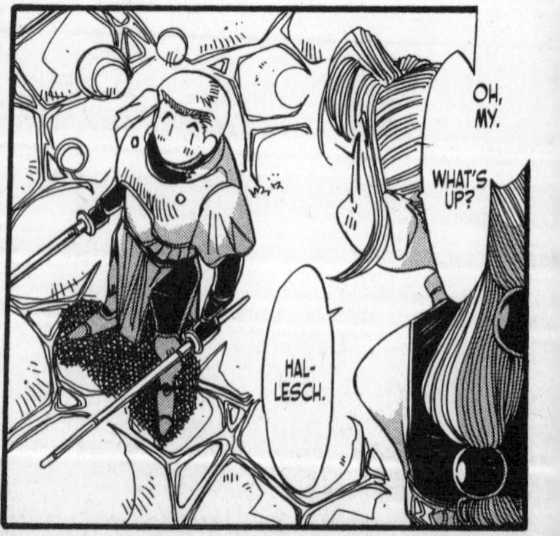
OH, MY.
WHAT'S UP?
HAL-LESCH.

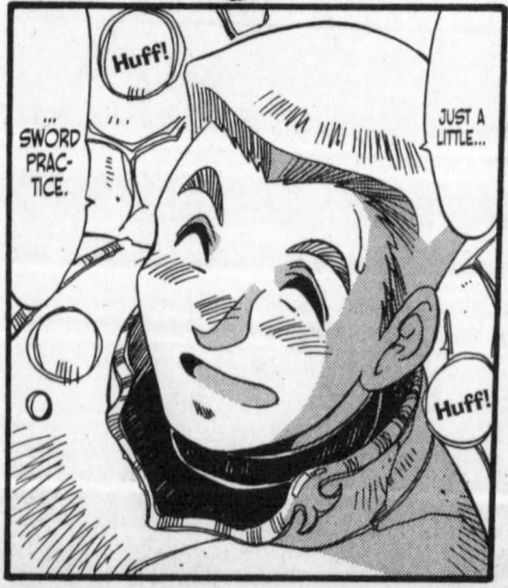
Huff!
JUST A LITTLE...
...SWORD PRAC-TICE.
Huff!

I HEAR...
...YOU MADE THIS CREATURE, MARIE?
Huff! Huff!
HE'S PRETTY TOUGH.
NNN, THEORETICALLY, HE'S A PERPETUAL MOTION MACHINE...
...AND WILL COME AT HIS OPPONENT UNTIL THE OTHER PERSON DROPS DEAD WITH EXHAUSTION.
Whaaa?!
YOW!
ONCE AGAIN, INFORMATION I COULD HAVE USED EARLIER.
OOPS.
DID I FORGET TO TELL YOU THAT?

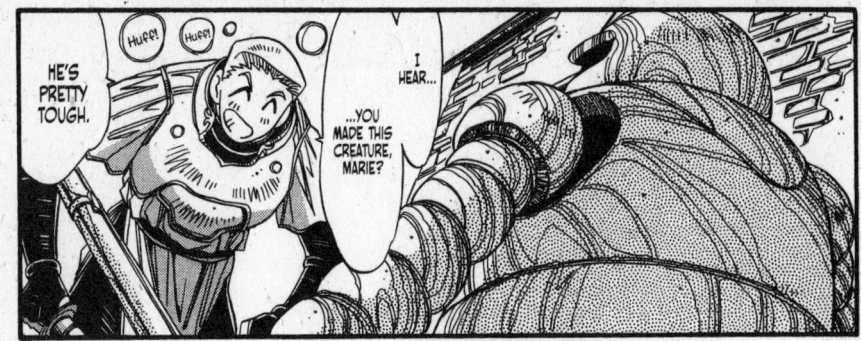

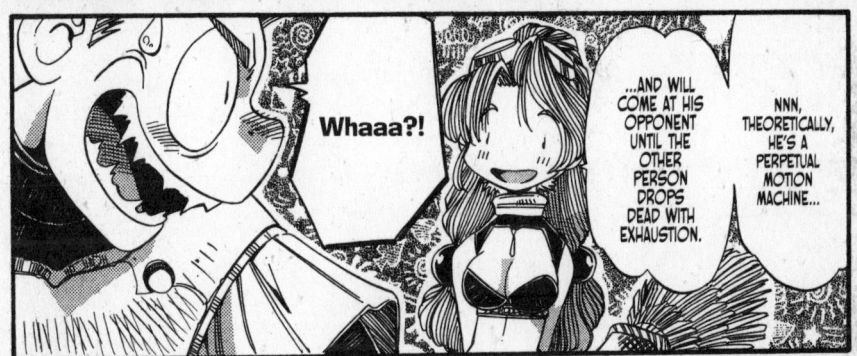

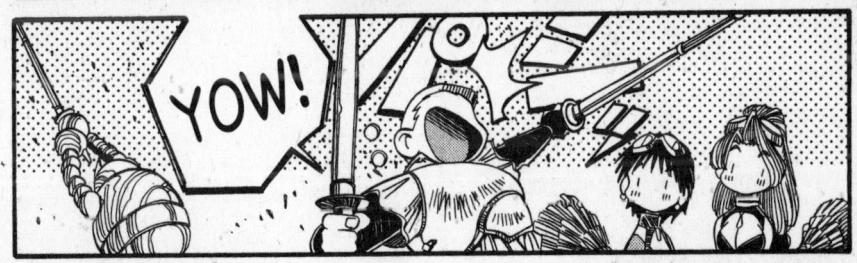

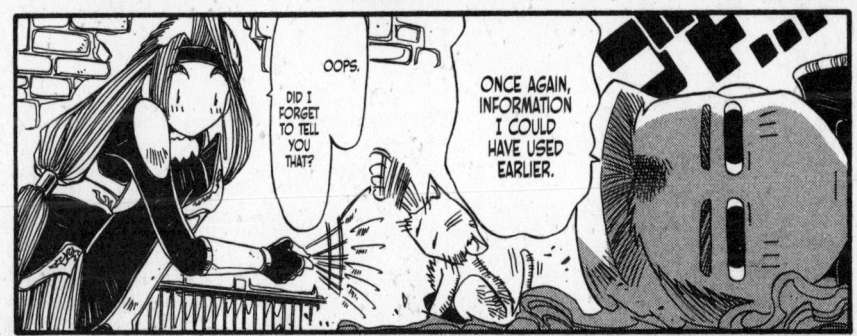

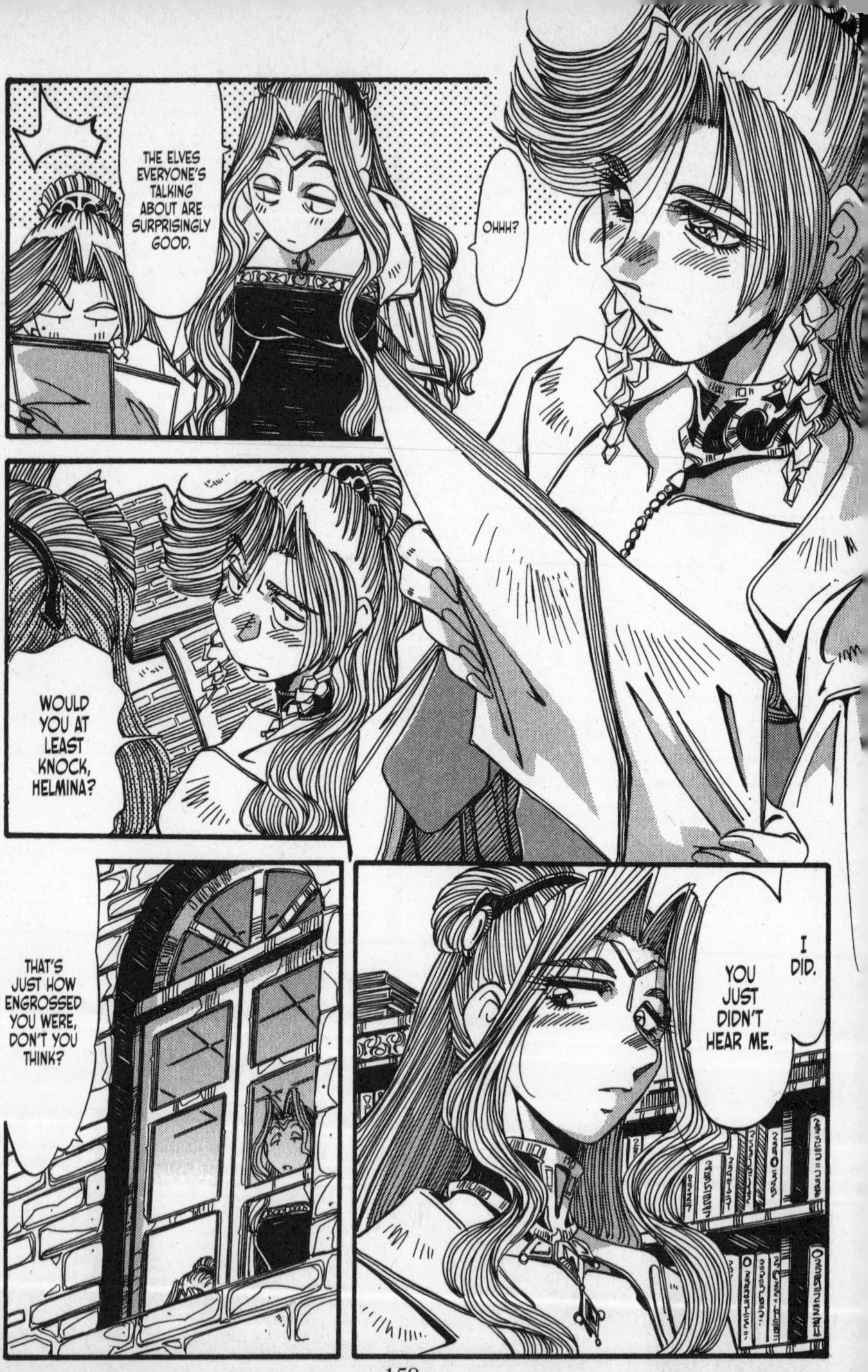
OHHH?
THE ELVES EVERYONE'S TALKING ABOUT ARE SURPRISINGLY GOOD.
WOULD YOU AT LEAST KNOCK, HELMINA?
I DID.
YOU JUST DIDN'T HEAR ME.
THAT'S JUST HOW ENGROSSED YOU WERE, DON'T YOU THINK?

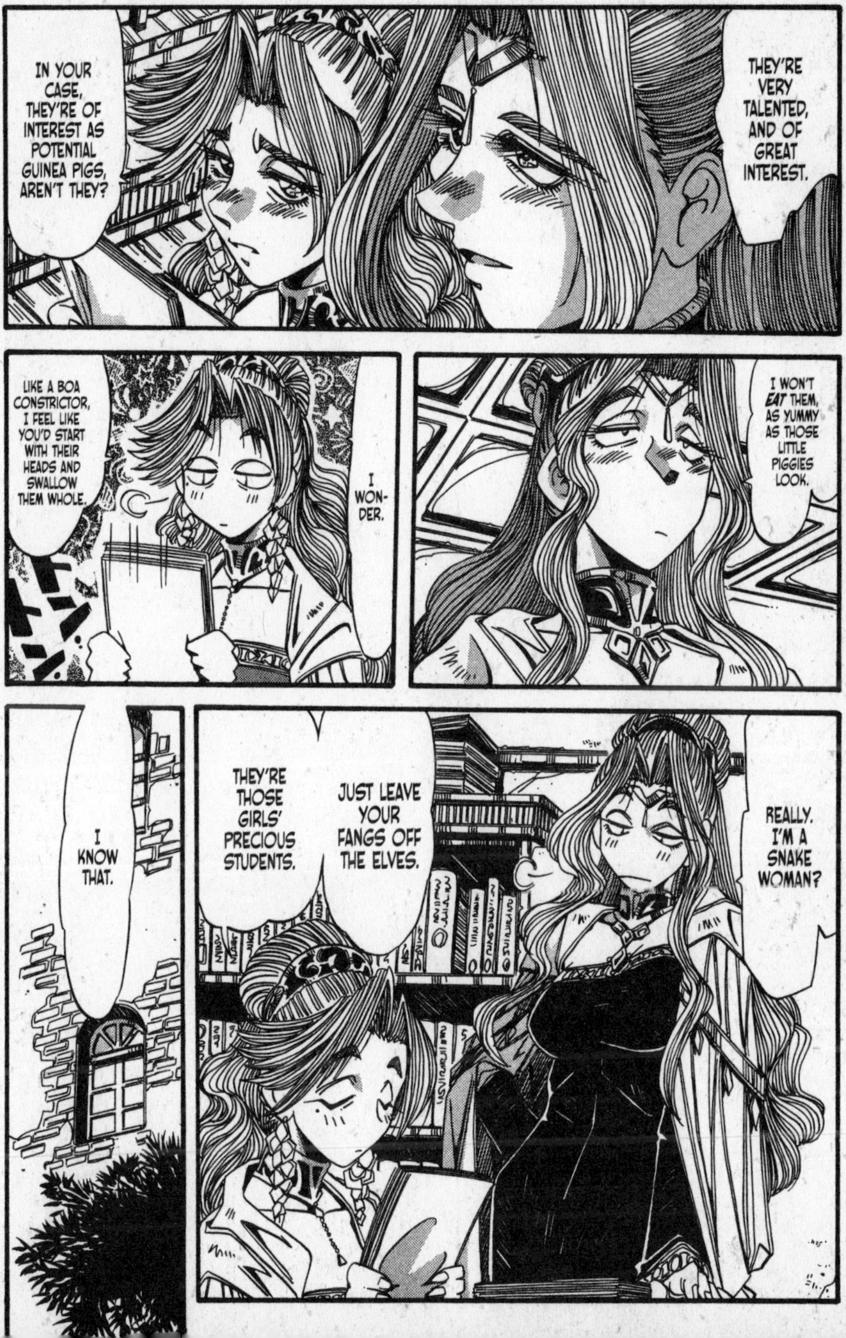
THEY'RE VERY TALENTED, AND OF GREAT INTEREST.
IN YOUR CASE, THEY'RE OF INTEREST AS POTENTIAL GUINEA PIGS, AREN'T THEY?
I WON'T *EAT* THEM, AS YUMMY AS THOSE LITTLE PIGGIES LOOK.
I WON-DER.
LIKE A BOA CONSTRICTOR, I FEEL LIKE YOU'D START WITH THEIR HEADS AND SWALLOW THEM WHOLE.
REALLY. I'M A SNAKE WOMAN?
JUST LEAVE YOUR FANGS OFF THE ELVES.
THEY'RE THOSE GIRLS' PRECIOUS STUDENTS.
I KNOW THAT.

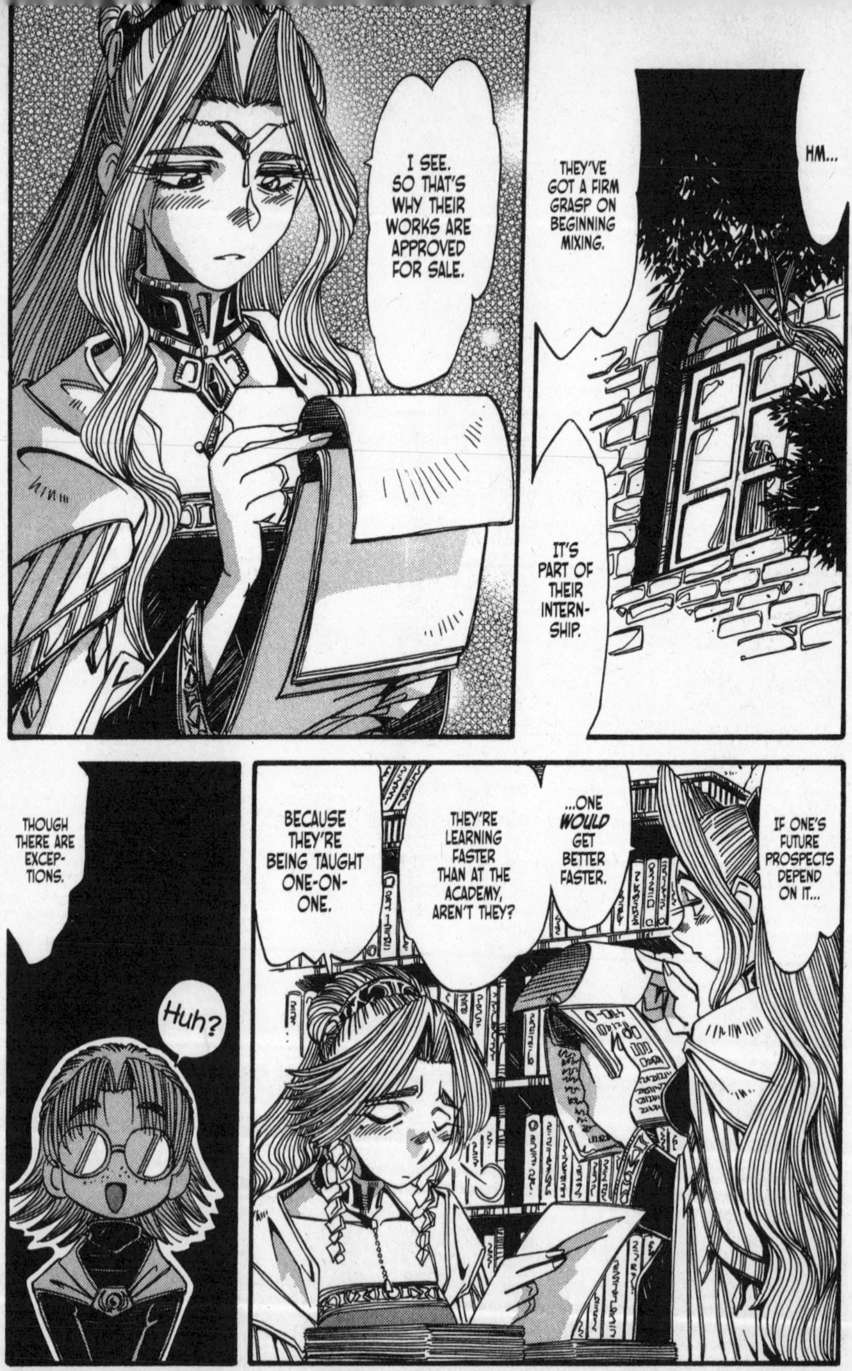
HM...
THEY'VE GOT A FIRM GRASP ON BEGINNING MIXING.
IT'S PART OF THEIR INTERNSHIP.
I SEE. SO THAT'S WHY THEIR WORKS ARE APPROVED FOR SALE.
IF ONE'S FUTURE PROSPECTS DEPEND ON IT...
...ONE *WOULD* GET BETTER FASTER.
THEY'RE LEARNING FASTER THAN AT THE ACADEMY, AREN'T THEY?
BECAUSE THEY'RE BEING TAUGHT ONE-ON-ONE.
THOUGH THERE ARE EXCEPTIONS.
Huh?

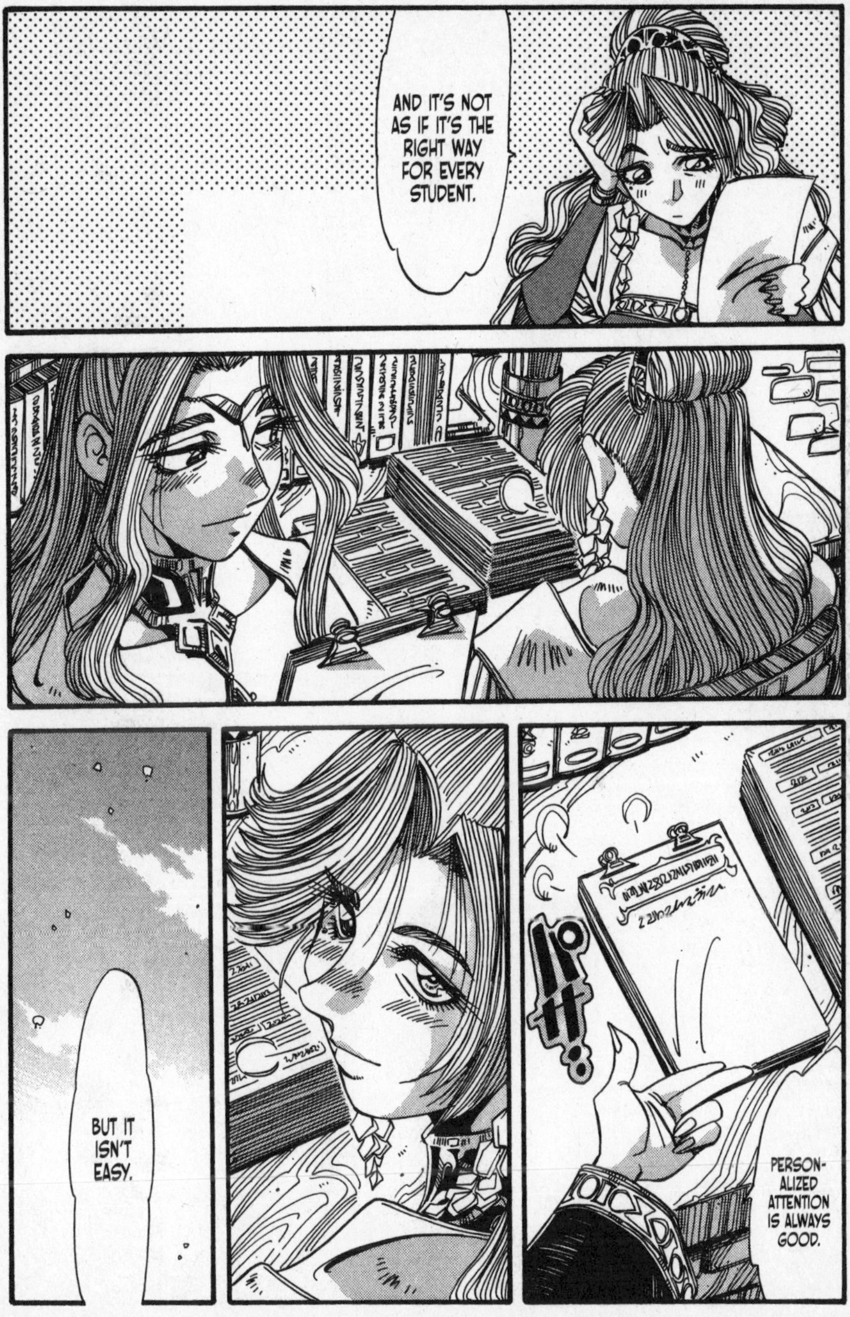
AND IT'S NOT AS IF IT'S THE RIGHT WAY FOR EVERY STUDENT.
PERSON-ALIZED ATTENTION IS ALWAYS GOOD.
BUT IT ISN'T EASY.

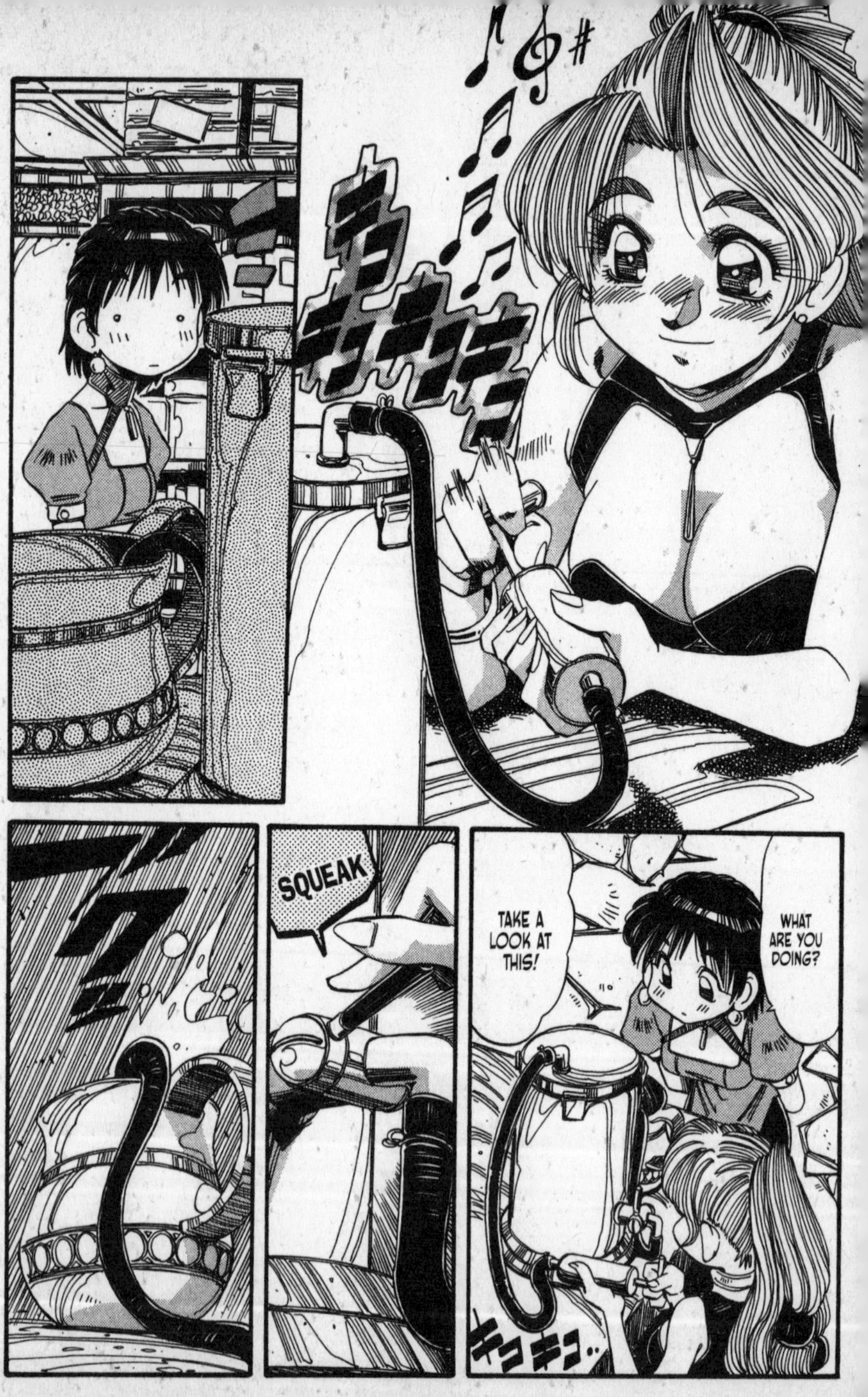
WHAT ARE YOU DOING?
TAKE A LOOK AT THIS!
キコ キコ‥
SQUEAK

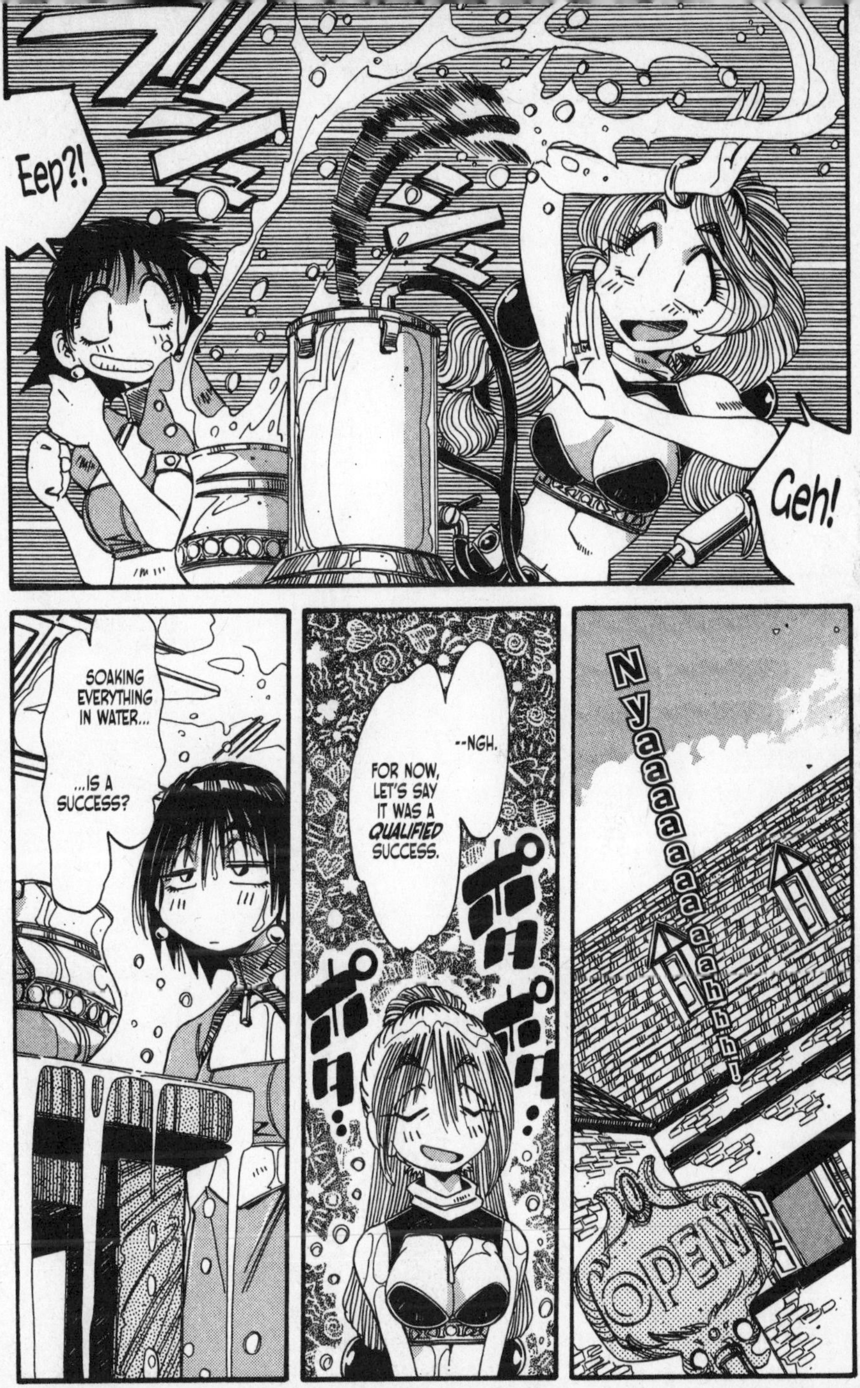
Geh!
Eep?!
Nyaaaaaaaahhh!
OPEN
--NGH.
FOR NOW, LET'S SAY IT WAS A *QUALIFIED* SUCCESS.
SOAKING EVERYTHING IN WATER...
...IS A SUCCESS?

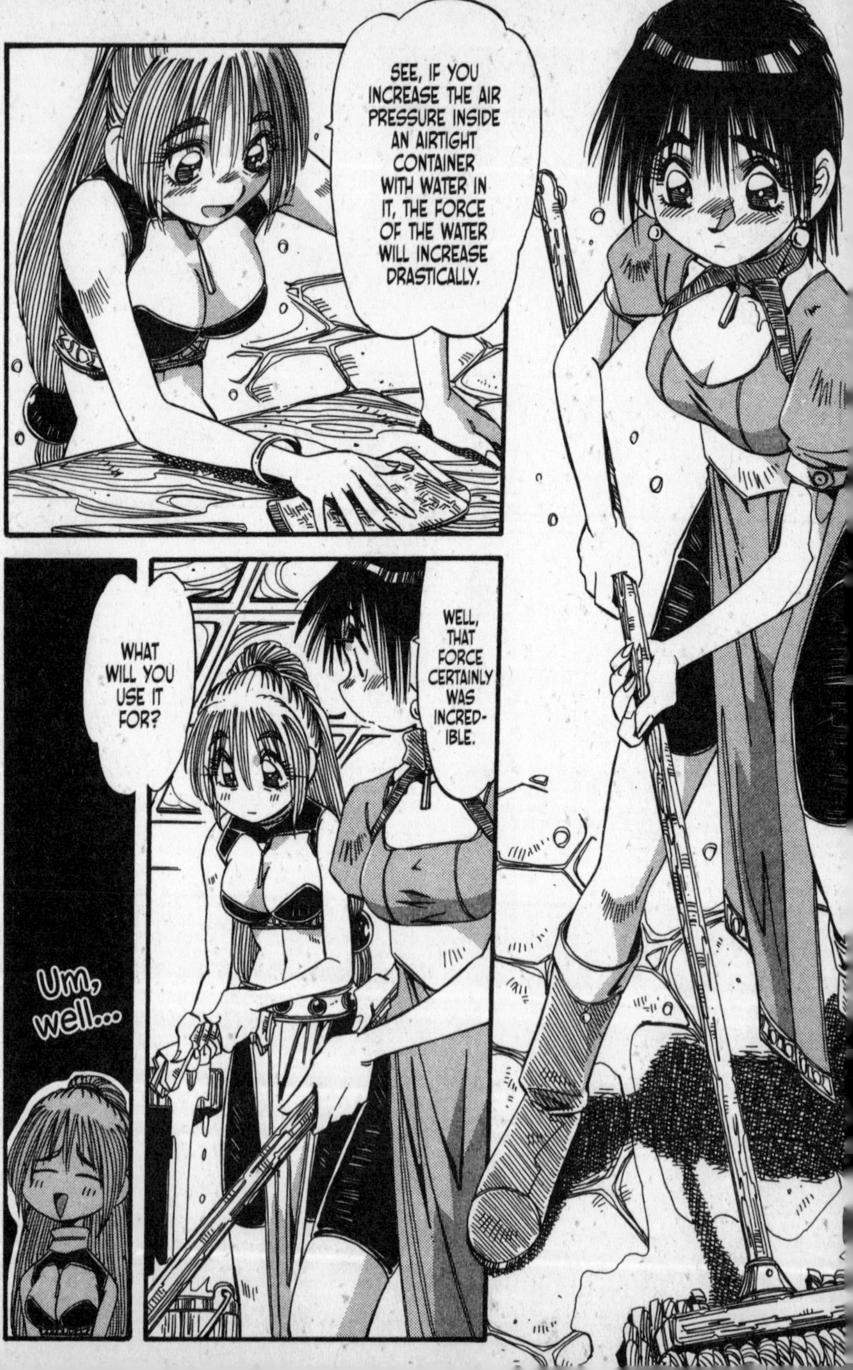
SEE, IF YOU INCREASE THE AIR PRESSURE INSIDE AN AIRTIGHT CONTAINER WITH WATER IN IT, THE FORCE OF THE WATER WILL INCREASE DRASTICALLY.
WELL, THAT FORCE CERTAINLY WAS INCRED-IBLE.
WHAT WILL YOU USE IT FOR?
Um, well...

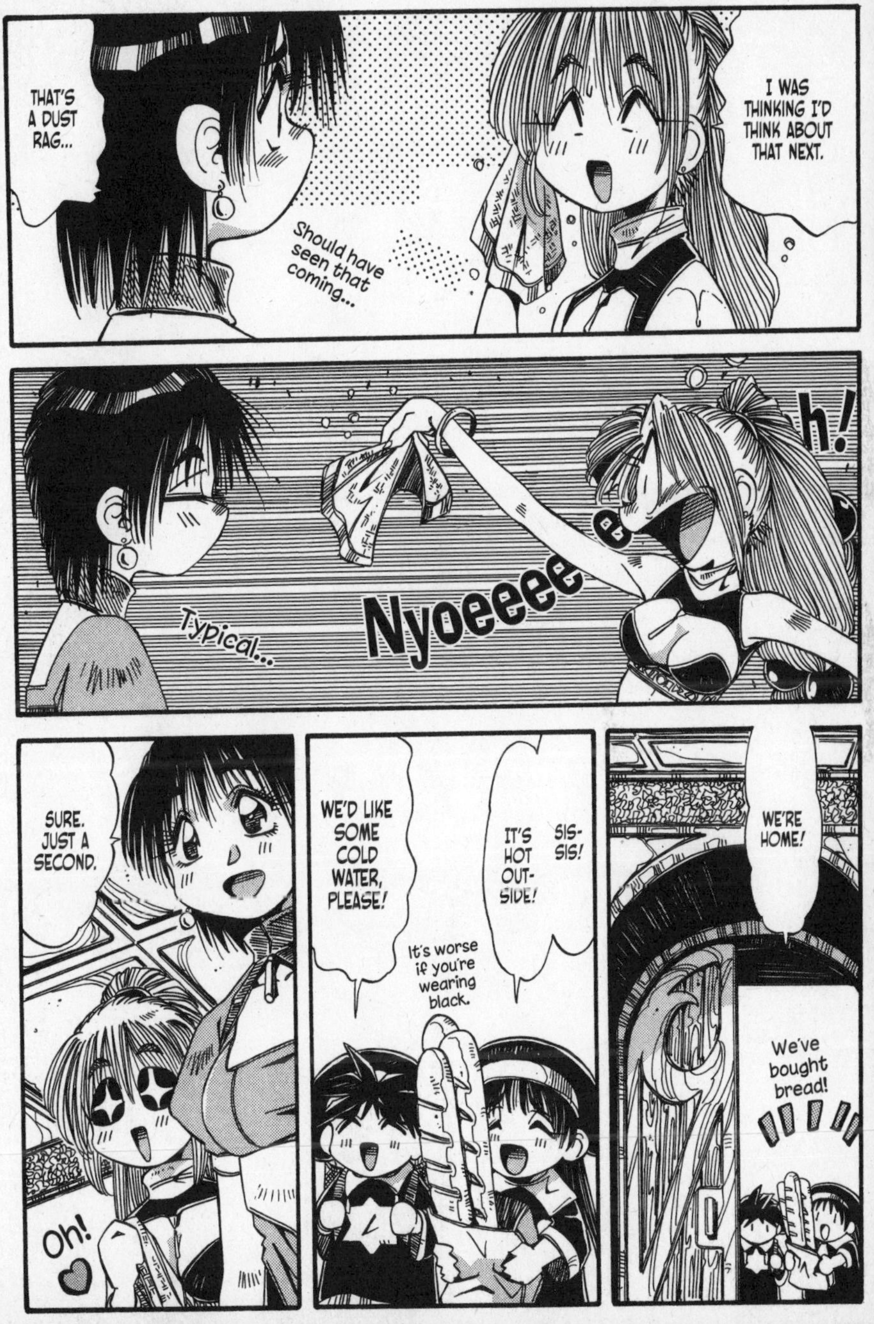
I WAS THINKING I'D THINK ABOUT THAT NEXT.
THAT'S A DUST RAG...
Should have seen that coming...
Nyoeeeeeeh!
Typical...
WE'RE HOME!
We've bought bread!
SIS-SIS!
IT'S HOT OUT-SIDE!
WE'D LIKE SOME COLD WATER, PLEASE!
It's worse if you're wearing black.
SURE. JUST A SECOND.
Oh!

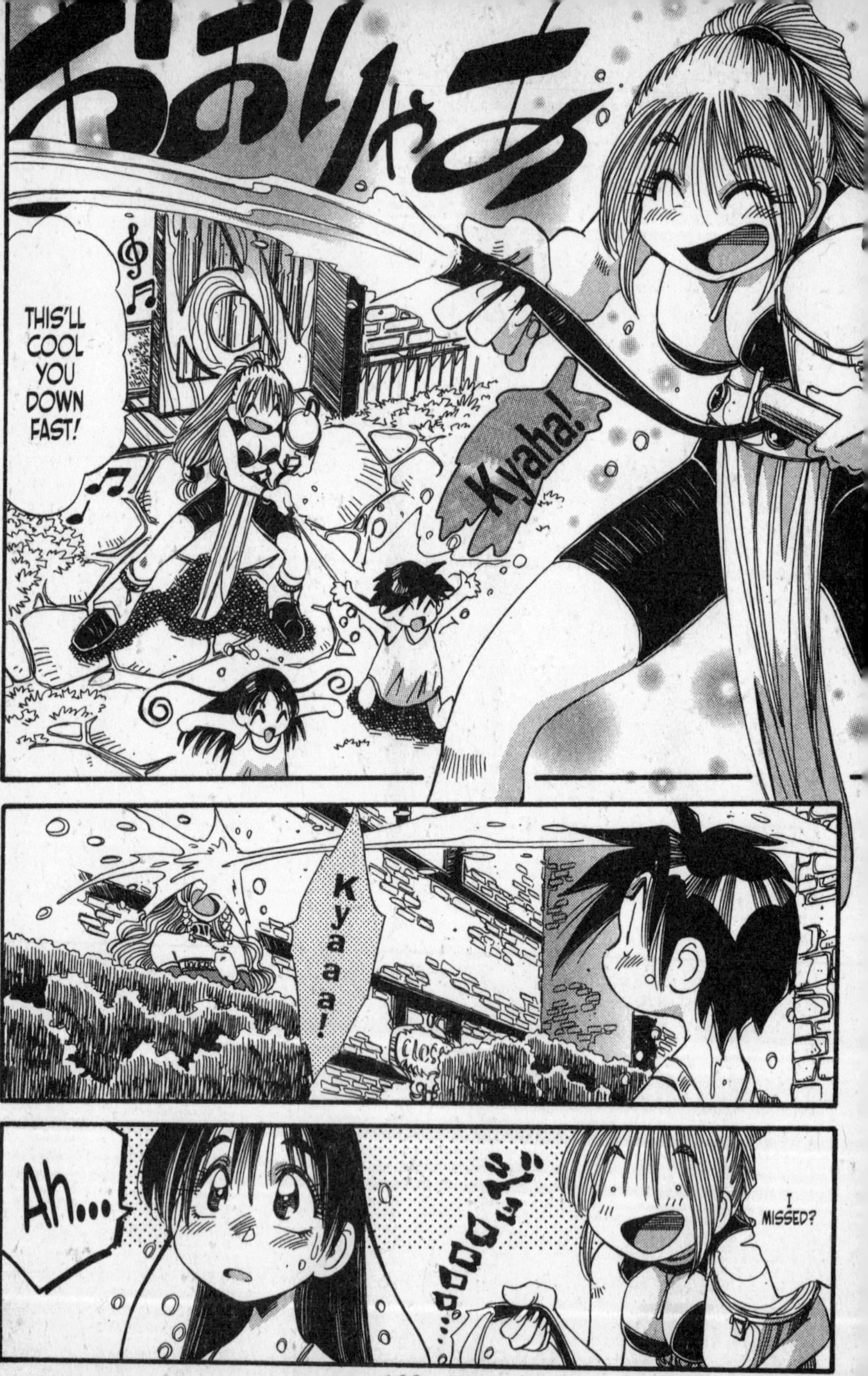
おおりゃあ
Kyaha!
THIS'LL COOL YOU DOWN FAST!
Kyaaaa!
I MISSED?
ジョロロロロロ…
Ah...

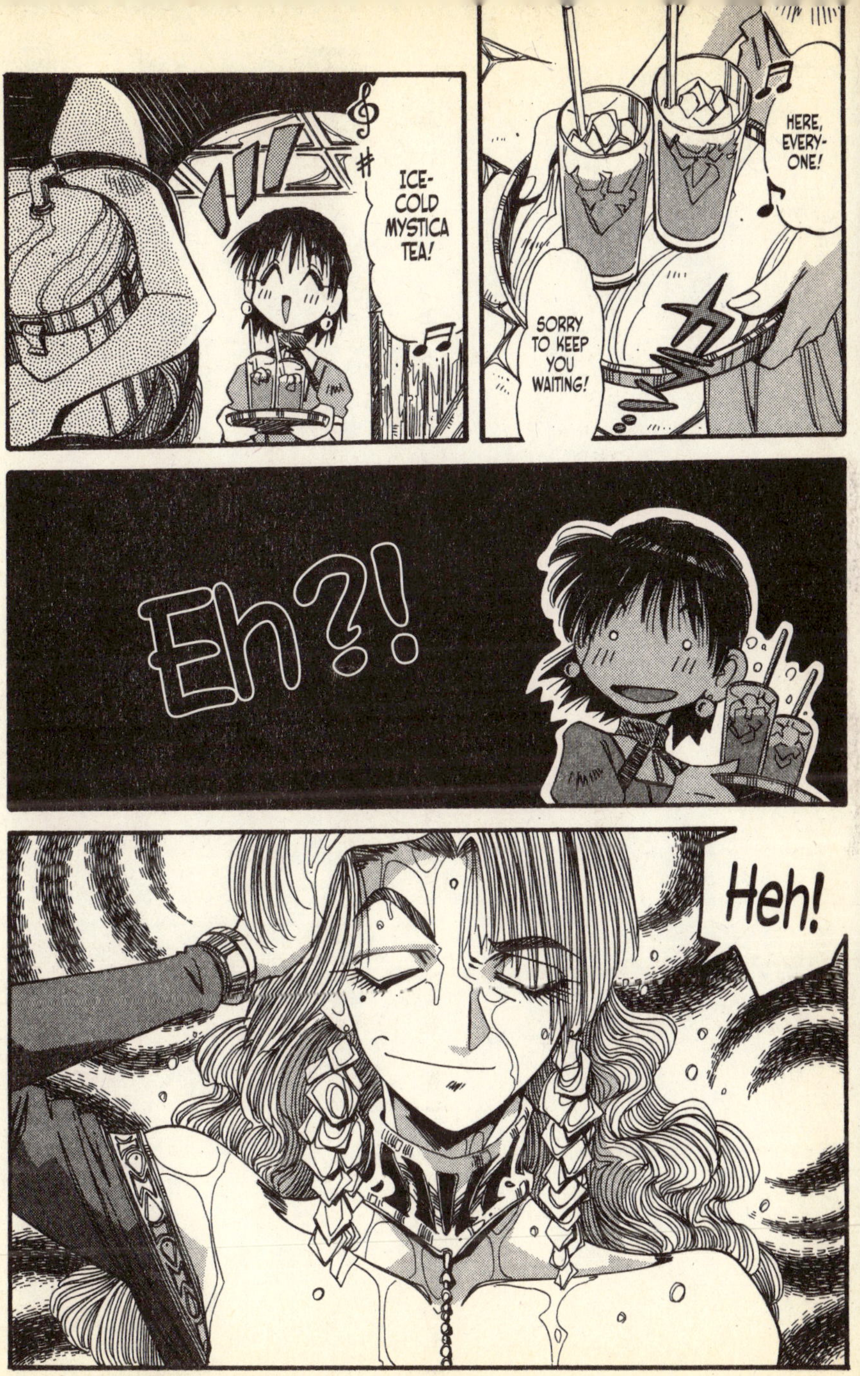
HERE, EVERY-ONE!
SORRY TO KEEP YOU WAITING!
ICE-COLD MYSTICA TEA!
Eh?!
Heh!

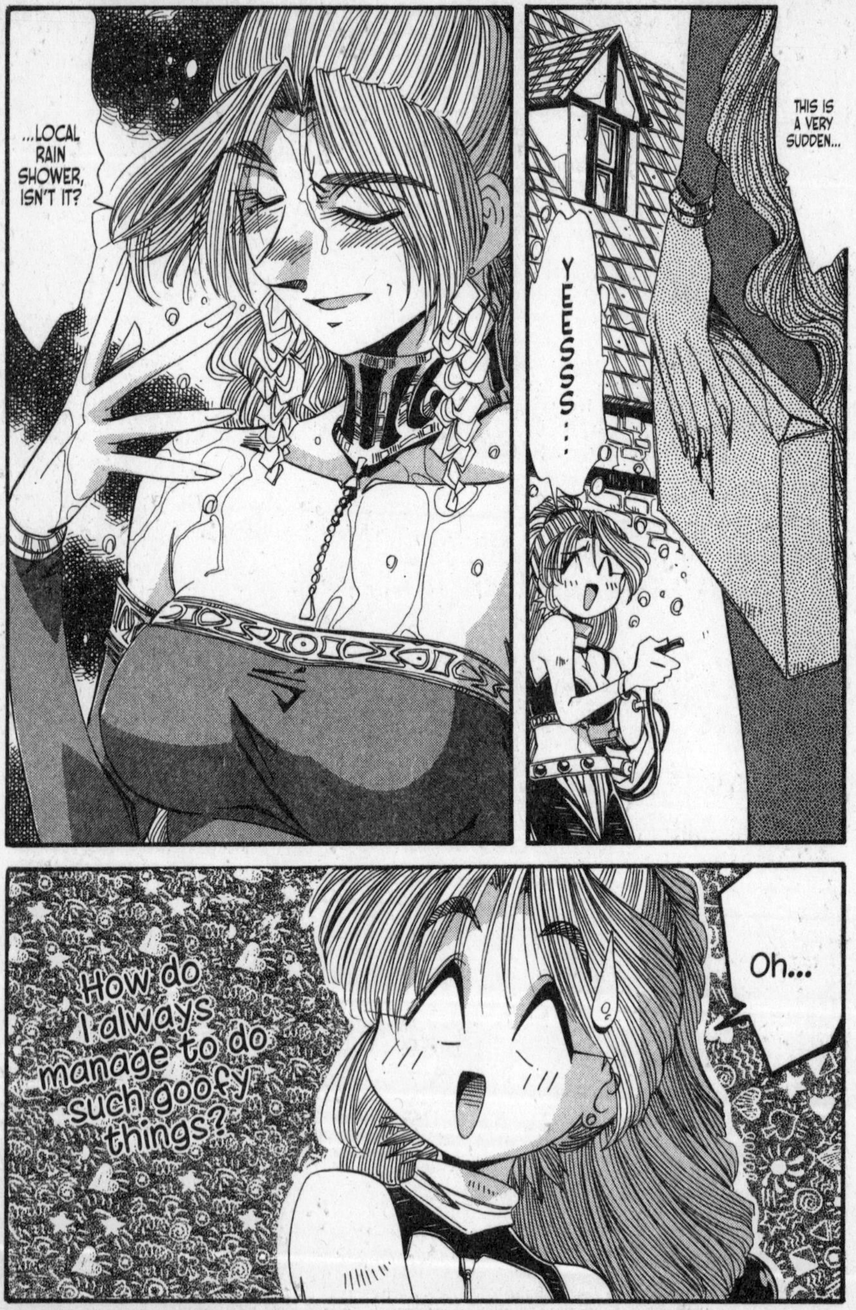
THIS IS A VERY SUDDEN...
YEESSSS...
...LOCAL RAIN SHOWER, ISN'T IT?
Oh...
How do I always manage to do such goofy things?

Volume 3: The End

After All Is Said And Done

WHOA! IT'S ALREADY VOLUME 3!!

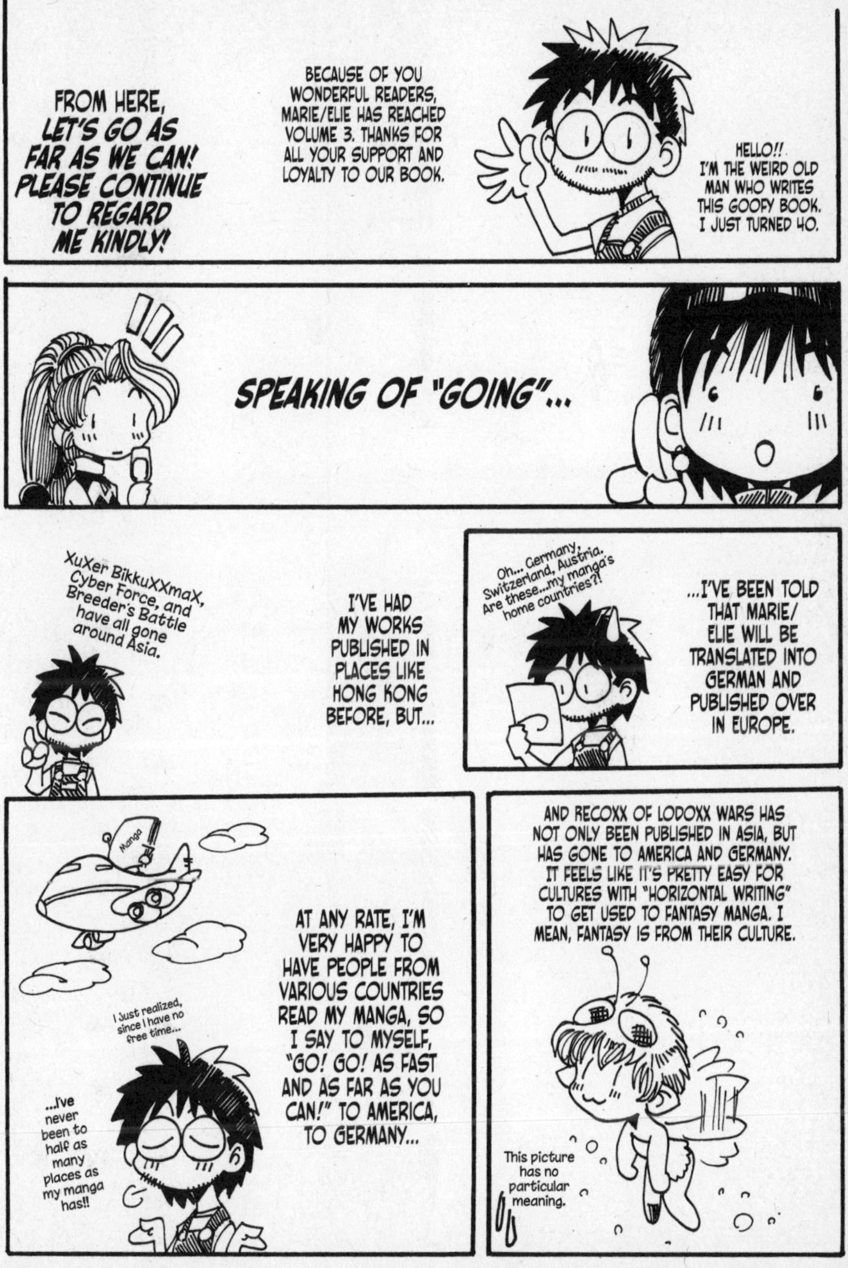
HELLO!! I'M THE WEIRD OLD MAN WHO WRITES THIS GOOFY BOOK. I JUST TURNED 40.
BECAUSE OF YOU WONDERFUL READERS, MARIE/ELIE HAS REACHED VOLUME 3. THANKS FOR ALL YOUR SUPPORT AND LOYALTY TO OUR BOOK.
FROM HERE, LET'S GO AS FAR AS WE CAN! PLEASE CONTINUE TO REGARD ME KINDLY!
SPEAKING OF "GOING"...
XuXer BikkuXXmaX, Cyber Force, and Breeder's Battle have all gone around Asia.
I'VE HAD MY WORKS PUBLISHED IN PLACES LIKE HONG KONG BEFORE, BUT...
Oh... Germany, Switzerland, Austria. Are these...my manga's home countries?!
...I'VE BEEN TOLD THAT MARIE/ ELIE WILL BE TRANSLATED INTO GERMAN AND PUBLISHED OVER IN EUROPE.
AND RECOXX OF LODOXX WARS HAS NOT ONLY BEEN PUBLISHED IN ASIA, BUT HAS GONE TO AMERICA AND GERMANY. IT FEELS LIKE IT'S PRETTY EASY FOR CULTURES WITH "HORIZONTAL WRITING" TO GET USED TO FANTASY MANGA. I MEAN, FANTASY IS FROM THEIR CULTURE.
This picture has no particular meaning.
Manga
AT ANY RATE, I'M VERY HAPPY TO HAVE PEOPLE FROM VARIOUS COUNTRIES READ MY MANGA, SO I SAY TO MYSELF, "GO! GO! AS FAST AND AS FAR AS YOU CAN!" TO AMERICA, TO GERMANY...
I just realized, since I have no free time...
...I've never been to half as many places as my manga has!!

Although I think that "folklore" from any country is fantasy.

IN THE NEXT QUEST OF MARIE AND ELIE

DEMON HOUND STRAFE MAY BE TRADING IN HIS WICKED WAYS FOR THE CHANCE TO SERVE AS MILLIE'S PROTECTOR, UNLESS KYRIE AND THE OTHERS GET IN THE WAY FIRST. MEANWHILE, THE WITCH UNA UNLEASHES THE SAME UNDEAD SERPENT THAT TERRORIZED THE CITY OF CASTAGNA WHEN ELIE WAS A STUDENT. WHO WILL FACE THE CHALLENGE *THIS* TIME?

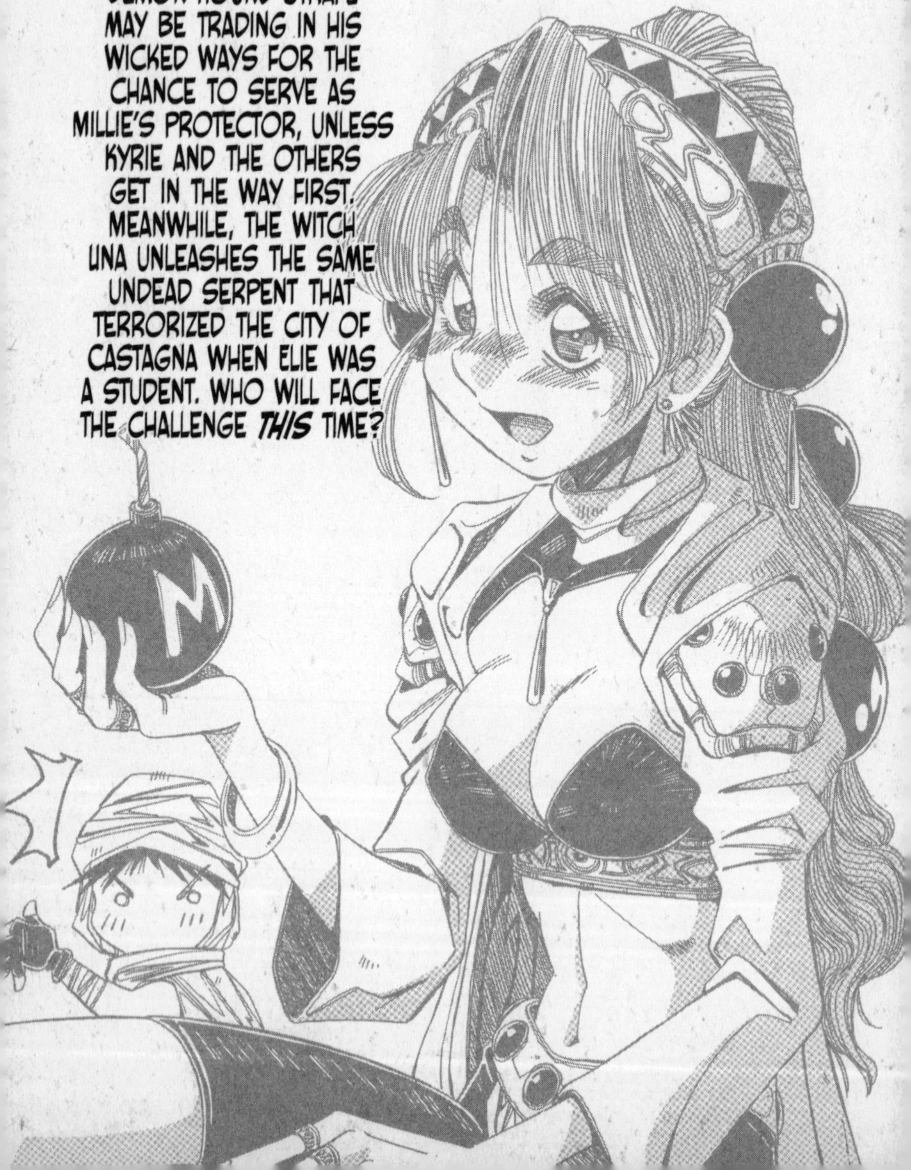

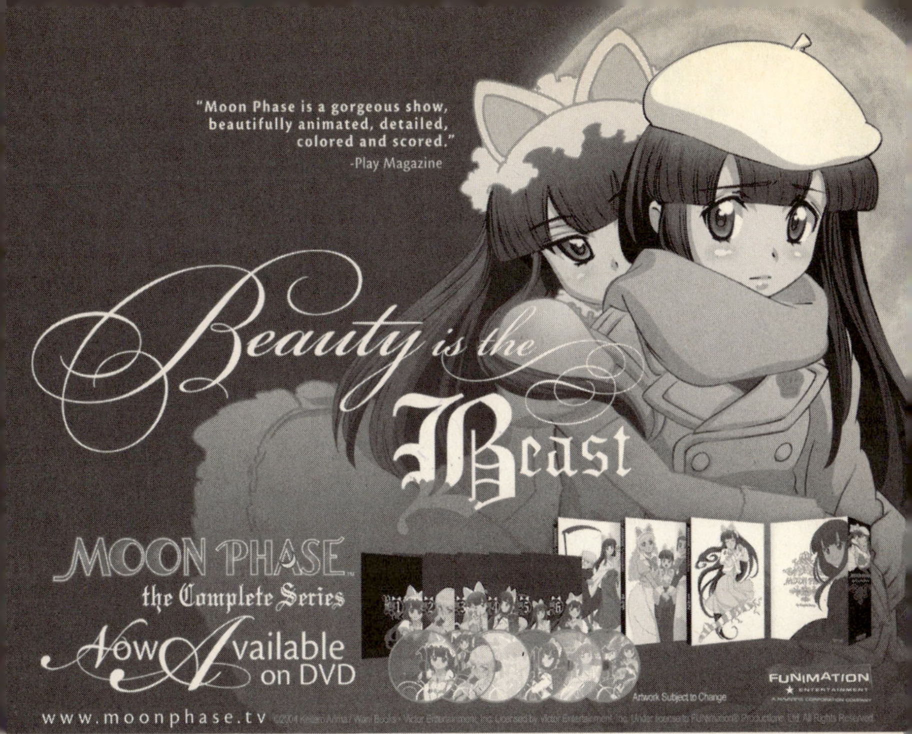
"Moon Phase is a gorgeous show, beautifully animated, detailed, colored and scored."
-Play Magazine
Beauty is the Beast
MOON PHASE
the Complete Series
Now Available on DVD
Artwork Subject to Change
FUNIMATION ENTERTAINMENT
www.moonphase.tv

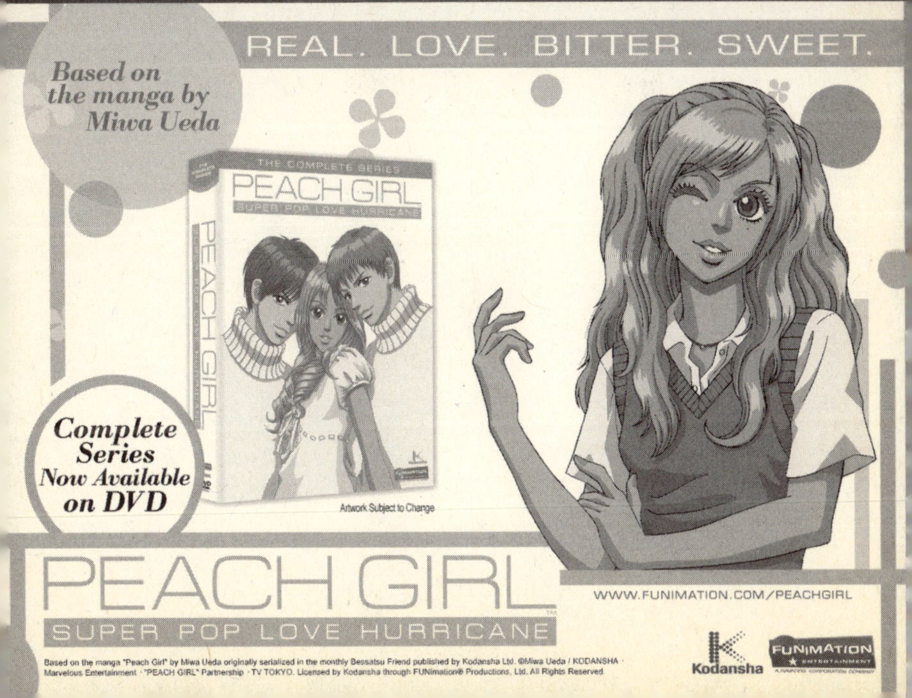
REAL. LOVE. BITTER. SWEET.
Based on the manga by Miwa Ueda
THE COMPLETE SERIES
PEACH GIRL
SUPER POP LOVE HURRICANE
Complete Series Now Available on DVD
Artwork Subject to Change
PEACH GIRL
SUPER POP LOVE HURRICANE
WWW.FUNIMATION.COM/PEACHGIRL
Kodansha
FUNIMATION ENTERTAINMENT
Based on the manga "Peach Girl" by Miwa Ueda originally serialized in the monthly Bessatsu Friend published by Kodansha Ltd. ©Miwa Ueda / KODANSHA · Marvelous Entertainment · "PEACH GIRL" Partnership · TV TOKYO. Licensed by Kodansha through FUNimation® Productions, Ltd. All Rights Reserved

TOKYOPOP.com

WHERE MANGA LIVES!

JOIN the TOKYOPOP community: www.TOKYOPOP.com

COME AND PREVIEW THE HOTTEST MANGA AROUND!

CREATE...
UPLOAD...
DOWNLOAD...
BLOG...
CHAT...
VOTE...
LIVE!!!!

WWW.TOKYOPOP.COM HAS:
- Exclusives
- News
- Contests
- Games
- Rising Stars of Manga
- iManga
- and more...

TOKYOPOP.COM 2.0 NOW LIVE!

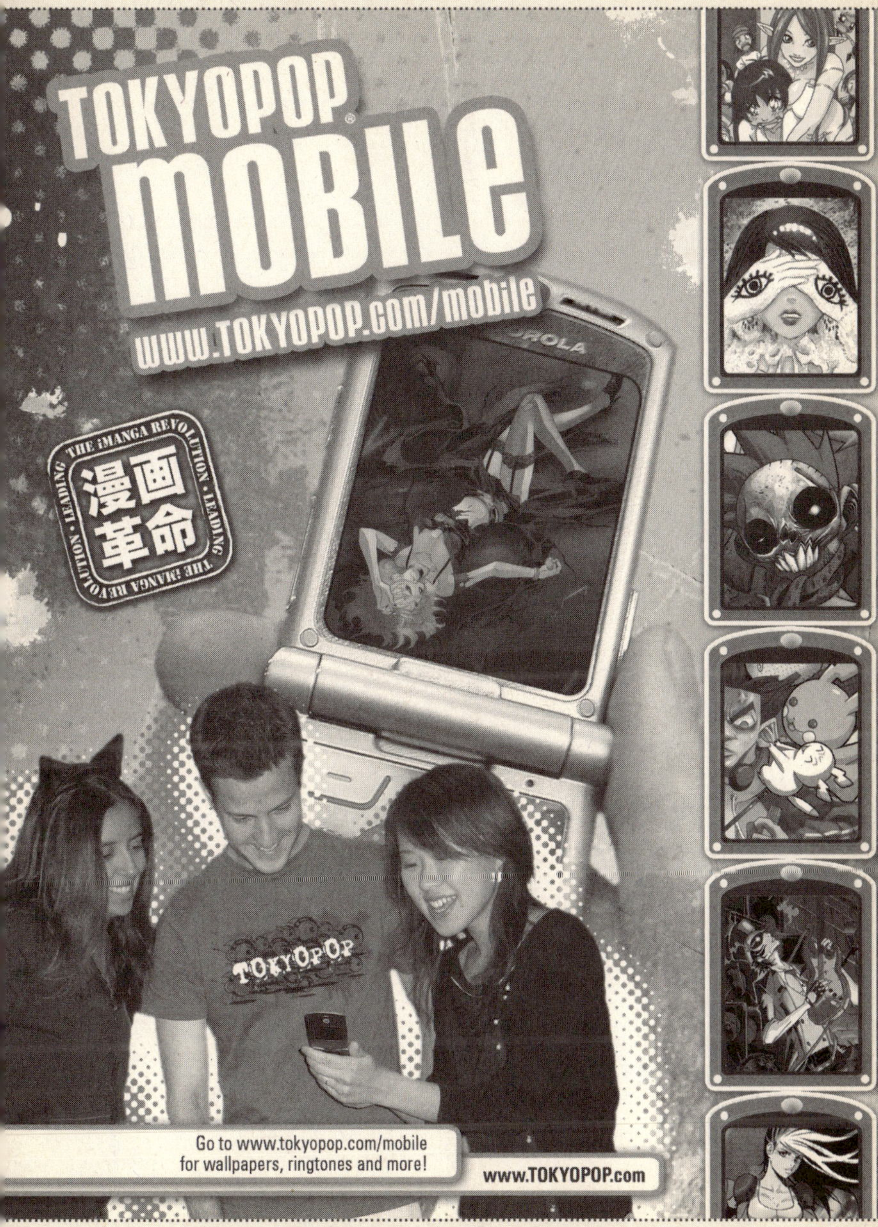
TOKYOPOP MOBILE
www.TOKYOPOP.com/mobile
THE iMANGA REVOLUTION · LEADING
漫画
革命
TOKYOPOP
Go to www.tokyopop.com/mobile
for wallpapers, ringtones and more!
www.TOKYOPOP.com

STOP!

This is the back of the book. You wouldn't want to spoil a great ending!

This book is printed "manga-style," in the authentic Japanese right-to-left format. Since none of the artwork has been flipped or altered, readers get to experience the story just as the creator intended. You've been asking for it, so TOKYOPOP® delivered: authentic, hot-off-the-press, and far more fun!

DIRECTIONS

If this is your first time reading manga-style, here's a quick guide to help you understand how it works.

It's easy... just start in the top right panel and follow the numbers. Have fun, and look for more 100% authentic manga from TOKYOPOP®!